THE AWAKENING OF A PRINCESS

The Awakening of a Princess
Book One of The Ashes of Eyrondale

Cover Design and Interior Formatting by: MythMaker Creations
Interior Artwork by: Samantha de la Porté
Author Photo by: Manon Denolle and Steffan Lones

ISBN:
Paperback: 978-1-0690717-0-5
Hardcover: 978-1-0690717-1-2
EPUB/e-Book: 978-1-0690717-2-9

First Edition
Published in all formats globally

Social Media:
Website: www.samanthadelaporte.com
Instagram: @samantha_delaporte | @ashesofeyrondale

THE AWAKENING OF A PRINCESS

THE ASHES OF EYRONDALE
BOOK 1

SAMANTHA
DE LA PORTÉ

DEDICATION

To the boy who made me long to believe in fairytales,
To the boy who showed me they could come true,
To the boy I let slip through my fingers,
To the man who built me anew.
To the same man who broke me,
To the one who came back time and again,
To the one that I should have held on to,
To the one who committed the original sin.

To the boy who
To the boy w
To the boy I wo
To the man who pr
To the same man wh
To the one I lost mys
To the on
To the one

To the boy who ... *,*
To the boy ...
To the boy I *gave* ...
To the man ...
To the same m... ...
To the one who I *shouldn't have* ...
To the one that I *should have stayed* ...
To the one ... *bt me to d*...

To the boy who haunted my d...
T... *who brightened my n*...
To the b... *t on a*
To the man who gave ...
To the same man who ...
To the one who cossea...
...*one that* ...
...

To the b... *years m*...
To the boy who I *pushed out of*
To the boy I *kept drowning* ...
To th... *m*... *I almos*...
To the sam...
To ...
To the one ... ...
To the one who tore

— From Katherine, who learned too late that love and
fate are never easy allies.

READER
GUIDANCE

B efore you begin your journey into The Ashes of Eyrondale
series, please take a moment to review the following content
and trigger guidance.

This romantasy series is intended for readers aged eighteen
and older. While The Ashes of Eyrondale is a work of fiction, and any
resemblance to actual events, places, or people is purely coincidental, it
includes emotionally complex themes that may be distressing or unsettling
for some readers.

The list below outlines potential themes and triggers that may appear
throughout the series. Not all content is present in every book, and this
list is not exhaustive, but it is intended to help you make an informed
decision about your reading experience while minimising spoilers. Please
also note that the emotional tone and thematic material deepen over time,
becoming darker and more mature as the series progresses.

The story of The Ashes of Eyrondale is designed to unfold gradually across multiple books. Some questions are answered early, while others are explored in later volumes. Each book reveals new layers of character, worldbuilding, and lore. Readers should expect that not every thread will be resolved within a single instalment, and that the full arc of the story comes into focus over the course of the series.

Content and Trigger Warnings (may appear across the series):

- Violence and torture
- Sexual content
- Referenced sexual assault
- Death and near-death experiences
- Substance abuse, including excessive consumption
- Strong language
- Graphic depictions of injury, blood, and other potentially distressing content

Your mental wellbeing is important. If any of the above content may be harmful or unsettling for you, please consider this guidance before stepping into Katherine's story.

CHAPTER 01
THE WELCOMING

The gold detailing on the fortified gates flickered as the fires hovering above either side of the stone entranceway flared brighter at the arrival of its guests. The sudden glow turned Emily's already vivid green eyes luminescent as the flames awakened others along the perimeter walls, offering her a glimpse into the dense, shadowy forest beyond. For a moment, Emily caught a hint of what lay beyond the defences of their supposed safe haven. But as the oversized gates swung forward, allowing passage to the line of jet-black town cars, the nagging sensation in the pit of her stomach vanished, her curiosity getting the better of her. As she gazed out at the corridors of old English oak trees that lined the seemingly endless driveway, awe at what had become her new reality was still settling in.

Before she could dwell on it, the car carrying Emily and her family rounded the forecourt's large fountain and came to a stop at the foot of the stairs. Their tall, silver-haired driver, Tom, opened the door, waiting to help them disembark. Emily knew that once the soles of her shoes crunched against the gravel beneath her, there would be no turning back. Brushing a strand of long black hair from her face, she glanced up at the moon as it danced across the night sky.

Many of the castle windows contained intricate stained-glass designs, handcrafted to complement the dark stone that housed them. Aged at least a thousand years or so, in Emily's opinion, this was the oldest building she had ever seen in person. Having taken a semester of Art History at university, she developed quite a liking for the architecture and artwork that emerged during the Middle Ages.

This can't possibly be real, Emily thought as a tall, elderly gentleman with near-white hair, dressed in a pressed, charcoal-coloured suit, stood waiting for them atop the landing. Serious, yet smiling, he opened the imposing, cathedral-style doors, their pointed archways stretching high overhead in a silent welcome. As dozens of gargoyles gazed down upon her from their perches on the walls' edge, the hairs on the back of Emily's neck stood tall, a shiver tracing its way down her spine.

∾

Emily recognised the man in the suit from the flight that had brought her and the others here. A few hours earlier, he had appeared on the private jet's television screen, attempting to explain why they had needed to leave their homes in the dead of night, and why their loved ones would be under surveillance for the foreseeable future.

She herself had not left her home or boarded the aircraft willingly. Well, not initially at least. Emily had awoken to the sound of her dogs barking at two heavily armed men pounding their fists on her front door. Fearful for her life, as her neighbourhood was known for frequent home invasions, it took the two men nearly an hour to convince Emily that they were not there to harm her but instead to take her to a safe location for her protection. Resistant and untrusting though she was, she had chosen to go along with them after they showed her a photograph of her best friend, whom she had not heard from in weeks, bound and bruised, holding a copy of that day's paper.

A quick ride to the nearest airfield had stirred a growing sense of fear and panic in Emily as she began to process the shock of seeing someone she cared for so dearly in such a state. But before she could spiral into a panic, the shorter of the two escorts blew a cloud of lavender-coloured smoke in her face, sending her into an instant sleep.

Though disoriented when she woke up on the aircraft, Emily was able to recognise her fellow passengers, who looked nearly as confused and scared as she felt on the inside. It had taken her a moment to grasp the fact that she was not dreaming before she noticed her sister, Layla, sitting in an armchair across from a couple who were taking up one of the cosy two-seaters at the far end of the room. Layla's brown eyes were wide, scanning the scene, and her fair skin was more pale than it had been in recent years. As Emily got to her feet and made her way towards them, she quickly greeted the others but was too desperate for answers to engage in polite pleasantries. She did wonder, however, how many of them had been taken like she had, or if she had somehow got off easy.

"Bayne? Layla? Jennifer?" greeted Emily nervously as she approached, doing her best to put on a braver-than-normal face.

Her cousin, Bayne, was quick to reply, looking less surprised to see her than she would have thought. "Emily. You okay?"

She nodded as Bayne's eyes narrowed and examined her. She was slightly taken aback at her cousin's seemingly calm demeanour amidst whatever chaos they had all just been thrown into. While the pair had never been on the best of terms, Bayne at least appeared to be relieved to see that she was alright.

Layla and Jennifer greeted Emily softly in unison as she sat down in an armchair near them. Looking around, it was evident that she had been the last to wake. Everyone else seemed alert and, for the most part, coherent.

"We can't have been in the air for that long," Emily hissed. "Where are we? Where are we going?"

Layla leant forward, strands of dark brown hair slipping into her face. "We've been wondering the same thing. We've spoken to a few of the others and figure it's been about six hours or so since we took off. From what we can tell, everyone's been told it has something to do with Katherine, but apart from that, they're in the dark as much as we are."

"Did you guys see the—" Emily started, but was cut off by a loud sound coming from the front of the aircraft as a large screen descended from the ceiling. The room went silent, and her train of thought came to a pause.

"Welcome!" greeted the grey-eyed man on the screen.

Emily saw a few of her fellow passengers exchanging nervous looks.

"You are, of course, wondering why you are here. My name is Alfred. Please, allow me to explain," he said in a soothing tone. "You are all bound together by your relationship with my master, Katherine, and as some of those she cares most about, we believe that it is our duty to ensure your safety and the safety of your loved ones until we can locate her. By now you would have all seen the most recent *gift* sent to us by her captors, providing proof of life. While we are still unsure as to how they managed to find her, our team has been able to narrow down the window in which she was taken to roughly two weeks ago, which aligns with when the first whispered rumours of her whereabouts being uncovered reached our ears."

Emily's stomach twisted with sudden dread as Alfred continued all too calmly for her liking.

"For those of you important enough to Katherine to earn a place on this aircraft, please be assured that your families and loved ones who have not joined you, those we have identified as potential targets, have had guards assigned to them who will monitor their movements and guarantee their wellbeing while you are away. This is in addition to doing what we can to shield them from various means of detection."

There was an outbreak of panicked chatter.

"What are you talking about?"

"Safety? *We're* in danger?"

"You've lost your mind!"

"This is clearly a joke."

"Silence!" came Alfred's voice over the noise, demanding their attention. "*Please!*"

The group went quiet immediately, the faint drone of the engines in the background was the only thing that broke the tension.

"All will be explained in due time, but for now, you must know that you need not worry for your lives. Our team is arranging for those of you who are able to work remotely for the time being or to file for unemployment benefits, in an attempt to maintain some semblance of normalcy in the days or possibly weeks to come."

Ignoring the rumblings of protest, Alfred pressed on, his rather white complexion turning the faintest hint of red.

"We are scouring the globe for Katherine as we speak and are confident that we will be able to return you to your regular lives before long. I will meet you all shortly after you land. Until then, Zachary will be giving you a summarised briefing in preparation for the jet to touch down. Please, I ask that you make this easier on yourselves and quickly come to accept what you are about to be told."

There was a pause before the screen went black, leaving Emily and the others to their racing thoughts.

"Can anybody explain this to me? Because I'm clearly missing something here!" said Jennifer irritably through her mane of red curls as she leant past Bayne, who had slumped his broad torso forward, head in his hands, to get a better look at the crowd.

"This can't be happening," he muttered from beside her, running his fingers frustratedly through his sleek, sandy-blond hair, dishevelling his usually neat appearance.

"Wait! What? Are we really going to believe this?" snapped Jennifer, all eyes and ears now on the pair, her eyebrows lifting as high as Emily had ever seen them go.

"You saw the photos, same as I did, didn't you, Jen?" said Emily, quickly trying to steer the conversation away from what would surely turn into an argument.

"Photos lie!"

"And all of this? Are you telling me all of this is what? Part of some elaborate hoax?"

"You're just quick to believe it because it's Katherine!"

Emily huffed, her blood pressure rising fast. The tips of her ears turned the brightest shade of pink. "And that's exactly why you're so quick to dismiss it. If it's believable enough for Bayne and Jamie," she said, pointing from her cousin to his slightly shorter, curly-haired best friend who stood near where the screen had descended, "that should be enough for you."

"Enough!" boomed Bayne's voice as his fist slammed down on the coffee table before them, silencing the bickering pair, snapping Emily back to the present and leaving Jennifer looking livid.

"I'd hop on board with this as quickly as possible if I were you. This is just the tip of the iceberg," called an amused voice from behind the curtain near Jamie.

Jamie's larger-than-normal brown eyes widened comically at the unexpected interruption behind his thick, rectangular glasses. Through the midnight-blue drapes that had, until now, gone mostly unnoticed, emerged a gangly, dark-haired, pale-skinned young man, clutching several files. His gaze shifted to each of them curiously. He walked with a kind of know-it-all swagger, chewing a piece of gum loudly as if this were nothing more than an ordinary afternoon.

"Zachary." He smirked. "I guess it's time we have a little chat."

Emily's recollection was cut short at the sight of what awaited them on the other side of the doors. From the outside, the castle was impressive enough, but she had not expected the interior to be even more striking. The bright white of the marble floor, with its distinctive black and gold veins, contrasted sharply with the darkness of the traditional stone walls. The shadowed wood embellishments and historical accent pieces brought warmth to the room, as did the flames hovering above the sconces and chandeliers, and those crackling in the fireplaces. As Emily watched the light bounce off the gold detailing above the door arches, she was overwhelmed by the opulence that seemed to welcome her with open arms.

Before the grandeur of the foyer could fully make an impact on its new visitors and suck them in with its more intricate details, a chime of "Für Elise" echoed around them, disappearing down the passages of the West Wing. Moving past them silently, Alfred waved open the heavy double doors to find a large wooden crate waiting on the landing.

As though already knowing what he would find, or not find, he scanned the night but saw only a pair of guards making their way back down the driveway. Emily and the others had been informed that only a select few were able to reach the doors without additional clearances. With another wave of his hand, Alfred sent the package into the foyer as easily as if it were being pushed by ten invisible men, causing many of them, Emily included, to stare in bewilderment. Zachary had made brief mention of a few of the more unnatural, or rather, supernatural, aspects of their circumstances, but for the most part, they had ignored it all as a bad joke.

Now in the room's centre, the crate towered over those who stood curiously at its base, a tiny note attached to it the only clue to what it concealed within.

As Alfred examined the note carefully, he muttered, more to himself than to anyone else, "Master Alek, I think this is what we have been looking for."

Pausing for just a moment, he removed the paper from the wooden panel and crumpled it in his fist. In a flash, it burst into flames, leaving no damage to Alfred's hand. Emily exchanged nervous looks with those around her, thinking that this must be some sort of trick, or rather, *hoping*.

After what seemed like less than a minute, the door to the left of the entrance burst open, causing most of them to jump out of their own skin as a young man strode out, brows furrowed with concern and a flicker of curiosity in his eyes.

"Ah, Master Alek! You received my message."

"Yes, thank you, Alfred," replied the man as he walked through the parting crowd, towards the package.

Alek was reasonably tall, with a noticeably built physique and a defined jawline. As he walked by, Emily's breath caught at the sight of his carefully styled short, dark-blond hair and striking green eyes that stood out against his tanned skin. He turned more than one head as he made his way to Alfred's side, commanding the room with his mere presence. Emily and the others quickly realised that now was no time to interfere.

Taking care not to touch it, Alek circled the mysterious delivery. He took his time, paying no mind to the group of strangers. After minutes of strained silence, with only the sound of his footsteps echoing around them, Alek stopped in front of the crate, satisfied that the only way forward would be to open it. He exchanged a hesitant look with Alfred and lightly pressed his hand to the dark panel before him.

At his touch, the walls of the crate crashed to the floor and Emily and the others hurried to avoid the sharp fragments of wood flying through the air. She and her companions could barely get back to their feet before a spine-chilling shriek escaped Layla's lips.

A glass box, as tall, wide, and deep as the space allowed, had been concealed by its encasement. Each edge of its walls was marked with strange symbols that neither Emily nor those around her could recognise. But that was of little importance. It was what the glass encased that had caused their panic.

❧

There, suspended from the ceiling of the box, was a body. Battered and bruised, mouth taped shut, wrapped in chains, and hanging by her wrists.

"Katherine!" Alek breathed, moving instinctively towards her in disbelief.

Cries filled the air. As each pair of eyes locked onto the near-lifeless body of their friend, Alek looked to Alfred to calm the nerves of their guests.

Looking pale, Alfred moved around the room, handing out glasses of kiwi water from a nearby table. He advised Emily and the others to keep a safe distance and assured them that everything would be alright.

Cautious and ignoring the sounds of panic that continued to bounce off the walls, Alek again stretched out his hand. Katherine, defeated though she looked, widened her light blue eyes and struggled against the chains that bound her. Too focused on getting her out of there, Alek placed his palm against the transparent pane.

At his touch, the enchanted prison trembled. The symbols lining the edges of the walls glowed bright orange as a large, luminous timer appeared at the top of each side.

～

In the second it took for the timers to start their countdown from the three-minute mark, the glow of the symbols began to move. Though the etchings on the glass stayed in place, their colour bled outward, flowing like tiny streams of lava toward the joins between the panels, merging to form a living seal at each corner of Katherine's cage.

As if being forged from within the fiery frame, small silver blades sprouted. Their razor-sharp tips swivelled towards the scared, wide-eyed, weakened body that hung there, helpless.

Although muffled by the tape on her mouth and the thickness of the glass surrounding her, Katherine's screams could be heard escaping as the white-hot knives took turns forcing themselves into her fair skin, retracting, and beginning all over again.

While her friends could barely stand to watch her being tortured right in front of them, they also could not bring themselves to look away.

～

The timers continued to tick loudly, and the more they did, the less Alek felt it would lead to anything good. He was not alone in his thoughts as he caught glimpses of the distressed faces of those around him. Almost every pair of eyes was transfixed on either Katherine's blood-soaked body, or on the final minute of the countdown. All of them were terrified of what could come next.

Tick. Tick. Tick.

Alek knew there was only one person who would dare put on such a grotesque display of power.

Tick. Tick. Tick.

He muttered something to Alfred, who immediately pulled out a notepad from his suit's inner pocket, scribbled on one of its pages, and gripped it tight until it, too, burst into flames in his hands.

Tick. Tick. Tick.

Emily, in tears, looked around as Katherine's muffled screams became almost inaudible. Her cousin's face was pale with fear as he stood frozen. Layla was crying into the chest of her husband, Brian. Jamie sat on the floor, rocking back and forth with his hands clasped around his knees. Matthew and Aiden, the two others who Emily had recognised on the aircraft but whose faces she did not know as well, were on the floor with tears in their eyes. Jennifer had her hands to her mouth in shock. None seemed able to say a single word. It was as though they were paralysed by the crippling idea that this was how it all would end.

Tick. Tick. Tick.

The bang of the castle doors pulled their focus away from their fearful thoughts, if only for a moment, as in marched a tall and slender man with short black hair and eyes as deep and rich as an early-morning espresso. He was panting slightly and wore a near-murderous look on his face as he strode past Emily and the others without so much as a flicker of acknowledgement, coming to a standstill at Alek's side.

"Marko," greeted Alek, checking the timer nearest him again.

There was a flicker of pain beneath the rage as Marko took in the reality of what stood before them. "Carter?" he asked through clenched teeth as any remaining colour drained from his already pale face.

"Must be. He's the only one who could have pulled this off. I just don't know what it means."

"He'll die for this. I swear it!"

"Brother, now is not the time. We need to get her out of there!"

The pair, who Emily and the others now took to be siblings, continued talking and snapping at each other as if they were the only ones in the room, adding to the collective panic.

Tick. Tick. Tick.

Only a few seconds remained, and all eyes moved to the clocks. The chatter between the brothers died out.

Tick. Tick.

Katherine managed a fearful look at the numbers before closing her eyes, waiting, terrified.

Tick.

There was a momentary silence before the dozens of blades retracted into the flaming edges of the glass walls, vanishing into nothingness, along with the molten glow, just as quickly as they had first appeared.

Before anyone could breathe a sigh of relief, a faint hissing came from the translucent cell. Katherine's eyes shot open and followed Alek's gaze to the timers, which had again started to count down. Seven minutes this time.

The hissing grew louder, calling the attention of the room to the water spraying from the joins of the cage into the bottom of its base. It did not take long for the sound to be drowned out by the water rising above its source. Katherine, weak and blood-soaked as she was, tried to fight her chains once more as it dawned on her, as well as her friends, what was going to happen if she was not able to break free.

"I c...can't do this!" Emily squeaked at the sight of her friend wasting what little energy remained on a doomed attempt.

Tears welled up in Katherine's eyes as they found Emily's. She realised there was little hope left of her escaping. This would most likely be the last time she would ever see them, any of them. Through a stream of tears, she held her friend's gaze as though to say her final goodbyes. They shared a silent exchange for but a moment before Emily gave her a nod and quickly wiped away her tears, as if Katherine had told her to be brave and unafraid. Aware that she had only a short time left, Katherine let her eyes sweep across the room, offering hurried farewells to those watching, and lingering perhaps a moment too long on Bayne's pale blue stare before snapping back to the threat rapidly rising beneath her.

~

The cold, wet, inescapable grip of the water touched the tip of Katherine's toes. If her mouth had not been taped shut, and if she had not already wasted most of what little energy she had, she would have let out a sharp cry at the touch of the frozen death that would soon engulf her.

Five minutes remained as Alek and Marko paced around the glass, throwing Katherine concerned yet encouraging looks every so often. But she had no time to focus on who they were, where she was, what her friends were doing there, or anything else but her need to survive.

As the water crept up her feet, surrounded her ankles, and began to make its way up her calves, Alek shook his head in frustration. "This is no use!"

"We could just break it?" suggested Marko half-heartedly, as though convinced it would not at all be that easy.

"Don't just stand there, do something!" piped up Layla, pulling herself away from the comforting arms of her partner. It seemed to take all the courage she had to find her voice and face the extraordinary scene unfolding before them.

"Who—" began Marko, but he was cut short.

"If all of this magic *nonsense* Zachary told us about is real, if everything Alfred's told us tonight is true, then save her. Do what you need to do and just *save* her!"

"Layla! Stop!" snapped Emily, who was trying to keep a level head.

"But they can do it, Em!"

"We will find a way," reassured Alek, finally acknowledging their presence and making eye contact, however briefly.

Emily shot her sister a quick look, silencing her before she could open her mouth to press on. Layla had always been the dreamer, while Emily, younger and shorter, had shouldered more responsibility as they grew up.

With mere seconds remaining before the countdown hit three minutes, the water had now reached Katherine's upper thighs.

⌇

"Screw it," said Marko angrily. "Break the glass."

"You sure that's a good idea?" asked Alek, hesitating at the thought of touching it again.

"Do it. If worse comes to worst..." Marko trailed off mid-sentence and exchanged a strange look with his brother.

"Okay," agreed Alek, clearly unhappy with the decision, but aware that they were fast running out of options. He picked up one of the broken planks of wood. "Let's do it then."

They took aim and, in unison, beat and hammered on the panels with all the force they could muster. The chain that suspended Katherine swung her body from side to side, but her cage remained intact. Not the faintest scratch to be seen.

Whatever hope Katherine, the brothers, and the others had been counting on faded from their eyes.

"It's no use," muttered Alek, sounding defeated.

⌇

"Carter." Marko scoffed, leaning his forehead against what would soon become Katherine's coffin as he watched the water continue to rise. "He's planned this too well. It can't have been anyone else."

"The real question is why. What's his endgame?"

Marko lowered his voice, panic starting to set in. "We have just moments left, brother. There's no guarantee that we'll be able to free her even after she's submerged. Even if we were, we'd only have minutes at most. What do we do?"

"We wait," whispered Alek after a brief pause.

"What?"

"We *wait*. Wait and hope that Carter has a better finale in mind, however terrifying that sounds."

"He wouldn't go through all of this just to send her into another life."

"Agreed. This wouldn't be how I'd end it."

"Fair point. We should send the mortals upstairs, though. They won't be able to handle more than this. Either way it goes."

"No," said Alek, his voice barely louder than a whisper. "If they're as important to her as our reports suggest, if they mean enough to her that their lives are threatened, then they need to stay. They need to be able to understand."

The pair looked up at Katherine and met her eyes as the water neared the top of her shoulders. She looked back at them and her heart sank, understanding that she was not going to survive this, no matter how determined these two seemed to want to save her. She gave a slight nod and braced for what she knew would be a horrific ending to whatever story her kidnapper was trying to write. A fitting end to the past weeks of torture.

Tick. Tick. Tick.

She did not want to leave them. She did not want to die. But as her breath wore out and the water seeped into her nose, her pointless struggling slowed.

Tick. Tick. Tick.

The chains stopped moving.

Tick. Tick. Tick.

Katherine's light brown hair flowed freely as she hung, suspended, motionless, the life draining from her.

Tick. Tick.

For a moment, her eyes remained open, taking in her final sights as the last bubbles of air disappeared.

Tick.

The cries of the crowd gradually faded, no one able to look away from the sight of Katherine's body, still and peaceful. But as the liquid finally reached the glass ceiling, it shattered along with the rest of the cage, sending Katherine crashing to the ground as water gushed across the floor, soaking everyone's ankles.

Alek rushed forward, grabbing Katherine in his arms. Without hesitation, Marko reached down and snapped the chains off her body with his bare hands as if they were made of nothing but cheap plastic. But the light had already faded from her.

The realisation that Katherine's body was now just that, a lifeless embodiment of all that their friend no longer was, began to dawn on those around her.

The last traces of colour left Bayne's face as his tall figure backed into a nearby marble column and sank to the ground in shock. Jennifer stood motionless, unwilling to believe. The others turned away, unable to face it. Though the sobs had softened to whimpers, one by one, Katherine's friends struggled to contain their emotions.

Tick. Tick. Tick.

CHAPTER 02
THE AWAKENING

They had been so distracted, blinded by their sudden grief, that they had not heard the ticking of the timer in all the chaos.

There, in one of the puddles, a single timer remained intact, flickering as it counted down on one of the unbroken pieces of glass.

"No," whispered Marko, hauling himself upright, away from where Katherine lay in Alek's arms.

Alek pulled himself together quickly, confirming, with a nod to his brother, that it was indeed counting down once more. The pair, exchanging an almost fearful glance, seemed to arrive at the same conclusion.

"She should have gone back when she died, shouldn't she have? To be reborn as a mortal again?" Marko asked Alek softly, his voice sounding as though it would break any minute.

"Apparently so. *If* the council is right. *If* that's what has been happening since she left."

"Do you think he's trying to get us to…?"

"Yes. It must be. It's the only other thing I can think of."

"Right? He'd never let it go that easily. Let *her* go that easily."

"That's what it's always been about, hasn't it? Isn't that why you started all of this in the first place?"

There was a strange excitement building in Marko's tone that gave Emily goosebumps. He grinned. "So, what do we do?"

Alek's eyes snapped up to Alfred, who was standing, ready for instruction. "It's time. *Finally*. We need to prepare."

Alfred's eyes lit up, and a smile appeared on his face, too, as he backed out of the room and slipped out of sight down one of the corridors.

Emily, like the others, was lost and confused, still in shock at their friend's death. The grief was too raw, the reality too harsh to accept. The sight of Katherine's lifeless body made it impossible to focus on anything, let alone wonder why these strangers' reactions were so different from their own.

Alfred hurried back into the room just as the timer marked eight minutes to go. He seemed quite pleased, considering the circumstances, as he crossed the foyer and handed Marko a bundle of dusty, tattered rags.

"Here it is, Prince Markovyas. Just as it was left."

Emily and Layla exchanged a confused glance.

"Thank you, Alfred," replied Marko, not taking his eyes off the package, his hands shaking.

Alfred nodded quickly. "Of course, sir. I have kept it close for this very reason."

"Brother, do you want to do this, or shall I?" asked Alek, a bit of fear sneaking past the coolness in his voice.

"You do it. She'll never forgive me if I do this to her, too," said Marko, unable to hide the regret in his eyes.

"Alright." Alek sighed. "So, now, we wait."

Tick. Tick. Tick.

The minutes passed and almost everyone was sitting on the foyer floor, not caring much about the extravagant artwork on the walls, or that the remaining water had all but ruined their clothes. All eyes were on Katherine, waiting for whatever the siblings seemed to be planning.

"What are you holding out for?" asked Emily through her silent tears, lifting her head from her arms.

"Don't worry, Emily," said Alek, his reassuring tone providing little comfort. "When that timer hits zero, everything will change. You'll see."

Their eyes met, leaving Emily fighting for breath as she spoke, nearly losing her thoughts in the forests of green looking back at her. "How can you say that? Everything h...has ch...changed."

Marko snickered, shaking his head at Emily's apparent innocence. "Like he said, you'll see. Your world is about to change. *Her* world is about to change."

Emily hung her head and buried her face in her arms again as Alek and Marko shot each other a knowing look. She was in disbelief at their cruelty, at their willingness to brush her friend's death off as a simple inconvenience, especially after they had appeared so eager to save her.

Tick. Tick. Tick.

The room became quietly restless as the time stretched on. The onlookers were fearful of what to expect when the countdown stopped, wondering what could be worse than watching someone they cared for die.

Tick. Tick. Tick.

Alfred continued to shuffle around Katherine, keeping his eyes locked on the package.

Tick. Tick. Tick.

With only two minutes left, it was as though life had been restored to both Alek and Marko as they finally broke the awkward silence.

Marko placed his hand on his brother's shoulder. "Almost time. Are you ready?"

"I have to be," Alek replied, still clutching Katherine's corpse. "Are you?"

"No going back now. It's either this or..." Marko gulped, not daring to speak his thoughts aloud.

"Definitely not that," reassured Alek hastily. "We're not giving up on her."

Emily and the others strained their ears as they watched on, not wanting to get too close, just in case.

"We're playing right into his hands, you know," muttered Marko. His voice shook as he began to unwrap the bundle of rags.

"Yeah." Alek sighed as more and more tattered bits of cloth fell to the floor, the package becoming ever smaller until, at last, a glint of silver could be seen in between the last few layers.

Emily squinted up at Marko to try to figure out what he was holding, but she did not need to wait long. He pulled out a small silver blade. Its pommel was made of reflective metal, housing a brilliant rose-gold stone. The grip was black, and the blade itself was a blend of silver and rose gold, with etchings that matched those they had seen on the glass box. It was beautiful.

Tick. Tick. Tick.

Marko handed the blade to Alek with care, who hesitated before taking it. Alfred stepped closer, preparing himself for whatever they might need.

Tick. Tick. Tick.

"Thirty seconds, Alek. Your timing needs to be perfect."

Neither Emily nor the others could take their eyes off the scene, their pain now overridden by their curiosity, tainted by mounting fear.

Tick. Tick. Tick.

Alek angled the blade downward.

Tick. Tick. Tick.

He hovered it over Katherine's heart, waiting for the signal.

Tick. Tick.

He could hear Emily gasp in the background as he took in a deep breath.

Tick.

"Now!" yelled Marko, shattering the air around them, his voice reverberating off the walls like a thunderclap.

With a surge of adrenaline coursing through his body, Alek drove the blade deep into Katherine's chest as the final digit on the timer dwindled to zero. The steel bit into her flesh with a sickening squelch. Gasps of horror broke through the fog of grief as a chorus of anguish and disgust erupted.

The crowd's reactions falling on deaf ears, Alek moved out from behind Katherine to lower her body onto the floor before standing up to take his place between his brother and Alfred.

"Now what?" he asked the other two.

"Give it a minute. Give it a minute," reassured Alfred, patting Alek's back.

~

A frigid breeze swept past Emily's petite frame, coiling around her ankles as it drifted towards her friend, whispering secrets of dark magic and forbidden power.

A loud gasp escaped Katherine's mouth as her eyes shot open, the cold, near-wet body of air taking visible form as it moved around her. Struggling for breath, she rolled onto her side and pushed herself up, rising to her knees. Hands trembling, she reached for the hilt of the blade and pulled the weapon from her chest, collapsing back to the floor immediately from the pain.

True panic attacked the room like a plague. Disbelief and shock striking each one of those still frozen in place on the floor, leading them to doubt their own sanity.

"How is this possible?" muttered Emily under her breath, watching terrified as Alfred and the brothers looked relieved, *joyous*, even. But her awe drew no attention.

The cold wind had taken on a blue hue as it encircled Katherine where she lay. Emily could not tear her gaze away as she watched the bruises on her friend's body begin to disappear, the air around her swirling faster with each turn. Katherine's cuts and wounds slowly healed themselves, and her scars faded. As the colour of her skin took on a healthier tone, her hair grew, turning the lightest of gold before she was obscured behind the spinning veil.

The paintings on the surrounding walls trembled, yet those that had been covered in white sheeting remained still, despite the wind growing stronger. It was as though it had a will of its own. The more it spun around Katherine's body, the brighter it grew, until Emily and the others had to shield their eyes from the light, only allowing themselves to take another peek as a loud thud came from within the sphere.

It slowed abruptly, and the light softened with each diminishing turn until only Katherine remained, sitting upright and glancing nervously around the room.

Unable to put into words what they had just witnessed, barely able to believe it themselves, Emily and the others stared gobsmacked between Alfred and the two brothers, amazed to find them unsurprised by Katherine's miraculous resurrection.

∽

"Kat? Katherine?" said Alek in a low, cautious tone as he made his way towards her, hands outstretched as if he was expecting her to run.

"Wha...what?" stuttered Katherine, looking at him as though she had no idea what he was saying.

"Katherine, how do you feel?"

"I...I don't kn...know."

"Perhaps you should lie down?" Alek suggested as he moved closer.

She looked taken aback, fearful, even, at his offer. "Where? Who?" Her eyes darted around the room at the faces that stared pointedly back at her, unable to recognise a single one.

Alek, exchanging a nervous glance with Marko, gently took hold of Katherine's arm. "Trust me," he whispered as she tried to pull away. "Let's get you checked over."

Afraid though she was, there was something reassuring in Alek's voice that Katherine felt was somewhat familiar. The panic that had taken root in her chest seemed to lighten at his touch, and, looking into his eyes, she could see no reason not to trust the stranger as he helped her to her feet. At least for now.

She nodded, the confusion on her face easing slightly as she chose to put her faith in something higher than herself. Alek smiled in return and led her away from the crowd, towards one of the passages into the castle's depths, leaving Marko and Alfred to deal with the fallout back in the foyer.

∿

"Someone better start talking! What the hell was that?" came a voice from near the castle doors.

"I agree with Aidan!" piped up Emily, her face stunned as she agreed with the tall, messy-haired young man she had recognised earlier.

Marko looked over at them and then turned to Alfred. "You mind taking this one?" He scoffed, patting Alfred's back as he walked past. "I need to get drunk!"

With a grimace, Alfred watched Marko head through the double doors that led to the main living room and slam them closed behind him, the force of their weight sending vibrations through the soles of their feet.

"So?" pressed Jennifer. "Are we just going to stand here, or are you people going to tell us what the hell just happened? Because, quite frankly, you're all insane!"

"Jen, stop it," came Bayne's shaky voice from behind her, the colour only just starting to return to his face. "I'm sure we all want to know what that was."

"Exactly," said Alfred. "However, for now, I think that each of you may be better served with a good night's sleep." He held up his hands as they started to protest. "Please! I promise I will explain in the morning. The castle keepers will lead you to your suites, and your luggage has already been taken up. They will provide you with something to help calm your nerves, should you desire."

Jennifer's face turned red. "But—" she urged, evidently tired of being treated like a child.

"Tomorrow," reiterated Alfred sternly, before leaving the room.

Silence fell over the group as half a dozen neatly dressed castle keepers entered the foyer and bustled around them, moving towards the centred staircase. The keepers, waist-height and exuding an air of whimsical charm, wore tailored uniforms featuring sleek, midnight-blue tunics adorned with intricate gold embroidery. Their matching trousers were neatly pressed, ending just above polished black shoes that clicked softly on the marble.

Some of them had pointy ears peeking out from beneath their neat caps, and others had curly hair that bounced with every excited step. Their oversized eyes sparkled with mischief and dedication, their lively nature evident in their playful movements. Despite their small stature, it was clear that they played an integral role in keeping the castle functional.

"Please, follow us!" called the shortest one, smiling as he ascended the stairs. He tapped rapidly on his tablet before issuing further instructions to the others.

Too tired to fight against it, Emily exchanged a look with her sister and was the first to follow the creatures to their suites on the first floor of the West Wing. Either she was about to awake from a really bad dream, or she was going to need her strength for whatever tomorrow would bring with it.

CHAPTER 03
THE DEEP END

"When Zachary briefed you on the jet, neither he nor I ever thought that what happened here last night would unfold as it did," Alfred said.

Emily had been startled awake a half hour earlier by a castle keeper gently knocking at the door to escort her and the others from their rooms. She had exchanged tired yet worried looks with Aiden, whose usually naughty brown eyes had lost their spark and looked strained, as he emerged from the room opposite hers. He, like the others, seemed to have got just as little sleep as Emily.

There had been no time for chitchat as the strange little creatures led them to meet with Alfred. They followed a different route through the castle than the one they had taken the night before, and with only a few restless hours of sleep, Emily found it far too confusing to keep track of.

Soon joined by Matthew, Layla, and Brian, and followed not long after by the others, Emily had been relieved to not have to wait in the dimly lit room alone. Having been served warm, much-needed coffee by the castle keepers mere moments before Alfred appeared at the door, there had not been much time for anything at all.

Alfred crossed the room to stand near the fireplace, then turned to address them, pacing almost immediately.

"While I may be unable to fully explain to you what has happened, I do hope that you will hear my words and take them in with an open mind. I will be brief, as there is much to do, and much still to be discussed."

There was a general hum of agreement as Alfred pressed on. Tired though Emily and the others were, they were all too eager to finally make sense of what they had witnessed.

"We initially believed that Katherine's kidnapping was the extent of the threat that faced each of you. We believed that once the princess was found, and the threat eliminated, you would be able to return to your lives and find some sliver of normality."

"Did you just say pr—?" a voice tried to interrupt, but Alfred merely paused, giving the room a stern yet sympathetic look that told them now was not the time to interrupt, before resuming his best attempt at keeping things simple and to the point.

"Unfortunately, yet fortunately still, our princess has returned to us, and a prophecy that was foretold at her birth is at last beginning to unfold. While I can only imagine the weight that has recently been placed upon each of you, and while I am sure that you are all in a state of distrust, you will need to accept that when it comes to the happenings within the castle grounds, or anything relating to this kingdom, anything is possible.

"You arrived here having learnt that your friend is more than who you have come to know. You have since witnessed real magic, and you have been exposed to circumstances that will surely disturb your thoughts now and in the future. While I long to tell you that you may return home, I am afraid that, as the prophecy has been set in motion, this will not be possible. Not for a while. Until it is fulfilled or until we deem it safe, you are to remain under the protection of our guards here in Eyrondale. This, at least as it pertains to your exposure to our world, is only the beginning."

Shuffling nervously on the oversized couch where he had flopped down earlier, Aiden piped up. The dishevelled brunette locks that dangled in his eyes were almost successful in masking the fear that hid within their deep brown corridors. "The beginning of what, exactly?"

Looking at him somewhat reassuringly, Alfred smiled. "There is much you shall still come to learn about your friend. But in this world, *her* world, you will be unable to escape the darkness that stems from the burden of knowing about this life, these secrets. However, while you are unable to change what lies ahead, the power she possesses, her immortality, or the danger you now face outside of these walls, you *are* able to control your own reactions."

The sound of Alfred's footsteps as his pacing slowed was quickly drowned out by whispers and comments of continued protest.

"Enough, please," he exclaimed, silence immediately falling among the crowd. "You will soon realise that the time for denial has long passed. Being granted access to this world is both an extraordinary gift and an unbelievable curse. While your friend's care for each of you puts you directly in harm's way, it is that same care that will ensure your safety. While her enemies would seek to exploit your importance to her, remaining under our protection ensures that we are able to shield you, as well as your families, from that which you would not be able to face alone."

"I...I...that doesn't sound too great!" Emily gulped. The others felt the same uncomfortable chill that was tickling the back of her neck.

"While this must be confusing for you, it would take a lifetime to explain in its entirety. All I ask is that you brave the coming days with a willingness to understand. The castle keepers will be here to help you at any point should you need anything, but for the rest, I ask that you not press too hard at the moment. For now, trust that you are safe."

"That doesn't really explain—" started Jennifer with a snap.

"It may not," said Alfred, cutting her off. "However, it is the only explanation that I am currently able to provide. The rest will come to light as this path continues to unfold. So, for now, I insist that you be patient." It was clear from his tone that the conversation was over.

After some quiet deliberation, Emily found her voice. "So, what do we do now?"

Alfred smiled. "Now? Now, you have breakfast. We shall concern ourselves with the rest later." He made his way over to the doors on his left, opening them with a wave of his hand. "Please. Your seats are marked. I am sure the others will be along shortly."

Exchanging unconvinced glances, their thirst for answers unquenched, the mortals followed instruction, allowing the aroma of fresh pastries to guide them around the nearest corner and down the corridor towards a magnificent dining room that awaited their arrival.

Although concerned for their friend, they found themselves drawn in by the castle and the lure of its secrets. There was something slightly comforting about being held within its walls that they were unable to shake. Alfred advised that once they finished breakfast, the castle keepers would help them become familiar with how to get from their rooms to the main areas of the wing and assist them in fabricating believable stories for their sudden disappearance from their everyday lives. Despite their initial objections, each of them ultimately succumbed to the realisation that they were not exactly in a position to argue, and that they may not be able to leave even if they tried.

While most of the day was spent recovering from jet lag and trying to settle into their accommodations, their second night in Eyrondale seemed to bring with it a more peaceful sleep than the evening before. While Emily suspected that the castle staff had dosed their dinner, she was not complaining. It had been too long since she was able to take time to truly rest.

The next days were spent collaborating with the castle keepers to fabricate the falsehoods that would shape their new lives, relinquishing control of their social media accounts and other means of communication for scrutiny and oversight, and gradually isolating themselves from the outside world.

With each passing moment, the gravity of their situation bore down upon them. While their lies ranged from being offered international positions within parent companies of their present employers to winning a fully paid holiday, none of them dared breathe a word of their new circumstances to anyone they needed to say their farewells to. Whether it was because they were under constant surveillance, or because they still had not yet fully come to believe, Emily and the others agreed to keep what happened within the walls of the castle a secret. For the time being. They could not, and would not, risk the safety of their loved ones.

As every inquiry and probe was met with the promise of more information becoming available to them upon Katherine's recovery, they longed for her swift return. Though they had not seen much of Alfred, and any encounters with one of the brothers were brief and marked by silence, the castle staff continued to offer reassurances, promising that the princess would regain consciousness soon and that answers would be provided.

Finally, hope came on the fourth morning when Emily woke in the castle to a soft knock just before sunrise – the sound of one of the castle keepers. Begrudgingly opening the heavy door and pining for the comfort of her bed, it took a moment for the news to sink in. Katherine had stirred.

Finally, thought Emily, breathing a sigh of relief that her friend was alright, the worry of a thousand hearts falling from her shoulders. That was all that truly mattered. *Right?*

Excitement grew within her and Emily raced to freshen, eager to see what the day had in store now that Katherine would be around.

Katherine opened her eyes that morning as a ray of sunshine broke through the clouds and caressed her face. She had been flickering in and out of consciousness for hours. Through the arched windows opposite, she could see the tops of the dark, full trees that stood at the edge of the castle's inner grounds. While her eyes took their time to fully adjust, a rustle from the corner behind her made her realise that she was not alone.

Looking around the room, Katherine noticed five other beds separated by glass panels, each area equipped with its own monitors, tools, and medical equipment. Locating the source of the rustling, her eyes stopped at the sight of the man who had led her to this room the night she had awoken without her memories. He was sleeping, arms folded, clearly uncomfortable as his body kept shifting in the navy-coloured armchair. Katherine watched him curiously for a moment when, as though she had called out to him, his eyes shot open, meeting hers in an instant.

"You're awake!" he exclaimed, yawning. He sat upright in the chair. "Do you know who I am? Do you know where you are?"

Katherine shook her head, hesitating before she responded. "I don't."

"You...you don't recognise me at all?"

Although doing his best to offer a reassuring smile, Alek was unable to hide the hint of disappointment in his voice.

Katherine bit her lip, staring at him as if waiting for something to click. But all that came to her was a flash of blurred images and drowned-out sounds.

Alek walked up to her bedside and took her hand. Katherine flinched, her hand twitching in his grasp as a spark of electricity was sent through her body, disappearing as quickly as it had come. But she did not pull away.

"Look. My name's Alek. We've known each other for most of our existence. You can trust me, I promise. I won't let you go through this alone. Okay?"

She could feel it somehow, his sincerity, his loyalty. There was something there, beneath the surface, something telling her that he would not lead her astray.

"Here." Alek turned to grab a heap of clothes from the nearby table and handed it to her. He gestured to the door opposite them. "Get showered. Get dressed. Knowing you, I'm sure you're starving. I'll take you down to breakfast. After that, I'll tell you anything you want to know.

Alright?"

Katherine, unable to outrun the growing fear of what would happen if her memories did not return, smiled and took Alek's outstretched hand, her stomach rumbling as she accepted his offer to help her down from the bed.

Katherine was less focused on the grand, white-marbled washroom she was steaming up and more concerned with trying to trigger a memory of how she knew Alek, as the warm water ran down her face. She figured that it...that he would be a good place to start. But the more she tried to make sense of who he could be, or who she could be, the more the incoherent, indecipherable flashes slipped out of her reach.

Frustrated, she turned off the large gold faucet, stepped out of the shower, and wrapped herself in a nearby towel. Fighting off tears, Katherine looked at the clothes and wondered how this *Alek* knew her clothing sizes. How well did he *really* know her? Her racing thoughts sent a jolt through her body, sharper even than the icy air whistling through the cracked window. Without a word, she hurried to put on the dark denim trousers, thick black sweater, and flat leather boots. *Whoever this Alek is,* she thought, examining herself in the mirror with a hint of approval, *he's got decent taste.*

Alek, who was waiting just outside the washroom, gave Katherine a wide smile as she emerged, as though to welcome back an old friend he had not laid eyes on in years. She looked comfortable yet flawless as she made her way to his side. A much better sight than when he had brought her in to see Dr Breme days before.

Katherine had seen no evidence of anything supernatural since she had awakened – nothing she could not explain away as more than a dream.

However, as Alek glanced back at her, his hand outstretched towards the intricately carved gargoyle door handle, she leapt as it suddenly came alive.

Having kept close behind her guide as they navigated the castle's corridors, descending past one of its bustling kitchens, Katherine knew there was no way she would have missed something like this. The figure's face bore a sinister grin, sharp fangs protruding from its gaping maw.

"Don't be afraid," said Alek, closing his grip around the creature's exaggerated tongue. The iron wings, once folded tightly against its back, rustled and shifted, curling around his hand. "They've been asleep for a really long time. I'm sure they were just as thrilled to wake up and resume their duty as we all were to see you back here."

Katherine could barely get a word out. Her eyes were transfixed on the wings as they caressed Alek's skin, acknowledging his right to enter before returning to their inanimate state and allowing the door to swing forward without force.

"Are you ready for this?" Alek asked, his eyes examining her from head to toe as pots and pans clanged from the room beside them, reverberating off the stone.

Katherine replied without thinking, her mind still struggling to make sense of what she had just seen. "How could I be ready if I don't know what to be ready for?" she asked, her voice carrying the same snarky tone Alek knew all too well.

He chuckled, shaking his head as he faced forward to lead her through the archway.

Every pair of eyes turned to them as they entered the dining room, and silence fell among her friends. It was easier for Katherine to take in the details of the large stone and marble room rather than meet anyone's line of sight. Worried that she would have no recollection of anyone there, she stopped beside Alek and admired the vaulted ceilings which matched the grandiose style of the foyer where she had initially awoken. The black and gold detailing, running like veins through the floor, contrasted with the white base and the deep mahogany of a large, solid wood dining table that could seat twenty quite comfortably.

Guiding her by the small of her back, Alek led Katherine to the seat at the head of the table, taking the open chair to her left as though it was a habit. Unable to avoid it any longer, she shot quick, nervous glances at those around her, shifting uncomfortably as a sharp pain seared through her head.

"Alfred!" Alek called to the white-haired, butler-type man in the corner of the room, who approached them at once.

Alfred bowed before leaning to whisper in Katherine's ear. "Anything you need, you only have to ask."

At the sound of his voice, another flurry of images ran through Katherine's mind. Although unable to make out any sort of clear memory, a wave of calm washed over her in the midst of the discomfort she felt at being the centre of attention. She knew Alfred somehow. He, too, was someone she could trust. She could sense it.

Alfred stepped back with a smile, and Katherine, who quickly snapped out of her daze, felt a little more at ease, even though the pain still lingered.

"How are you feeling?" called a woman's voice from down the table.

"We were so worried. Just can't believe..." started another.

"You look amazing!" said a young, light-eyed man from near the middle.

There was a rush of agreement as Katherine looked between them, unsure of what to say. She did her best to fight off more incoherence in an attempt to gain some semblance of quiet control, but she merely managed to push the chaos aside, compartmentalising the pain that would not let her be.

Through the growing chatter and the tangled web in her own mind, Katherine heard a voice that ignited a flicker of warmth in her chest. "What do you remember from that night?"

Conversation slowed as the room turned to watch Katherine seek out the face of the young, black-haired man seated to her right. Finding herself unexplainably locked onto the intensity of his deep chocolate gaze, she paid no attention as Alek stopped buttering his toast beside her, giving the man a look that should have stopped him dead in his tracks.

Ignoring his brother's death stare, Marko pressed on, this time with more urgency. "What about the two weeks before that?"

"Marko!" snapped Alek. "Enough!"

Katherine traced an invisible pattern on the table, her voice barely above a whisper. "I don't remember anything."

"You don't remember anything *yet*," reassured Alek, his face softening as he turned from his brother to face her. "You went through a lot these past few weeks. We can't expect you to be back to full steam at the drop of a hat."

Katherine grimaced and reached for a cheese croissant on the tray of pastries in front of her. Not wanting to push, just as their hosts had asked, most of the diners returned their eyes to their breakfast.

"Ma'am?" came Alfred's voice from over her shoulder once she had finished the last bite of her buttery indulgence. "If you would like to join me for a stroll, I might be able to assist."

Alek nodded in approval, as Katherine stole a hesitant glance at him. She excused herself from the dining table and chose to trust that her feelings about them were guiding her towards the right choice. As she followed Alfred through one of the arched doorways to her right, which led to a large stone courtyard, she heard murmurs from the table as the discussion about her memory loss resumed in her absence.

The courtyard was breathtaking. The stone-paved square was cornered by the castle walls on two of its sides. A grand, sweeping staircase centred each of the two adjacent edges of the area, each lined with large pots filled with an assortment of roses, leading down into the seemingly endless grounds that surrounded them. At the far corner, opposite where she and Alfred had entered, stood a large gazebo, its stone columns covered in white roses that crept up and over its roof.

Katherine turned to face the towering walls, taking in the beauty of the ivy-covered stone, arched windows filled with stained glass, and columned balconies that sprung out overhead. It was absolutely enchanting. Her jaw dropped as she fought to stay grounded in the sheer awe of it all before more images of a life once lived teased her mind.

"What *do* you remember?" asked Alfred. His grey eyes filled with a warm kindness, encouraging Katherine, as if he knew what she had been thinking only moments before.

She sighed, shoulders slumping as she shook her head, feeling a pang of disappointment in herself for failing to provide the answers that she, Alfred, and the others were longing for.

"Ah! I see," he exclaimed with an affectionate smile, gesturing for her to leave the outdoor dining area to walk with him. "How about we start with the most pressing of matters?"

Nervous, but with curiosity getting the better of her, Katherine kept to Alfred's peaceful pace as they strolled down the garden-lined walkways. It was clear that he would prefer not to be overheard.

Alfred moved in silence, hands neatly clasped behind his back. Occasionally, he paused to inhale the fragrance of the flowers they passed, their sweet blooms filling the air with a cloudy haze. Katherine thought she caught them turning to glance at her once or twice, but she dismissed it as a trick of her mind.

"You may not believe this now—" Alfred said. "But, before long, I expect your memories will return and all of this will become clear."

From his tone, Katherine gathered that it would be far better if she remained silent and listened to what he had to say. That suited her just fine – her thoughts were too muddled with questions to settle on just one.

"I suspect that, at this very moment, you are attempting to sort through a cloud of confusion inside your mind. Wondering, perhaps, what may be reality and what may be fiction. I encourage you, Princess Katherine, not to dismiss any memory or emotion."

She was certain she had misheard him, her surprise evident to Alfred.

"Yes." He nodded. "Before you journey down a road of disbelief, take a look around. Look at where we are this very second. Whether you believe this to be a dream or reality, either one has you here, at this moment in time, for a reason."

Katherine held Alfred's gaze as he studied her, searching beyond the surface for a reflection of an open mind and heart. His smile widened as he continued.

"Having been by your side since the beginning of my existence, Princess, I have always known that it would be my responsibility, no, my honour, to guide you through the inevitable events to come. The prophecy that was created by your birth would always come to pass, and regardless of how many ages it has taken to be set into motion, my readiness for the path ahead has not been shaken.

"I have notified the Consilio Statera as to the events of the night you arrived here and have informed them of your return to consciousness. Now that you are awake, they will look to move ahead almost immediately. Messengers have already been sent to each of the kingdoms, calling for their representatives to join us at court tomorrow evening, where you will be presented to the communities of power, and we will bear witness to the formalities of the champion selection for the upcoming trials."

The pain in Katherine's head intensified as a wave of panic took hold. "Who are...? Trials?"

"All in time, Princess. Please, allow me to continue. We have much to go over and a limited amount of time in which to do so."

"I ca...this is too much."

"Indeed. There is much to take in, Your Highness. Of that, I am acutely aware. However, I will be by your side to assist you through it all. While you may not recall who you are or *what* you are at the moment, the communities of power need you to be who they know you to be, regardless of whether you are aware of the truths that surround that. They need to be confident that you are indeed the princess they are putting their hopes in, the princess whose return they have awaited for so long. Even if only for now, you need to pretend."

Katherine's mouth hung open, but she was unable to form a single audible sentence. *He's serious*, she thought, a sinking feeling in her stomach pushing the notion of reality out of her mind. *It's impossible, but he's serious.*

"Princess, we unfortunately do not have the luxury to waste time on questions or doubt. Nothing I can say will convince you of what you feel is true deep within. I understand that I, that *we*, are asking for more than you may currently be able to give, but rest assured that I will assist you in being as convincing as you could possibly be until such time as you are once again able to recognise the throne of Eyrondale as rightfully yours."

Alfred was unable to mask his sympathy for her as Katherine took on the impact of his words. But no matter how much he clearly wished he could explain it more eloquently, the urgency in which she needed to come to terms with her role seemed to outweigh any feelings of his own.

"While the council moves to begin the proceedings that will lead to the prophecy's fulfilment, every eye in that room, whether magical or mortal, will fall upon you tomorrow. You will need to face our world's other leaders, the five other kingdom masters, and their court representatives. Believe me, Princess, it is better if they do not see you as vulnerable."

Alfred's voice suddenly turned cold, stressing Katherine's need to pay attention.

"Each kingdom will be rooting for their prince to succeed in these trials. It is important that you do not underestimate how far they will be willing to go to ensure their master's victory in this. If this prophecy is to bring about what it says it will, you and the victor are fated to give rise to some of the most powerful magic this world has ever seen."

They reached the gazebo, having passed the pond in the middle of the courtyard gardens, and having emerged from the pathways lined with artfully arranged roses and statues. Katherine, still unable to fully comprehend what Alfred was saying, found herself overtaken by an unexpected sense of acceptance. It was as though the scattered fragments of her memories were slowly aligning, yet she remained lost in the haze of her own mind. However, there was something undeniable that brought her an inexplicable sense of peace.

"I…I believe you," she whispered at last, the feeling in her gut urging her to follow the path being laid before her. She could tell from the look in Alfred's eyes that, no matter how crazy his story sounded, he was sincere. "I'm not sure why, but I do."

Alfred smiled and looked out towards the forest that surrounded the edge of the inner grounds. "I will explain as much as I am able before tomorrow's festivities. For now, come. Let us begin our preparations for what is essentially your re-entrance into a quite extraordinary world."

"What…" Katherine's throat tightened. "What would I need to do?"

"You need to be able to make them both love and fear you at the same time. Princess, you have been lost to us for seven lifetimes, and with the fate of the natural and supernatural worlds in the balance. You need to show no fear, no fault, no doubt. For they will eat you alive if they sense any sort of trepidation."

His tone carried an intensity that eclipsed any words Katherine could muster. Whether he had meant to instil a sense of fear that churned her stomach and made her want to bring up her croissant, or had another intent entirely, it was as though some deep part of her opened its arms to his tale, absorbing it like a black hole starving for light.

"It was long ago foretold that upon your revival in the thirteenth minute of mortal death, Fate would begin a series of trials that would allow for a pure descendant of the Strands of Power to bring into existence an heir of their own, one that would give rise to a new kind of force entirely. For millennia, our communities have either longed for this day while fearing that it would never come, or they have dreaded it, desperately wishing it to be merely the whispers of ancient folktales. That night…" Alfred sighed, turning his back on the grounds. "The prophecy was proven to be true with your awakening. And believe me when I tell you, Princess, even the faithless and the forgetful cannot escape the new realities that these next weeks shall bring to life."

He started back towards the castle, motioning for Katherine to join him.

"I will teach you how to conduct yourself as the princess you truly are. Enough to make them all believe it, for now, at least. Enough to pass their judgemental gaze with flying colours until you remember. Until you understand."

They walked in silence for the rest of the journey, Katherine replaying Alfred's words on a loop in her head as she desperately tried to quell the queasiness she now felt. Approaching the same entrance they had used before, she was relieved to see that the dining room had been cleared. Happy at the thought of not having to answer any more questions, her lingering headache eased.

Their footsteps echoed as Alfred led Katherine through the West Wing, guiding her up staircases, through hallways lined with suits of armour, and beneath countless intricately detailed arches, too many for her to keep track of. Finally, they reached a set of double doors at the end of a corridor on the third floor. Beaming, Alfred encouraged her to step inside.

"Apologies, Princess," he exclaimed as Katherine entered, the wonder evident on her face. "The Monarch Suite, which you had been renovating, sealed itself shut at your disappearance from our world, along with other parts of the castle. This is only temporary until you are able to recall how to lower the seals."

Barely able to take in his words, Katherine walked through the large sitting room. At each opposite end of the seating area stood a roaring fireplace, flanked by a set of comfortable yet elegant-looking couches and armchairs. The style matched the mix of contemporary elegance and traditional architecture that she had seen throughout the wing. The balance between the cold of the marble and stone and the warmth of the furnishings and fires was so familiar, stirring a longing for a home she wished she could remember.

Katherine passed through the doors that stood open opposite the suite's entrance, into a magnificent bedroom that held all the comforts she could need. A giant four-poster bed stood against the right-hand wall, framed on either side by arched double doors with stained-glass panels. Through them, Katherine caught a glimpse of the balcony, easily as large as a studio apartment, that overlooked what appeared to be some sort of small arena and the back of the grounds. Opposite the bed, she peeked through an opening and into the en-suite washroom. It matched the theme of the one she had used that morning, but with a tub large enough for three, and a shower that could easily, in Katherine's opinion, fit a small horse.

Alfred, who had been watching her patiently, gave a quiet cough and walked into the room. "This way," he said, gesturing for Katherine to follow him through the door to the left of the en-suite entrance.

As they crossed the threshold, the room filled with light as the peaceful flames hovering above each sconce grew bright, revealing a collection of clothing, accessories, and jewels that any woman would surely envy. Leaving Katherine rooted to the spot, her eyes wide as another display of power stole her speech, Alfred searched the rows. It was not long before he returned holding some of the most beautiful gowns Katherine had ever seen – or, at least, so she assumed.

"This is certainly not all of it. I have spent the past fortnight preparing for your possible arrival."

Alfred hung the selections on a rack that stood alongside the floor-to-ceiling mirror and dressing area to Katherine's left.

"While Prince Aleksander and Zachary may have been doubtful, I had hope, hope that your kidnapping, the first trace of your whereabouts we had heard whispers of since your disappearance, would signify your return. The more modern designs are closest to you, the range dating back the further you walk. However, I have taken care to limit your immediate selection to the past century. For anything else, you only need to ask either myself or a castle keeper, and we will be happy to search for whatever you desire in one of the other closets, or have something made to your liking."

"Alfred, I..."

"Tomorrow, my dear," he said softly, placing both hands on her shoulders, his eyes twinkling as the flames of the nearby fireplace danced in place. "You will shine bright enough that they will think you are a shooting star. Pick one. We have a lot to discuss before then. Trust me, Princess, you shall remember who you are soon enough."

CHAPTER 04
THE LEGEND

"Alfred should be on his way soon," said Zachary, his voice calm as he reassured them. The depths of his brown gaze held a hint of sadness as he looked out at the mortal faces he had only recently come to know through his research into Katherine's lifetimes away from the castle.

Emily exchanged a quick glance with her sister and took a breath. "Are we finally going to get a reasonable explanation for what's going on? Alfred said that we needed to wait for Kat to wake up. Well, she's awake."

Having led them into one of the vacant ground-floor guest rooms that boasted a spectacular view of the forest in the distance, Zachary could not help but appreciate the irony of this moment. He smiled. This was the room where he had, not once, but twice, heard news that would come to shape the course of his life. The first, after Katherine had saved him from certain death hundreds of years earlier. He had awoken to her kind touch and the news that the wolves who held him and dozens of others captive had been slain, and he had been rescued. The second was the night he had been told about Princess Katherine's sudden disappearance from their world.

Zachary stood with his hands in his pockets, taking a moment to admire the sea of green that stretched towards the horizon before turning to face the room. He reached for a wooden stool nearby and invited the mortals to make themselves comfortable.

"Take a seat," he said, glancing towards the door, hoping that Alfred would join him sooner rather than later.

There was a bustle to find somewhere to sit down, but it was not long before silence fell.

"Now, I'm going to try to make it as simple to follow as possible, but please, pay attention. It'll go a whole lot quicker if you'd let me finish before you start chucking questions my way." Zachary narrowed his gaze. "Okay?"

Emily and her friends shuffled in their seats, agreeing, however reluctantly, eager to hear more than the bare minimum they had been told so far.

With a theatrical wave of his hands, heavy black drapes appeared at each of the windows, blanketing the room in darkness. With a whoosh, the flames that had been crackling loudly in the fireplace behind Zachary dimmed, the glow barely bright enough to keep the figures in the room visible.

"Princess...okay...*Katherine*," he started, calling a flicker of fire to his outstretched palm and watching as it scurried across his skin, climbing to the top of his hand as he turned it over. The flame brightened and darted back and forth a few times before settling on his fingertips, where he rolled it effortlessly from one to the next in a fluid motion, like a coin slipping between practised fingers. "She is one of the leaders of the Six Kingdoms of Power that exist here, in our reality." His voice trailed off as he tossed the flame gently into the clearing in front of him, where it hovered a few inches above the floor. "Obviously, she is the ruler of this kingdom, Eyrondale."

Without warning, the flame that moved so gracefully before them multiplied, another five balls of light bursting into life. Layla gasped from nearby, but none could tear themselves away from Zachary's story. His animated gestures continued to captivate their focus even through the shadows.

"Prince Aleksander, who you met briefly when you arrived in Eyrondale, and then again as he's popped in and out since, rules Keldorne. His brother, Prince Markovyas, who you've also had the pleasure of meeting, rules the kingdom of Neighlore."

Two of the flames travelled to claim areas of the floor a little away from Katherine's representation.

"Alek and Marko have three other brothers – Prince Dàikonos, ruler of Azrallus, Prince Kaëden, ruler of the kingdom of Cardinallis, and Prince Cartesius, ruler of Callidusius."

The three remaining flames made their way to their own sections of the room. Zachary glanced at the attentive audience, the areas around his eyes almost hollow-looking.

"With me so far?" he asked, squinting through the darkness to focus on Emily's face, which was fixed intently on his display.

"Um, I think so," she said, looking up at him. "So, basically there's magic, it's an actual thing, and Kat is...a fairy princess?"

Zachary let out a loud chuckle at the snark the mortal had let slip through in her voice. "No, no!" He laughed. "*Believe* me, Katherine is the furthest thing from a 'fairy princess,' as you put it. No, no, she and the princes are...something *older*. Something...*else*." He paused as a sudden chill tickled their skin at his words.

Knowing that Emily could not be the only one suddenly feeling they were being told considerably less than they should be, Zachary scanned their faces. His eyes caught the flickering light reflected in Bayne's narrowed gaze as he stood, arms folded, leaning against a nearby wall. Though he could not see the mortal's expression clearly from where he sat, Zachary could imagine it – hard, full of doubt and distrust. His attention quickly shifted back to the room as he spoke again.

"You've all heard the stories of how magic has consequences," he whispered. "But where the traditional limitations and consequences of magic and power apply to anyone else born or turned to it, and especially those who have had to learn it, like me, they don't apply as such to Katherine and the others like her. She...*they* are able to wield powers like nothing I have seen in my hundreds of years on this planet. Even so, pushing themselves and their abilities past the breaking point is what brought us all into being in the first place."

From each of the little fires sprang tinier versions of themselves as Zachary spoke. The scent of anticipation that had wafted from the mortals was quickly soured by a trace of fear.

"Each catastrophic misuse of power brought into life a new line of magic, a new kind of monster, a different type of *being*. This eventually led the Consilio Statera to take action. They harnessed untouched energy from the Three Spheres of Power to limit these abilities and minimise consequential damage." There was a momentary silence. "Whether born to power, turned by it, or having learnt to wield abilities unlike anything you've ever seen, each of us exists because of a breach of our world's laws in one form or another."

As the flames continued to multiply, shrinking in size and brightness with each cycle, Zachary focused on maintaining the delicate balance of the magic. He let the murmurs of disbelief wash over him, giving no outward sign that he heard them.

The hypnotic crackle of the flames, reaching into the far corners of the room, was drowned out by a voice that seemed to find its courage from behind a mane of thick red hair. "How is that possible?" asked Jennifer. "How is it possible that magic can even exist without anyone noticing?"

Zachary could practically feel her brown eyes rolling as she spoke. However brave or dismissive the human was trying to sound, she was unsuccessful in masking her unease.

"My girl," came a quiet voice from the doorway behind them. "Can you honestly tell me that you have never seen or experienced magic in your life?"

"Ah, Alfred!" exclaimed Zachary in surprise before Jennifer could reply. "You snuck in without making a sound."

"I have just left the princess and thought you might need a hand. How would you put it?" Alfred smiled. "Ah, yes! Sooner rather than later, I am sure."

A smirk tugged at the corner of Zachary's lips. "Well. You *did* promise to take over."

"Oh, no! Please, go ahead," Alfred said, shuffling his way past the group to Zachary's side, avoiding the multitude of flames that continued to put on quite a display. "You are doing a fantastic job."

Zachary scowled as quietly as he could, getting to his feet. Alfred knew how much he disliked having to talk to anyone unless he really had to. He much preferred the company of computers to that of man.

"Fine." Zachary sighed. "Now, tomorrow will be the first time in a long time that representatives from *all* the kingdoms are going to be in the same place at once. In an effort to maintain discretion, for the duration of your stay here, *you* will serve as the representatives of Eyrondale."

"Indeed," added Alfred. "Traditionally, a full court of leaders would gather, one or two from each branch of the kingdom's reach, to represent their respective communities. However, aside from the activities in the East Wing, this will be the totality of Princess Katherine's court."

The mortals became restless at Alfred's words. Whether it was the way in which he had phrased it, or whether they simply took him to be more serious than Zachary, there was something about the way he spoke that made each of them feel an instant burden placed upon their shoulders.

"So," came Jamie's calm voice through the dark, "say we believe you and go with this."

"Jamie!" whispered Layla's husband from where he sat next to her. Beads of nervous sweat were clearly visible as they ran down his near-balding scalp, his thinning light-brown hair not helping to keep them at bay. "What are you doing?"

"Brian, just go with me for a second here." Jamie left the comfort of the couch to stand nearer the flickering display, picking at the fair skin of his chin as he attempted to articulate his thoughts.

Zachary, just as surprised by the human's willingness to get involved as the rest of them, stood back and leant against the fireplace, waving his hand in encouragement. "Go ahead. Have at it."

"Say we believe everything everyone's said so far, believe everything we've seen, why would an all-powerful *being*, or whatever..." Jamie's voice cracked as he struggled to say it aloud with ease as if it was meant to be an everyday, rational concept. "Why would Katherine care so much about people she would have only known for a tiny fraction of her existence? Why can't we just go back to our day-to-day and have guards like the others do?" He shook his head, a deep furrow forming between his brows. "Wouldn't having us head into a room with people... or things...who may want to kill us be a tad redundant if you're trying to keep us safe."

Alfred and Zachary exchanged an uncomfortable look. It seemed that, from the sounds of fidgeting around him, Jamie had triggered a question that none of the mortals had been wanting to ask them aloud – one that neither Alfred nor Zachary had particularly wanted to answer.

"Actually," said Alfred, apparently deciding that it would be best to be truthful here. "We are not able to provide you with the answers you seek. Your importance to Princess Katherine is something that she alone will be able to explain. For the time being, we are only able to place trust in those within the castle walls until we are able to determine the reach of the threats against this kingdom. As such, seeing as we cannot allow you to leave, we ask that you accept the roles that have been given to you and participate in keeping up the necessary pretences. The easiest way to ensure your safety is to have you in plain sight, where there will be too many eyes on you for anyone to attempt anything. All we know is that each of you was brought to our attention for a reason, and we ourselves are seeking to understand Fate's rationality behind it."

"I have a few ideas," muttered Emily, barely above a whisper, as she cast a few cautious glances into the darkness.

Bayne's voice suddenly cut through the shadows. "Wait." All eyes turned to where he stood.

"Yes?"

"You...you speak of fate like it's a person or something."

Attention snapped back to their storytellers and Alfred gave a small, knowing smile. "And if *Fate* is indeed a person...or *something*? Then what?" His eyes narrowed with quiet amusement. "That discussion, however, will have to wait until another day, I am afraid."

"Yes, Alfred. Let's continue," pressed Zachary, before anyone could make the scene more uncomfortable than it was quickly becoming. He beckoned everyone to return their attention to the dancing lights before them. "Throughout the ages, the kingdoms and the lands they are made up of, have maintained peace, have dived into war, have been destroyed, and have been rebuilt."

The calm flames that represented Katherine and the five princes took turns rising to meet their gaze – clashing, uniting, then dividing. As Zachary continued his story, the fires took cues from his words, acting out key details before their eyes.

"Now, this is the important bit. Let's go back to just after the birth of existence when the Spheres of Cosmic, Magic, and Destiny brought about the beginning of ages. Each sphere divided into three distinct lines of untouched power that would see the universe and planes of being maintained."

Zachary could tell that his audience was captivated, however difficult this was becoming for them to process. With an encouraging gesture from Alfred, he did his best to keep his explanation brief.

"The presence of these strands, however, were too much for existence to withstand, threatening its very foundation. Able to manifest only briefly without risking total collapse, the Nine Strands understood the need for balance. To preserve reality, they created a plan to weave their essence into the very fabric of life, death, and all that lies between. From each sphere, one strand would be absorbed into existence. One would shape all that lies beyond. And one would take form as a physical embodiment of power.

"Now, it is said that, in their greed, Creation and Destruction worked together in secret, bringing about the Age of the Gods, by birthing creatures known as the Celestials, the physical manifestations of Cosmic

Power. The same was not true for Void, who was unable to take physical form and instead made its presence known in all that cannot be touched or seen. Void was joined by Spirit, representing the Magic Sphere, and Soul, embodying the Force of Destiny."

Even Alfred, who had heard the story a million times, seemed to be enjoying the animated tale that the mortals were so hypnotised by.

"In this, Arcane was absorbed into the corporeal worlds, to be harnessed and channelled by users of Magic. Fate, stemming from Destiny, was also absorbed into the universe, charged with guiding all paths of being."

"So what does that make—"

"Now," continued Zachary, shooting an annoyed look in the direction of the voice that had so rudely tried to interrupt, "that brings us to, well, the reason you're here, I guess."

Having been snapped out of his trance, he looked to Alfred to take over, who quickly cleared his throat.

"Indeed. Just as the others had been acknowledged, so too were the lines of Elemental Magic and that of Time, the final branch of Destiny Power. However, the Cosmic strands had jumped the gun in a race for control, creating their embodiments as fully developed beings whose powers were volatile and whose minds were their own. Seeing the threats that the newly formed Celestials already began to pose to existence, the remaining two strands sought to bring balance by slowing the growth of the vessels destined to carry their power, ensuring these physical forms could better withstand what they were meant to embody. It was here that five sons were birthed as a means to house the power of the elements, while a daughter was birthed to Time as a product of both light and dark."

Alfred was taking great care in his choice of words, evidently trying to avoid inciting more panic or fear than was necessary.

"Upon the birth of these descendants of power, it was said that Fate dared to gather the Nine Strands one final time, risking all of existence to lay down the prophecy that has brought you here. At that moment, Fate foretold that the lines of power would one day merge, reshaping all that is destined to come."

"Now that means," interrupted Zachary, quite amused, "that as Alek is a son of Elemental Magic, it's up to him or one of his brothers to fulfil the prophecy. It resulted in them basically becoming royalty in our world."

Alfred let a judgemental cough slip out.

Zachary smiled slyly as he continued. "While the eyes of the communities of power will be on Princess Katherine and the princes tomorrow, the faster you accept that there is no going back to your lives right now, the better. You're entering a world that you could only ever imagine, that comes with dangers your wildest dreams couldn't even begin to summon."

Zachary knew his carefree attitude did little to inspire confidence. He could feel their unease, but he remained relaxed. *Too* casual perhaps. Alfred opened his mouth, likely ready to step in, but Zachary waved him off. They needed to understand, and they needed to understand now. Feelings be damned.

"The dominos that had to fall to trigger the other night's events were too intricate to attempt to explain. This isn't just the result of seven lifetimes worth of preparation, but thousands – many thousands. What has happened is no accident, and because of that, I'd encourage you to take time after today to read up on our histories, on what you've all fallen into here. We have a large enough library to answer most of what you could possibly think to ask about the world you're about to be fully exposed to, but you have to understand that Katherine's memory needs to come back in its own time, so don't push her before she's ready. I'll get you guys going with a brief rundown of all this, but there's no time for us to pull focus from what we need to be doing to babysit."

"But—" Emily started.

"This being said," Zachary cut her off, raising his voice a little, "there are rules when it comes to your being here. While we live in plain sight and have our arrangements with those that govern the mortals out there, they can never know what goes on here in *our* world. Do you understand? You'd be risking the lives of those you care about if you expose them to our truths, any more than they already have been."

"Sounds more like a lecture than an explanation," muttered Jennifer snarkily, crossing her arms. It was clear that she did not like the idea of being stuck in the middle of all of this, no matter how safe they were promised to be within the walls of the castle. That this was all a little too far-fetched for her.

Emily and the others seemed to wish to say something too, and longed to react, but the flicker of darkness that flashed across Zachary's face suggested that they would be better off keeping their thoughts to themselves.

"Young Zachary is not wrong," said Alfred, his eyes glinting as he looked out at their worried faces. "But, while you are prohibited from sharing what happens here with those outside of these walls, you will soon learn the benefits of being at court."

With a wave of Alfred's hand, the flames vanished, and the drapes dissolved into a wisp of black smoke, flooding the room with sunlight once more.

"Come!" he instructed as Emily and the others adjusted from the shock to their eyes. "The castle keepers are on their way with a selection of clothing options for tomorrow's event. You may select any outfit you would like, and they will have them fitted to your measurements."

"Wait a sec..." piped up Jamie.

Alfred ignored his protest and placed a hand on his arm, leading the mortal towards the exit.

"Unfortunately, we do not have long before delegates from the other kingdoms begin to cross our borders. You should know that while *we* are aware that Princess Katherine has a form of memory loss, the rest of the communities of power do not, and *cannot*, know. It is imperative that you remain on guard tomorrow and stay 'tight-lipped,' as they say. You never know who may be listening. We will, of course, be nearby should you feel you need assistance, but for now, please excuse me. I will rejoin you later on." Not waiting for them to respond, Alfred left Jamie's side and exited through the door.

"Well, I guess this is where we end off for now then. See you all downstairs tomorrow around four. Do try to get your rest before the festivities, you'll need it," said Zachary loudly as a stream of castle keepers entered the room, each carrying armfuls of various bags and boxes, with racks of gowns and suits following behind them as if instinctively knowing where to go. "You're in good hands."

He followed Alfred's fresh trail out of the door and down the corridor, leaving the mortals at a loss for words, having had not nearly enough time to take it all in and feeling as though they had been thrown into the deep end, *again*.

"You know this is crazy, right, Em?" whispered Layla, watching as, one by one, their friends were surrounded by castle keepers, who soon became annoyed at the mortals' lack of willingness to participate. Whether simply deciding to give in and accept their new reality, or not daring to get on the bad side of the waist-height creatures who seemed able to appear anywhere within seconds, the sisters watched as the others, even their cousin who was usually so level-headed, followed their instructions.

"True," Emily admitted as a bouncy, long-haired young castle keeper made her way towards them, arms overflowing with shiny dresses she had pulled off of a nearby rack. "But I kinda wanna see what happens next."

"From what it sounds like, it can't be anything good."

~

"May I enter, Your Highness? It's Aimee," came a voice from the other side of the suite's large double doors.

Katherine, who sat in an armchair nearest the fireplace, welcomed the distraction from reading and re-reading the files Alfred had left her the day before – documents that contained a breakdown of the evening's key participants and an overview of what would be required of her.

"Come in," she instructed, removing the pencil from between her teeth and tucking it behind her ear.

"How's it going, Princess?" squealed Aimee with an excited bow after shutting the door behind her.

Katherine smiled at the optimism that the short, pointy-eared castle keeper exuded. "To be honest? It's all a bit much to take in."

"Yet you seem so quick to accept it. If you don't mind me saying?"

Aimee tilted her head in quiet interest, her large blue eyes tracking Katherine as the princess got to her feet and moved to warm her hands over the flames.

"That is a *complicated* question."

"Well then, we have a little while longer before I am to escort you downstairs. If you'd like, you could tell me all about it while I clean up?"

Warmth spreading through her at this small stranger's genuine empathy, Katherine agreed, feeling quite comfortable in her presence.

"I could definitely use the company and, preferably, more to go on than just the summaries of the kingdoms and tonight's guests that Alfred gave me. Would *you* be able to help me with that?"

A wide smile spread across Aimee's porcelain face as she conjured a duster from thin air. "I wish I could, Your Highness. I can assist you with any questions you may have about the files. Beyond that, however, I think you would be better served with Alfred."

"And why is that?"

"We've been asked to allow your memories to come back to you when, and how, Fate has intended."

"So you think my memory loss is part of this whole prophecy thing, and not because of what Alfred told me happened the other night?"

Aimee bit her lip. "To be honest, I couldn't tell you. But personally, I don't believe in coincidences."

"Something tells me neither do I."

"Well then, why don't you ask me what you'd like to know, and I'll see if I can answer."

"Thank you. Aimee, is it? That means a great deal, all things considered."

The castle keeper's wide smile returned, and she bounced around the room, cleaning and dusting as she went. Katherine wondered just how much Aimee would really be willing to tell her – even if she asked.

CHAPTER 05
THE EAST WING

L ayla scowled as Matthew catcalled her and Emily when the siblings arrived in the main living room. Having not seen each other since parting ways at breakfast to attend to their final fittings, and having spent most of the previous day preparing for the festivities, the mortals had agreed to gather a few minutes before Alfred instructed them to meet in the foyer to leave.

Jamie grabbed two glasses of champagne from the table and handed one to each of them. He appeared to be growing rather used to castle living. "Looking good there, ladies!"

"Well, you clean up nice yourself, Jamie," said Layla, looking him up and down, evidently approving of the modern black suit and bright purple tie he had chosen to wear, which suited his broad frame.

"Ah! And here come Jen and Bayne," Matthew exclaimed, pulling on his dew-green jacket as the couple arrived just in time. He had been the only one brave enough to wear a lighter suit – the rest had thought him slightly mad for choosing a colour so close to that of his eyes. Although his dark blond hair remained as artfully unkempt as ever, he pulled the look off quite well. "Come, join us!"

Jennifer had chosen a more classic style and dazzled in a cream gown fitted tight to her tall, slender frame. It contrasted the pink of Layla's dress and the black of Emily's dramatically. She bent to hug the siblings and greeted the others as a tight-lipped Bayne shook hands with Brian and Aiden before joining the rest of their group. Although he looked quite comfortable in his classic black suit and light blue button-up underneath, Bayne appeared more on edge than any of them. There was a strange darkness that framed the pale blue of his eyes, a glimmer of something eating away at him beneath the surface.

Not wanting to acknowledge the obvious tension in the air, Jamie raised his glass. "Oh, well! Here's to getting through whatever happens from here on out, together."

"I'll drink to that," said Emily, raising her glass to his. The others, however hesitantly, followed suit.

Their small talk was short-lived as Zachary entered from the dining room next door, looking unexpectedly sophisticated in a gunmetal grey suit that he had clearly been itching to take out for a night on the town.

"It's almost time," Zachary announced, adjusting his silver cuff links. He strode through the room towards the foyer, gulping down a glass of champagne along the way.

Exchanging quick looks, Layla and Brian – who had chosen a larger-than-normal bow tie that matched the colour of her dress – followed Zachary out of the room, leading the rest. None of them felt as though they had drunk enough to prepare them for the night ahead.

❧

"Good evening, everyone!" came Alfred's booming voice from atop the landing as Layla and the others entered.

A flurry of greetings filled the air as he descended into the foyer.

"You all look wonderful."

"As do you!" said Zachary playfully, twirling in place for him to get the full effect of his ensemble. "Absolutely spiffy!"

"Oh, stop," muttered Alfred, rolling his eyes in annoyance at the childish behaviour. He joined the group at the bottom of the staircase and reverted to his pleasant and reserved demeanour at once. "Everyone, town cars are waiting outside to transport you to the East Wing. Once you arrive, you will make your way into the Grand Hall, seating yourselves at the front, on the left-hand side."

He paused, lingering his gaze on each of them in turn to ensure they understood his instruction. Satisfied that they were all paying attention, he pressed on.

"This evening, as best as possible, avoid interacting with members of the other courts. There will be a number of representatives in attendance who do not take as kindly to mortals as some of us do. There will be castle keepers watching over you at all times. However, for your own safety, it would be best not to go off alone – or to go off at all. There will be many questions surrounding the events that you have witnessed, and we would prefer to maintain manageable control of the narrative, considering the present circumstances. Therefore, I remind you to treat your time here as confidential. Be pleasant, be wary, and remember to keep an open mind. Any questions?"

There was a moment of silence before Jamie's rational thought process kicked in.

"Hold up. First, if we're supposed to stay inside the grounds for our protection, why are we heading out of the gates to get to the other side of the castle? Second, if it's so dangerous, why are we going in the first place?"

"Can't fault him on that one," muttered Matthew as he puffed out his broad chest, scratching at the stubble on his chin.

"There's technically no way to access the East Wing from here. Not for you, anyway," said Zachary, a little too quickly. "Only the castle staff can transport themselves between the wings using the servers' portal in the kitchens. The passages that connect the two wings sealed themselves shut as soon as Katherine left and won't open for anyone. Any other way, underground tunnels included, isn't exactly an option for you. So, gotta take the long way round."

"Not *exactly* an option?" prompted Jamie, Zachary's choice of words not lost on any of them. "What does that mean? Not that I'd like to muck about in some creepy old tunnels. But still."

"That is of no concern to you," interrupted Alfred, steering the conversation away from the touchy subject. "However, as for your second question, that is simple to answer. Should you not form part of the court of representatives for this kingdom, we would need to gather others willing to serve the cause."

"I'm sure that would be easier, wouldn't it? Then none of us would be stuck in this mess," came Jennifer's snarky side commentary that Alfred was quickly growing impatient with.

"The true representatives of this kingdom, the collection of leaders who rule over their respective communities," he snapped in a hushed tone, "some of them would cause even your most terrifying of nightmares to be afraid of the dark. You seem to be forgetful of who, of *what*, you are dealing with here. I warn you, do not press the limits of those with abilities you know not. While you are under the protection of this house, we would prefer that you not provoke the very beings that we are doing our best to avoid inviting inside these walls – nor the ones that already reside here.

"Calling Eyrondale's true court to service would mean allowing such beings free rein within the West Wing. It would give them access to all of you. To secrets best left guarded until Princess Katherine can advise who she deems trustworthy enough to allow back into the fold. Until we are able to determine the truth surrounding her kidnapping, we cannot be sure of who may have played even the smallest part in the events that have led you all here."

Alfred waited for a retort, but none came, and the quiet that followed his words only added to their weight. The sound of the melodic doorbell broke the uneasy silence. With a wave of his hand, the arched set of doors opened to reveal a collection of black cars waiting in a line down the drive-way, ready to round the elaborate centrepiece and collect their passengers.

"Please," Alfred said, gesturing for the mortals to make their way towards the vehicles, "I will see you there shortly."

Although they were nervous, Emily and the others started towards the exit, visibly relieved not to have to face the dangers of the night alone.

Alfred noticed Jennifer exchanging a furious look with Bayne, who, it seemed, had been just as unimpressed with her tone earlier. It was an exchange that turned more than a few heads.

Bayne looked more tired than usual, the circles under his eyes deeper than any of them had seen since the mortals arrived at Eyrondale Castle. Catching Alfred's watchful stare, Bayne quickly averted his gaze, as if to avoid making things worse, and sped up to Aiden's side.

The town car made its journey down the winding driveway, towards the golden gates of the West Wing's exit. Security noted down the vehicle and driver's details before allowing them through. Katherine tensed up the moment they passed through the gates. She was anxious enough as it was without the worry of the lowered protection outside the castle walls. Alfred, during their earlier discussions, had promised that she would be completely safe, but her gut told her to keep on guard.

They turned left onto the main road, a thick corridor of tall trees lin-ing their way, and Katherine quietly promised herself to not let her nerves get the better of her. She was a firm believer in things happening for a reason – or, at least, she assumed that she was, seeing how quickly she had agreed to go along with all of this.

Unlike the West Wing, which was situated quite a drive from its entrance gates, Katherine was able to see the lights of the East Wing from the moment they reached its security post. Logical though it was to her, considering the types of guests that would be in attendance, it was still quite daunting to see such a vast difference in the number of visible guards. While she assumed that there must be even more roaming the inner corridors of the wing and its surrounding grounds, Katherine hoped they would not need to do any more than they were at present. She shuddered at the thought of the power the guards must possess if they had the ability to keep such a large gathering of supernatural and magical beings from ripping each other apart.

The castle walls bathed them in shadow as the car drove not towards the main driveway, where countless cars were lined up waiting to drop off their passengers, but down a road to the right that led to a private entrance. Tom, the pasty-skinned, blue-eyed driver Alfred had introduced Katherine to earlier, hurried to open her door and assist her exit. His slender figure bent into a low bow as Alfred rounded the back of the vehicle to escort the princess inside.

Alfred smiled and held his arm out to guide Katherine up the stairs. "Deep breaths, Princess. I will be right here."

Following his lead through the foyer into a large, dimly lit study, Katherine was barely able to take in its beauty before two of Alfred's most trusted castle keepers and a near waist-height, dark-haired woman who was wearing a slim floor-length dress and sporting a daring pixie cut, entered.

"Excellent timing," exclaimed Alfred, his eyes gleaming with pride as Katherine responded to their bow in the manner he had taught her.

"We've brought your gown, Princess. If it would please you, may I assist you in getting ready?" asked the woman.

"Ah, yes! Princess, this is Heleen, one of your handmaidens. Now, while you have always been firm on the fact that you require no assistance, I thought this would be the best time to make use of her skills. Now that you cannot object, that is." A soft chuckle escaped the handler's lips. "She will be here to assist with anything you need."

Catching a glimpse of his encouraging smile from the corner of her eye, Katherine nodded. Alfred rubbed his hands together, clearly pleased, and advised that he would return to escort her to the Grand Hall once she was ready. She watched as he left the room, muttering instructions to the castle keepers, who struggled to keep up with his pace.

Heleen's violet eyes widened. "The gown you have selected is lovely, Your Highness," she exclaimed as she removed it from the garment bag and hung it from a hook on a nearby closet's door.

Katherine smiled. She was more nervous than she would allow herself to let on.

"I understand this might be strange. Alfred has informed the West Wing staff that your memories continue to elude you. Just know that we are here to assist in any way we can, Princess. We have not forgotten the kindness you have shown us, and we are all eagerly awaiting your full return. There is no doubt in my mind that you will get through this with grace."

With a hardly noticeable bite of her lip, Katherine nodded as Heleen bustled around the room.

∾

One by one, the mortals' cars arrived from the West Wing, joining the queue of high-end, highly armoured vehicles.

"Great," muttered Aiden, rolling his eyes theatrically. "Of course, they're all rich, too. Like there isn't already enough to worry about."

Emily stifled a giggle as Layla shot him a stern look. But the nearer they drew to the castle, the more real everything was becoming. They passed two entrances to the museum area of the wing as they waited for the remaining few cars ahead of them to move out of the lineup. Emily said a quick prayer, hoping that someone, somewhere, would hear it and guide her through whatever was next to come.

She and the others got out of the car when it was finally their turn and joined the rest of their friends atop the stairs, just outside the entrance to the castle where they, and Alfred, stood waiting. Exchanging a worried glance with Layla and Aiden, Emily recalled what Alfred had told them earlier about who would be attending that evening. While she and the others were still clinging to the last shred of hope that all of this was an elaborate hoax or illusion, it was the sheer extravagance of this fantasy that seemed to be the common thread between their feelings of disbelief and doubt.

They waited for only a moment before Alfred led them to the Grand Hall. They passed through an entrance that put the West Wing's foyer to shame. Though its stone walls, white and black marble floors, and gold detailing were similar in style to that of the West Wing, Emily could tell that this side of the castle was purposefully designed to take their breath away. Its walls were multiple stories high, held by marbled columns that branched out towards the crystal ceiling as though seeking to grow in the light that emanated from it. Hundreds, if not, thousands of white butter-flies danced above their heads to the gentle sound of a harp playing in the distance, while pots overflowing with deep-red roses lined the path to the set of arched doors to their right, blocking any access to the other parts of the castle. There was something enchanting about the way the flowers bowed as Emily and the others walked by, their petals falling to carpet the floor while new buds began to bloom.

The mortals followed Alfred's lead up the steps and into the opulent hall, where he guided them down the aisle, where more red roses bowed to them from the ends of the solid wooden pews. From what Emily and the others could see, doing their best to avoid eye contact with curious onlookers who had settled in before them, the hall had been divided into three sections of pews on either side. Alfred guided them towards the very front rows on the left.

The enormity of the room could not be lost on them. It was impossi-ble. Oversized, arched windows lined the wall to their left, where between the stained glass stood three sets of double doors that appeared to lead out to a large courtyard. The doors on their right looked to lead into the rest of the wing, and above them, a large tapestry spread across the wall, its images moving to the music that danced through the air.

Alfred quickly excused himself to attend to other guests as Emily and the others took their seats. Overwhelmed by the extravagance of it all, the mortals did their best to take in as much as they could while they had the chance. Before them, atop a handful of stairs, stood a raised platform bearing a large throne. The seat of power's gold detailing mimicked the vine-like style they had seen in the entrance, sparkling under the abundance of candlelight that filled the room. The curved double staircase that framed the dais was lined with golden candelabras, leading to a balcony above and a set of golden doors that were columned by red roses blooming in a constant cycle.

The sound of the harp was soon challenged by the whisperings and murmurs of the crowds that were filling the rest of the hall. Sweat gathered on Emily's palms. She, like those she cared for, was thankful for the clearly visible security team that was stationed throughout, and for Zachary, who was staying close to keep an extra pair of eyes on them.

Emily, like her friends, had prepared herself for the possibility of locking eyes with a werewolf's piercing gaze, encountering the devilish grin of a vampire, or facing some other wild creature, given everything they had recently learnt. But as she and the others scanned the room, their senses alert, they found no obvious signs of the supernatural among the attendees. Apart from the diminutive castle keepers scurrying about, there was no telltale hint of a supernatural presence other than the castle itself. Yet, an eerie sense of foreboding hung in the air, as if the very walls that surrounded them whispered secrets they could not quite grasp.

Having harboured a slight hope of encountering one of the mythical creatures she had only ever imagined, Emily found herself suddenly disappointed. Despite the undeniable hints of power they had witnessed since arriving in Eyrondale, she had anticipated more than just the occasional display of magic – mere door openings or the whimsical dance of a measuring tape.

⟲

Heleen took a step back and sighed happily. "There. Absolutely beautiful, Princess. Would you like to take a look?"

Katherine, still too nervous to say a word, nodded and moved towards the mirror, closing her eyes. She had not wanted to see herself until Heleen finished, fearing it would only add to her unease. *No escaping it now,* she thought, taking a breath that filled her lungs with the sharp breeze that floated in through the window.

Her eyes widened as they met her tall reflection, and a barely audible gasp escaped her lips. Although Katherine knew the brilliant blue eyes that stared back at her to be her own, there was a twinkle in them that made them suddenly come alive. She gaped at the mirror, admiring how the light-golden locks that framed her porcelain face fell to her waist and contrasted with the dark, flowing backdrop that was her gown. As the cold air put its arms around her, caressing her bare shoulders, the faintest of her hairs stood at attention. She knew this was real. She just knew it.

"P...Princess...are you pleased?" asked Heleen, twisting her fingers nervously.

Unable to find the words, Katherine hoped that her smile was enough to show her thanks. Her handmaiden's fair skin flushed red with pride.

≈

The rest of the Grand Hall was completely full. As far as Emily could tell, theirs was the only section with rows of seating left, which, unfortunately, was drawing the attention of many of the other guests. The arrival of a shorter, round-faced gentleman, who was wiping sweat from his forehead, marked the last of four others who had joined them, including Zachary. Their party had taken to the far-left ends of the rows, keeping to themselves while the chatter among the crowds only grew.

All the attendees were eager to catch a glimpse of the princess, even if many of them had long ago declared the prophecy a myth.

Silence fell upon the hall as the doors closed loudly behind a group of three elderly men, where only the sound of the harp continued to air its voice. Bayne and Aiden shuffled nervously in their seats, turning to catch a good look at the three guests, who were clearly of great importance.

Each of these men wore a champagne-coloured cloak that only just hung on the floor. The tallest of them appeared to be the leader, his blue eyes sparkling in the candlelight as he led the others down the aisle. The slim man to his right wore a blank expression, his silver eyes looking down disapprovingly at the shortest and roundest of the three. On his left, an elderly man with a neatly trimmed grey beard beamed behind his spectacles, waving cheerfully to the guests as they passed. As the trio reached the landing, the tallest of them made his way to a podium and held his hand out to silence the harpist.

"Welcome!" he said, his voice booming through the room. "Thank you for making the journey to join us here this evening. Tonight, we gather to represent the Six Kingdoms of Power, and together, we will bear witness to the beginning of events that will shape the future of the balance."

There was an outbreak of applause that could easily have grown to be deafening.

"Let us welcome back to her rightful throne, Princess Katherine of Eyrondale."

꙳

Katherine took a deep breath and exchanged a nod with Alfred as the golden doors opened before her as if encouraging her to return to the life she had been trying to piece together for the past two days. The moment they let out a creak, every eye in the Grand Hall snapped to her, and the rumblings of bodies rising to their feet were soon drowned out by a silence so loud it seemed to overpower Katherine's racing thoughts.

She did her best to focus on Alfred's earlier instructions as she held her head high and made her way down the staircase to her right. She dared not directly meet the gaze of the crowd of onlookers that bowed low as she descended. Instead, she focused her gaze on the three old men, who beamed warmly at her from their place on the dais, though an air of seriousness lingered in their expressions.

They must be the council, Katherine thought as she walked for what felt like forever, hoping that she looked as elegant and graceful as she was attempting to be, her long black cloak fluttering softly at her ankles. Alfred had done his best to explain the role of the Consilio Statera in his notes, but it had been a lot to digest. Katherine, though having repeatedly gone over the files he had left her, still could not quite understand it all. From what she had managed to decipher, each member of the council acted as a final authority for their respective Sphere of Power, having been created to channel the whispers of untouched energies and mediate the relationships between the Nine Strands.

All eyes faced forward, fixated on the princess as she reached the landing and moved to stand before the throne – her throne. Its beauty was undeniable. It was as though, amidst the chaos and confusion, it called out to her, muting the crowd who had taken to applause at seeing her in her rightful place. It took Katherine more effort than it should have to pull herself away, but she met the council's bow with an acknowledgement after a delay that was barely noticeable. The noise of the guests died down as the tallest of the three council members called for the room's attention. Katherine's heartbeat was too quick to measure as she took in the sea of faces before her. The warmth of the candlelight brushed against her bare shoulders as Heleen removed the cloak, draping it over her arm before retreating to stand by the wall near Alfred.

It had been too long since the throne of Eyrondale had been occupied. Even Katherine's mortal friends could not help but admire how easily she seemed to fit in. The vintage black and emerald gown that she and Alfred had decided on the previous day glinted in the light, its gold detailing dancing before their eyes. As the crowd settled back into their seats, Katherine scanned the room, her eyes lingering a moment on a flicker of pale blue that made her stomach lurch, telling her that there was something important she should be remembering. But there was no time to dwell on the feeling as words echoed throughout the hall.

∾

"The day has finally arrived," said Horus. Authoritative and commanding as his mere presence was, his ocean-blue eyes were unable to mask his excitement. "The prophecy has been triggered, and it is unfolding before us this eve. We, the mouthpieces for the Spheres of Power, have been waiting for this day for a very, very long time.

"Here before you, the representatives of each of your kingdoms, you will witness the ritual for the Selection by Fire. As each of the five princes presents himself to the will of the prophecy, his sacrifice will bind him to the outcomes of the trials as Fate so declares."

Horus took a step backwards. His mid-length white hair, only a shade darker than his complexion, narrowly missed hitting his fellow council member as the shorter of the three moved to take centre stage.

"Each prince shall come forward this evening to be formally selected by the orb that houses the Breath of Fate," said Herlock, his green, almond-shaped eyes gleaming out at them all. "Once their life force has been drawn and their offer accepted, the fire representing the princes' participation in the trials will be lit, and each will take their place at the point of the symbol as the flame instructs. As we move through the five trials, Fate will decide whose light shall continue to shine and whose shall dim and fade into emptiness. While the road ahead may be long and unforgiving, the prophecy and its power shall decide the future of all beings by, at long last, uniting two lines to give rise to a new power. Let us begin."

CHAPTER 06
THE SELECTION BY FIRE

The council moved in unison, chanting quietly as they circled a large orb that Herlock had retrieved from his robes and placed in the middle of the dais, in line with the throne. Emily, although one of those nearest the front, could just barely see what appeared to be white smoke moving within the sphere. Not breaking their concentration, the council focused their energy on the orb until a bright white light shot from each of their hands, encircling it before being absorbed into the cold floor.

The ground beneath Katherine's feet rumbled as if the very earth was stirring to life. The base of the sphere before her shimmered with a mesmerising glow that was visible from across the room. Before she could blink, tendrils of light emerged from it, weaving a delicate tapestry on the dais to form an intricate pentacle and carving themselves into the ancient stone below. At the junctures where the pentacle's points met the outer ring, circular placeholders materialised, pulsating softly as though the very essence of power was manifesting before her eyes.

Herlock gestured for Katherine to step into the symbol's centre as the ground grew quiet. Apprehensive as she was, a part of her gravitated towards it without fear or hesitation. As she crossed the outer lines, the light turned to flame around her, dancing wildly as she took her place beside the smoky sphere. Dying down as quickly as it had first appeared, the flame retreated into the ground, leaving only the carving of its creation behind.

The waves of chatter and hushed whispers were lost to her ears. All Katherine's mind could focus on was a growing feeling that she was finally where she was meant to be.

Emily could hardly believe her eyes, but there it was, right in front of her. Again. Exchanging awestruck looks, those in the first few rows of the hall were no longer able to hold on to the tiniest of chances that this was some game or joke. It was too elaborate. Each of them could feel another dose of reality set in. Many, including Bayne, flashed back to the events from the days before and felt the sharp sting of the undeniable truth as the spectacle continued.

"Now," said Horus, holding his hands out towards either side of the aisle, beaming at the crowd. "Your Highnesses, rise if you would."

Katherine's eyes snapped away from the carving at her feet as five hooded figures rose and stepped into the walkway from the head of their respective kingdoms' pews. Although she heard the crowd more clearly now, their murmurings remained dull.

As if rehearsed a hundred times over, the cloaked beings made their way towards Katherine and the council, drawing the gaze of those they passed. Without a word, they came to a stop at the base of the dais and stood side by side, waiting. Even if Katherine was able to recognise the faces around her, she would still not have been able to guess which of the five men before her were which. Their identical black cloaks hung neatly at their ankles. The matching gold detailing along the fabric's edges reflected the light. The hoods that darkened their faces draped neatly on their shoulders.

It was only in the flickering of the candlelight that Katherine noticed the slight differences between them. Through the darkness, she saw traces of intricate designs on each cloak fastener that appeared to distinguish the figures from one another. From what she could make out, each was detailed with the likeness of a different animal, some resembling noble beasts of myth and legend, while others bore the likeness of creatures more mundane.

The council bent low to the floor, greeting the five princes that now stood before them, the rest of the event's attendees rising to their feet and following suit. Katherine nodded in their direction, recalling Alfred's instruction that she need not bow to those considered her equal. At least, not while they were guests in her home.

Horus called for calm, preparing to continue. "Your Highnesses!" he exclaimed, turning from the princes to Katherine and back again as he spoke. "Tonight will forever be remembered as the beginning of a new age of power. For what was long ago foretold now comes to pass."

Herlock handed his fellow council member a battered and weathered scroll that he had pulled from the safety of his cloak, beads of sweat starting to form at the base of his receding grey hairline.

Horus cleared his throat and pressed on, merely shaking his head at Herlock's lack of decorum. "While those of us who were there remember it as though the dawn of power was yesterday, the legend of the prophecy has been handed down through generations of beings. It has been distorted, translated, and mostly forgotten, yet its message remains clear."

Silent as the hall had now become, there was a faint rustling as many shuffled eagerly in their seats. For most, this would be the first time they would hear the prophecy as it was foretold, not merely a cheapened version of it. Many had only ever heard it whispered to them in the darkest of nights as if it were a secret not to be spoken aloud.

Katherine noted the anticipation and hunger in the countless eager gazes that swam before her. She herself felt butterflies in her chest as she realised that this would be her first time hearing it properly, too. She wondered what, if anything, Alfred had failed to mention to her.

Her heart raced faster than it had all evening.

"As it was told, so shall I speak its truth." Horus returned his attention to the scroll and began to read aloud, his words turning into a familiar tongue by the time they reached the ears of those in the hall. While Emily and her fellow mortals could faintly hear the distant echoes of the strange words that left his lips, they were drawn to the low hiss of those they could actually understand.

"From both light and dark, she has been born,
But from power, she will be torn.
In her mortality, she must die,
In a magical minute, she must be revived.
By Fate's blade, she must be set free,
In her wake, she becomes the key.
Five will rise to challenge Fate,
One will be chosen to be her soul's mate.
From the fire, Fate will decide,
Together with whom she will bear a child.
The ultimate power will be bestowed,
Dark and light magic like never before known.
The child becoming the holder of each,
Bringing about peace, or laying siege.
The future of power will be decided,
Forever together or forever divided."

As the last of the many whispers reached those in the farthest corners of the room, the crowd's momentary silence was short-lived as the meaning of the prophecy sank in. Preconceived hope gave way to flashes of fear. Excitement was quickly tainted by worry. Although faithful to those who led them, the idea of a singular power influencing the balance appeared to trouble even the most loyal. There was a hint of desperation that soured the air, each kingdom longing for its leader to raise it to new heights.

"Our world has awaited this day for so long," whispered Horus. "The day the hands of Fate reach out and touch us all."

"Let us proceed," said Herlock, moving to stand at the symbol's outer circle.

"Your Highnesses," instructed Herlock, "as your name is called, please remove your cloak and make your way to join me. You will make an offering of your life force to bind yourself to the power of the prophecy and take your rightful place."

"Presenting Prince Markovyas of Neighlore," announced Horus. His tone carried a mix of eagerness and unease.

Whatever whispers and worries had broken out among the crowd quietened as the tall, hooded figure that stood to the far left took a step forward, removing his cloak and letting it drop to the floor. Katherine recognised him from the dining room the day before, and from her brief time in the foyer before that. A flash of distorted images and sounds entered her mind as she looked him in the eyes. She knew this man, she was sure of it. She knew him well.

Climbing the small set of stairs, Prince Markovyas held Katherine's gaze as he made his way towards the outer edge of the carving. His brown eyes, both kind and secretive, held an intensity that made her feel as if he could read into her soul – if she let him. She was unable to deny that he looked enchanting in his black-on-black suit.

The finely tailored ensemble, woven from the richest velvet and embroidered with subtle, glistening thread, accentuated the sharp angles of the prince's frame. A high-collared jacket, fastened with onyx buttons, draped over his shoulders, while a silk cravat, as dark as midnight, rested against his throat. His short black hair, effortlessly tousled, framed a face of sculpted perfection – pale, yet strikingly handsome.

Mysterious and dangerous, Katherine thought. *Probably just my type.*

Marko came to a stop and raised his right hand, Herlock taking it quickly with his own. Every eye watched eagerly as the council member took the same silver-and-rose-gold blade the mortals had seen on the night they arrived at the castle and ran it across Marko's palm. Without flinching, maintaining eye contact with Katherine, the prince allowed the dark crimson life force to drip down his wrist and into the grooves of the carved circle below.

Herlock stepped back as the etchings on the floor came alive with light that turned into a brilliant white flame. It moved along the outlines of the pentacle, dancing until it reached one of the circular placeholders behind the princess, simmering down to a small ring of fire that waited for its champion.

Laying a hand on the prince's shoulder, causing him to finally break eye contact with Katherine, Herlock guided Marko to where the flames welcomed him excitedly. As the dark-eyed mystery took his place within his circle, Neighlore's court broke out in celebration, while members of the other kingdoms applauded along politely. The prince turned his sights back to the rosy-cheeked council member and waited patiently for the ceremony to proceed, the twinkle in his eyes not fading as a satisfied smirk crept across his face.

"Prince Dàikonos of Azrallus!" squeaked Horus.

A tall, slightly built figure stepped forward from the line, lowering his hood and dropping his cloak as he moved to stop at the edge of the circle. He, too, wore a black-on-black suit that caused Katherine to go slightly weak at the knees.

She examined Deacon's pale face. The prince's lips curved into a boyish smile as he swept his dark brown hair from his eyes. Katherine found herself intrigued. A mere moment of blurred thoughts held her captive before she snapped back to the welcoming call of his chestnut gaze.

Unlike Marko, Deacon seemed able to break his focus away from her, turning his attention to Herlock as he pressed the glistening blade to the prince's palm. As the rose gold of the blade's stone caught her eye, Katherine was suddenly curious as her stomach gave a tiny jolt. She could tell that the gem was important somehow.

As Deacon's life force saw the light of the symbol appear again and grow into flame, it quickly led him to take his place at another of the pentacle points. He broke out into an even bigger smile as his court cheered loudly.

"Next," Horus's voice rang out, though slightly unsteady, "Prince Kaëden of Cardinallis."

The tension in the hall heightened, and they watched with eager yet cautious anticipation as the next tall figure in line stepped forward, letting his cloak fall to reveal his face.

Katherine had to catch her breath as she looked into a pair of the most brilliant green eyes she had ever seen. Distorted visions came in and out of view as she took him in. The barely audible gasps of the crowd were not enough to distract her.

His short, sandy-blond hair framed his symmetrical face, and his expression was as hard as the stone his jaw seemed to be chiselled from. Katherine took the room's reaction as a sign that she should either fear or admire the handsome man standing before her. Kaëden's green eyes, although cold, seemed to have a hint of hope in them that was doing its best to stay hidden.

As Herlock cut open the prince's palm, directing his life force onto the circle, Kaëden's face remained unchanged, his eyes never quite meeting Katherine's.

The white flame danced with slightly more aggression as it twirled along the symbol, turning into a smaller yet just as fierce version of itself that directed the prince to his place on Katherine's left. As his noticeably well-built frame walked past her, Katherine felt a cold whisper of warning move through her body.

The members of Cardinallis's court celebrated with victorious roars, pulling Katherine away from her worries as Horus announced the next champion.

"Presenting Prince Aleksander of Keldorne!"

Alek lowered his cloak and moved towards the waiting council member. Relief washed over Katherine, glad to see someone she recognised from more than just glances or Alfred's files. The prince walked with more authority than she had seen him do thus far, but this *was* the first time she had seen him in front of anyone from his kingdom. *He's quite something, isn't he?*

As Alek's flesh opened, dripping glimmering liquid onto the stone, he shot Katherine a reassuring wink. Again, the light ignited into flame, tracing the carving that lay at their feet. It stopped to the right of her, and Alek took his place at the pentacle, his adoring court beaming at him and cheering with admiration. *He seems to be the most loved of them all,* thought Katherine, as Horus took a breath to announce the final participant.

All eyes now turned to the only remaining hooded figure. The sudden silence was unnerving.

"P...presenting Prince C...Cartesius of Callidusius," Horus stammered, his voice barely above a whisper. The nervous nature of his tone did not slip past Katherine.

With long, slow, intentional steps, Carter moved forward.

When he dropped his cloak, Katherine was one of the few beings in the room who did not flinch. Carter was slightly shorter than his brothers, well-built, though wider. His olive skin was complemented by his jet-black, chin-length hair. Katherine's eyes found his. They were deep, black and beady, quivering with excitement as his face twisted into a grin. A primal warning flared within her.

The prince held out his hand, and Herlock accepted it with a slight shake. As the blade slid across his palm, Carter turned and closed his fist to squeeze out every drop of fresh power onto the carving.

The entire hall seemed to hold its breath. The moment stretched, heavy and unbroken – until, all at once, the prince's face hardened.

"Give me the blade!" demanded Carter, his hand stretching out to Herlock.

He sliced open his palm once more, watching as even that failed to summon the white light they had come to expect.

"What's going on?" he asked the council with a sneer that made Katherine's neck hairs stand tall.

Facing Carter and his apparent rage, Horus was hesitant to respond. "We...we..." he whispered. "It appears you have not been selected to participate in these trials, Prince Cartesius."

"You will need to step aside while we discuss what this might mean," said Herlock quickly, his tone firm despite his evident worry.

Carter directed his angry gaze towards the third council member, whose already pale complexion seemed to take on a grey tinge to match that of his chin-length hair. "Dolos?"

"I am afraid that we do not control the outcome of the trials. Fate has decided, Your Highness, that you will not be able to proceed as expected," said Dolos, though failing to meet the prince's eyes.

Carter scowled at them. It looked as though he would have liked to throttle them with his bare hands. Angry cries emanated from Callidusius's court as the prince quickly turned to move towards Katherine. There was a fire in his eyes that roared with a determined hatred so intense that it warmed the air around him.

As his foot touched the boundary of the symbol's outer circle, crimson flames roared to life, halting him in his tracks. It shot him backwards, hurtling him through the air, down the aisle. Commotion broke out in the Grand Hall. The courts began to argue with each other, yelling insults and making threats. It was clear to Katherine that something had gone horribly wrong.

The flames died down around the princess as Carter got to his feet, his eyes firmly upon her. He roared with a fury that sent tremors through the hall, the glass of the windows quivering under its force. Without pause, the prince took large strides back to the dais, pushing aside anyone who dared to stumble into his way, as though they were cardboard cutouts. He pulled a silver butterfly knife from his belt and flipped it open as he neared the front of the room.

The other champions were unable to move from their points on the symbol, just as Katherine was frozen in her place in its centre. The spell that bound them to the power of Fate's prophecy was holding them there until the Selection by Fire was complete.

While there was no reason to doubt the seemingly protective power of the symbol, there was a part of Katherine that knew that the prince, clearly determined enough, would find a way around it. She only hoped that someone, anyone, would stop him before he could. Something inside her hinted that she was very likely to die by his hand this night or another.

It was as though everything was happening in slow motion. Katherine, concerned for herself as well as for the surrounding innocents, braced for what she was sure would be a nightmarish ending to what had been an extravagant daydream.

Her eyes, drawn towards the terrified faces of the mortals she had met in the West Wing, widened as the vengeful prince passed the pews that housed them. Whether it was sheer stupidity or an instinctual drive, forgetting all logic, the blue-eyed mystery she had caught sight of earlier leapt out into the aisle.

Followed closely by a fearful yet brave Jamie, Bayne stepped in front of Carter, blocking his path. The guards, who were battling to control the crowds, were nowhere near enough to intervene, and the council, it seemed, was doing what it did best according to Alfred's notes – allowing things to unfold until there was a dire need for intervention. The prince entertained Bayne's attempt to disarm him for only a moment before sending the mortal flying into the hard, unforgiving stone at the council's feet without any effort.

Emily and the others, Katherine included, were unable to tear their gaze away from where Bayne lay, battling to breathe as he spat out a few drops of blood and massaged his ribs. Pushing Jamie aside, Carter advanced, seemingly annoyed to have to get the pesky mortal out of his way.

His actions proved to be the final straw for the council, however, who were seething at the prince's unprovoked attack on two innocents. Wielding their power, they swiftly moved to wrestle Carter into security's custody, intending to expel him from the property. They called for an immediate halt to the chaos that had erupted. Bayne, using the least battered and bruised of his hands, struggled to prop himself up off the floor, his senses and rationality only just returning to him.

The doors closed on Carter, and the majority of those who remained managed a sigh of relief as his yells faded to nothing. Although furious at their leader's expulsion, many of the representatives of Callidusius returned to their seats, curiosity overshadowing their desire for action as, without warning, light flooded the Grand Hall.

The council turned towards where Katherine stood rooted in place, their eyes wide. Emily's face mimicked theirs, as did the faces of so many in the crowd. The light turned into a white flame once more and made its way around the circle. It soon took its place and lit the final remaining marker of power.

Gasps echoed like ripples into the furthest corners of the room as all focus turned to Bayne, whose face was marked with a mix of disbelief and confusion, mirroring the collective sentiment. Katherine's mouth fell open, realising what the Consilio Statera had just pieced together as they advanced towards the symbol, sharing frantic whispers.

Ignoring the furious stare of his silver-eyed counterpart as the council went silent, Herlock laid his hands on Bayne and steered him towards the flame now holding a place for him.

"Impossible..." Herlock muttered as he guided the reluctant mortal into position. "Simply *impossible*."

As Bayne stepped across the fire with apprehension, taking his place at the marker, every inch of the carving erupted in flames that towered over the six of them before shifting to a brilliant shade of blue and dying down to an ankle-height glow.

"We have our five champions!" came Herlock's booming voice, gesturing towards the group of men who now surrounded Katherine.

While the champions were applauded, sized up and wagered on by members of the different courts, Katherine's attention was on the section of seats in front of her – *her* court, as it were. She discreetly took in the reactions of those who had been sitting nearest the man who now stood beside her. As the echoes of applause rang in her ears, her mind wandered, not towards the apparent darkness of the man the flame had so quickly rejected, but towards the one the fire had seemed so determined to accept.

Why are they looking at me that way? Why is everyone so on edge if this is
supposed to be an honour?

~

Emily stood paralysed as Dolos instructed Katherine and the princes to
head through a narrow door off to the left of the hall, Bayne along with
them. This is impossible, she thought as her mind raced over what had just
happened. She barely registered the council's farewell as they bid everyone
a good night. It was absurd enough that her best friend was really a being
of power. Now her cousin, it seemed, would be forced to compete for a
love he had once let slip through his fingers so easily. Impossible.

It was nearly a minute before Emily noticed one of the castle keepers
trying to get her attention as the council chanted once more. The flame
that lined the symbol travelled back into the orb, taking the carving with
it and leaving nothing else behind as Herlock tucked the sphere safely
away in his sleeve.

Confused and fearful, Emily reluctantly joined the other mortals in
following the castle keepers' lead out of the castle and to the waiting town
cars.

There was silence among them, nobody too sure what to say or believe. Each of them wondered what was happening back in the East Wing,
behind those closed doors. Each of them was too stunned to come to
terms with the now all-too-real consequences of their time in Eyrondale.

CHAPTER 07
THE RULES INTRODUCED

They stood in silence as they waited for the council to join them, in the same room where Katherine had got ready earlier, each of the champions eagerly awaiting an explanation for what had just gone wrong. However, their questions would only multiply as the Consilio Statera entered to elaborate on what the next few weeks would demand of them all.

Dolos waved his hand, encouraging everyone to gather in front of him. They did so, Bayne with some hesitancy.

"From the moment your essence was accepted by the power of the prophecy, an oath was made that cannot be broken or undone. The punishment for trying to escape Fate would be severe, I am afraid," explained Dolos.

"It is for this reason, Master Bayne, that your place in this cannot be ignored, wished away or overruled," said Herlock, looking at the mortal as though empathetic to what he would come to face on this path.

Bayne shuffled nervously, not knowing how to respond, shaking his head in disbelief. This was proving all too difficult for his overly logical mind to comprehend.

"Young man," continued Dolos, his eyes narrowing to the point of shutting themselves. "You have stumbled into an ancient form of power that governs us all. Neither Princess Katherine nor the council can free you from this now."

"The gravity of the punishment that would befall any of the other champions would be extreme. For you, as a human, even more so. I fear that should you not do your best in these trials, death may be a kinder end than what Fate might have in store," advised Herlock. "Therefore, young master, heed the words we speak with care and caution. You are, as of this moment, chained to the fate of us all."

Bayne wanted to protest but opted against it, fearful that instead of words, it would be this morning's breakfast making its way out of his mouth. If this would indeed be his new reality, there would be no stopping it – he had learnt enough during his short time in Eyrondale to be able to admit that to himself. He had always been considered highly intelligent, but even he had to confess that if this were truly how he would be spending the next few weeks of his life, he was in over his head. *Magic? Trials? Death? How could I possibly come out of this alive?* he thought.

A lump formed in Bayne's throat, but he made no effort to clear it as he attempted to shake off the judgemental glares that held him frozen in place. But even as his heart thundered in his chest, certain that those around him could hear it, something deep within urged him to stand still – to let Fate weave his plan, undisturbed. *Something.*

"Now. Let us proceed," instructed Dolos before anyone could question the situation further. "Horus?"

Bayne noticed Alek and Marko exchanging worried looks, but they remained silent, allowing the council to continue without interruption. It seemed that the princes knew better than to question the will of pure power.

Horus cleared his throat. "Five trials. Five trials are what stand between you, power, and the fate of the magical and supernatural worlds.

These trials will test you, your abilities, and your heart. At the end of every trial, each of you will need to offer your life force again, just as you have done here this evening.

"After careful consideration, the flame will decide which of you is worthy to proceed through the next trials and who will see their light and hope fade. As this matter concerns all six of the kingdoms, Eyrondale will host a ball after every trial is completed so that each of your lines may bear witness to Fate's decision. As one's course can change in an instant, it will only be as you embark on the next phase that the Breath of Fate will carry its instructions on the air. While we are unable to see beyond the broad scope of each trial at this point, all will come into view as we move ahead."

"The first trial," continued Dolos, picking up where Horus had left off, "appears to be simple at face value. But we would caution you to be prepared for whatever may come your way."

Breaking the champions' silence, Marko voiced what they were all thinking. "So, what is it?"

Herlock smiled, but there was something unsettling about it. "Quite simply, Your Highness? 'Tis a kiss."

Alek let out a barely audible chuckle. He and Marko shot each other a sideways look that implied they were sure this would be *anything* but simple.

"We begin tomorrow evening, where we will first select the order in which you will participate," said Dolos, shaking his head at the two princes. "Next, we shall oversee the first participant as he completes his task. We will allow for a day of rest, then we shall move on to the next champion. Do you understand?"

Katherine and the others quickly agreed.

"For now, rest," advised Herlock. "For we all await what is to come as dawn breaks."

Dolos and Horus nodded in agreement and bowed before they turned to exit, leaving Katherine and the five champions still struggling for speech. The three men broke out into a hushed yet rapid discussion of the evening's events as the door creaked closed behind them, their hastened departure not providing any comfort to those left behind.

~

Katherine and the champions replayed what had just happened in silence for close to fifteen minutes, each feeling uneasy at the council's words, when there was a sharp rap at the door.

"Enter," instructed Katherine, her eyes darting between the men in front of her as none of them dared to make a sound.

"Sorry to disturb you, Princess," said Alfred as he opened the door and entered the study.

"N...not at all," replied Katherine, still pretending to know exactly what she was doing.

"Whenever you are ready, we have drivers waiting to transport you and the champions back to the West Wing." Turning to face the princes, Alfred continued, "I have instructed that the additional suites be ready before your arrival, and luggage arrangements have been made with your handlers. Feel free to take some time to finalise any other matters before you join us."

Marko took a sharp breath, drawing Katherine's attention. "Thank you, Alfred."

"Now, the council has briefed the other handlers, and myself and has asked me to remind you that upon being chosen to participate in these trials, your abilities have been limited to work only on those who are not bound by the power of the prophecy. This means, Your Highnesses, Master Bayne, that for the duration of these events, you will not be able to influence each other with supernatural talents or do harm to one another via these means. The *only* exception to this, within the boundaries of the castle's grounds, will be the training yard. There, your power will be more accessible, but it will still be subject to the rules of Eyrondale and its enchantments."

Alfred's tone had gone from pleasant to strict, one that neither prince, princess, nor mortal would want to try their luck arguing against. He took a breath, stared them down knowingly as he pressed on.

"The council and I have seen to it that the power protecting the castle and those within it remains firmly in place and has been strengthened for the duration of these events. None other than those who, from tonight, dwell inside of it will be able to gain entry without it being granted by me, the council, or yourself, Princess," he said, nodding at Katherine. "Additionally, measures have been put in place to enhance the protective barrier that surrounds the outer castle grounds to ensure that no amount of force, whether mortal or magical, shall cross.

"The gates at the entrances to the castle grounds have had more guards assigned to them to assist with monitoring those who enter and exit, and the East Wing's role as a local museum has been temporarily suspended to deter unwanted attention and visitors. Each prince's handler has been authorised to come and go from the grounds, and each will be allocated a suite to aid in the managerial oversight of each of the kingdoms until the trials are completed.

"Each of you has been assigned a dedicated town car and driver that will be available to assist with your transportation needs, and the castle staff will be there to tend to anything else you may require. They have been instructed that secrecy and discretion are of the highest priority during this time and that any request be addressed with urgency. The council has also advised that silencing enchantments are being placed within the boundary line in order to dull any enhanced hearing abilities to maintain fairness and ensure a balanced competition."

While not really sure what they were agreeing to, Katherine and Bayne followed the lead of the others, nodding as if they had understood every word.

"After you, Princess. Dinner should be ready within the hour." Alfred gestured towards the door. "I will finalise the preparations for the others' stay while Tom takes you and Master Bayne back."

"Thank you, Alfred," said Katherine, crossing the room, quite relieved to be able to take some time to process the evening's events.

"Master Bayne," called Alfred as the mortal started towards the door.

Startled, Bayne responded, his voice shaking as all eyes turned to him. "Um...yes?"

"The council would like a private word before you join the princess. Please, follow me."

Exchanging an apprehensive glance with Katherine, Bayne hesitated only briefly before following instructions.

Bayne climbed into the car and sat next to Katherine, a wave of dread crashing down around them in an instant. The silence that set in as soon as Tom closed the door behind the champion was broken only by the soft mutterings of disbelief that escaped his lips as he stared blankly out of the window.

As the high walls of the East Wing disappeared from view, Bayne felt Katherine shift in her seat before finally giving in to whatever thought had been pressing at her.

"I need to know something," she said, breaking Bayne out of his trance.

He whipped his head around to meet her gaze with a suddenness that seemed to catch her off guard. She was staring back at him with those familiar eyes he knew so well.

"Yes?" asked Bayne, keeping his expression carefully neutral.

"I was just wondering," Katherine muttered, nervously running her fingertips across the smooth lines of her gown. "How...how do I know you?"

Her eyes searched the champion's as though they were reaching into his mind in a desperate attempt to find the answers she sought. There was a sharp pang in his chest. It was a look she had given him many times before, and he knew all too well that if he was honest with her, the story would only end up with one or both of them hurt.

"It's...it's not something we really speak about," replied Bayne eventually, trying his best to keep his cool.

"Alright then." Katherine's eyes narrowed. "Different question. Back there, in the Grand Hall, when I looked out at the sea of unfamiliar faces staring back at me, I found yours." She spoke hesitantly, but the determination in her tone made it clear she would not accept a second dismissal.

Bayne swallowed hard. *She's really going to do this,* he thought. *Now?*

"I can't explain it. But at that moment, when you looked back at me, the room faded." Katherine paused. "Kind of like it's doing now."

Bayne shifted uncomfortably, the brief flash of headlights from a passing car catching in Katherine's eyes before fading into the night. A warmth stirred in him – a warmth he had long forgotten, yet deeply missed. He knew *exactly* what she meant, but wondered how he could possibly say it aloud. For one, where would he start?

"Then, when that man tried to attack me, you jumped in the way. You, being a mortal, from what I understand. I...I just need to know why."

Bayne let out a loud sigh as he broke Katherine's captivating stare and ran his fingers through his hair. He shook his head. But he was unable to stop a twinge of pain from flashing across his face, which only seemed to add to Katherine's curiosity.

"Yes?" she pressed.

"Katherine," Bayne said, wincing as her name left his lips. "You and me...it's...complicated at best. Yes, we know each other, but the *how* that goes along with that will only bring up questions I can't face answering right now. Not after everything that's happened."

"Yet you're a champion set to take part in dangerous trials to win my heart?" Her irritated tone was not lost on him, though he chose to ignore it.

"Like I *said...complicated,*" he muttered with a slight smile.

Clear that there would be no satisfaction to her curiosity, Katherine leant back, and they sat in silence for the remaining minutes before Tom pulled up to the stairs leading to the West Wing's entrance. Katherine and Bayne thanked their driver as he held the car door open for them and the pair headed into the castle without another word to each other, the double doors opening for them intuitively.

Emily and the rest of the mortals had already gathered for dinner by the time Katherine and Bayne made their way through the foyer and into the living room. Before facing the awaiting crowd, the two exchanged a look that sent fire through Katherine's chest. The thought of him knowing more about her past than she could recall was hitting her harder than expected. She had a feeling that his lack of transparency was more than a simple character trait and that there was so much more to his reasons for withholding information than he was letting on. She wished she could remember how all of this pieced together, how she was connected to all of this.

Lost in thought, Katherine entered and crossed the dining room. But as she was about to take her seat, she paused.

"Princess? Is everything alright?" came Alfred's voice from beside her.

She scoffed and, with a forceful shove, pushed her chair back into place, the sound echoing around them, before storming back towards the living room. Each step was deliberate, leaving behind a trail of unanswered questions in her wake.

A few of those who had known Katherine and Bayne well during her time as a mortal shot glances of concern at him throughout the rest of dinner, hoping he would address what had just happened – or at least say something about what he had learnt after the ceremony. Anything. But Bayne kept his eyes firmly on his plate, speaking to no one.

Amidst the heavy silence, a few brave souls attempted to break the tension with light conversation, their voices hesitant and strained. But their efforts were lost in the mounting worry that hung overhead. Though each of the mortals longed to have their questions about tonight's events answered, they were still in too much shock to address the issue with rationality. With Bayne maintaining his resolute silence, they were reluctant to push the subject until he brought it up himself. But as they tiptoed around the multiplying elephants rapidly filling the oversized room, their thoughts raced with endless concerns, worries and fears about their uncertain future. It was becoming increasingly evident that they would not be leaving anytime soon, trapped in an uncomfortable limbo between their world and this one.

The mortals braced themselves for whatever blow was next as they followed one of the castle keepers into the living room after dinner.

Despite their visible apprehension, it was not Alfred's arrival that held their attention, but rather the conspicuous absence of Katherine. Her missing presence seemed to cast a shadow over the room as they awaited Alfred's address. Many, if not all of them, had hoped that they would find some comfort in hearing about what was going on from Katherine herself.

"Thank you for your time, ladies and gentlemen."

As the pitter-patter of rain reached their ears from the open doors, Alfred quickly waved them shut and gestured for the flames that crackled gently in the fireplaces to grow tall.

"Now, I assume that you are all still coming to terms with what this evening's outcome evidently means for you and your time in Eyrondale. And, while we understand that such a realisation will take time to fully digest, there are matters that need to be attended to in the meantime. While we may not be holding full court in the West Wing due to the new circumstances surrounding the trials, there are several traditions and rules that we still need to follow."

There was a slight murmur of protest that could be heard over the sound of the fires. The mortals were too tired, physically and mentally, to argue.

"As part of Her Highness's court, you are to welcome the champions upon their arrival. It is customary that any visiting royal or their inner council be greeted by the hosting court. Before they arrive, however, I must advise you to take caution. The princes and their handlers are some of the oldest, most powerful beings you will meet during your stay here. Not all of them are as tolerant and understanding as Prince Markovyas and Prince Aleksander, and even then, it would be wise to be mindful. By now, the other princes will have learnt about Princess Katherine's memory loss from their respective handlers, a fact that, thankfully, the council has advised, is part of the first trial."

Emily exchanged concerned looks with those beside her, as the spark of worry in Alfred's voice was undeniable.

"While I may not know Prince Dàikonos and Prince Kaëden on a level near as well as I know the others, I can assure you that it would be best to stay on their good side. I have seen the destruction that Prince Kaëden can lay in his wake, and he has gone to war more times than I care to count. He can be ruthless and violent. Prince Dàikonos, I knew only before maturity, but he is rumoured to play it slightly fast and loose when it comes to the rules, showcasing a penchant for unpredictability."

"You've got to be kidding me," came the voice that Alfred had grown to expect at any mention of anything other than what was considered *normal*.

"Yes, Jennifer?" Alfred sighed. He had hoped that they would be too preoccupied with their own thoughts to make this any more difficult than it already was.

"Exactly how serious is this?" she asked, her voice betraying her attempt to mask the obvious panic and her desire to be anywhere other than where she currently was.

"I would suggest that you be mindful of who you trust. *Always*. Now, follow me."

Ignoring Jennifer's attempt to press for a clearer answer, Alfred led them into the foyer. There was silence as each member of the group wondered about the possible horrors that inevitably awaited them during the trials. If the past few nights were anything to go by, there was indeed much to be wary of.

～

The mortals lined up on either side of the castle entrance, just as instructed, creating a pathway to the centre of the foyer where Alfred and five castle keepers moved into position to wait for their guests. It was only a few minutes before Alek made his way down the stairs to join them, a slightly shorter, golden-haired man following behind.

As the living room clock chimed nine-thirty, Alfred opened the large double doors with a wave of his hand to welcome the three waiting champions. Each stood alongside their handler. Among them was Marko, the dark-haired prince the mortals had first encountered in this very spot several nights ago, whom they had scarcely seen since.

He was accompanied not only by his handler but also by two large dogs that reminded Emily of some breed of terrier. The creatures' mere presence was unnerving as they stood beside him, their demeanour alert yet restrained.

The sight of the formidable canines drew swift attention from one of the castle keepers, who promptly approached and nervously led the animals towards the kitchen. The beasts' paws clicked softly against the polished marble as they followed without hesitation. It was clear they were no strangers to the castle.

Emily felt a surge of relief as she glanced down at her dress, grateful that she had not changed out of it yet. However large the part of her that wished to flee the dangers of their situation, there was a stronger desire to make a good first impression on those who effortlessly captivated the attention of so many with their dark allure. Adjusting her posture, she resolved to present herself with confidence and poise, determined to put her best foot forward.

"Welcome, Your Highnesses!" greeted Alfred with a low bow, the rest of the welcome party following his lead as the six new guests stopped before him.

The immortals' expressions were hard. Even Marko appeared eager to hurry through the formalities as his eyes scanned the room. Whether it could be attributed to the unforeseen events that had unfolded mere hours earlier, or their evident disdain for having to associate with lesser beings, the princes and their companions seemed less than thrilled to be greeted by Emily and her friends.

"Everyone, please welcome Prince Markovyas of Neighlore," said Alfred, gesturing to the prince and the pale figure to his right. "And this is his handler, Lucien."

Emily and the others bowed again as Marko and Lucien acknowledged their greeting in return. She could practically feel the judgement seeping out of Lucien's pores as his tall, slender frame reluctantly bent towards her. While neat in appearance, it was his negativity that made the true impression. There was a darkness there that went beyond just the black of his eyes.

Alfred turned to the next pair. "Welcome, also, Prince Dàikonos of Azrallus and his handler, Rawson."

Again, Emily could feel the disdain that neither the prince nor his slightly taller, pasty-skinned counterpart tried to hide as they returned the mortals' greeting.

"And Prince Kaëden of Cardinallis with his handler, Daniel."

The handler, who had not taken his striking blue gaze off of the mortals since he had been welcomed into the castle, gave more of a nod than an actual bow. Emily barely got a glimpse at the top of his moderately cut tuft of dark hair before his eyes snapped back to stare them down. Although slightly less built and shorter than the prince, who avoided all eye contact, Emily got the feeling he could be just as terrifying.

"And, of course, you have already met Prince Aleksander of Keldorne. This is his handler, Greyson."

Unlike the others, Alek's handler gave them a slight smile as his golden locks whipped towards the floor and back again.

"Now," continued Alfred, gesturing at Emily and her friends. "Allow me to introduce you to Princess Katherine's guests for the duration of these trials. We have Emily Burke, Aiden Edwards, Matthew Moore, James Campbell, Layla and Brian Alwyn, and Jennifer Farrows. And this is Bayne McAllister, whom you have not had the pleasure of formally meeting yet."

"No Katherine?" asked Deacon with a raised eyebrow as soon as Alfred had finished introducing the mortals. The prince's handler's dark eyes narrowed with suspicion as they scanned the room again.

"The princess is...uh...not feeling herself this evening. She sends her deepest apologies and has requested that I welcome you on her behalf."

Emily could tell that Alfred was improvising. Before any of Alek's brothers could press the issue, the prince quickly smiled and added, "You'll get used to it."

Alfred turned to the waiting castle keepers. "Please, join your designated champion and their handler and escort them to their suites."

Needing no further encouragement and unable to conceal their excitement, three of the keepers moved to join their assigned guests. The one assigned to Alek hopped to stand next to the gentleman who had remained within arm's reach of the prince since they had entered the room, which was met with a soft giggle from the handler.

"Master Bayne," said Alfred, all eyes turning to him now as the fifth castle keeper reappeared, picking the last of the loose, wiry canine hairs from her shirt. "For the purpose of these trials, I have volunteered to be your handler. Please join Aimee, who will escort you to your new accommodations."

Emily caught the slight falter in Bayne's movements, as if the news had taken him aback. Nevertheless, he nodded and made his way across the foyer. Though he tried to mask it, Emily could see the tension in his jaw, as if the council's words were still echoing in his head. She doubted he wanted to flaunt his nerves in a room full of supernaturals. His gaze flicked towards Jennifer, who looked even less impressed than their new castle-mates. Still, with clear reluctance, he joined his guide, fully aware that he had a lot of explaining to do.

Emily watched as, one by one, the four princes and their handlers were led up the stairs by their castle keepers, heading in the direction of the Royal Suites, which were the closest to Katherine's temporary suite on the third floor. Alfred lingered behind as Bayne followed Aimee out of the room to thank the group and wish them a good evening, promising that the morning would bring them more answers.

∼

Aimee had lagged behind the other champions and their handlers to introduce herself properly to Bayne – and to give him a moment to gather his thoughts. Unlike the other castle keepers, who had led the princes up the foyer staircase to their suites on the third floor, Aimee took a different route. She guided Bayne through a door flanking the staircase on the right, turning immediately into another set of vaulted doors. She pushed them open, flashing a smile over her shoulder just as Bayne's expression betrayed his quiet awe.

Taking the corridor to the left, they passed a narrow staircase on one side and, to the right, a vast vaulted chamber that housed a towering set of doors. Something about them called to Bayne as his gaze lingered a moment too long, but he quickly snapped himself away. He sped up to where Aimee was rounding the corner of the secondary kitchen, where Bayne caught the hurried exchange of gossip between castle keepers inside. The scent of fresh bread and herbs lingered as they turned left at the music room's entrance, taking the corridor that led to an arched doorway. There was no handle, yet the door seemed to sense their presence – swinging open instinctively as the pair approached.

Bayne stepped inside and had to catch his breath.

A grand tower stretched upward, its domed ceiling swallowed by darkness. A magnificent helical staircase curved along the walls – but it was the fire at its heart that held Bayne still. Thousands of tendrils drifted upward in slow, hypnotic waves, their colours shifting between molten orange and spectral blue. The flames did not lash or crackle but flowed, whispering against the stone as though carrying voices too soft to hear. Bayne and the castle keeper ascended. Narrow windows revealed glimpses of the castle grounds – vast and empty beneath the night sky. At the top of the tower, Aimee led him through a set of large wooden doors, stepping onto the third-floor landing.

Bayne had not explored much of the West Wing since their arrival, but he should have known that the floor housing the Royal Suites would be nothing short of sickening in its opulence.

As he followed Aimee's lead, Bayne's footsteps echoed softly against the floor before quickly getting lost in the whistling of the breeze that danced through the open set of windows at the end of the corridor. Moonlight streamed through the stained glass windows to his right, while the imposing elegance of the paintings on the walls to his left – especially those shrouded in sheeting – left Bayne with an eerie sense he could not shake. The comforting warmth of the crackling fireplaces and flickering sconces clashed against an unsettling coldness that seeped into his very bones. There was an unmistakable feeling of displacement that set his nerves on edge.

"This is where Prince Dàikonos will be staying," Aimee said, glancing over her shoulder and pointing to the first arched doorway on the left. "Then you're at the end there."

As though sensing his apprehension, the miniature gargoyles that sat perched atop the prince's suite's door stared him down like silent guardians as he passed by. Even the suits of armour that flanked the entrance seemed to watch his every move. He felt as though the castle itself was judging him, questioning his belonging.

"Don't worry. So am I," Bayne muttered.

"Did you say something, sir?" came Aimee's voice as she turned around quickly.

"Oh, um, no. Nothing."

"Are you sure, sir? I am sure that you have at least a question or two."

"Well..."

"Ah! Too many to choose from?"

"Now that you mention it."

Aimee giggled and gestured for them to continue towards the furthest set of doors. "Alfred will be able to answer most of them. So, no rush."

"Actually," said Bayne. He hesitated but ultimately gave in to his inquisitiveness. "What...what exactly does Alfred, being my handler, mean?"

"That one's easy! For each of the Nine Strands of Power, a representative was created to oversee the impact of that power on existence. These beings were created by the Consilio Statera, who serves as the spokespeople for the Three Spheres. For the pure descendants of power that aren't part of the Cosmic Sphere – like Princess Katherine – these representatives are what we call 'Handlers.' They raised these physical descendants until they reached maturity and were deemed ready to take over the management of the manifestations of their power."

Bayne's thoughts spun. "So that makes Alfred—"

"Second in charge of everything...well, in Eyrondale, anyway. He basically oversees everything related to the kingdom and keeps the wheels turning."

Bayne let out a low sigh and rubbed his hands over his face, taking a moment to glance out at the view of the sprawling grounds that met a body of water in the distance. Deciding that there was no reason to avoid it any longer, he joined the castle keeper at the entrance to his new suite.

"So what does that mean for me, exactly?"

"Means that you, as a mortal, may not have a kingdom or power going into this, but Alfred will be there to help you play your cards right so that you walk away with one or the other, or more. If that's what you decide you want, that is."

Bayne was silent. It was all too much to take in already, and he feared that his thoughts would finally overwhelm him.

"Would you like to do the honours, sir?" Aimee asked, prompting the champion towards the grand doors that stood before them like the entrance to a fortress, guarded by its own stone creatures and armoured figures that leered at their visitors.

His apprehension was evident. Bayne was still trying to get used to the more animated quirks of the castle. As his fingers tightened around the gargoyle handle's tongue, the wings that had stood firm came alive, wrapping their cold iron around his wrist. Bayne jumped. Before he could even muster a protest, the wings' grip tightened, urging him forward. With a quick squeeze, they released their hold on him, allowing the champion to step back as the door obediently swung open, revealing what lay beyond.

Aimee attempted to stifle her quiet laughter, but Bayne still caught her giggling out of the corner of his eye.

Upon first look, it was clear that the suite was certainly better suited for royalty. The doors led him into a large living room, complete with a fireplace to the right and a handcrafted wooden bar in the corner. Large black couches and white wingback chairs faced the flames, and a plush rug tied the room together with matching ottomans.

"I'll show you around," said Aimee excitedly, clearly eager to see his reaction to the rest of it.

She moved past the seating area and pushed open the double doors that stood beside the fire, revealing an enormous bedroom that welcomed them with a cosy lounge and led out to a fully furnished balcony overlooking the northern grounds. Turning left, Bayne's eyes fell upon the inviting sight of a magnificent four-poster bed, its luxurious presence promising comfort and respite from his lingering pain and bruises. Wooden dressers and nightstands dotted the room, their sturdy frames adding warmth to the space against the backdrop of dark walls. Above, the painted ceiling captured his attention, its complex designs whispering tales of bygone eras and forgotten legends, calling him to lose himself in their timeless narratives.

Aimee led Bayne through a door in the wall to the left of the bed, into a bathroom he could only ever have imagined. White marble and gold detailing complemented the glass and stone, adding a modern touch to the room, and matching the theme of the West Wing. Bayne, who had always enjoyed planning renovations, had never seen such a grand en-suite in person before. There was nothing about it he wanted to change. It was as though the his and hers basins, oversized walk-in shower, and free-standing claw-footed bathtub had been taken out of a magazine filled with spaces in which he dreamt of living.

After a quick run-through of where everything had been placed throughout the suite, and after showing Bayne the walk-in closet that was accessible from the bathroom as well as through the door on the right side of the bed, Aimee made her way towards the exit.

"I'll just go grab your lady, sir." Still smiling, she gestured for Bayne to settle in and relax.

"Thank you, Aimee," said Bayne, taking her advice and sinking into the couch closest to the seating area's roaring fire, relieved to have a few moments alone.

~

Having made their way up to the first floor not long after the champions had been led off, Emily and the rest of the mortals embraced the warmth of the dual fireplaces as the icy ripples of the night's events threatened to overwhelm them. Seeking some semblance of solace in the largest of the first-floor living rooms, they wasted no time before diving straight into it.

As soon as Aiden shut the doors, ensuring that they would not be overheard, Emily rounded on the others.

"Alright, we need to talk about this," she said firmly, her voice betraying a mix of anxiety and determination. "We're clearly not leaving anytime soon. Are we?"

The group exchanged uneasy glances.

Aiden cleared his throat. "Emily's right. Now that Bayne's—"

"Now that Bayne's *what*, exactly?" came Jennifer's unsteady voice from where she stared absently into the fire.

The hesitation to answer barely had time to settle in.

"Somebody," she urged. "What exactly does this mean?"

"Jen—" started Jamie, his eyes soft and sympathetic.

"No! I mean, we're all thinking the same thing, aren't we?" Jennifer turned to face the group. "Tonight just changed everything. Please, someone tell me that I'm wrong."

"I—"

"Jen, I..." muttered Emily. "We always knew that we'd be here for a while."

"Just not like this."

"No. Not like this." Emily shrugged, massaging her forehead with her fingertips as she took a seat in a nearby armchair. "Anyone feel like throwing out some ideas about what the hell happened tonight?"

"Your guess is as good as mine," said Aiden, following Emily's lead as the others, too, chose to make themselves more comfortable. "Mistake, maybe?"

Matthew set down a tray of whiskies that he had rounded up from the bar in the corner and handed them out. "You'd think so, wouldn't you?"

"I wouldn't," whispered Jennifer as Matthew sat down on the couch beside her.

More than a few eyebrows suddenly raised.

"Seriously?" asked Brian, a flash of confusion crossing his face.

Jennifer scoffed. "If you knew their history, it would make more sense."

"Bayne and Katherine's?"

"Jen, don't—"

"You're going to tell me I'm wrong, Emily? What about you, Layla? You two should know better than anyone."

The sisters exchanged a look that only seemed to confirm what Jennifer had been thinking.

"Exactly."

The rising unease in the room was unmistakable, and Aiden quickly jumped back in. "I seriously doubt that whatever happened in the past is the reason for all of this. It's probably just some sort of fault in the spell thing or whatever."

Jennifer clicked her tongue. "Don't be naive."

"Hey! I get that you're a bit pissed right now," Aiden snapped, clearly less sympathetic now that she was taking her frustrations out on them. "But this isn't just about you. Sure, Bayne somehow got sucked into this, but it could easily have been Jamie. He was in the thick of it with that lunatic, just as Bayne was."

"I didn't—"

"Think about it that way? Figures!" Aiden scoffed. "If you think about it. *Logically*. What's more likely? That Bayne is some special *chosen one*, or that some shit went down with that line when it fired up against the prince? It doesn't help to overthink this. It happened. That's that." He turned his attention away from Jennifer and continued. "Look, Alfred said they'd tell us more in the morning—"

"That's what they keep saying, but—"

"But," said Aiden, raising his voice, "maybe they also need a bit of time to figure out what happened. They seemed just as shocked as we were."

"You're right," said Jamie, finishing off his drink well before the others. "They can't give us answers if they don't have any to give. Doesn't help to speculate before tomorrow. We're just going to lose more sleep than it's worth."

There was a polite knock at the door, startling the group.

"Y...Yeah?" called Emily, thankful for the distraction.

Aimee's head popped into view as the door opened. "Sorry to bother. Miss Jennifer? Are you ready to head up to your new suite?"

Caught off guard, Jennifer coughed on her whisky. "I...I..."

"I have already taken some of your belongings upstairs. Master Bayne is awaiting your arrival."

Jennifer flinched at the sound of Bayne's new title escaping the castle keeper's lips – a reaction Emily and the others could not miss. She glanced around the room as if searching for an escape that would save her from having to face the conversation they all knew she was about to have. But no one came to her rescue.

"I...uh...guess I better head up then. G...goodnight, guys."

"Night, Jen," said Emily, exchanging another nervous glance with Layla.

"Night."

"Night, Jen."

"See ya."

As the door closed behind the apprehensive redhead, Aiden let out a long sigh.

"And that?" said Matthew, getting to his feet to grab them another round.

"Wouldn't like to be in her shoes is all."

"His neither."

"Not a chance."

"Think we're actually going to get answers tomorrow?" asked Layla, cuddling into Brian's chest for extra warmth.

Aiden avoided her gaze. "Not the answers we're looking for, I think."

"Can't say I don't agree with you on that," muttered Emily.

"Listen. Why don't we just get some shut-eye after this one?" asked Matthew, setting down the tray.

"Who'll be able to sleep?"

"Hey, no offence, but after the day we've just had, I'm going to crash as soon as my head touches that pillow."

"Guess you're right. Wouldn't hurt to get out of this dress and get some rest."

Aiden raised his glass. "We're gonna need it."

∾

Bayne had sat there in silence, listening to the crackling of the fire, for what felt like an hour before there was a knock on the door, and Aimee entered the suite with Jennifer in tow.

"Master Bayne, is there anything else you will be needing this evening?" asked the castle keeper, hands behind her back, smiling.

"Um, no," replied Bayne with an apprehensive glance towards Jennifer. "No, thank you. That will be all for this evening."

Aimee left with a quick bow, leaving the couple alone.

"So," said Jennifer as soon as the suite's doors closed behind Aimee's mousey blonde locks. She took a look around the room, clearly less impressed with the grandeur of it all than Bayne had been. "When are we leaving?"

At hearing the harshness of her words, Bayne's chest tightened. "What do you mean, *leaving*?"

"So you're honestly expected to go through with whatever this is? Why can't we just leave? Let them sort out their own prophecy."

"Jen," Bayne began, not quite sure of how to approach the subject. "I...I can't leave. I have no choice. It's literally life or death here."

Jennifer scoffed. "Of course! And it's not because of *her* at all, right?"

"Jen, don't start. Please. These people are serious. *This* is serious. It doesn't matter what I want here. This is just the way it is, and we need to get used to that...*quickly!*"

"Are you kidding me? You, of all people, are willing to go along with all of this?"

"I'm bound by blood here—"

"Oh, please. You're telling me that they're powerful enough to keep us 'safe' but not powerful enough to let you out of this?"

"Jen—"

"Bayne, don't 'Jen' me. I need you to be serious right now."

"I *am* being serious, Jen." He moved towards her, but she recoiled at his touch. "You weren't there. You didn't hear what they said to me."

"So, they're not even going to try to get you out of it. Are they?"

There was no dancing around it. "No," Bayne whispered, his eyes heavy with the guilt of disappointing her. "They aren't."

Whether her lips had started to tremble from anger or whether she was about to allow the tears that were welling in her eyes to consume her, he could not be sure.

"Jen—"

"Tell me something."

"Anything."

"What does *she* have to say about all of this?"

Bayne threw his arms into the air. "She doesn't even remember who I am, Jen. What could she possibly say?"

Jennifer pursed her lips. There was a moment's pause as she nodded, staring at the fire. "You'd think that if her feelings for you were strong enough to rope you into all of this...well, maybe she remembers more than you think she does."

"Jen—"

She held up a hand to silence him. It was clear that she was holding herself back from breaking down. "Stop," Jennifer muttered, shaking her head as she walked towards the open bedroom doors. "I can't. Not right now."

Bayne heard the en-suite's door slam shut. *This is a nightmare,* he thought, sighing. *It can't possibly be real. But yet?*

He gave the fire a last look before making his way through to the bedroom and flopping onto the bed. As he stared up, past the drapes of the four-poster, at the beautifully detailed ceiling, he wondered what awaited him in the morning, eventually falling asleep as he waited in vain for Jennifer to return.

Waking up to the sound of Jennifer exiting the suite sometime around two, Bayne was too exhausted to fully pull himself from his dreams to go after her.

Katherine sat on the edge of the balcony, the cool breeze flowing around her as she took in the beauty of the night, thinking back on the events of the evening. While her memories of the champions continued to evade her, she could not help but wonder if, just perhaps, this was in fact a blessing.

She had escaped the dining room earlier to seek solitude, a quiet place to steady her thoughts. After a long, hot shower, it was no longer her title or power that plagued her. As she stared out towards the dense forest in the distance, it was not the arrival of the princes that drew her curiosity, but rather the reaction of the fifth prince that had led to the night's chaos. That, and the uncomfortable car ride that had followed. Something inside of her would not let go of whatever it was that called for her to keep these thoughts front of mind.

Lost in contemplation, Katherine found herself caught between the desire to unravel the mystery and the need to find peace within herself.

Inner dialogue echoed in her mind, a chorus of questions and doubts. *Why did the prince's reaction seem so personal?* The thought tugged at her consciousness, teasing her with elusive fragments of memory that slipped through her fingers like sand.

With a furrowed brow, Katherine pressed her fingers against her temples, willing herself to piece together the puzzles that haunted her thoughts. The answers remained stubbornly out of reach, leaving her feeling adrift in a sea of uncertainty. Drawing a shaky breath, Katherine forced herself to set aside her doubts, if only for a moment, and focus on the present. The night was wearing on, and fatigue settled deep in her bones as the light rain continued.

The sun threatened to break through the night sky by the time Katherine finally pulled herself away from the window, seeking comfort in the refuge of her bed, hoping that sleep would offer some respite from the turmoil of her mind. She was sure that she had heard Alfred knocking at the door earlier, but he seemed to respect her decision to be alone. As she embraced her blanket's welcoming arms, she let out a deep sigh and stared up at the hand-painted ceiling. It did not take long for her eyes to close, her mind putting her new reality temporarily on pause in favour of more pleasant dreams.

CHAPTER 08
THE MORTALS SETTLE IN

S oon after the sun had fully risen, Katherine awoke to the sound of rain pouring in through her open balcony doors. Rushing to close them, she was suddenly much too awake to go back to sleep, no matter how exhausted she still was. While the fires continued to burn, as always, the gloominess that the thick black clouds brought with them seemed to darken more than just her room. It was as though the skies were choosing to play an amusing game with her by mimicking her mood. She glanced at the clock and sighed, deciding to have a shower to ease her worries before breakfast.

The warm stream of water that hit Katherine's back as she turned on the gold faucet almost took her breath away. It took her a minute to adjust, but soon it felt more like a comforting hug than a crushing weight. It took everything in her to not collapse to the floor and allow the heat to take away her fears.

"You can do this, Katherine," she muttered as the steam tried to blind her.

She was resolved to face the day with more grace than she had shown after arriving back at the West Wing the night before. The more she gave herself permission to linger on the questions that continued to race around her mind, the more she wondered if it was more than frustration that she had felt after the awkward drive back. More than surprise at the sudden turn of events. More than the fear she had felt as Prince Cartesius stared her down so hungrily.

"Breathe."

Her heart refused to calm down. Even the rejuvenating water proved powerless in her ultimate struggle for tranquillity.

"Just breathe."

Finally, accepting that escape was futile, she turned off the faucet, surrendering to what she knew she must face.

It was not until Katherine noticed her fingers shaking as they tried to tie the laces on her boots that she realised what it was she was feeling.

Hurt, she thought, snapping her eyes to the closet mirror.

It's hurt.

Confused at how she could feel something without knowing its true cause, without remembering whatever it was that clearly lingered in the back of her soul, Katherine did her best to shake it off, knowing that such vulnerabilities were best left concealed. It was already troubling enough that those around her knew more about her past than she did, but she would be damned if she allowed anyone to exploit that knowledge to manipulate that which she was not yet able to comprehend.

Arriving early to try to catch Bayne before anyone else came down for breakfast, Emily had taken her seat at the dining table just as the last of the pastries were being perfectly positioned by one of the castle keepers. She was determined to find out what exactly had happened the night before.

But, unfortunately for Emily, Bayne did not grace them with his presence until well after many of the others, Matthew having been the first to join her. Bayne entered within only moments of the other champions. As Alfred directed each of the princes to their designated seats, the other handlers took their places against the walls behind those they had spent their entire existence protecting, pulling out their devices and attending to the needs of their respective lands.

Emily felt somewhat envious that she was sandwiched in between two mortals while Brian was the one to have the mysterious, dark-haired prince, Deacon, seated next to him. But even she had to admit that from where she sat, she had quite the view. As nervous as Brian was looking at this point, it seemed to be the general mood around the table, so his slightly sweaty brow went mostly unnoticed.

Alek looked directly at Alfred as he sat down. "Is she—?"

"As far as I know, on her way, sir," Alfred replied from the corner.

Emily and the other mortals, who had been unsettlingly quiet since the champions entered, seemed to be visibly more on edge than usual, prompting Alek to break the ice.

"So," said the prince, stabbing his fork into a cream-covered waffle and taking a bite. "Tell me, how freaked out are you, exactly?"

The mortals exchanged nervous glances. It was becoming clear that Alek was doing his best to make them feel included and safe, but that did nothing to make them feel so under the judgemental gaze of his brothers.

"Listen." Alek laid down his cutlery and rubbed his hands together. "Yeah, this is strange. I get it. *We* get it. You're going to see things, learn about things, and do things that might challenge every belief you've ever had. But the reality is, you're a part of this world now." He chuckled. "Crazy as it sounds, this is Katherine's life. And none of you would be here if she didn't care about you deeply. None of us are sure how long this is going to take, so I reckon it would probably be best to just treat each other like equals and try to make this as comfortable as possible. For *everyone* involved."

As the prince looked around the room, many nodded in agreement, however reluctantly or nervously.

But Marko, it seemed, had reached his limit. He scoffed and locked eyes with his brother, his expression one of unmistakable defiance.

"You know, you're trying so hard, but nothing's going to change the fact that there's danger around every corner and they should prepare for that. Even in this very room," said the prince, throwing his hands up and looking around.

"Don't start," snapped Alek.

"What? Why not? I mean, they should know what they're in for, shouldn't they? I mean, one of them's even a champion."

"Markovyas!"

"What exactly are you saying?" came Deacon's voice from further down the table, opposite Bayne. His chestnut gaze darkened as it fixed on Marko.

"Well, *brother*, let's just say that when it comes to anyone, mortals included, those of us on *this* side of the room are a bit more trustworthy." The prince sneered and took a large sip of his freshly poured bourbon.

"How dare you!" Deacon narrowed his eyes in anger. "You automatically think that just because you're you, we're the ones that are going to go off the handle and skirt the rules. *Hurt* them?"

A shadow crossed Marko's face. "Not just them, brother."

"We haven't even been here a day and already you're jumping to conclusions."

"Enough, both of you!" objected Alek, his voice raised.

"It's true, though. Why lie to the mortals? If they knew the number of heads Kaëden's rolled with just a wave of his hand, they may be a bit more prepared going into this." Marko scoffed and cast a disgusted look at his brothers. "Or how about the number of times Deacon has run people through just because he couldn't control his temper or because he thought it'd be *funny*?"

Alfred dared not get involved. He seemed to know better. His eyes simply darted back and forth, as if he was readying himself to react in an instant should things escalate too far. His fellow handlers followed suit. Emily had no doubt they had seen far worse temper flare-ups over the centuries. To them, this was probably barely the beginning of a little spat.

"And *you're* going to take this?" asked Deacon, gesturing to Kaëden, who looked all too comfortable, glass in hand, at the head of the table to Emily's right.

A single, sharp expression from the eldest prince immediately silenced his brother.

"You see? And there it is!" Marko pointed out with a scoff. "Even Deacon is scared of you, Kade!"

"I think you've had enough, brother," said Alek, raising his eyebrows at Marko's handler. "And the day's only just begun."

"I'm just saying, *brother*, this is life and death, after all. No point in sugarcoating that fact."

"Enough," came a voice from the doorway over Kaëden's shoulder.

Silence fell immediately as Katherine entered. She looked around, visibly disappointed at their bickering, and crossed the room.

Reaching her chair, Katherine turned to face them all, taking the glass of liquor that Alfred held in his outstretched hand. She took a sip before allowing a slow and controlled breath to escape her lips.

"I'm sure that there are a ton of unsettled disputes that each of us is bringing into this," she said, glancing up at her guests. Her voice was barely more than a whisper, but it called for their attention like no other as it shook with frustration. "However, you are in *my* kingdom, *my* castle, around people *I* care about. I will not have this become a problem."

Emily caught the hint of approval in Alfred's eyes. Katherine had evidently taken to heart what he had told her about maintaining an appearance of strength and authority until her memories fully returned, especially now that the princes understood the connection between her memory loss and its role in the upcoming trials.

The mortals assumed the royals and their companions would never dare disrespect Katherine's rules in her own home, not when the threat of inevitable retaliation loomed over them. And judging by Alfred's expression, the princess had proven herself more than capable of commanding respect.

All eyes were on Katherine, and not another snarky remark was passed. Her face was hard, cold, and bothered. But it showed no fear.

"Alfred, what time do we begin?" She glanced towards the golden clock that was seconds away from chiming eight-thirty.

"The council will be here at five, Princess. If everyone could gather slightly earlier in the courtyard, perhaps?"

"Excellent. Seeing as nobody seems to be able to play nice, I will see you all at four-thirty then."

She left without another word. Disappearing *again*.

~

"You heard her," called Alfred in a loud voice, turning the room's attention away from Katherine's sudden exit. "Please gather in the courtyard outside at four-thirty this afternoon. While there will be no representatives of the other kingdoms here for the actual trials, it is still important to adhere to at least the most basic of courtesies. So, please do not be late. While there is no formal dress code, I ask that you still present yourselves respectably, as I am aware that many mortals enjoy conducting daily business in their... pyjamas."

Emily let out a giggle as a faint smile shot across Alfred's face.

"Please, should you need anything during the course of the day, there are many castle keepers at your disposal. You are welcome to explore the wing further than you have since your arrival or take the time to settle in properly, as you are now all aware that your stay will be longer than originally anticipated. However, I ask that you refrain from venturing onto the grounds just yet, until you have become more familiar with the property. It has only been a week, and I am sure there are many curiosities you are eager to uncover."

Marko snickered as he took another sip of his bourbon. Clearly, he had dismissed his brother's disdain towards his coping mechanisms and had decided that a morning bender was the best way to begin the trials.

"Should you need electronics, clothing, or anything else to make your extended stay here more comfortable, please head up to see Zachary in the armoury." Alfred turned to point over his left shoulder at a door in the corner of the room. "Simply ask one of the castle keepers to show you where it is if you have not found your way there yet."

Zachary waved his hand dramatically from where he sat beside Alek, stuffing another roll in his mouth. "Even you can't get lost," he said between bites.

"Champions, the same goes for you. We are going to be here for a while, and the princess would want me to ensure your stay in Eyrondale is as pleasant as possible." He took a quick look at the clock. "Zachary, shall we?"

"Oh. Right," said Zachary, rushing to get out of his seat, hesitating only to grab another roll from the table before following Alfred's lead past the diners and into the main living room. "Oh," he added, popping his head back into view, "the rain should clear up by noon."

They were gone in an instant, leaving the mortals feeling rather vulnerable, despite having the other handlers in the room.

"I'd suggest heading to see Zachary first for those of you needing to arrange with your employers to extend your remote working privileges, or if you're in need of finding something more permanent to do around here," advised Alek, getting up from his seat. "Your cover stories will need to be able to last as long as these trials go on at the very least, so best you flesh those out ASAP. Zach's IT team is excellent, and they'll be able to help you with pretty much anything."

The prince walked past Katherine's seat, towards the door Alfred had pointed to, and opened it to reveal a dimly lit staircase.

"The armoury is up there, or at least the parts of it you'll need. My advice, take liquorice! Bribery will get you far with Zach." Alek chuckled.

As he left the room, Kaëden's and Deacon's handlers moved towards the table and began conversing with the princes at a rapid pace. Marko rolled his eyes at their micromanagement, another bourbon in hand. Whatever Kaëden's handler was saying to him must have been serious, as the prince got up immediately, buttoned his blazer, and quietly excused himself from the room.

"Must have someone to kill, I bet," remarked Marko with a laugh.

Deacon shot him an angry look but bit his tongue.

"Oh, come on!" Marko leant back in his chair and propped his feet up on the table. "It was a joke."

Rolling his eyes, Deacon got to his feet and gestured for Rawson to follow his lead to discuss kingdom business in private.

"*Kinda,*" Marko muttered under his breath, soft enough for the youngest prince not to hear as the pair left the room.

Emily exchanged a look with a few of the others that suggested they leave the champion to drink in peace. As if understood by them all, the mortals finished their meals and left. Some stopped in the living room to discuss what to do with their day or to gossip about what had just happened, and others headed to the armoury's staircase to await Zachary's return.

Bayne did not seem inclined to rehash the morning's events – or to spend the day surrounded by others. Instead, he made his way straight to the armoury, where only Matthew and Layla had decided to begin their day. Emily doubted Layla would press their cousin with anything too personal, and as for Matthew, she suspected he would avoid making a scene in front of the castle staff.

While Emily had missed her opportunity to talk to her cousin once again, she thought that Jennifer may just be the easier target. She *needed* to talk to someone about what was going on, and if Bayne was reluctant to open up, maybe his better half would. She joined Jennifer and Aiden, who were locked in conversation with Jamie and Brian.

Brian was a jolly young man, a tad on the larger side, but had a boyish smile that was contagious even if you hardly knew him. Emily had only met him once or twice before he and her sister had decided to marry, but she had immediately seen the kindness in his light brown, almost hazel eyes. Jamie, on the other hand, Emily had known for most of her life. Bayne and Jamie had been childhood neighbours and best friends, so Emily saw him at least every summer when she and her sister stayed with their aunt.

Jamie's dark eyes lit up behind his rectangular glasses as he saw Emily approaching. Truthfully, she had been aware that he had harboured a bit of a crush on Layla for the longest time, though he had never acted on it. Still, it was she and Jamie who had always got along best.

"Emily," he exclaimed happily, "these three were just telling me that they're off to stock up their closets. What are *your* plans for the day?"

"I...uh," she mumbled. "I was thinking that we should all probably have a talk about what we're gonna do here."

"What do you mean?" asked Aiden, confused.

"Well, all I'm saying is that I know we said we'd wait for them to give us some answers, but that hasn't happened yet. I think we should come up with a game plan so we don't get caught up in the crazy."

"You mean in case something bad happens, we have an escape route?" Jamie asked with a raised eyebrow, smirking. "So much for a good night's sleep, eh?"

"Exactly." Emily scowled at him. "And I'm pretty sure you got just as little sleep after we said goodnight as I did," she muttered.

"I don't know about you guys, but I agree," piped up Jennifer.

Jamie and Brian exchanged a hesitant glance, but Aiden barely noticed.

"Guys. Seriously? We've been over this. You've gotta give them a break, too. It's barely nine, for crying out loud. You all seem to keep forgetting that until Kat remembers who she is, who *we* are, we're at a bit of a disadvantage here."

"I say to hell with it, and we pack up and leave," Jennifer said, her voice cold as she glared at Aiden.

"Come on, Jen!" started Emily. "You can't ask us to do that. You can't have us choose."

"Besides, even if we managed to get Bayne out of this, we were brought here because they're trying to protect us. Or did you forget that while you were focusing on the grudge you hold against Kat?" interrupted Jamie before Emily could say any more.

Jennifer's eyes narrowed, and her fists clenched tightly, but she said nothing. Emily could tell she did not want to cause a scene – not now.

"Alright then," continued Jamie, rubbing his hands together. "Let's go get a bunch of free stuff and drink whatever tension this is away." He glanced at the fiery redhead beside him. "Unless he told you something last night that suggests that we're *not* stuck here for the foreseeable future?"

Jennifer was tight-lipped again.

"Thought so. Alright, guys, you coming?"

There was a slight stench of unease, sharp in their nostrils, but the rest of them nodded and followed Jamie's lead, calling on the first castle keeper to cross their path.

❧

"Ah!" came Zachary's voice as the three mortals entered the armoury.

He spun out of the chair where he had been rocking back and forth at the workstation nearest the stairway and made his way over to greet them.

"Hello again, Layla...Matthew," he said, waggling his fingers in greeting before approaching Bayne, curiosity written all over his face.

Layla and Matthew replied in unison, quite taken aback that Zachary had managed his way to the armoury so quickly after having left breakfast with Alfred.

Zachary circled around Bayne before coming to a stop before him and bending into a low bow. "Master Bayne."

Bayne was unable to stop his face from turning a bright shade of red. He simply nodded and muttered a barely audible greeting under his breath.

"Come now," exclaimed Zachary, gesturing for the trio to follow his lead as they descended the nearby steps towards a round table situated in the middle of the lower level. "Don't be shy, mate. You've got it better than anyone else around here. You just don't know it yet."

"Um, who are all these people?" asked Layla, looking around the armoury, which was playing host to at least a dozen others, her question distracting focus from Bayne's evident discomfort.

"Oh, well, let's see then. Everyone against the wall with the workstations behind us is part of the surveillance and intelligence team. The big guys heading in and out of the door on the other end of the room are a few of the tactical leaders."

He leant in to carefully select an apple from a bowl on the round table, his tongue sticking out in concentration as he searched for the deepest shade of red. Happy with his choice, Zachary rubbed it against his sleeve and took a bite before continuing.

"Then, the ones moving around us like they're kind of awkward, those are the Interchangeables. They're not part of intelligence or tactical, but they make sure the armoury is always fully stocked, every camera or microphone is up and running, and any and all paperwork is sorted. You know..." He took another bite. "Wheel turning."

"And this is all it takes to run a kingdom?" asked Matthew, eyebrows raised as he took in the small warehouse-sized room around them.

Zachary let out a loud chuckle mid-bite, sending pieces of apple to the floor. "My dear boy!" he said, trying to catch his breath as he looked at the fruit with a sense of betrayal and threw it into the nearest bin. "That's not even everything it takes to run this castle."

Noticing their puzzled expressions, Zachary composed himself.

"Listen, I know it's a lot, but you'll get there. Basically, this room, and the one above it, is where myself and my team keep track of magical and non-magical incidents occurring in Eyrondale and everywhere else under Princess Katherine's rule. It's our central base of operations where we work with tactical leaders, informants, etcetera to keep the kingdom, and the places, groups, and companies within it, running right."

"And it's all tech?" asked Bayne, his curiosity getting the better of him.

"Yes and no, Master Bayne."

"You don't need to call me that!"

"I'd take it if I were you!" Zachary laughed. "It's not every day that someone, let alone a human, gets a title from the council."

Bayne mumbled something about not wanting to talk about it, his face turning a darker shade.

"I've been around for...well, a long time. Over the ages, we've learned to adapt to the times and find ways to join the efforts of power and technology to create something truly beautiful. If you'd like, I could show you sometime, Master Bayne?"

"I...um..."

"Don't worry. From what I hear, you're more than capable of keeping up. So, whenever you need an escape, this room never stops."

Zachary threw his hands in the air and spun around dramatically, Layla giggling at his silliness.

"Now then, let's get you what you need. Take a seat."

With a quick wave of his hand, three chairs rolled forward to meet the mortals as they returned to Zachary's workstation, guiding their attention to the screens. Before they could ask what their host was doing, their profiles had already appeared on the nearest monitors.

"So, Master Bayne, how 'bout we start with you?"

"I...um...sure."

"Alrighty." Zachary reached for the tablet that lay on his workstation and turned to face the nervous-looking champion. "So, after last night, it doesn't look like you'll be heading back to work anytime soon, mate, even if the others get to. We're gonna have to play this one a little differently."

"How so?"

"Well, even if we get the green light to let everyone else head home, you're in this until you're not. You know?"

Bayne's insides squirmed. He understood precisely what it meant – unfortunately.

"Right," Zachary said, taking the resounding silence as a yes. "So, I was thinking that, in your case, it may be best to put in your notice and tell everyone you've picked up another gig overseas. Whatcha think?"

Slightly overwhelmed, Bayne was reluctant to let go of one of the few threads of sanity he had left. "I'm sure when I get kicked out at the first trial, I'm still going to want that job when I get back to my normal life."

Zachary hesitated, biting his lip – anxious, it seemed – before finally broaching the subject. "Listen. I get it. At this point, it's easier to hold on to some semblance of hope that this is all a bad dream. How 'bout this?" He turned back to his station and typed away frantically for a minute or two before turning back to face them. "There," he said, clearly satisfied. "Now you get to go back whenever you choose, once this is all over. Your family's going to think you're heading off to consult on a site at the office in Germany."

"I guess that's easy enough to believe—"

Layla giggled. "Yeah, they probably don't even realise you've left, anyway."

"Hey!"

"What? It's not like you text or call them more than once every week or two."

"I...I guess," Bayne muttered, not too thrilled that Layla had decided to call him out on his busy schedule. "But," he said, turning his attention back to Zachary, "how is that going to work exactly? My bosses aren't just going to let me take more leave. It was difficult enough to swing it for this long."

"All taken care of." Zachary smiled, a hint of naughtiness flashing in his eyes.

Bayne was almost afraid to ask. But, thankfully, his cousin beat him to it.

"How *exactly* is it taken care of?"

"Oh, that's easy!" Zachary shrugged. "I just bought it."

"You bought what?" asked Bayne, suddenly more worried than he had been all morning.

"The company."

"Wait. What?"

"Yeah. That way, anyone who questions anything gets the boot, and you get to enjoy a cushy gig that lets us keep an eye on you if, for whatever reason, we'd need to."

"You can't just—"

"Oh, trust me. We can."

"How?"

Clearly amused, Zachary narrowed his eyes. He tilted his head and pressed his fingertips together thoughtfully. "You're actually asking me that, after everything you guys have seen?"

"But that company's worth—"

"Let me ask you something. You ever seen a city made of gold?"

"What?"

"Let's just say that Eyrondale has more than one under its wing." Zachary laughed, turning back towards the screens to enlarge Layla's file. He pulled his legs up onto the chair, crossing them on the seat.

The mortals shared a stunned, disbelieving glance.

"Is he serious?" mouthed Layla, her eyes wide.

"You know what? I kinda think so," muttered Matthew, glancing nervously at the back of their host's seat.

They barely had time to linger on Zachary's words before his voice met their ears again, snapping their focus back to the agenda at hand.

"Layla, your turn."

She gulped. "Alright."

"This one's a bit easier. We actually have a few islands in need of your services that are close to where you've already set up shop. I'm going to put in an internal transfer for the two of you that comes with an extended holiday as a condition of your promotion. Boom! Done. Nobody's going to be asking any questions till the end of next month. And if you're still here by then, I'll send out a few ghost workers for you. Nobody will know the difference."

"Why not just do that to start off with?"

"Well, this way, you can tell your folks that you've decided to treat Emily to some time on the island while you and Brian are getting settled." Zachary pulled open the drawer beside him, then shifted his attention to an empty jar behind one of the files on his desk. "They should find that pretty believable now that I'll be sending in Emily's resignation."

"You're what?"

"She's been having issues as is with that boss of hers." He sighed, looking quite disappointed. "Damn – no liquorice. Figured this would be the best thing for her."

Layla raised her eyebrows, her expression stern. "And you've asked her about this?"

"Oh, no need! She's been actively looking for something new for a while. This way she doesn't have to worry about it till she has to. I'll even help set her up in one of our holdings. That way—"

"You can keep your eye on her if need be?" came Bayne's voice, the hint of disapproval making Zachary smile.

"See it how you'd like, Master Bayne, but Katherine's always taken care of those she cares about. Even long after they've disappeared from her life."

"Oh?"

"A story for another day." Zachary shot them a wink.

"Right."

"Anyway, that just leaves you, Matt."

"Hey, man," said Matthew, leaning back in his seat and stretching out his arms. "I'm down for whatever."

"My kinda man. Alright, how about setting you up with your residence here and your own brewery? I'm thinking...a little town just outside of Oxford? You can say it's been in the works for a bit and you got a good deal?"

"Not like I haven't been looking into moving over here."

"Exactly. Should give you a good six weeks before you could travel back home."

"I'll take it. One question, though."

"Shoot!"

"Do I actually get the brewery when this is all done?"

Zachary let out a laugh so loud that two nearby Interchangeables shot him dirty looks. "You guys didn't think we were doing all of this just to *pretend*, did you?"

"Sweet," exclaimed Matthew, clearly happy with his winnings.

"Okay. Moving on. Let's get you set up with the rest."

Bayne and Layla exchanged an apprehensive glance, but Bayne knew that there was no fighting against it. They spent the majority of the day with Zachary finalising the arrangements that would see them easily slip away from the world for the next month, at least, without too many questions. From automated social posts to recording messages to their loved ones for later use, Zachary had truly thought of everything they would need to disappear from prying eyes.

CHAPTER 09
THE FIRST TRIAL

E mily met Aiden and Matthew at the top of the staircase leading down into the foyer. They were locked in rapid, hushed conversation. As she approached, they went silent.

"And that?" asked Emily, looking between them.

"Nothing, Em," said Aiden, half shrugging.

"Sure. Somehow, I don't believe you."

"It's nothing," said Matthew. "It's just...this is all so crazy! You won't believe what happened to me today."

"I know. Layla gave me the memo when she got back from the armoury. Can't say I'm upset to be rid of that place. And you? A brewery?" A wide grin spread across Emily's face. "There are a few benefits to being here, at least. But, insane as it is, I can't find anything that faults it. It's becoming more and more real at every turn. Like that *Alek* said this morning, we don't really have another choice but to accept that we're in this."

Aiden raised his eyebrows playfully. "So, you're agreeing with our idea to just go with it for now?"

"Nothing we can really do besides that, I guess."

Aiden's lips curled into a smirk as a slow, amused breath escaped his lips. He tipped his head towards the ground floor, motioning for the others to follow. "C'mon."

They descended the stairs, past the warmth of the fires in the living room, and out into the courtyard as the sunset quietly approached in the distance. The days of late had been growing darker earlier and earlier.

The trio joined Layla, Jennifer, and the rest of the mortals who were gathered near the dining table to their right, near the castle wall. As they approached, they could sense that everyone else was just as on edge as they were.

As they waited and the group whispered among themselves, Emily couldn't help but take in the surrounding beauty. She had not had a chance to spend time in the courtyard since they arrived.

From the large clearing, she looked out towards the pathways lined with gardens, admired the fountains, and longed to get a closer look at the statues scattered throughout the blooms. It was more beautiful than she had noticed through the castle windows. Emily wondered what lay at the bottom of the grand staircases leading to the vast, inviting grounds, while her gaze was drawn to the forest as its depths called to her.

Having got lost in her thoughts, Emily shifted her focus back to the group as Alfred made his way into the courtyard, champions and their handlers in tow.

"Good evening, everyone," he greeted loudly, leading them to the middle of the clearing.

"Hello, Alfred."

"Hi."

"Good evening."

Smiling, Alfred turned to the handlers and instructed them to join Emily and the others and take a seat wherever they would be most comfortable. As he did, Katherine emerged through one set of open double doors, the sheer white drapes that lined them whispering peacefully in the wind as she passed.

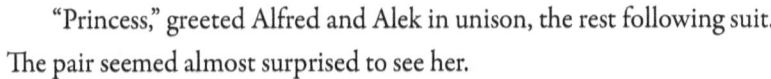

"Princess," greeted Alfred and Alek in unison, the rest following suit. The pair seemed almost surprised to see her.

"Gentlemen," Katherine replied with a curt nod.

Emily was unable to miss the way Alek's gaze lingered on Katherine – as if he had noticed she still seemed troubled – but for now, he chose to let it go.

"Your Highness, the council should be here at any moment," Alfred advised, examining the princess's expression as if trying to X-ray her insides. "Would you like me to go and greet them? Or would you prefer one of the castle keepers to lead them in?"

"Go ahead, Alfred. We'll be fine," replied Katherine, giving the handler a reassuring look.

All eyes were glancing between Katherine and the champions, curious, waiting for someone to say something. But the mortals were left wanting. It was not long before Alfred returned with the three elderly gentlemen from the night before following closely behind.

"Ah!" exclaimed the tallest of the three, gesturing towards the group of royals. "Your Highnesses, wonderful to see you all again!"

He stopped before them, the other two council members at his side, and bowed.

"And the humans, how lovely!" he said, straightening up and giving them a once-over. "My name is Horus. This is Herlock."

Horus gestured to the man on his right, the shortest of the three, whose green eyes sparkled behind his glasses.

"Hello," Herlock greeted with a slight smile, just visible behind his beard, which was shorter than the other two's.

"And this," said Horus, gesturing to his left, "is Dolos."

The tall elder with dancing silver eyes smiled coldly at Emily and the others as he looked them up and down, a flicker of disapproval on his face.

"Welcome! These are indeed unusual circumstances," Horus continued, his eyes lingering on the mortal champion. "Well, I suggest we proceed while the night is young. For none of us truly know what is to happen next, and I am sure we are all curious to gain enlightenment."

Emily heard a loud gulp amidst the uneasy shuffling. Even she had to admit, her heart was beating faster than it had in the time since she had arrived at the castle, faster than it had at the Selection by Fire. She was almost sure that her face was no longer capable of hiding her nerves.

～

"First," said Herlock, his eyes narrowing, "I ask that each of you be aware that whatever is to happen during the course of these trials, none will be allowed to interfere. While those here, including ourselves, are powerful, the prophecy has now begun to unfold and thus, Fate is the only force capable of shaping what is to come."

He reached into his cloak, withdrew the orb that they had seen the previous night and placed it in the centre of the courtyard clearing.

Just as they had activated its power at the champion selection, the council circled the orb, chanting until white light shot from their hands, sending the Breath of Fate into the floor below. Unlike before, the sphere itself seemed to melt seamlessly into the stone, leaving behind only a carving of its creation – identical to the one that had been etched into the dais of the Grand Hall.

A small flame ignited, tracing the symbol's lines before splitting into five, each fire settling at a marker of power, waiting for its champion.

Katherine could have sworn she heard the whispers of the fires flying on the breeze to fill the council's ears as their eyes turned a snowy white.

Dolos, not a moment later, his eyes taking on their familiar shade of silver, waved his hand, and summoned one of the wooden tables that stood nearest them to his side. "Interesting," Katherine heard him mutter as he handed Herlock a magenta drawstring bag from inside his sleeve.

Kaëden exchanged a dark look with Daniel that did not escape Katherine's gaze. It made her nauseous. But there was no time for her to question why the prince had suddenly managed to make her feel so uneasy.

"Now," said Herlock, addressing the champions as he emptied five small, marble-like objects into his hand, "we have enchanted each of these spheres to represent you during these tasks. Princess Katherine will reach into the bag before each trial commences and select the order in which you will complete it."

Horus cleared his voice to take over as Herlock returned the representations to their velvet housing.

"We informed you last night that the first trial would be a kiss."

The sound of Jennifer's sudden gasp was acknowledged by no one.

"We also advised that we would not know the exact nature of each trial until the Breath of Fate reveals it to us. This trial, it appears, Princess," said Horus, a single bead of sweat appearing on his brow, "will return to you that which you have lost."

Katherine stared at him, waiting for a better explanation.

"Indeed!" added Herlock with a bit more excitement than his fellow council member. "With each champion's kiss, it appears that your recollections of them will return to you. And, at the completion of the final task, you will have regained not only your memories but along with them, your power."

Katherine was beginning to understand. This is what they had meant by her amnesia being part of the trials. Finally, some insight as to why she could so far only grasp a small fraction of her existence.

"Simple as it may seem," Herlock continued, "these challenges are designed to test your resolve, your power, your mind, and so much more. From what we have been informed, with each kiss, your memories of that particular champion will return in order. However, you will not only remember them, you will also *experience* them."

"What?" blurted out Alek, unable to keep his mouth in check.

Looking at him, Horus let out a deep sigh, clearly having hoped that they would be able to get through this with as little distraction as possible. He turned back to face Katherine. "You will relive each encounter, Princess. You will feel every emotion. Just as if it were happening for the first time."

The shuffling became more frequent as Horus set out the terms of the trial. Katherine could practically feel the apprehension his words had fuelled among not only the champions but also the mortals who continued to watch, fixated on each syllable that dripped so smoothly from the council member's lips.

"That is not all, I am afraid. Upon entering the symbol, you will be shielded inside it until the task is complete. More daunting still, to fully open yourself to the possibility of an eternity together, Fate would have it that each champion join you on this journey."

"You're trying to say something. What is it?" asked Katherine, her tone of suspicion interrupting what she and the others were quickly starting to think of as a purposefully vague explanation.

"Well," said Herlock, unable to dismiss her apprehension, "you will not only be reliving your own memories. It will be as though your very essence inhabits both your body and that of the champion for the duration of the kiss. You will each experience your own emotions as well as the other's, experiencing both the physical and near-physical encounters of your history. What will be only a few minutes out here will seem like years, decades, or even centuries in *there*."

"What does—"

"This trial is designed to bring up any and all pre-existing feelings that have an influence over your hearts. It is designed to bring each of you into this series of trials, more aware of where you stand moving forward. You shall live through recollections that you were both a part of, as well as any moments that included the mention of one's name from the lips of the other, assuming that you were both within the range of each other's heightened hearing abilities at the time." Herlock paused, allowing time for his words to sink in. "While Fate is seeking to open your eyes to more than just what once was, we remind you that you will not be privy to each other's thoughts, nor the conclusions drawn by one another from each experience. Nor will you gain insight into that which occurred outside the reach of your enhanced abilities. In other words—"

"In other words," interjected Dolos, "you will know the truth of what once was, but not the reality of what is or the possibility of what could be. So be warned."

"Please, Princess, approach the table and select the order for this trial," instructed Horus, determined to press on without further delay.

"You're still leaving something out," whispered Katherine under her breath as she neared them. *I can feel it.*

Katherine reached into the bag and searched around. There was no way for her to tell whose sphere belonged to whom. With a deep breath and a quick pause, not wanting to scare herself by replaying the council's words, she pulled out the first of the five and handed it to Herlock.

"Prince Markovyas of Neighlore," he announced with a smile.

What looked like a half-hearted grin spread across Marko's face as he attempted to conceal his hesitation. In fact, each of the champions seemed rather apprehensive about what the trial was to bring.

Katherine reached in again and pulled out the next sphere.

"Prince Dàikonos of Azrallus."

The youngest prince seemed slightly more willing to dive in than the others, judging by the way he was nodding in acknowledgement.

A barely audible gasp escaped Bayne's lips as Herlock's voice reached him, saying, "Master Bayne McAllister." But his reaction was quickly overshadowed as the next names were called.

"Prince Aleksander. Which means that you, Prince Kaëden, shall be the last to participate," Herlock concluded, nodding towards the eldest prince before returning their representations to the bag and handing it to Dolos, who tucked it safely within his cloak.

Not wanting to risk more questions, the council raised their hands towards the symbol and the ankle-height flames flickered with more intensity.

"Princess, Prince Markovyas, please make your way to the centre," instructed Horus.

Katherine looked back at Marko before taking a breath and doing as she was told. The prince joined her a moment later, standing a foot away, facing her, and looking as uncomfortable as she did.

The five flames lifted from their markers, dancing along the outer circle of the carving. They grew higher, enclosing the royals in the barrier.

"Whenever you are ready, Your Highnesses."

CHAPTER 10
PRINCE MARKOVYAS
OF NEIGHLORE

"**A**ny idea what we're about to dive into?" asked Katherine half-jokingly, trying to break some of the ice.

She was nervous – not only because of what was about to happen. As she looked into Marko's warm stare, she felt herself being pulled in. Katherine could not help but admire how handsome he was. Just as when she had looked into his eyes at the champion selection, her stomach gave a lurch, hinting at something that she was eager to learn more about. Thankfully, unlike with the Selection by Fire, there was not the added pressure of having hundreds of supernatural and magical guests watching her every move. At least, here in the West Wing, it was safe.

Marko smiled. "That would spoil all the fun now, wouldn't it?"

Smiling back, Katherine blushed. She quickly averted her gaze, glancing at the ground.

Marko took a breath and inched nearer. Like he had been waiting for this forever. With one hand, he reached for Katherine's chin, lifting it so that she had no choice but to be held captive by the intensity of his eyes. With the other, he took hold of her waist.

As Marko's thumb delicately traced the curve of Katherine's lower lip, the anticipation that had gripped everyone seemed to ebb away, like a veil lifting, leaving behind an atmosphere charged with a different kind of energy entirely.

She stole a glance at the onlookers, noting their discomfort, yet for Katherine, the world narrowed to the feeling of Marko's hand on her face, the warmth of his skin against hers. Her heart fluttered – each beat echoing a tempest of unnamed emotions. At that moment, Katherine found herself strangely cocooned in the prince's presence, as if his touch created a bubble of calm amidst the storm of uncertainty. As all worry faded into the background, leaving only the pair of royals suspended in their own realm, her nerves melted away, replaced by a growing sense of familiarity.

As Marko's stare held hers, she realised she did not need to know what to expect. All that mattered was the here and now, the firmness of his touch, the quiet mystery beneath his cool exterior. And in that realisation, Katherine found a newfound sense of courage, a willingness to surrender to whatever awaited them.

She swallowed as Marko's lips bridged the gap between them, parting slightly as his eyes shut. Her heart racing, she lifted onto her toes, their lips touching in a moment as natural as breath.

It was as though Katherine's essence split itself in two. One half remained in her body, the other entered Marko's. Not only was she able to see into her own mind's eye, but she was able to see into his, too. Sensing that Marko was experiencing the same in-and-out-of-body sensation as she was, she barely had time to adjust to the darkness before being snapped back into her toddler self.

It was strange. She could see what her younger self saw and feel what she felt but had no insight into the thoughts that gave it all context. At the same time, she was able to see herself from across the room, playing with a doll that Alfred had made for her, feeling the sting of jealousy as the toddler version of Marko seemed to long for her prized possession.

Marko felt the rough material against Katherine's fingers as she ran her hands over the doll, its uneven stitches pressing into her skin. He warmed at her joy as she held it close to her chest, just as he could feel his own envy rise. But the memory did not last long. It was cut short by the sting of Marko being knocked over by something, or *someone,* neither of them was able to see. As the young prince ran from the room, the scene changed.

They relived the few times they had interacted before reaching maturity and setting out to rule their respective kingdoms, though many of those visions were hazy as well. They barely had time to wonder why before the memory of the first time they saw each other after taking their thrones unfolded.

The first *clear* memory the two shared.

Katherine watched herself through Marko's eyes as Alfred led him towards a blonde, slender figure, standing in a moonlit garden nestled within a quiet monastery at the meeting point of Eyrondale's two main lands. She felt every shudder as the prince's nerves tried to get the better of him. She caught his hesitation as he came to a halt at the entrance, nodding for Alfred to announce him.

"Princess, you recall Prince Markovyas of Neighlore?" said Alfred softly as he bowed the son of Magic into the light.

Katherine turned from the white lilies that she had been captivated by to greet her guest. As their eyes met, she paused. The look they shared took Katherine's breath away. There was a warmth in Marko's eyes that seemed to stop her heart mid-beat, even if only for a second. He moved forward, bending into a low bow, never taking his gaze off of hers. As the pair were suddenly trapped by the instantaneous connection they had once shared, neither Katherine nor Marko could prevent the endorphins from washing over them as they relived the true beginning of their story.

"Princess," Marko greeted in a confident, smooth voice, "it really has been too long."

"When I last laid eyes on you, you were barely grown. And now..."

"And now?" Marko asked, a playful glint lighting his eyes as he edged closer, his tone low and teasing.

Alfred shuffled his feet beside one of the columns lining the corridor back to the monastery, and a wave of quiet impatience tightened in Marko's chest, pressing against Katherine as if she could sense his silent wish for the handler to take his leave.

"And now you are...*taller* than I would have expected." She cleared her throat. "That is all."

Marko bit his lip before a grin spread across his face. "As long as it pleases you then, Princess."

"Alfred?" Katherine called, not diverting her attention as she fought to contain a smile of her own.

"Yes, Your Highness?"

"Leave us. *Please.*"

Marko was consumed by the force of what she had felt, the waves of energy rolling off him, each one threatening to knock her off her feet. Her heartbeat pounded in her ears, a rapid, unrelenting rhythm that the prince could feel thrumming through her.

"Are...are you certain, Princess?" asked Alfred, his eyes darting between the pair as they remained transfixed on each other.

"I am certain, yes. Thank you, Alfred, that will be all."

"Of course. Have a lovely evening, Your Highnesses." Hesitant though he seemed to leave them, Alfred bent into another low bow before making his way down the corridor.

It took a moment, but Marko was the first to break away, relieved as Alfred disappeared from view. Turning, the prince placed one hand behind his back and gestured for Katherine to join him with the other. With a nod, she agreed. They walked in silence down the cobblestone pathway that led them through the garden until they reached the other side, far from potential eavesdroppers, each trying their best to tame the fire that had awoken within.

"My apologies for the intrusion, Your Highness," the prince began, moving to admire a nearby rose bush that stirred at the sound of his voice just as a group of fireflies brushed past Katherine's cheek. "Many whom I trust hold you in high regard, and I would like to discuss a potential alliance between our southernmost lands."

"An alliance? Mmm, go on."

As the pair relived how their playful banter had blossomed into an alliance strategy destined to become one of the region's most powerful, Katherine and Marko found themselves unable to shake the exhilaration born of the strength they once drew so effortlessly from each other.

~

Kaëden had taken up against the castle wall behind the dining table, away from the rest of the onlookers. While visibly uncomfortable, his reaction was less obvious than those of the other three champions, from what Emily could see. She noticed how her cousin, watching apprehensively yet trying to appear unaffected, seemed to be having his whisky glass refilled more frequently than normal.

As hushed whispers and the clinking of glasses filled the air, a chill set in that saw Emily's arm hairs stand at attention. She was not the only one who felt the sudden shift in the wind. But brushing it off as inconsequential, she returned her focus to the objects of everyone's gaze.

~

Mere minutes after agreeing on an accord, the sound of Marko's heartbeat quickened as he pulled Katherine closer and pressed her against a nearby stone pillar, the sensation reverberating through her mind, tilting her balance between memory and reality.

Without a word, he kissed her.

And, at that moment, he felt more alive than he ever had.

They both did.

Taken by surprise, Katherine had no choice but to give in. Give in to a man she had only just re-met. Their chemistry, however, was undeniable. The spark wove through Katherine's veins, humming along every path, wrapping her in a shield of unseen fire. It sizzled beneath her skin, alive yet barely perceptible, a faint glow lingering at the edges of her form as Marko finally tore himself free.

Nearly breathless, they exchanged a look, neither uttering a word. A sharp sting pricked Katherine as Marko bit his lip. He hesitated before backing away, his gaze tracing every detail as if committing it all to memory. Once he was out of the princess's line of sight, he instinctively ran his fingers over his lips, still lost in the haze that had caught them both off guard.

The hairs on the back of Marko's neck stood tall as the cold surface of the column touched Katherine's skin while she braced herself against it. The electricity that had quickly taken root within her morphed into something unparalleled, faster than it took for her to stare up at the night sky. As the scene faded, the prince felt the exact moment when Katherine had known that her heart would be forever changed.

However quickly the world outside their minds was moving, they would never know. For them, it was as though time had no end. The wind picked up and carried light clouds into the view of their onlookers, but Katherine and Marko continued on their walk down memory lane, all concepts of their present reality lost.

Among the flood of recollections, most of them incomplete, there were flashes of clarity. As the pair was plunged into what could easily have been their hundredth interaction, Katherine felt her hands tremble as Marko removed the ring from his finger and slid it onto hers, a shudder running through him at the chill of the metal gliding over her skin.

Katherine's heart eased as she looked down at her hand, and the prince was finally able to understand just how deeply his gesture had impacted her very being. Just how quickly her heart hurtled into a free fall, convinced that no matter what, she would never wish to let go of this feeling, that a part of him was now irrevocably hers, and hers alone.

The two royals experienced the wonders of first love for the second time and fully embraced the grip that their past had tightened around their throats, neither desperate to escape its clutches as they dived head-first into memory one hundred and one and beyond.

"And this, my love?" Marko asked, whispering in her ear as he held Katherine from behind, gesturing to the white sheet that hung in front of the entrance to his private library. Her body trembled.

"Well," said Katherine as she turned in his arms, "you have been so supportive of late that I simply wanted to express my gratitude."

She caressed her fingers along his face, kissing him gently on the lips before waving her hand, causing the drapes to vanish in a whimsical puff of blue smoke.

The prince's eyes widened, and his mouth fell open in silent astonishment. Where a set of rounded arched doors usually stood that allowed him to so successfully flee from court, was a creation of Katherine's own design. As the princess's heart lifted with pride at his reaction, a sharp pang struck Marko's chest as he relived one of the many acts of unconditional love she had shown him during their time together.

Framing the doors was a dragon. Its horned, metallic black tail lay carved in stone on the left side of the door. Its body lined the archway, its talons wrapping around the exposed entrance, and its large, deep-blue wings stretched out above them. Its long neck lined the right-hand side, with a monstrous head extending out towards the corridor, black eyes gleaming in the light from the torches that remained lit along the castle's walls.

"It is magnificent!" Marko exclaimed, moving closer to the expertly carved creature. It was cold to the touch as he ran his hands along it, admiring the workmanship. Even the solid wooden doors that the beast guarded had been updated. They were now a dark wooden colour, iron vines covering them, each sporting sharp thorns. "Come on!"

The prince took Katherine's hand and led her inside. He pulled her into a passionate kiss, lifting her into the air as the room sealed itself, granting them complete privacy.

He felt the intensity of his touch as it exhilarated her. How his kiss had become a near-addiction. How the heat of his breath on her neck ignited an intense flame deep within that could not, and would not, be extinguished by the judgement of lesser beings. It was almost primal.

Marko lay Katherine down on the plush fur that blanketed the stone before the roaring fireplace. "Would you give me your virtue?" he whispered.

His question hung in the air like a delicate promise of forever. It was more than a request for something physical. It was, instead, a tender plea for her trust. Her vulnerability. A wave of feeling surged through Katherine, a fierce desire to give herself wholly to this shared journey, to the spell he had unknowingly cast upon her heart, binding herself to him in ways beyond words.

"What I have left is yours to take," she breathed, pulling Marko close enough for his long eyelashes to touch hers.

As they succumbed to the longing and passion they had been holding back for so long, all kingdom business was forgotten. All threats were put far out of mind. In each other's arms, it was as though they were one. It mattered not that they were defying Fate and the ancient prophecy that would surely see them torn apart in favour of potentially uniting Katherine with one of the prince's brothers. It mattered not that, at this moment, they were each choosing love over duty. All that mattered was their unspoken promise to never let each other go.

The sun had already set by the time the pair took time to slow down. As they lay before the crackling fire, fantasising about a future where their feelings would prove more powerful than their destinies, both Katherine and Marko were completely and utterly content. It was only as their eyes started to tire that they allowed themselves to truly dream.

"I am not sure," said Katherine as Marko held her in his arms, the sound of waves crashing against the rocks beneath the castle lulling them to sleep as the breeze carried it through the open window. "Perhaps two or three. That is it, yes! Three. A boy, a girl, then another boy."

"Are you to tell me that the subject of a certain prophecy is suddenly a disbeliever?" Marko teased, running a hand through her hair, twirling the strands between his fingers.

"How could I believe in something that would see you and I punished for how we feel?" She scoffed, her fingers idly tracing infinity symbols on his bare chest. "Besides, you were the one who wanted to play this game. Your turn. If we were able to, how many would you want?"

"Four."

"Four?" Katherine gasped, taken aback at the prince's quick response. She propped herself up beside him.

"Yes. Four."

"So am *I* to believe that you have this all planned out, then?"

"Oh, of course I do." Marko smiled. "From the first moment when I saw you in the moonlight. Sethius Kohën, Karaleia, Kalēb Sc..."

The sound of Katherine's heart pounding drowned out the rest, and Marko could feel how her entire being ached to pull itself into his. While the realisation that without the prophecy being fulfilled, neither could actually produce an heir, let alone three or four, weighed on their minds, it proved no match for the potential of a future filled with love instead of forced proximity and tainted destiny.

As Katherine relived the comfort and safety she had felt when she and Marko were together, she sensed all that she had meant to him, too. How his body seemed to scream at him that perhaps this was the one he was meant to be with, the one who would understand every part of him, the one he could not imagine anyone else taking the place of.

But for every happy memory, an unhappy one lurked in the shadows – or a wave of fragmented ones that swept them into a relentless emotional whirlwind. And, as the clouds grew ever more dense over the heads of those watching the pair's embrace, time seemed to move even slower, throwing the royals into a memory that the young prince had long since tried to put out of his mind.

After the highs of such excitement, Marko's heart suddenly shattered as if it were made of glass as a younger version of Katherine looked into his sad eyes. Things were starting to make more sense as they relived how she had ended their relationship so unexpectedly. Having experienced all that they had until this point, Marko was finally able to piece together the reasoning behind her actions all those centuries ago.

He had always wondered about Katherine's true motivation, and as the answer finally settled in, a wave of relief washed over him. It was not that she had not loved him. It was that she had been so afraid of losing everything she so desperately wanted, with no control over it, that she pushed him away at the very moment she needed him most. Before either could accept what they had felt, the scene changed, then changed again.

~

The fire in Marko's chest rose as the princess entered the room, followed closely by Lord Mikhael, who, despite wearing higher-than-normal shoes, only managed to close the gap in their height by an inch. The depth of his rage saw his eyes darken to midnight at the sight of Mikhael's smirk as the firstborn took the hand of the one the prince desired. It was Katherine's first exposure to a taste of true hatred, all at the disgust of having to put up with the wavy-haired fool's smugness.

The pair took a seat as the Consilio Statera stepped out from behind the library desk.

"We have gathered you here because prominent figures within the communities of power have raised concerns," said Horus, skipping past greetings and pleasantries. His tone was firm and his eyes hard. "Far too many for us to ignore any longer."

Mikhael's stockier frame shifted nervously in his seat beside the princess. It was a strange sensation, unlike anything Marko had experienced until now. The pleasurable feeling of Mikhael's skin on Katherine's was sickening. If he could have leapt up to throttle the little prick, he would have – not caring which of the two bodies he inhabited would get the job done better. But the prince remained trapped within the confines of the vessels that lived on in this memory.

"It has come to our attention that while the two of you are no longer together, it is Princess Katherine's choice of current companion that concerns you as well, Prince Markovyas?"

Marko scoffed and folded his arms, leaning back in his seat, his anger only growing at the council's interference.

"Alright. Then are we to assume that there is no longer an issue to be addressed?"

The prince remained silent, holding his tongue.

"Your Highness," said Horus, turning to face Katherine, unimpressed with the royals' behaviour. "Pardon my directness. But is this romance between you and Lord Mikhael serious?"

Sensing that there was no way out but through, Katherine rolled her eyes and opened her mouth to reply. "We have held hands but *once* before today," she said, voice shaking from upset. "Why are you so insistent on getting involved? Especially in something that has existed for no longer than the passing of a comet. Should we not be allowed to make our own mistakes?"

"Of course, Princess," came Herlock's voice from next to the stargazer. "We merely wish to provide guidance. Please do not take it as an offence."

"Of course not," she replied coldly. "However?"

"However, we cannot simply sit by and allow it," muttered Dolos, his nose scrunching up as he stared down at the nervous product of power.

"Excuse me?" Katherine exclaimed, her brow furrowing.

"Please, Your Highness," said Herlock quickly, rushing to quell the princess's temper as her hands clenched into fists. "You are aware of the p—"

"Are you honestly telling me that you are concerned with the prophecy? Now? After Markovyas and I—"

"*Prince* Markovyas," interrupted Dolos, his voice raised, "is a son of

Magic. At least he is one of the five. He is well aware, as are you, that you are to be betrothed to a pure descendant of power, not a product of its consequence, nor their descendants."

"How dare you—"

"How dare *I*, Your Highness?"

"Dolos! Enough!" Horus implored as Katherine's eyes flared scarlet.

"Horus," she hissed through gritted teeth, her voice trembling with restrained fury. "Herlock, I suggest that you remind your fellow council member of his place."

Seething at the princess's insolence, Dolos narrowed his eyes and yanked his arm free from Horus's grip before stepping forward. "Best you learn yours, *Princess.*"

"I—"

"Now, now, Princess Katherine," spluttered Herlock, stepping between where she had leapt to her feet and started towards Dolos, who stood, daring the princess to succumb to her anger. "Give us a moment. *Please.*" He turned to the others. "Dolos, Horus, join me."

The council left Katherine to stew in her anger as they conversed softly in the corner for what seemed like far too long before returning to address the room.

"May I ask a question, Your Highness?" asked Herlock, locking his gaze on the prince, who had remained seated, watching the show with a near-sinister smile on his face.

Marko nodded, not wanting to allow his thoughts to escape his lips.

"Could you see yourself and Princess Katherine married?"

Katherine snapped her head around to look at Marko as he answered with nearly no hesitation at all, leaning forward and staring Herlock in the eyes. The council had taken her completely by surprise. A nervous shake passed through her hands as that single second seemed to drag on in her mind.

"If I could, I would marry her today."

The instant the words left him, Katherine's mouth fell open. That was the last answer she would have expected to come from his lips after everything that had happened between them. The sincerity in the prince's voice caused her rage to melt away, folding in on itself.

"And you, Princess?" asked Herlock, turning towards Katherine, serious yet suddenly smiling as if he was daring her to say no. "If we were to appeal to the Nine Strands to allow you to marry, if we could find a way, would you risk it knowing that there is a chance that you would be ripped from each other should the prophecy come to pass? Would you be prepared to risk heartbreak in order to be together without any knowledge or certainty of what the future might bring? Spend your days together without the promise of a child? Would you be able to, if and when the time comes, not stand in the Fate's way if it means that, until then, you were able to be together?"

Forgoing all common sense, forgetting that Mikhael sat behind her, and ignoring every lesson Alfred had instilled in her upbringing, she whispered, "If I could, I would marry him, too."

The hope within Marko was restored, all anger vanishing without a trace.

Mikhael got to his feet and muttered a half-hearted goodbye from over Katherine's shoulder that fell on deaf ears, the colour draining from his olive skin, knowing that he no longer stood a chance – that he had never truly had a chance.

Before the council uttered another word, the prince got to his feet and marched across the room. He placed his hands on the sides of Katherine's face and kissed her with a passion that could have sparked the creation of a thousand new worlds.

A raindrop landed on Emily's cheek, breaking her concentration as she, like the others, continued to watch Katherine and Marko's embrace, which had seemed to stop them in time. Looking up at what only moments ago had been a mostly clear sky, Emily grew cold as more droplets pattered against the ground.

The sky darkened as the last gaps in the clouds closed and Alek, who had taken to sitting on a stool near the dining room doors, got to his feet. Concern spread across his face as he looked between Katherine and the impending storm.

"You worry too much, brother!" called Deacon loudly, shaking his head at Alek's obvious mistrust of the thunderous roar echoing in the distance. "Always the worst-case scenario, isn't it?"

"Enough," came Kaëden's voice, stopping Alek's retaliation. "This is no time for your bickering."

Reluctantly, Deacon wiped the smirk off of his face and turned his attention back to the centre of the courtyard. Not even he dared fight against his eldest brother.

~

The spiral stairway that led to the top of the Stargazer's Tower was lined with an assortment of white candles that hovered close to the floor. With every step Marko took, Katherine felt his heartbeat quicken, his nerves tightening.

As the prince approached the topmost stair, the sight of Katherine staring out of one of the arched windows that lined the room stole the air from his lungs. Moonlight glistened on her porcelain skin and the silver of her dress seemed to fade into its light.

Sensing his presence, she turned, the candlelight catching in her eyes like captured stardust as her lips curved into a smile, slow and utterly disarming. Had he been none the wiser, Marko might have believed the white lily woven into her blonde locks was a crown of the divine and that she had been sent to him by those beyond the heavens. A light in the dead of a darkness that had long plagued the prince's land.

His hands were clammy as he reached to kiss Katherine's cheek. For a moment, there was a distortion of the scene before it was restored – the prince on one knee, pulling a glass box from his overcoat. She was barely able to lip-read how he was unable to imagine his existence without her and how he longed to be at her side forever. Marko's proposal of marriage was barely audible, yet at the same time clear as day.

Katherine wondered whether the faults in the recollection were due to yet another mention of someone or something she was not allowed to remember just yet, but she had no time to dwell on the thought before all traces of the anomaly vanished.

She stared down at Marko's trembling hands. Set in a delicate band of white gold, the ring held a striking rectangular sapphire, its depths shifting like the endless currents of the sea. On either side, two perfectly cut diamonds gleamed like reflections upon still water, their clarity enhancing the sapphire's ever-changing hues. A piece not merely crafted, but meant, as if shaped by Time himself, for Katherine. Handcrafted in the fires of one of Neighlore's most deadly volcanoes and sealed in the abyss of its treacherous waters.

The prince beamed as he slipped the ring onto Katherine's finger. Tears welled in her eyes as she trembled, tracing its delicate setting. A breath hitched in her throat, a soft, disbelieving smile breaking across her lips. Every detail was perfect, a showcase of how Marko always seemed to know exactly what she needed before she ever spoke a word. Always seeking to be the one to fulfil her every desire. But while the prince was overcome with Katherine's elation, the experience left him with a sinking sensation in his stomach, as he knew which memories were still to come.

∾

"It's only getting worse!" shouted Aiden, as the rain pellets stung his skin with their power.

"Here!" yelled Alek, sending a burst of vivid green light from his hands to shield them overhead. It turned into a haze that diminished the rain's intensity as it fell down upon those in the courtyard, the light flickering with the wrath of a thunderstorm as it absorbed the power passing through it.

"Hold on, Your Highness!" yelled Alfred, his suit drenched from the downpour that had come on just as quickly as the clouds had darkened the skies. Running to stand beneath the barrier's centre, the handler held his hands upwards, fuelling its energy.

Suddenly relieved by the capabilities of the world of power, Emily longed for the warmth of her suite, and for dry clothing. But as the storm showed no signs of slowing, she and the other mortals huddled under the protection of their hosts' enchantments, waiting for it all to be over.

~

Katherine absorbed Marko's longing for his handler to stay silent, just as he desperately wished for the whispers to be false. As the prince braced himself for whatever was to come, a deep sadness took hold of her, unmistakable and raw.

"My men say that Prince Cartesius has been asking a few too many questions concerning the prophecy of late, Prince Markovyas," said Lucien, running his fingers nervously through his dark, uncharacteristically unkempt locks.

Marko spun around on the spot, stomach lurching. "What? What kind of questions?" he asked, the fireplace crackling behind him.

The heat from the flames was a relief to Katherine as a chill moved through the prince's body at Lucien's words.

"I have been unable to find a witness who is prepared to come forward. However, there have been more than a handful of whispers about a wizard in his kingdom who has been looking for a means to bring about the death of a pure descendant."

"Nonsense, no weapon can kill us. One would have been found by now if it were—"

"Actually, Your Highness," interrupted Alfred from the corner where he had remained silent until now. "I am afraid to say that there is, in fact, a way."

"How?"

"It is an ancient legend, as old as the prophecy itself. I cannot say with absolute certainty, nor would I dare to speak the words aloud, but there *is* a way."

Whether the prince believed in the prophecy made no difference here. Any rumour of such a means to bring about their destruction, even the faintest of whispers, was enough to provoke swift action from the royal, his deepest fears taking him captive and sending him on a path he had never wanted to venture down.

"Alfred, summon the council. Now. They need to be made aware of this."

Somewhere in Katherine's mind, this was familiar. As with a handful of previous memories, she had not been there at that moment, but she was able to sense the presence of the body of her younger self nearby.

"If these rumours prove true, how close would he be to getting what he needs, Lucien?" asked Marko, standing before the fireplace, the heat of the flames snapping at his heels as Alfred left the room to get a message to Herlock as discreetly as he could.

"We do not know, but such rumours are not born from nothing. However, given your brother's penchant for vengeance and chaos, it would most likely be only a matter of time before he pieces it together."

Lucien handed his prince a brandy, and Marko accepted it as though it were a lifeline.

"These stories. *This* legend…from what I have heard in the echoes of the susurrations of ghosts long since doomed to the darkness, such matters have not been spoken of in many an age. Something is happening, Your Highness. Darkness has begun to creep through the Valley of Aldone."

The prince ran his fingers through the waves of his hair and loosened the silk ties at his throat. Katherine felt his frustration. His disbelief. His anger. His worry. "Cartesius's involvement alone proves that nothing good lies on the horizon. Weapon? Spell? It matters not! She will only be the first one he comes for."

"I agree, sir. Cartesius knows that should the prophecy be triggered, he has a near-nil chance of being victorious—"

"And we all know what my brother will do for power."

"And, your bond to the princess aside, sir, should it be fulfilled, Katherine—"

"Would use whatever it is to go after him instead." Marko sighed, his face haunted by threats from both sides.

"Indeed."

"What would you have me do, Lucien? What would *you* do?"

"May I speak plainly, sir?"

"Always."

"Trigger the prophecy yourself."

Taken aback, Marko turned to face his handler. "What?" he whispered, the colour fading from his cheeks, hoping he had misheard.

"Well," said Lucien, setting down his glass. "Should it be triggered, you would have the most advantage. She loves you. There is no possible way that even Fate could deny that. Which, with your wedding day upon us, could be the very fuel behind Cartesius's quest."

"But this weapon, this spell—"

"What you need is time. We do not know what it is he seeks, but with enough time, there would be a chance of finding out. A chance of keeping her safe." The handler sighed. "It speaks of the princess having to die as a human, correct?"

"This would see me banish her to life without love. Without me. There is no guarantee that—"

"Please, Your Highness, we may have very little time."

Reluctantly, Marko answered, "From what I can recall, yes. She would need to die as a mortal in order to be reborn. But..." He scoffed, pressing his fingers to his temples. "The last time I heard the prophecy was when I was a child. I am sure I recall about as much as you do, seeing as you were the one who told it to me. After it has been retold and filtered down through the ages, there is no way to say which variation of the story is true. Not without asking *them*."

"My suggestion, sir, is to speak to the council. Voice your thoughts. They will be on their way as soon as they receive your summons. They may just agree to this, just as they agreed to allow you to wed. Send the princess into safety. Make it impossible for Prince Cartesius to find her. Find whatever it is that he can use against one of you, and destroy it. Then, when the time comes, fight for your rightful place at the princess's side."

Marko contemplated Lucien's words, and a hollow dread settled in his core as he realised that his handler's plan may be the only way to protect both his love and his chance at ultimate power.

"Protect her from Cartesius and trigger the prophecy once we are certain the danger has passed?" said Marko, more to himself than anyone else, his words barely more than a breath.

"Yes. This way all but ensures that Cartesius will be powerless against the two of you once it comes to fruition," said Lucien with a sly smile.

"You have given this much thought—"

A rap on the door interrupted them before Alfred entered with the council in tow.

"Ah, Prince Markovyas!" greeted Horus, looking quite concerned. "We came as soon as we heard."

Dolos raised his eyebrows. "Alfred has enlightened us to the news. How can we be of service, Your Highness?" he questioned, drawing out the words with a slow, languid ease. Almost as if indulging in a tiresome formality.

"I have come to a decision," said Marko, his glass refilling itself. "As it is my responsibility to keep Katherine safe as her future husband, prophecy or not, I cannot allow Cartesius to succeed in his endeavours. I need you to send her away. Do what only you have the power to do."

"But, Your Highness, Prince Cartesius will be able to sense her power," said Horus. "Sending her away will not be of any help."

"You know full well what I am asking."

"You mean...make her *mortal*?" asked Herlock, adjusting his glasses, eyes narrowing as they looked Marko up and down. "Set into motion the course of events that will lead to the fulfilment of the prophecy?"

"My brother has found a way to kill a pure descendant of power. Or is close to finding a way. He is gaining too much strength too quickly for me to thwart him without an advantage, and Katherine's loathing of him will all but drive her headfirst into ruin. The only way we can stop him is to cut him off at the knees."

"Are you sure about this, sir?" asked Alfred, clearly uneasy at what the young prince was suggesting.

"I can spare a few years without her to ensure that I can spend the rest of eternity at her side."

The council exchanged dark looks. There was a loud pounding in Katherine's ears. Whatever Marko had felt at this moment was taken over by her realisation that he was the one who had started all of this. And now that some of her past was becoming known to her once more, the white-hot knife of betrayal burnt brightly in her very core.

"Once done, it cannot be undone," advised Dolos. "Perhaps you should discuss this with the princess? Or your brothers? This is not how the prophecy is meant to be—"

"No!" exclaimed Marko. "She would never agree, and the fewer people who know about this, the better. The only way to defeat Cartesius is to take away whatever he may have in his sights and overpower him. *This* is the only way. Only Fate can confirm how things are meant to be set into motion, and unless you can tell me what that is, this is the way it will be."

The prince's eyes flared, daring them to try and overrule him.

"She may never forgive you," muttered Alfred.

"She need never know. And *you* never need tell her," the prince snarled, his fists clenching at his sides as flames erupted around them, crackling and sparking like embers on the verge of a blaze.

"Your Highness, I—"

"Very well, Your Highness. If this is your decision, so be it," said Herlock reluctantly, interrupting Alfred's protest. "We are here to serve the will of Fate and the Nine Strands."

"Alright then," said Marko, the warmth in his eyes fading as the fire within them died out, darkening to mere shadows of themselves. "Today!"

Katherine, shaken at the revelation of the prince's betrayal, longed for the task to end so she would not have to witness what was inevitably to come. Marko, in his mind, desperately longed for the same. But no such end came. At least, not before they faced the last of their recollections.

Marko sensed a subtle shift in Katherine as her handmaidens laced up her dress, pulling it tight enough to accentuate her figure without restricting her breath. A thrill of anticipation stirred within her as they placed a diamond and sapphire tiara on her head. As she stared at her reflection, a quiet certainty settled in – she knew this would be forever.

~

The dark steel of the chairs grated loudly against the floor as the storm continued to torment those within the castle's grounds. The umbrellas shook in the wind, threatening to uproot themselves from the stone that held them in its clutches. The rain had escalated to the point where those in the courtyard were barely able to see three feet in front of them, even with the protective shield that remained lit overhead.

"This is too much," yelled Alek over the sound of the rumbling black skies and snaps of lightning.

"It'll rain us out if we aren't careful!" shouted Deacon.

"Take care of the furniture. I'll get us some more cover. Kaëden, help me!"

Kaëden reluctantly took his hands out of his wet pockets, straightening himself from where he had remained against the wall, watching, without much concern for the downpour.

He joined his brother and together they fired balls of light into the sky.

Whether it was because of the enchantments placed on the castle that Alfred had warned them about, or whether it was because the prophecy would not allow them to interfere with the trials, neither Alek nor Kaëden was able to quell the storm entirely, merely slow it down some.

Meanwhile, Deacon was shooting sparks towards the movable objects that were being whisked away in the chaos.

Between the three princes, their handlers and Alfred, who ensured that the mortals were sheltered from the worst of it, the immortals were able to contain the majority of the damage resulting from the kiss. Even if only just.

The council, however, appeared unperturbed by the weather, their focus solely on the two royals standing at the centre of the symbol, drenched and unaware.

~

Katherine tried to mute her own feelings as they slipped into the next memory, eager to reach the end of the story.

Regret washed over Marko as his toes touched the stone where the icy whirlwind had teleported them, the sleeping princess cradled in his arms. As the prince moved towards the waiting council, the fire on the ground before them reflected on the crystals that protruded from the cave walls to create a spectacular show of colourful dancing light. Katherine could do nothing but watch as her immobile vessel became a mere pawn in the prince's chess game.

"Please, Prince Markovyas, enter the Waters of Herion," instructed Herlock, gesturing towards the shallows where the turquoise surface shimmered as the royal approached.

Marko stepped into the pool, the warmth of the water immediately creating steam around them.

"What do I do?" asked the prince, eyes transfixed on the rippling depths that now covered him to his waist.

"Place your hand on her chest, over her heart. You will need to pierce her flesh until she bleeds."

"I..."

Katherine could feel the hesitation spread through Marko's body as his bones cried out for him to find another way out of this.

"Once we lay down the orb and begin the ritual, there will be no stopping what is to come. As the waters around you move, be sure not to remove your hand until they turn calm."

"What happens then?"

"Then, her power will be contained, her body bound to the Waters of Herion, and she will be reborn into a new life until the prophecy is triggered by her mortal death."

"And what if we are unable to put an end to Cartesius's plan? What if we are not able to locate the weapon before that mortal life ends?" asked Marko, voice shaking as he admired Katherine's beauty, determined to remember this moment and his motivation to make this all worth it.

"She will be reborn again, repeating the cycle until she dies in the way the prophecy intends."

"And nobody will know where or when she will—"

"No, Your Highness. She will be as lost to others as she will be to you."

Katherine could hardly believe it but, as Marko appreciated what he knew would be their last moments together for a stretch of time he dared not attempt to predict, she almost felt sorry for him. His lips quivered as they brushed against her skin, pressing a kiss to her forehead before he placed a trembling hand over her heart.

Herlock removed an orb from his cloak and placed it on the floor before them. As the council circled it, they chanted, and a bright light emerged from their hands and drifted towards the hypnotic sphere. It absorbed it and then, as if pausing to decide its next move, the light flickered before shooting outward straight for the princess. The moment it touched the waters, the pool came alive, bubbling fiercely around the royals.

Meeting Herlock's gaze, the prince hesitantly pressed his fingers into Katherine's chest.

"Forgive me, my love," Marko whispered.

As Katherine felt his touch pierce her flesh and break through her bones, the life force that spilt over into the water around them coalesced into a cloud, rising to form a shield of turquoise and crimson until it hid the pair from view.

Suddenly, the veil crashed back down, leaving Marko standing alone as the light flickered out and the Waters of Herion drained into nothingness, leaving behind only dry stone.

"It is done," said Horus softly, his voice wavering, the sound raw as if torn from him unwillingly.

Pausing to give the now-dead source of power one last look, the council turned their backs on the prince and, in a whirlwind of fire, they were gone.

"Should we leave, Your Highness?" asked Alfred, looking defeated, from where he and Lucien stood waiting.

"'Tis for the best, Alfred. You know it is."

"Of course it is, sir."

Their time together faded as the storm around the royals intensified, rising into an unrelenting force.

Through the sheet of rain before her, past the fires of power, Emily could only just make out as Katherine and Marko were pulled apart and, as if repelling each other, flew out to slam into the flaming barrier that contained them.

Unable to get to her feet, Katherine surrendered to the ease of the stone, clutching her chest as she struggled to breathe, her eyes barely able to keep themselves open. Marko, soaked to the bone, tried to crawl towards her, his limbs trembling with exhaustion. But before he could reach her, his strength gave out, and a dark blue light erupted from the spot where he and Katherine had stood.

It spread outward, dancing along the lines of the carving as it moved towards the circle that marked Marko's place in the trials. The radiant force flared as it focused all of its energy on the placeholder below, transforming it into an ancient symbol for water. Satisfied, the light launched itself outwards to meet the fire, turning the flames blue before they shot into the sky, ending the storm without another raindrop touching the ground. The clouds folded into themselves before vanishing completely.

All that remained were the same ankle-height flames that had called to the champions before the task. The flames that so desperately longed to be fed.

Cries of worry met their ears as Katherine and Marko fought to recover from the lingering ache inside and push themselves to their feet. Alek and Alfred dried off the mortals using a quick wave of the hand and stood waiting, visibly concerned, for the princess to join them.

Emily wanted to run to her friend, as did Alek, but neither dared ignore the council's warning. Katherine knew that many of the onlookers wanted to intervene, but they could not. Not until the royals stepped beyond the symbol that held the others so perfectly at bay.

"What should we do?" said Zachary to Alek and Alfred, failing at keeping his voice low enough for only them to hear.

Alek held out his hand out to deter others from making any sudden moves. "Just wait, Zach. It should be over soon."

"I think the kids are a bit freaked," said Deacon, glancing around at the mortals, many of whom appeared to be rooted in place.

"Quiet!" snapped Alek as he followed Deacon's eyes. "You're going to make it worse."

Before they, or anyone else, could make a sound, Herlock cleared his throat. He and the other council members approached the royals from where they had been watching, conveniently shielded from the storm from the moment it had begun.

"You may exit once you are ready, Your Highnesses," advised Herlock, examining the pair in the hope of gaining an idea of what had happened in their minds.

"Are you alright?" came Marko's voice from behind Katherine.

As she turned to the prince, she was unable to hide her pain. Her eyes were wide, fast filling with tears. Her expression alone was enough to silence Marko immediately. Not wanting to allow the others to see her physical weaknesses, let alone what hid beneath the surface, she held on as best she could, straight-faced, trembling lips, but as composed as possible.

Katherine sensed every eye in the courtyard on her – waiting. Looking past the prince in the direction of the council, she inclined her head in greeting before turning on her heel to leave the power of the symbol. She left a trail of water as she walked, still soaked from head to toe, but steaming on the inside.

Alfred and Alek exchanged sideways looks as Katherine marched past them on her way into the castle. But neither commented. She caught the tension in Alek's stance as he shot Marko an angry look before following her inside, while Alfred motioned for the others to stay back.

∾

Alek entered the living room, the doors shutting themselves instinctively behind him. The heat of the fire offered little comfort as Katherine stood, her eyes fixed on the sheet that concealed the painting above the room's main fireplace. There were many paintings she had seen during her limited exploration of the castle that had been hidden away behind similar white fabric. No matter how hard she, or the others, had tried, they refused to reveal themselves.

Alek moved to stand beside her. He folded his arms across his chest and followed her gaze. "You okay?"

"You know," Katherine said, her lips pressing together briefly before she spoke, her tone steadier than it had any right to be. "I would never have guessed what lay on the other side of that sheet. And now that I know, I still can't make any sense of it. Alfred conveniently left all of this out of his files."

"Listen, I'm not too sure what's going on in that head of yours, but I can't imagine it's anything good based on what happened out there. Here, let me dry you off!"

With a wave of his hand, the prince sent an orange glow towards her – heating her from the outside in, her clothes and hair dry in an instant.

"No. It is not," she said after a momentary silence, shaking her head and mirroring Alek as he crossed his arms again. "And *thank you.*"

"So, does this mean you remember me too now?" said the prince half-jokingly, nudging Katherine's shoulder with his arm. "Because I'm pretty sure I'm in more than just a few of those memories."

"Apparently, it is not that simple. It was like I could see every memory that Marko—" She took a sharp breath. "*Markovyas* and I had shared together. I could feel what he felt as well as what I did. I could even see things that happened when I was near him, but for whatever reason had been unable to use my power to know it at the time—"

"But?"

"But there is still a disconnect."

Alek furrowed his brow. "What do you mean?"

"I...I can't explain it. I can't tell if I'm dissociating because of how difficult that just was, or if I'm not able to fully embrace it because so many of the recollections appear half of what they should be."

There was a long silence before she turned to face the prince.

"Like you said, you should be in more than a few of them, and yet, *nothing*. It is as though some memories are distorted versions of themselves. Incomplete."

Katherine met Alek's gaze, her eyes brimming with unshed tears, but beneath them lay a resilience he had always admired.

"Well, you certainly sound a lot more like yourself. The accent's back at least." Alek sighed. "What would you like to do about these then?" he said, nodding his head towards the painting, his eyes not leaving hers.

"Something tells me I'm the kind of person who would rather leave the wound open and ignore it than be unaware of its existence in the first place."

"Well, if we're being honest here," Alek replied with a smirk, "you *do* have this tendency to burn things to the ground. Only happens after you're pushed to your breaking point, though. Normally you're the master of compartmentalising."

"Oh really?" Katherine said, almost smiling now. "Well then, maybe I know myself a little better than I thought."

She reached for the painting and grasped the fabric in her outstretched hand. In one swift motion, she pulled the drape to the floor, dust particles whooshing into the air. She turned, marching towards the foyer as the sound of hundreds of drapes hitting the ground echoed throughout the castle.

Katherine crossed through the arched double doors, only to stop mid-step.

"Leave them up. Something tells me that when I *do* remember everything, I'm going to need a reminder of just how much this all hurts," she instructed, leaving Alek staring up at the painting that had been commissioned of her and Marko at their engagement in 1515.

CHAPTER 11
THE MEMORIES BEGIN
TO RETURN

E mily and the others waited nervously for Alfred to signal that it was safe to enter the dining room for dinner. Not that any of them were hungry. Her mind was racing, but she dared not say anything until she could figure out how everyone else was feeling about what had happened.

It was but a minute after Alek had gone after Katherine that Marko disappeared down the steps into the grounds. The council had soon after greeted the princes before taking their leave, too, using the route that led around the front of the castle to not interrupt Katherine and Alek. While there were a few whispers here and there, it seemed that even the two remaining princes were holding their tongues.

Once given the go-ahead, the group made their way inside and settled in, most eyes on Alek, who sat in his usual seat as if nothing had happened. Katherine's presence did not go unnoticed.

"Please, enjoy, everyone," said Alfred, convincing the fireplaces to add more flames as the castle keepers entered with trays of aromatic family-style dishes that made Jamie's and Brian's stomachs suddenly growl.

As if triggered by the scents of home filling the room, they dived into their meal, nobody really knowing what to say or even if they should say anything at all. With none of the mortals brave enough to press for answers on where Marko had run off to, or why Katherine made no appearance at dinner, they were unable to ease their minds. And, as the evening drew on, and the princes left to attend to kingdom business with their handlers, Bayne excused himself, most likely to seek solace in the gymnasium, leaving his fellow mortals to face the last remnants of dessert on their own alongside a visibly disgruntled Jennifer.

～

Katherine had made her way to her suite on the third floor. Now that a portion of her life had returned to her, she was able to more easily navigate the castle without running into anyone. After she closed and bolted the door behind her, she leant her back against the solid wood and shut her eyes. From beneath her eyelashes, beads of tears fell softly onto her cheeks as she struggled to contain all that she felt inside.

There was still a distortion to her newly acquired memories, that she was sure had to do with her having to wait to kiss the other champions, but things were slowly moving into place. She took a few minutes to compose herself, breathing deeply as she willed her body to remain as numb to her emotions and recollections as possible.

Katherine opened her eyes after a few breaths and crossed the sitting area to close the windows that were allowing a chill to wisp its way into the suite. It was clear that the castle keepers had recently been in the room to neaten things up.

Kneeling on the soft carpet in the bedroom that remained warm from the fire, she stared hollowly at the flames. The dancing images drew her in, trapping her in a world of what once was until she fell asleep, burning as she drifted into the depths of her mind.

~

"I have a feeling that a whole lot of change just hit us," came Jamie's voice as the fires in the dining room dimmed, encouraging them to turn in for the evening.

"Didn't have the guts to bring it up with them around, hey?" joked Matthew with a grin.

"I just think that we don't really know who we can trust yet, so best to keep things tight. We might be going along with all of this, but we still gotta keep our guard up."

There was a murmur of agreement around the table as the mortals enjoyed some mulled wine.

"Why don't we find out then?" piped up Aiden with a hiccough as the drink turned his usually pasty cheeks quite red.

"What do you mean?" asked Emily, curious and quite brave from drink herself.

"Well," said Aiden, the smell of fragrant spices wafting out of his mouth as he spoke. "Didn't Zach and Alfred mention that there's a library in this place?"

Layla exchanged an excited look with Brian and Emily. "We haven't been in there yet. Where is it again?"

"I kind of remember one of the castle keepers pointing it out. Follow me!"

Layla and the others got to their feet without hesitation, ready to follow Aiden bravely through the dark corridors of the sleeping castle.

"I think I'll go to bed instead," said Jennifer as they walked through the living room.

"Why? What's up, Jen?" asked Layla. The rest of them turned to hear the answer.

Jennifer's eyes avoided meeting anyone else's. "I just need to be alone for a while, okay?"

Emily pulled her into a consoling hug. "Sure thing. You do what you need to do."

As the rest of them bid Jennifer a good night and watched her head up the staircase in the foyer, they heard the sound of the castle keepers scurrying to clean the rooms they had just left.

"Come on," instructed Matthew, motioning for the group to keep moving. "Let's get going."

Wasting no time, they followed Aiden's gangly frame in search of the library that they hoped housed the answers each of them so desperately, however secretively, sought.

Not wanting to sleep in the suite on the royal floor and risk running into Katherine, Jennifer chose to head to the room she and Bayne had stayed in when they first arrived, just as she had the night before, after leaving him. As she took the corridor off to the left of the staircase, she nearly bumped full-bodied into Alek.

"Oh!" she exclaimed, startled, having been lost in thought. "I'm so sorry!"

"No, don't be," replied the prince, having only just missed her. "Everything alright? You're going the wrong way, aren't you?"

"I…" she began, not knowing how to interact with him without anyone else around. "I just can't s…sleep upstairs r…right now."

"Ah!" he said, holding his hands behind his back, looking at her with understanding. "I take it you're nervous about Bayne's turn?"

"How did you…?"

Alek smiled as he whispered rather loudly and theatrically, "Just because we don't say anything, doesn't mean we don't know everything about all of you."

A faint grin flickered on Jennifer's face as the prince managed to take some of the tension out of the air.

"Listen, this is difficult for everyone. But trust me, if something is meant to be between two people, then it will be."

Alek reached out and squeezed Jennifer's shoulder before bidding her goodnight and heading off in search of Marko, allowing her to make her way to the room in peace.

"Push, don't pull it, you moron!" snapped Matthew as Jamie continued to yank on the door handle. The gargoyle laughed at the foolish attempt to gain entry, rustling its wings against the grain.

Shaking his head, Matthew leant up against the wood and, without a struggle, the door opened inwards, revealing quite the sight within.

An instant rumbling of 'oohs' and 'ahs' echoed far into the depths of the library as they entered.

The floor had the same gold and black crackle detailing that matched the rest of the West Wing, but, for some reason, it was as though they had entered a different world entirely.

"Wow!" exclaimed Aiden, looking around the room, stunned.

"Didn't Alfred say this was just a smaller version of the one in the East Wing?" muttered Layla, her eyes widening at the sight of the starry ceiling above that mimicked the constellations.

The tall white marble columns were adorned with golden accents, as were the arched windows on the opposite side, which overlooked the gardens separating the two wings. Although only three stories instead of five, as its sister room had, the home to the West Wing's collection of knowledge was still an impressive display of architecture and design. Dimly yet adequately lit by the tiny orange fires hovering above each sconce that extended out of the columns, the room had an air of mystery and magic that called out to them.

"Alright!" said Jamie, clapping his hands together after he set his drink down on one of the nearest tables. "Everyone, pick a floor, pick a row, and let's see if we can find a bit of history on this place."

Whether stumbling or fumbling, each of the mortals found their way into the wonders of the library. Searching through its many sections, they gathered anything that looked remotely useful. Once there was a large enough pile on the table, they each took a book and skimmed through, looking for relevant information to relay to the rest of the group.

It did not take long for Emily and the others to get lost in the world of magical wars, politics, and stories. Their drinks refilled automatically as the night went on, thanks to Aiden, who had convinced a castle keeper to cast the spell, and they stayed up well into the morning, diving into Katherine's world until they fell asleep beneath the light of the stars.

CHAPTER 12
PRINCE DÀIKONOS
OF AZRALLUS

Wings brushed the air outside the window, the sound barely audible. But Katherine lay still, eyes closed, holding onto the silence a little longer. She had been lying there for hours, her mind racing just as it had the night before. Although she had slept, she had not rested. Dreading what awaited her with Deacon in the next part of the trial, she curled up into a ball under her soft blankets and granted herself some more time before getting ready.

What am I supposed to say to them? she thought, imagining having to face Marko and the others, knowing there was still so much more to learn about her own life – things that only they knew and that she could only dream of. *How am I supposed to go back to running my kingdom without being whole?*

She tossed and turned as the questions in her mind plagued her. They followed her into a warm shower, then into a fresh set of warm clothes. But a lingering pain in her chest saw Katherine spend the day away from her guests, in quiet recovery before facing them again.

~

Breakfast had come and gone before Layla woke up with a piece of paper stuck to the side of her face. As she peeled it off and looked around the library, a dull pounding took hold of her head, confirming that she had indulged a little too much the night before.

"Em!" Layla whispered, leaning across the table to shake her sister gently on the shoulder.

Begrudgingly glancing up from where she had rested her head on her crossed arms, Emily looked nearly as rough as Layla felt.

"I take it we found the library," muttered Layla, attempting a smile.

"But what else did we find?" Jamie mumbled through a yawn, from the floor nearby as he sat up and stretched.

"Not so loud!" said Matthew from beside him, eyes tightly closed, slapping Jamie on his leg to shush him.

"Aspirin. Now!" muttered Emily.

Rummaging in her bag, Layla pulled out a small bottle of pills that she tipped out onto the table. She quickly swallowed two before handing some over to Brian and her sister.

As they struggled to wake fully, it took a while for them to become stable enough to place their focus back on the evening's mission.

"Well." Jamie clapped his hands together, startling the others. "Seems we need to go over a few things, don't we? Someone round up some water?"

Aiden offered to head to the nearest kitchen for fresh bottles and to sweet-talk a castle keeper into repeating a certain spell. The door had barely closed behind him when Emily pointed out the first problem as she turned to their research.

"Wait!" she exclaimed, pointing to one of the open books on the middle pile. "Can anyone read that?"

Gathering to get a closer look at the text Emily was referring to, the others saw that it, along with the others, was not written in any language they recognised.

"How did we read these last night without a translator?" asked Layla, her eyes darting to each of them. "How drunk were we?"

"The way my head feels? Plenty drunk," muttered Jamie, picking the book up and squinting at the page. He let out a loud gasp, his grip faltering as he nearly dropped it. Shaking, he lowered it for everyone to see.

The instant his fingertips met the pages, the words changed. It took mere seconds before the entire text lay in his hands, written in English.

"No way!" Emily gasped, rushing to grab one of the others and watch the magic at work.

"Well then." Jamie smiled. "I guess we might not have been that drunk after all. Come on, guys, let's get cracking."

~

The morning of the trial saw Bayne arrive in the courtyard earlier than anyone else. He had woken up alone in his third-floor suite yet again and had spent the day in the gym to work off his frustration. Having successfully avoided the others since halfway through dinner after Marko's trial, not knowing they had spent almost every moment since in the library, even mealtimes, it had taken more self-encouragement than he would have thought necessary to agree to witness another kiss. But he knew that if there was any way he was going to survive this, he needed to know exactly what he was in for.

"Master Bayne!" greeted Alfred as the mortal walked through an open set of doors that led out of the dining room. "I began to grow concerned when neither you nor the others arrived for breakfast yesterday. Then, even more so when breakfast turned to lunch. The true worry set in when they managed to make their way to dinner, and then breakfast again this morning, without you. If it were not for the castle keepers running food up to your suite, we would have had no choice but to send out a search party."

"I'm alright, thank you," reassured Bayne as he took a seat at a nearby cocktail table, noting the hint of a smile on Alfred's face. There was something so comforting about his presence.

"Are you certain, sir? As your handler, I am here for whatever you need."

"I appreciate that, but I know it's only a matter of time before I'll fail out of this and watch her end up with someone better suited to her." Bayne shrugged, realising he was being a touch more honest than he would have liked. "I just need to keep Jen and me afloat until then."

Alfred's grey eyes were warm and genuine. "My dear boy! You have yet to realise just what a feat it is to have been selected for all of this."

"Exactly. There's no way this turns into anything more than a situation that will leave us all hurt. It was a fluke. A cruel distraction that—"

"And all the other times you and she were thrown together? Or the times your souls passed right by each other in the depths of the night? Were *those* flukes as well, Master Bayne?"

"I...I think you may be misunderstanding here, Alfred—"

The handler held up his hand and smiled. "One thing you should know about my role here, sir, is that I am aware of approximately ninety per cent of what happens with regard to the princess, even if I do not say it."

He gave Bayne a quick wink before leaving him to greet Layla and Brian, who had just arrived to join his table. Not sure if it would be the best idea to dwell on Alfred's words, Bayne welcomed the pair and tried his best to look cheerful.

Emily and Aiden arrived soon after, heading for one of the other tables, followed by Matthew, Jamie, and finally, Jennifer. As Jennifer greeted Bayne with a quick kiss on the cheek, Alfred signalled for the castle keepers to serve drinks to help ease everyone's nerves. The handler soon left to welcome the council, returning with them at his heels minutes later.

While chatter bounced off of the stone walls, Alek made his way to the courtyard from the castle grounds, followed by Kaëden, who entered from the direction of the armoury, and Marko, who appeared silently at the dining room doors. The council had only just greeted the champions when Katherine arrived to join them.

An unshakable stillness settled over the group as she made her way towards the council, at last able to recall who they were and greet them accordingly. They exchanged pleasantries just beyond earshot before Katherine informed them that she was ready to proceed.

"Where is he, Rawson?" asked Dolos, eyes narrowing at the prince's blonde-haired handler, unimpressed.

"I'm here, I'm here!" came Deacon's voice in the distance.

~

Deacon's dark brown eyes seemed to lead into the wide, near-endless corridors of his soul. There was a twinkle in them that almost outshone his boyish smile. A flutter in Katherine's stomach made her want to dive deep into the layers of mystery she saw within him.

As the prince walked across the clearing in the courtyard to meet her, one hand casually in his pocket, Katherine wondered what kind of pain awaited her once they kissed. What memories would fall into place? She had been unprepared for the effects of the task with Marko, but this time she was going into it with more strength, knowing more of who she was and what she was truly capable of.

"You look worried, Princess," Deacon whispered to her from behind a grin she could hardly take her eyes off of as he stepped over the ankle-height flame, stopping just short of her.

The prince swayed back and forth on his heels, reminding Katherine of a nervous child about to do something he knew he should not. The fire around them surged, sealing them inside the symbol.

"Should I be?" Katherine replied, somewhat seriously.

"Compared to my brothers?" he said, shrugging. "This should be a walk in the park."

A soft giggle escaped Katherine's lips. Hesitant though she was, she had a feeling he was not lying. *After what happened with Marko, how could it get worse?* she thought, trying to put the anxiety out of her mind.

Katherine and Deacon faced the council, who had decided to take a seat at one of the additional cocktail table sets that Alfred had positioned around the clearing to accommodate the guests. The first task of the trial had seen him optimise the courtyard's layout so that each onlooker would have a clear view of the symbol while providing enough room for him and the others to step in should things take a turn for the worse.

"Please," said Herlock with a nod. "Proceed."

The royals turned to one another, and Deacon's smile faded as he moved toward Katherine, his breathing growing more uneven with each step.

∼

Not for the first time since arriving, a flicker of jealousy stirred within Emily. In all the chaos surrounding power, prophecies, and princes, she had mostly been able to put out of her mind the fact that she and her friend were at opposite ends of a spectrum. While make no mistake, she would hate to be the one having to go through the process of these trials, there was so much about Katherine's life that Emily had long wished for.

As she watched Katherine and Deacon about to embark on the first leg of their tasks together, Emily almost wished that it was *her* standing before the prince. *Tall, brown hair, brown eyes, slightly built...what more could you ask for?* Emily thought. While Deacon's snark irritated her at times, there was something behind that smile that tempted her.

Out of the corner of her eye, Emily saw that she was not the only one with mixed feelings about this kiss. She knew her cousin well enough to know that he was uncomfortable, even if he was hiding it particularly well today. Just past Bayne's table stood Marko. Leaning up against the doorway to the dining room, the prince held what Emily guessed was a glass of bourbon in his hand, his expression cold and vacant. Even Alek, who had moved to stand alongside his brother and Alfred, was cross-armed and stone-faced.

Deacon flashed another boyish grin before licking his lips as he took Katherine's face in his hands. Without the slightest hesitation, he moved to kiss her for the first time.

The leaves that had fallen to the floor throughout the day now rustled as they tumbled towards the clearing. As the onlookers watched the royals' embrace, their curiosity was evident as to how intense its effects would be – whether they could take shelter quickly if needed, or whether what had happened with Marko had been the exception, not the rule.

~

Deacon smiled as Katherine sat on the wooden plank on the other side of the garden, swinging back and forth and staring up at the sky as though listening to the whispers of the universe. Katherine surrendered to his pure joy as the child version of the prince made his way towards her, passing a patch of grass that was home to tiny yellow blooms.

The ground crunched beneath her feet as Katherine stopped and watched the dark-haired royal approach.

She smiled as he held out his hand and, just as she reached out to take the yellow flower he had picked for her, Deacon's stomach flipped, and he quickly leaned forward to kiss her cheek. Her face flushed a brilliant shade of red. Giggling, the young princess laughed at the prince, who grinned before turning to run back inside.

While Katherine wanted to believe that all of their memories would be this pleasant, she refused to allow herself to be that naive.

~

More and more leaves were drawn towards the barrier flames as the wind gained force. What was at first a light breeze was turning into a sharp wisp. The other princes watched as the air circled the pair of royals, gathering debris, ready to react at a moment's notice should anything pose a threat.

Emily and the mortals huddled into their cloaks and coats, wrapped themselves in blankets that Alfred had pre-emptively set out, and covered their ears to keep the whistling of the wind from deafening them.

Katherine absorbed his sense of pride as the young prince stood before the large, closed doors. His excitement and eagerness pulsed through her, undeniable.

"Your Highness!" greeted Deacon, bowing low as the princess approached.

"Prince Dàikonos," she said with a smile, returning his gesture. "It has been too long."

"That it has," he said, turning to stand beside Katherine as she came to a halt. He offered his arm to escort her into the room.

"Are you here to flatter me, or are we to discuss the division of the western territories?"

"Even as a child, you were always so serious," muttered the prince, taking Katherine's arm in his. A simmering mix of amusement and insolence built within him that threatened to spill over as he tried to sidestep the topic.

"We *are* still children, Dàikonos."

"We are now of age," he said, his eyes finding hers. "We are finally able to pave our own paths in this existence. Finally able to create kingdoms of our own design. So, no. We are no longer children. But that does not mean we cannot enjoy this."

Katherine sighed. The boy who had once been so full of life seemed to be consumed with ambition and a relentless need to prove himself.

"Well then, let us join the others," she said, the doors swinging open before them.

A veil of obscurity fell as the pair walked through the doorway, and the memory faded into another without Katherine learning much else.

"It's getting worse!" shouted Emily as the wind that circled the barrier strengthened.

As it spun with greater speed and aggression around the trapped royals, the air whipped nearby objects into motion, building toward a growing whirlwind. The mortals gripped tightly onto the nearest piece of furniture to keep themselves steady.

They recalled the few times they had seen each other, even in passing, since they had come of age, but the experience was short-lived, as Katherine and Deacon had never really been close to begin with. As the pair relived their brief exchanges, those who watched on waited in suspense.

The whole thing was over as quickly as it had begun. The wind died down as soon as the royals broke apart. Though they staggered briefly, each stabilised with ease as a bright yellow haze rose from their feet.

It moved towards the lines of the symbol until it consolidated its energy at Deacon's marker, glowing as it morphed into a symbol for air. The light made its way to the barrier, turning the flames into a luminescent yellow that could have rivalled an endless field of sunflowers. The royals watched as the fire pulled the haze towards them, causing it to spin faster before flickering out in a sudden burst and exploding into a puff of dust that blanketed the clearing.

Emily swiped the hair from her face. As she and the others straightened their clothes and shook off the residue that had so gracefully settled on them, the flame returned to burn low in wait.

Katherine and Deacon shared a look as they paused to catch their breath.

"What did I tell ya?" muttered Deacon, rubbing his chest to ease the slight discomfort that lingered within it.

"Definitely a walk in the park." Katherine smiled, looking rather relieved. "It is good to see you again, Your Highness."

The familiar boyish grin spread across the prince's face, and he let out a soft chuckle, the light dancing in his eyes. "It's been too long, Princess Katherine."

They bowed to each other, then made their way over flames. A strange sensation found its home in Katherine's gut as her recently recalled histories continued to string themselves together.

~

Katherine noted the audible sighs of relief from the mortals, who were grateful to have escaped with so little damage, as the two royals stepped out of the symbol without a scratch.

"So," exclaimed Alek, throwing up his arms comically. "That was it?"

"Must have been, brother," said Deacon, heading to join his siblings for a drink while Katherine offered to walk the council out.

It was not long before the princess returned, having bid farewell to her guests. Taking a drink from the nearest castle keeper, she gave into the idea that perhaps participating in the evening's events might be the best move for now.

"Should we serve dinner earlier then, Your Highness?" asked Alfred from behind her.

Katherine smiled. "Yes. Thank you, Alfred. Actually, if we could do dinner out here this evening, that would be wonderful. Would you see to it that the fires are told to burn a little brighter, please?"

"Of course." Alfred gave a curt nod and left to oversee preparations.

"Oh! You're joining us then?" asked Alek in a rather snippy tone, as Katherine took her place at the head of the large wooden table.

"Do you always talk to me this way?" She sipped on her drink as her guests followed suit, most choosing to match their assigned seats at regular meals.

As a short-haired, petite castle keeper bustled out from the dining room, whispering to the fires around them to add more heat, Alek

laughed.

"You just wait!" warned the prince, a large grin spreading across his face. "You're going to remember me soon enough."

There was something about Alek's words that sent Katherine into a silent fit of giggles. From everything she had found out about him so far, she could see why the pair had been said to be the best of friends. The prince spoke to her without fear or hesitation, as a true equal. It made her feel at ease. *Safe.*

"Ah, Princess!" called Alfred, appearing alongside her as if out of thin air moments later.

"Yes, Alfred?" she prompted, as the other diners conversed among themselves.

"I have arranged for the chefs to serve tonight's meal outdoors as requested. They should begin preparations momentarily. I have also seen to it that two of the castle keepers bring out a few charcuterie boards in the meantime."

"Thank you, Alfred."

With a wink, the handler was gone.

Katherine felt a wave of relief at how much easier today had been. She looked out at the table of those she had come to know over the past days, remaining relatively discreet as her eyes lingered on each of the champions. With each memory she regained, she grew more and more curious as to how the rest of them fit into everything, particularly the human who seemed to be incredibly uncomfortable around her, yet at the same time, so at ease.

As she watched Bayne and Jennifer strike up a conversation with Aiden and Brian, Katherine wondered why on earth Fate would want a mortal involved in all of this mess. *What's the end goal here?* she thought. Taking a sip of her drink, she turned her attention to the others.

For the rest of the evening, it appeared as though each of them had chosen to put their questions on hold and enjoy the calmness of the night. They made light chitchat and spoke nothing of the possible perils that lay ahead. Kaëden was mostly silent as usual, Deacon remained as sarcastic and opinionated as always, and Jamie was growing ever more confident in the royals' presence.

As they feasted on an array of meats and cheeses, followed by cold salads, steaming pasta, and freshly baked goods, Katherine caught sight of Alfred in the corner with the other handlers. He was watching them, a smile crossing his face as he took in the rarity of such a moment.

~

"Um, Katherine?" came Emily's voice from over her shoulder as the princess selected a new drink from one of the more nervous castle keepers at the bar.

Turning around, Katherine found it somewhat difficult to reconcile the memories of who she once was with the hint of humanity that she felt at the mortal's words. The fragments of her human life and her time apart from the princes had slowly been coming into focus since the first task, yet they remained frustratingly elusive.

Katherine noticed Emily falter briefly before pushing forward. "Could we talk for a moment?"

"Sure," said Katherine, leading the mortal closer to the nearest fire.

"So, the next kiss..."

The look of worry on Emily's face made Katherine even more curious than she already was. "What is it?"

"You're going to be kissing Bayne. It's...it's just that you two have, um, *history.*"

Katherine's eyes narrowed. "I figured as much."

"Well, I just want you to be prepared. That's all."

"I'm sure that I will be alright in the face of a few mortal memories. Compared to the past few days, how bad can it be?"

Before Emily was able to open her mouth to respond, they heard Alek's booming voice from close by.

"Katherine! Emily! Here you two are."

Emily's sigh was soft but telling, and Katherine guessed that Alek must have heard enough to decide he needed to step in.

"Emily, your friends are looking for you. If you'll excuse us?"

Without waiting for permission or acknowledgement, the prince gently took Katherine by the arm and smoothly steered her away from the topic of her next task. Katherine noted the way Emily hesitated before seeming to take it as a sign to let the matter unfold on its own. *Naturally*.

From the corner of her eye, Katherine spotted Emily's cousin slip out of the crowd and head inside. She saw the moment Emily decided to follow, turning her attention to Bayne instead, since Katherine was too closely watched to be left alone even for a moment.

~

"Bayne!" called Emily, struggling to keep pace as her cousin chose the route past the library and second kitchen, towards the north-east tower.

He stopped, however reluctantly, and turned to face her. "Yes, Em? What is it?"

"Hey!" she started angrily. "Don't *you* talk to me like that. Especially when I came here to warn you."

"What—?"

"Not here, follow me!" Emily instructed, gesturing for Bayne to follow as she sought privacy in the music room.

"Seriously, what is it, Em?" Bayne asked, closing the doors behind him, irritated.

Making sure they would not be overheard, Emily wasted no time in cutting to the chase. "You know how she felt about you, right?"

"What?" asked Bayne, his mouth hanging slightly open, taken aback at the sudden punch to the gut.

"Don't act stupid!" she continued, her voice pitchy as if scolding a child. "You know that I know exactly what you meant to her, and you know that means I have some idea of what's coming."

Bayne shuffled his feet uncomfortably, but before he could protest, Emily pressed on.

"You need to be careful."

"Wait," Bayne muttered, eyes narrowing as he snapped away from his racing thoughts. "Careful? Me?"

"You know what I mean. You're going to be experiencing everything you felt, as well as—"

"It'll be fine."

"You're either lying or delusional—"

"Em..." Bayne sighed, rubbing his forehead. "What is it that you think Katherine and I had, exactly?"

"Well..."

"Listen, I appreciate you looking out for me. That, in itself, is strange, but respectfully, don't make assumptions about what you don't know."

"Well, from what I remember, things didn't end well," Emily snapped, raising her eyebrows. "I know *that* at least!"

Bayne clenched his fists in frustration. Did he dare admit that nobody really knew the depths of what he and Katherine had shared? Before he could react in anger, he made the conscious decision to ignore her words and continue with the version of the truth he had so adamantly narrated all this time.

Emily let out a sharp laugh, shaking her head. "There we go. Typical!"

"Em! Don't start, please."

"Whatever!" Emily said, raising her hand as she turned to leave. "I came here to tell you to prepare for the intensity of her memories of you, that's all. Whatever you actually felt for her...well...that's clearly your business. I've done my part. I just hope you know what yours is in all of this."

Without wanting to go into it, especially with Emily, Bayne chose to let it go, allowing her to leave the room without offering a retort. Taking a few deep breaths, he did his best to calm the pounding in his head.

Left to himself and his ever-wandering thoughts, Bayne's frustration was eased as he looked around. He chuckled, noticing a row of blue guitars on the opposite wall. *Typical Katherine*, he thought as he made his way over to them. *Even here, everything has to be blue.*

Ignoring the electric guitars, he reached for one of the acoustic steel-strings. It had been years since he last played, and his fingers felt stiff as he positioned them on the frets. Bayne sat down and started to play a song he had learnt as a young boy, the only one he could still remember how to. Knowing that Jennifer preferred to be alone for the night, *yet again*, he played the tune over and over until the darkness engulfed him, as if commanding him to go to bed. Nervous though he was, he knew that rest would be the only thing he could still do to prepare for what lay ahead.

CHAPTER 13
MASTER BAYNE MCALLISTER

er mind overrun with Emily's words from the night before, Katherine had taken to slipping into the library unnoticed, just as the sun began to rise. Despite recalling substantially more than on her first examination of Alfred and Zachary's research, she still felt uncomfortably in the dark about many things. In addition to playing more catch-up than she would have liked regarding the running of her kingdom and the management of her communities of power during her absence, she was more determined than ever to learn more about the mortal whom Fate seemed to deem more worthy as a potential suitor than a pure descendant of power.

The slow return of some memories allowed her to better navigate the historical archives. Thankfully, though fragments of her past – unrelated to the champions – remained blurred, navigating the realm of social media was like second nature. While her ability to speed-read remained locked away with her power, Katherine spent the day before the next part of the trial researching everything she could about the man she was about to kiss, as well as those who knew more about their history than she did. Until now, her focus had been centred on the immortals. Between the enigma that was Bayne and the mystery of why she had so few memories with Deacon, Katherine dived headfirst into a sea of information, only resurfacing at the sound of the library doors creaking open.

It was after midday when Alfred managed to locate her on the first floor. "Princess!" he exclaimed, relief evident in his voice. "You missed breakfast, *and* lunch, yet again. We were concerned."

She smiled at the friend who had weathered the ages with her from behind one of the only two computers installed in the room. "Are you not always concerned, Alfred?" she asked, raising her eyebrows playfully.

"You jest, Your Highness, but it has really been much to take on without you here."

"Thank you for those kind words. I have missed you, too."

The handler smiled. "Everyone else has eaten. Would you like to have the kitchen bring you something?"

"Yes, thank you. I will join everyone for a drink before the festivities tomorrow afternoon if you would arrange that for me, please, but until then, I believe my attention needs to remain here."

"Of course, Your Highness," replied Alfred at once with a bow, seemingly happy to be ordered around by the princess after too many years apart. "I will see to it that you are not disturbed as best as possible."

"Excellent. Thank you, Alfred, that will be all."

The handler smiled again before hurrying out through the nearest exit. Katherine let out a soft chuckle, not missing the hint of relief in his movements, as if he felt reassured by the return of some long-lost sense of normality.

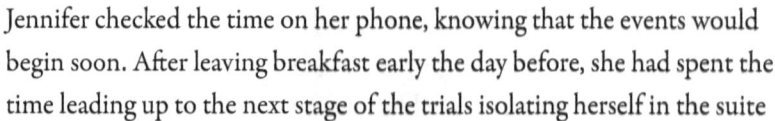

Jennifer checked the time on her phone, knowing that the events would begin soon. After leaving breakfast early the day before, she had spent the time leading up to the next stage of the trials isolating herself in the suite on the first floor, wondering how she would be able to make it through what was to come without her true feelings betraying her.

She had not seen Bayne since he disappeared from dinner after Katherine and Prince Dàikonos's kiss, and she was rather relieved that he had respected her wishes to be alone after she had learnt of his obligation to see the trials through. While happy to avoid the stares and hushed whispers of those in the castle, she wondered whether the man she loved was wishing that he had never met Katherine, or whether he was secretly happy to know that she held him in such high regard for him to be selected as a champion.

Unable to avoid it any longer, Jennifer finished getting ready and made the final preparations to endure something she thought she had long since put behind her. Though she and Bayne had been distant since arriving at the castle, Jennifer trusted he would never do anything to truly threaten their relationship. She stepped out of her suite, hoping this would be the only trial he needed to complete.

Joining Jamie and Brian at the end of the corridor, Jennifer was relieved to find them trapped in a debate about sports teams and not talking about her, Bayne, or Katherine. Although she did not know much about the teams they were talking about, she made her best effort to be involved in the conversation and distract herself from her thoughts as they moved through the castle, taking the nearby stairs that led down past the main kitchen.

The sound of clanging pots and pans was soon drowned out by laughter that filtered in from outside as they walked through the dining room, and their conversation trailed off.

The trio was met with waves and calls from Emily and Layla to join them and the princes. Almost everyone looked as though they were already a few drinks in. While Bayne was yet to make an appearance, Jennifer agreed to join the others for a round before facing what she had always hoped she would never have to witness.

Sunset was nearly upon them when Alfred walked into the courtyard, accompanying a nervous-looking Bayne, who had spent the majority of his time in the armoury with Zachary since they last saw him. As the pair walked across the clearing towards the group waiting at the other end, he sensed Emily watching him. He kept his eyes forward, unwilling to acknowledge her judgemental gaze. Handing the champion a stiff drink to calm his nerves, Alfred patted Bayne on the shoulder reassuringly before leaving to await the arrival of the council.

"So..." started Alek, hopping off of the chair he had seated himself on and walking over to clink glasses with Bayne. "You ready?"

Looking as though he would rather answer any other question, Bayne replied rather quickly. "No backing out now."

"Hey, man, listen," Alek said, now talking low enough that only Bayne heard him. "It's apparently a lot rougher than it looks. Just brace yourself. Okay?"

Bayne gave a brief nod as the prince slapped him on the shoulder and headed back over to his brothers, allowing the heavy-hearted champion to greet the rest of the mortals and have a moment with Jennifer before Alfred returned to the courtyard with the council.

"Master Bayne!" called the handler, gesturing for him to join them. "It is time!"

With a quick, slightly awkward hug, Bayne turned his back on Jennifer and made his way forward, stopping just short of the flame.

Everyone, from the princes to the mortals, the castle keepers to the handlers, settled in, their curiosity only mounting as they waited for Katherine to arrive.

～

Alek's words echoed through his head and Bayne's mind drifted to the warning Emily had given him two nights before. Why now? What do they know that I don't? What have they assumed?

His nerves were making him ill at the thought of what reliving the memories would actually mean, when he caught part of the hushed conversation the Consilio Statera was having nearby.

"...and what of the fact that he is mortal?" asked Horus in a barely audible tone.

"If this is what Fate has decided, who are we to argue?" whispered Herlock.

"We will not be able to interfere—"

"And nor should you!" came Katherine's voice from the living room. All conversation was halted as her words carried across the clearing.

"Ah! Princess!" exclaimed Dolos, turning on his heel and opening his arms to greet her.

"Oh, please do not become silent on my account," she said, smiling with a knowing look in her eyes.

"Apologies, Your Highness!" stammered Horus. He and the others bowed as she approached.

"We are all aware of the consequences of standing in the way of Fate. We proceed as we are instructed to. No exceptions," Katherine said firmly as she took her place at the edge of the carving.

"Of course, Princess," exclaimed Herlock from beside her as if to reassure them all that they would never suggest otherwise. "Whenever you are ready."

Katherine turned her gaze away from them and faced the flames, drawing a breath before taking her first step across the lines.

∽

Bayne and Katherine looked as though they would rather be anywhere else than where they were at this moment. Each avoided looking at the other.

Bayne's mind raced as he struggled to admit to himself how they had never allowed anyone to witness their feelings for one another, not really, which was what made it all worse. People had only ever seen glimpses of them together, never understanding how they could say so much to each other without so much as a single word. Now, not only were they being forced to enact a public display of affection, but they had to do so under the most awkward of circumstances – in front of those they cared for most. Those who thought they knew their story. Those who just assumed how it had, or had not, ended. *Jennifer.* Bayne's chest tightened under the weight of crushing anxiety, and he almost wished to be in Katherine's shoes, not able to remember any of this beforehand. He had done so much to put it all out of his mind until now.

Katherine's stomach was uneasy as she tried to gather the courage to look at Bayne. She had read and re-read the files that Zachary had compiled on him, and had looked into his online history without being able to recall any of the times they had been seen together over the decades. While Zachary had done a fantastic job at wiping clean most of her digital and physical footprints from her past lives, he and his team were only just beginning to fully erase the trails left from her most recent one, as the Katherine that knew Bayne. Whether it was to ensure that they found every last trace of her past presence, or whether Zachary was purposefully taking his time to give Katherine a slight advantage during this task, she was grateful to have some insight where her mind seemed to hold only darkness.

However, Katherine suspected that the second she looked into those pale blue eyes, she would lose control of her expression. That she would want to blurt out every burning question that had been brewing in her head over the past few days. Though her memories lay scattered like puzzle pieces across a thousand forgotten realms, she found it easier to accept those she held as an immortal than to comprehend how a single mortal lifetime could leave such a profound mark on a prophecy far beyond her own power.

Bayne shuffled his feet. He was not a generally nervous man, but the thought of having to kiss Katherine again after all of these years scared him. Whether he wanted to admit it or not. *Will it be different from before? Will things have changed now that she has...all of this in her life?*

"It is time," announced Dolos, his voice breaking both Katherine and

Bayne away from their internal debates.

Looking up, they finally met each other's gaze. Katherine felt it at once. So did Bayne. This task would reveal how far they had – or had not – truly come over the years. Staring into his hesitant eyes, there was a sudden flutter in Katherine's stomach, just as Bayne fought against a jolt in his, a familiar feeling that had made his knees go weak every time he thought of her in the past.

Bayne's breathing grew shallow with each step as they moved closer, the barrier flames rising and trapping the pair inside. *How is this fair? To me? To her? To everyone? Anyone?*

Katherine's lips trembled as Bayne drew closer to her. Each seemed to be doing their best not to cower in the face of their fear.

They moved closer.

Closer.

And closer still, until their faces were an inch apart.

Bayne released a slow, measured breath, its warmth brushing against Katherine's lips as he rested an unsteady hand on her waist. No matter what came next, it would lead nowhere good.

As Katherine summoned the courage to make the first move, she leant up and let her lips find his. Bayne's parted instinctively – as if welcoming hers home. Their eyes drifted shut, and in a heartbeat, the years between them, the prophecy, and even the uncertainty of memory all fell away.

Everything else was lost to them.

Jennifer hardly had the strength to look at Bayne's lips on Katherine's. Oh, how easily he seemed to forget that anyone in the courtyard existed, including her. She turned from the scene, covering her mouth, tears in her eyes. She knew that he had no choice but to commit entirely to the rules of the trials. She understood that – or was trying to, at least – but it still hit her. Hard. Somehow, she always had this feeling that Bayne never stopped caring for Katherine, not really.

As Jennifer wiped her face, she caught Emily's smirk, which felt like a sharp contrast to the ache in her own chest. Almost as if sensing her distress, Emily's expression softened. A quiet sigh escaped her lips before she shifted closer, as if unsure whether to offer comfort.

Jennifer just shook her head before turning away to focus on the crowd instead. Through blurred vision, she took in the sea of faces – mortals and supernaturals alike – all watching Katherine and Bayne with curiosity. She could hear some whispering about the power that might emanate from this moment, while others, council members in particular, appeared to be speculating on how it would shape the trials.

Just then, a low rumble broke the evening silence, and the ground beneath trembled.

Oblivious to all that was transpiring around them, Katherine and Bayne were transported back to the memory of their first meeting. Brief as it was, neither of them could have known what would unfold the next time they crossed paths. Yet, in that moment, each felt an undeniable pull toward the other, one they could neither explain then nor now.

Bayne had been warned that within the Memory Kiss, they would inhabit each other's minds, hearts, and bodies – reliving every moment together, every feeling, every time they had been close yet only dared to whisper the other's name. But this was far from what he had allowed himself to imagine.

Experiencing his own actions and emotions again was one thing, but splitting his very being between himself and Katherine was beyond anything he had ever read about in books. He felt the thud of her every heartbeat alongside his own, the sting of her every emotion – each sensation overwhelming in its intensity. It was a dream. It had to be. A beautiful, cruel, sadistic little dream. In truth, the only thing Bayne could imagine making this worse was if she could hear his thoughts, both then and now. Worse still, if he could hear hers.

The pair was thrown into the body of Katherine's younger self, sitting across from a boy with whom she had exchanged little more than a greeting until now. As Bayne found himself staring at, well, himself, the anxiety he had tried to fight earlier was replaced by something that he could, to this day, remember all too well. All too quickly, he was lost in the magic of the trial, surrendering to that which brought power to the memories.

As they revisited their second encounter, it was clear that something had shifted between them that night. It was as if Katherine was noticing Bayne for the first time. A spark had ignited a connection that neither of them could resist. They may not have exchanged many words that evening, but Bayne felt the high that coursed through Katherine with every stolen glance – as if she had never met someone who consumed her so effortlessly. Similarly, Katherine was flooded by the rush Bayne felt as he teasingly danced on the edge of a very fine line, fully aware that the object of his intrigue was on the arm of another.

They relived how neither of them had cared that their loved ones noticed every folded serviette sent flying across the table at Katherine's head, or how eating their bread rolls with cutlery had somehow become an excuse for flirtatious glances. Lost in the simplicity of days long since passed, Bayne and Katherine watched as the moments, stored in neat little boxes for far too long, broke free as the power of the kiss shattered their defences.

∼

The ground beneath shook more violently and cracks splintered through the stone. Bracing for the worst, Alek cast a spell beneath the onlookers' feet, creating a protective layer to ensure they would not be swallowed by the earth if it decided to open up beneath them. While they were unable to predict what was still to come, Alek's knowledge of Bayne's history, however much was still to be uncovered, saw the prince eager to take proactive measures.

As the fissures widened and spread, Alek exchanged a glance with

Emily, who seemed to share his unspoken question of how bad things would get before Katherine and Bayne could walk away from this. No matter how much the mortal cared for Jennifer, Alek was certain Emily understood that those she loved needed to face this trial to free themselves from the chains of their past.

Before either Katherine or Bayne could catch their breath, they were thrust into the next memory. It felt as though they were being swept through space and time, each high and every low crashing into them without warning or pause. Yet it was their first kiss that brought with it a dizzying rush of destiny.

Katherine moved slowly towards Bayne. Her breathing was shallow and controlled. Bayne felt her heart leap as if to say to her that this would be the true test of what she felt for him. That this would confirm all she held within was more than just a passing hope.

"Close your eyes," she whispered as she used the tips of her toes to lean in towards him, her lips hovering so close to his that she could almost taste him. "Don't move." Katherine took a nervous breath, closed her eyes and then gently pressed her lips to his. Without thinking, one foot lifted behind her, its toes barely grazing the ground, as if caught between earth and the soaring rush of her heart.

Bayne had never felt anything quite like it either. As Katherine's lips left him, he opened his eyes – only to find himself lost in the brilliant blue depths of the potential of forever, left breathless, weightless, and utterly undone. Time seemed to stand still. The air around them pulsed with the energy of every heartbeat and every breath, each one synchronised in a rhythm that tethered them together, darker than evening's shadow and as fierce as the rising dawn.

As the waves of their emotions crashed into each other, they tangled into an inescapable web. Their first kiss destroyed any illusions the pair had of making it through this unscathed. If that recollection alone had struck them with such force, Bayne feared that what lay ahead would break them before it ever set them free.

The good memories, however, were not all they were forced to live through. They were soon thrown into the first time they saw each other after Katherine ended their relationship. Though Bayne was grateful not to relive the moment his heart ripped open upon reading that text message just weeks earlier, he still felt a ripple of pain before hurtling into the next.

A rising dread filled Katherine as she sat there, in Bayne's living room, with Layla and Emily. She paused mid-sentence, hearing a car door slam in the distance. His chest tightened as hers had, just as a deep, bracing shock settled in at the reality of seeing her again so unexpectedly. Until now, Bayne had always assumed that Katherine's discomfort stemmed from her desire to keep him at arm's length. But he was beginning to think that what he had mistaken for unease was actually her shame. Shame at her prideful nature, accompanied by a desperate longing to possess the power to alter time and change things, and the hope that he would see through her brave disguise.

As the pair struggled to come to terms with how each had so determinedly hidden their pain from the other in the desire to not be the first to break, Bayne and Katherine were subjected to the polite pleasantries they had so hated to endure, yet secretly craved, as it meant they could be near each other, even if only for a moment.

She bid him farewell after he had offered to walk her out. Bayne felt the warmth of her tears trailing down her cheeks as she fought to keep up appearances until she was out of his sight. As she drove out of the gate, leaving him wishing he had the courage to say something, anything, Bayne was knocked off balance by the unbearable ache of Katherine's heart and mind breaking as she rounded the corner and pulled into Jamie's driveway. It only worsened his regret as he was forced to sit through the pain of her sobbing quietly in her car for hours.

It was here that Bayne finally understood that Katherine had not dismissed him out of a lack of love, but because of the overwhelming fear she had carried. She had not been ready for forever then, and deep down, she had known that was exactly where things were heading if they had stayed on that path. As she whispered to herself that she would be ready for him one day, only hoping that by then it would not be too late, Bayne longed for this torture to end. Not only for his sake but for hers, too.

But this would not be the most painful series of events the pair would experience.

More anger.

More love.

More heartbreak.

Suddenly, Katherine collapsed onto the floor of Jamie's shower after another of his legendary parties, and Bayne was hit with yet another glimpse of just how much she had hidden from him. Despite all the convincing performances of moving on over the years, the hurt that followed still hit with the same crushing weight as if it were the first time. Painful, silent cries slipped between each shallow, convulsive catch of her breath, and Bayne was unable to escape the hand that tightened around Katherine's throat as she choked out his name. It was almost too intense for him to believe that he had caused her this much hurt. Almost too paralysing for him to accept that she had really held on to the thought of him for so long.

Even if he had, in fact, done the same.

The shaking worsened as vines emerged from the earth, twisting up from its shadowed depths. Creeping across the courtyard, they took on a life of their own, wrapping themselves around the surfaces closest to the onlookers. Determined to keep the mortals safe, Alek instructed Emily and her friends to remain in their seats, knowing it would be easiest to protect them if there was as little chaos and panic as possible.

But without warning, the ground went still.

Bayne and Katherine's loved ones watched in awe as tiny buds sprouted along every vine, no matter where they spread. Nearer the council, tendrils coiled around an artistic display of pots, crushing them beneath their suffocating grip. Soon, each bud burst into continuous bloom, unfolding into the most beautiful white roses any of them had ever seen – perfect in every way imaginable.

As a sweet aroma filled the air and drifted into waiting lungs, the crowd watched as the world around them became overrun with thousands of white flowers, blanketing the courtyard like fresh snow. For a moment, even Alek allowed himself to get caught up in the beauty of it all.

Katherine and Bayne drifted from one interaction to the next in chronological order, growing increasingly aware of how much things between them would change now that each knew certain truths about the recollections of a life once lived. Whether for better or worse, neither could shake the feeling that nothing would ever be the same again.

The more questions were answered, the more questions arose. If he could, Bayne would have been yelling for it to end. He longed to be free of the endless half-goodbyes, to avoid reliving the dread and hopeful anticipation of the next inevitable hello. He wished to continue ignoring how each ending had always come an inch too soon. Bayne's ears rang as Katherine's heart screamed into the darkness whenever their paths crossed, and he could no longer pretend that she had only ever seen him as a fleeting thought or placeholder. The truth of the consequences of their actions was thrust upon them.

The inescapable grip of his own pain was one thing, but what truly unsettled Bayne was Katherine's ceaseless cycle of realising, time and again, that he would never muster the courage to act. Knowing now that part of her had remained frozen, clinging to the hope of one day feeling the full warmth of him again, made it that much harder for him to hold the fractured pieces of himself together. It was only when Bayne's spirit was on the brink of crumbling under the sheer force of pure human emotion that Fate finally deemed their trial complete.

Katherine was slammed back into her own, present-day body, and she opened her eyes, meeting Bayne's, just as the roses stopped blooming. In less than an instant, her body collapsed to the floor in unparalleled pain. She clutched her head in agony, a raw, guttural scream tearing from her throat as Bayne's knees gave way beneath him, sending him crashing onto the floor. Pain lanced through every nerve, every memory she had of him flooding back in unbearable clarity. She could barely keep her eyes open, her vision blurring, but through the haze, she saw streams of crimson tears carving paths down the champion's cheeks.

The crowd ran towards the pair, dodging the obstacles created by the effects of their kiss and stopping as close to the barrier circle as possible. There was nothing they could do but watch as two of their closest friends lay there, tortured by the relentless onslaught of their history.

Bayne let out a yell that quickly turned into a spluttering cough as blood shot out of his mouth. He did what he could to stop the flow, but it was futile. As Katherine glanced up to meet his eyes, she knew that he felt it too – the physical pain of their memories was twisting into a deadly echo of everything they had once felt for each other. Everything they still felt.

Cries bounced off of the castle walls as Jennifer and the other mortals feared the worst. Even the other champions appeared to be more concerned than they had been at any of the previous tasks.

Katherine watched as Bayne, on all fours, crawled towards her. The look in his eyes sent a chill deep into her bones – the champion knew he was going to die tonight. And at that moment, she realised he needed her to understand. To know that he was sorry. Just as she needed him to know that she had never meant to cause him pain.

Seeing him fight with what little energy he had left caused Katherine to find a sliver of strength beyond the hurt. She reached Bayne just as he collapsed to the ground once more.

This can't be how our story ends.

Turning him onto his back, Katherine forced a slight smile, masking the torment clawing at her insides as she tried to ease his suffering. Unsure of whether it would work, Katherine could think of only one way to save him, to save them both.

She hesitated for only a second before launching into a rapid chant, her words spilling out in a dialect lost thousands of years before. As she spoke, light glowed within her eyes, brightening with every syllable.

With all the power she was able to summon, she rammed her fingers into Bayne's chest, over where his heart was beating ever slower. A harrowing, earth-shaking scream tore from his throat, echoing through the castle and beyond the grounds, a cry of unbearable pain that shook the very air around him as her nails pierced his flesh.

From the corner of her eye, Katherine saw Emily turn away, unable to bear the sight. The mortal became sick in an instant. Most of the onlookers, many castle keepers included, recoiled as Katherine's other hand battled its way into her own chest. Fighting to stave off the death creeping closer, she was desperate to outrun the clock measured by her own blood spilling out onto the stone.

The flowers that had bloomed from their kiss let their petals fall. With each painful, strained breath, Katherine continued to chant. The pair's friends and family watched in terror as every soft curl of the roses inched towards the barrier circle. Gathering in a slow wind that grew ever faster, the petals circled Katherine and Bayne, forming what looked like a whirlwind, until they were completely lost in a shield of white. Unable to interfere, Alek and the others stood helplessly.

The rose veil exploded seconds later, leaving Bayne and Katherine exposed in its centre. They lay on the cold stone, eyes closed as the spilt blood that surrounded them turned into streams that crept their way back to the bodies from where they had originally come. It was an incredible sight to witness.

As the last traces of crimson vanished into them, sealing their wounds shut, Katherine and Bayne awoke, unleashing a brilliant green light from where they lay. It traced along the carving's lines until it reached Bayne's marker, turning it into the symbol for earth.

They battled but managed to sit upright, meeting each other's eyes in a look so fierce it made Jennifer's breath catch mid-inhale, just as the barrier flames turned green and erupted outward, streaking across the courtyard in a ring of light. As the glow faded into the evening, taking with it the last remnants of the task's consequences and leaving little trace of the havoc it had wrought, Katherine and Bayne crawled to exit the symbol, unable to speak a word before the crowd rushed to their aid.

Getting to his feet with help from Prince Dàikonos and Greyson, Bayne struggled to stay upright, knowing that his thoughts might not be easily calmed. He staggered as he made his way to sit with his back against the cold wall. He waved off the concerned advances of his friends, but his mind would not release its grip, calling questions to the surface that he had long since thought buried and breathing life into feelings he had so desperately tried to stifle.

He had seen how Katherine had cried for him. Felt how she had hated him. Experienced each time she felt love for him. And he lived through what he was sure was not the extent of the times she had buckled from how badly she had been broken by that love. Bayne's heart sank at the knowledge that if he had just been honest with her, with himself, just once, everything could have been so different.

Nearby, Bayne watched as Alek helped Katherine to her feet, steadying her as she leant against him for support before guiding her to the closest chair. Even from a distance, Bayne could see the strain in her movements – the way her hands trembled, the way she clutched at her chest as though trying to hold herself together. She looked as if she were unravelling, not just physically, but in a way that ran far deeper. As though something inside her was fracturing. The humanity of it all. It had to be.

The realisation that they had both held back the truth in a misguided attempt to protect each other's happiness hurt almost as much as knowing they had no one to blame but themselves for how close it had brought them to death. Before the thought could settle in his mind, Bayne's world faded into darkness as what little energy he held onto trickled away.

Katherine succumbed to her exhaustion only moments later.

Hiding his concern behind a composed exterior, Alek advised the council that the pair should be taken to Dr Breme. Quick to agree, clearly just as curious as the rest were about how Katherine had just managed to display such power without access to her abilities, the council summoned the nearest castle keepers to carry Bayne to the medical ward. As another pair hurried forward to attend to Katherine, Alek waved them off, taking her in his arms. The prince carried her through the castle himself as Alfred and Zachary were left to attend to the concerns of the mortals and other champions. The council quickly took their leave, immediately locked into what appeared like a heated conversation about what had just happened.

Clearing his throat loudly, Alfred called for attention. "Everyone," he said, "please do not be concerned. We will update you all on the status of Princess Katherine and Master Bayne as soon as Prince Aleksander returns. For now, I urge you to remain calm as they appear to be, for the most part, out of any immediate danger. Rest will be the most restorative medicine for them now. Please, it has been quite an evening. Follow me into the dining room for something to eat. I am certain that the prince will join us shortly."

Emily and those around her were unsure how to react. Jennifer appeared to be in a state of shock but nodded silently and made her way inside as if on autopilot, her eyes red and puffy, her face pale. The rest followed. As they stepped into the room, which was soon filled with the rich scent of freshly roasted beef and fragrant herbs, they remained silent, struggling to process what they had witnessed.

The princes were almost as taken aback as the rest of the onlookers. Eager to hear from their brother about Dr Breme's findings, they too followed Alfred's advice to settle their stomachs.

∾

"So?" Marko scoffed as he settled into his seat. "Anyone care to explain what the hell that was?"

The group was silent. Only the fires seemed willing to voice their opinion as they spluttered and crackled from the fireplaces.

"Nobody?"

"The same as when you kissed her, I guess, brother?" replied Deacon, furrowing his brow as he shot a glance at Kaëden, who seemed too locked in his own thoughts to answer.

"Don't play dumb, Deacon! It's beneath you," snapped Marko, throwing up his hands in frustration.

Emily saw the anger that flickered in the youngest prince's eyes.

"He's a champion. What are you misunderstanding?"

"You know exactly what I mean, Deacon!"

"And we're going to go through this again, are we?" came Alek's voice from over Marko's shoulder as he stepped through the doorway at the bottom of the armoury's staircase.

"You're telling me that you don't think it's strange?"

"That *what's* strange?"

"He's a *human*," Marko spat. "He's known her for how long in comparison to any of us?"

"Oh, so you're jealous?" replied Alek irritably as he took his seat opposite his brother. "By the way, they're both fine if anyone wants to know rather than further their own agenda."

"Jealous? Don't start. We all knew what would come with entering the trials. I knew what I was walking into. But him? You tell me, *brother*, were you expecting that or did it blindside you, too?"

Alek shot Marko a deadly look as he stabbed at a bread roll with more force than necessary, causing Matthew to jump in his seat beside the ill-tempered prince. "I'd let it go if I were you. If you want to know what he means to Katherine, I'd suggest you pluck up the courage to ask her rather than making speculations about something you know nothing about."

Jamie and Aiden snickered from where they sat across from each other, while Emily and the rest of the mortals either sank low into the dining room chairs or stuffed their mouths with food, pretending not to be listening to the bickering. Each of them was, in some way, thankful for the distraction.

Marko looked stunned at Alek's retort and turned to Kaëden. "And *you*? Anything to add?"

Kaëden's eyes snapped up. He looked down at his brother from the far end of the table, pressed a napkin to his mouth, and cleared his throat to speak. His tanned face was hard and unsympathetic.

"Markovyas," Kaëden said coldly, leaning forward as he laced his hands together before him. "Would you really like me to weigh in on this conversation, or would you rather leave the topic for a day when you are a little less...emotional, brother?"

"Never mind." Marko scowled, obviously having hoped that his short-fused sibling would entertain his frustration. The prince turned his attention to his plate and aimlessly reached for whatever food lay in front of him, not wanting to argue with his eldest sibling.

The rest of the meal passed mostly in silence. Jennifer excused herself before anyone else had finished. There was an unspoken understanding that she needed space. Once alone, she bolted the bedroom door behind her and sank to the floor, no longer holding back the emotions she had suppressed at the table. Tears streamed down her face as she replayed the events over and over until exhaustion overtook her, and she eventually fell asleep where she sat.

The others escaped to their bedrooms soon after they ate, each coming to realise how close tonight had really come to ending in disaster.

With effort, Katherine forced her heavy eyelids open, her vision clouded and blurred by the distant haze of flames. Her small burst of energy faded almost instantly, but not before she saw the outline of Bayne's body that lay in the bed beside hers.

As her world dimmed, Katherine managed to mutter, "You should have told me."

Just as everything went black, she could have sworn that, in the distance, she heard someone say, "You should have told me, too."

CHAPTER 14
THE NEED FOR KNOWLEDGE

atherine opened her eyes around dawn. For a moment, she allowed herself to take in the sight of Bayne lying in the bed alongside hers. Even if she had not just relived the last time she had smiled as she caught him sleeping, she would have had the same reaction. Her eyes lingered before a wrenching pull seized her, forcing her to suppress the pain that suddenly shot through her heart. Moving as quietly as she could, Katherine got out of bed, crossed the room and snuck through the door, leaving Bayne to get some much-needed rest.

She chose the most direct route to the armoury and, even though the medical ward was not far off, Katherine had to fight to keep herself from questioning her recollections from the task. It had been difficult enough for her to come to the realisation that she was who she was, but it was a completely different struggle to try to reconcile that with a person she had been for only a blink of an eye. *Yet somehow...?* she thought, before shaking her head back to its senses.

As she approached the first-floor entrance to the armoury, Katherine made sure to be extra careful, now knowing full well that Zachary had ears like a hawk, even if he would never admit it. But she also knew that he valued his sleep and that the usually bustling, two-story room would most likely be empty at this hour. Pushing the door open as carefully as possible, Katherine snuck inside and made her way down the stairs, past the surveillance room, and through the shut frosted-glass door at the end of the wall that housed the large display screen. She slipped through and breathed a sigh of relief, taking solace in the soundproof entryway to her private rooms.

Not having accessed them in hundreds of years, Katherine took a moment to laugh at how Alek and Zachary must have felt when they inevitably failed to uncover the secrets that lay within. They had always wondered what awaited beyond the doors of the places in the castle that nobody but she could enter. With a drop of her life force, the stone entrance, framed in elegant mahogany that Alek must have added when the armoury was renovated, slid open with a grate against the floor.

Even as her memories continued to unveil themselves, Katherine had barely taken a breath to allow herself to appreciate just how much she had truly missed magic and power. She paused in awe as the room lit itself with a soft blue glow upon her arrival as if it was trying to make her smile by choosing her favourite colour. She took in the elegance of her handiwork, admiring the complexity of a creation that not only concealed her deepest confidences but had always given her unparalleled clarity.

The faint scent of aged parchment and dust filled the air, a familiar presence that clung to the centuries-old chamber as she descended to the lower floor. It was a scent woven into her memories, one that spoke of knowledge, mystery, and time itself. She made her way past the shelves of rare books and scrolls, and ignored the spine-chilling whispers that crept from a collection of spheres said to be the keys to the forbidden plane. Katherine strode to a bookshelf at the far end of the room and rummaged through its abundance of papers until she pulled out a tattered page that hummed at her touch.

"Gotcha!" she whispered, smiling to herself.

She looked down at a collection of ancient symbols that glowed a brilliant gold as they swirled into place. She folded the parchment carefully
and tucked it safely away on her person. This piece of moving text, once
spoken aloud, would grant her the ability to read at an astonishing speed
until its effects returned to the page and waited to be called upon again.
While she could not explain how she had tapped into a vein of power to
keep Bayne from slipping into an eternity of darkness, she concluded that
nothing prevented her from using her collection of enchanted objects to
gain a bit more of an advantage.

Katherine took comfort in the room's urgency to seal itself tightly
behind her as she exited into the armoury. Having created a multitude
of rooms just like this in castles and palaces across the various regions of
Eyrondale, and all over the world, many of which housed more complex
security systems, Katherine felt that her memories could not come back
quickly enough.

There was too much to figure out.

Too much that could no longer afford to remain hidden.

Too much at risk.

Heading for the library, she snuck a lemon poppy seed muffin from
the kitchen to fuel up for a long morning of reading.

Awoken by the tall, bustling silhouette of Dr Breme who, for some reason,
had started her cleaning earlier than usual, Bayne was relieved to finally
get permission to leave the bed he had occupied for the past two nights.
He had spent his time wondering whether he had only dreamt of Katherine lying in the bed beside him or if it had been a wicked trick played
by his own mind. Although his physical pain had greatly subsided, he
was unable to prevent his mind from replaying what had happened as he
headed to his third-floor suite, desperate to escape the judgemental gaze of
his caregiver's cold grey eyes, and determined to freshen up and figure out
his next steps.

He arrived at an empty room, but Bayne had almost come to expect Jennifer's absence. As far as he knew, neither she nor the others had visited his bedside, whether by their own choice or under Dr Breme's instruction, he could not say. He stepped into the steaming hot shower. The warm water cascaded down his muscular torso, which bore no signs of damage or harm. His mind soon betrayed him, conjuring 'what if' scenarios and playing them on a loop. *No!* he thought, his stern tone echoing in his head. *You can't think this way. You can't let them see.* Spending more time in the shower than he probably should have, it was a while before Bayne once again felt clean.

~

On her way to brunch, Emily met Aiden and Jamie, who were just as excited at the news that Katherine and Bayne had regained consciousness as she was. The mortals had endured the past nights, fraught with worry, even though Alfred had done an excellent job of ensuring that the castle keepers kept them distracted. Having awoken to a handwritten note informing them that their morning meal had been postponed and inviting them to dine outside, Emily and the others looked forward to enjoying a bit of sunshine, along with the relief of knowing their loved ones had recovered from their injuries.

Though she had yet to fully process what had happened to her cousin, Emily willingly accepted the group hug forced upon her just before the trio joined the others out in the courtyard.

"Thanks, guys," Emily muttered, not quite wanting to dampen the mood.

"Hey," Jamie said gently, giving her another quick squeeze. "You doing okay?"

"Just been a tough few days. A lot to digest. But thanks."

"Absolutely, kiddo," he replied, his voice warm and steady. "We're all in this together."

"Okay, let's get out there before they come looking for us," prompted

Aiden.

"Yeah."

An assortment of freshly baked pastries met their eyes as the three walked through the living room doors. An array of fresh fruits, fragrant preserves, and a variety of cooked eggs and meats made their mouths water. If there was one thing that the castle keepers excelled at, it was providing a proper feast.

As the remaining guests began to arrive, it was a surprise to everyone when Bayne showed up and dived into the nearest croissant without any explanation or mention of the trial. Their eyes widened as Jennifer joined them, taking her usual seat without acknowledging the elephant in the room either. Even Alek and Marko exchanged confused looks before deciding to go along with it, as it appeared Bayne would make no mention of it at all.

Alfred emerged from the dining room, discussing the day's duties with three castle keepers. As he approached the table, the question lingered – would Katherine grace them with her presence, or was there more to her continued absences than anyone had yet realised?

Before they could dwell on it, a faint humming drifted on the gentle breeze. Those familiar with the sound took a moment to recognise it. It was Katherine. As the diners glanced towards the courtyard, eager for the princess to join them, more than one smile appeared at the table at the sight of her pausing to inhale the scent of a newly bloomed royal-blue rose.

"Your Highness!" Alfred exclaimed, making his way up the nearest walkway to meet her.

"Hello, Alfred. How are you this morning?"

"Well, thank you for asking, Princess. However...are *you* alright?"

"Of course, Alfred," Katherine said as a smile crept across her face. "*Be the embodiment of strength*, if I remember correctly?"

"So you *do* listen when I speak?"

"On occasion," said the princess with a light giggle.

"Well then, I must admit that it pleases me to hear it. Would you please join them for a meal?" Alfred asked, gesturing towards the table where most of the diners had paused their efforts.

"Of course. I had intended to," Katherine replied, resuming her path towards the scent of fresh, buttery pastry.

～

Taking her seat at the head of the table, her back to the castle, Katherine put on a spectacular smile as every pair of eyes, including Bayne's, focused on her.

"You feeling alright?" asked Alek, pausing mid-bite of his sausage.

"Never better," Katherine replied, taking the coffee Alfred had brought her alongside a freshly made mimosa. "Why?"

Lowering his fork, Alek finished his bite with a hard swallow. As he rubbed his hands together, his face turned stern.

"Well, do you think you're ready—?"

"Ready for?"

The prince jumped up from his seat beside her, startling those around him. He ran his hands over his torso with a slow, exaggerated motion. Chuckling, he flashed a grin. "Ready for all of this!"

Katherine let out a laugh, as did many of the others, having thought that Alek would try to provoke a serious discussion about her emotional or physical well-being. She was relieved to see that all she had read about him during her research proved to be true.

Smiling, Alek sat down and grabbed the closest stack of pancakes, the warmth of the syrupy scent sweetening the air as he drowned them in an obscene amount before diving right in.

Relieved by everyone's clear willingness to set recent events aside, at least for now, Katherine relaxed and joined in the polite chitchat.

It was only after deciding that he could not eat another bite that Alek turned to Katherine and whispered under his breath, not joking this time, "You sure you're up for this?"

A quick nod was all it took to convince the prince that there was no getting around proceeding with the next step of the trial today. Alek sighed and, stuffed though he was, gave in to the longing look of the last of the pastries on the plate before him.

"Everyone!" called Alfred over the buzz of chatter, which died down instantly as the diners turned their attention towards him. "The council has advised that they will be arriving earlier today in order to allow adequate time to deal with any potential aftermath that the next task could bring."

"Wait," said Alek suddenly, mouth full of custard tart. "What?"

Marko let out a snicker, lifting his glass to take a sip. Katherine was grateful the prince had done his best to keep his distance since their kiss – whether to give her time or himself. But with him assigned to the seat beside hers, avoiding each other was impossible at the mealtimes she bothered to attend.

"You, uh…" said Deacon loudly, Marko's snickering clearly contagious. "Think that all those years of wars, the ups and downs of *best* friendship, perhaps got the council thinking that *this* kiss might be the worst of them all?"

Shooting his brother a furious look, Alek swallowed and started to respond but was cut off before he could get a word out.

"*Or* that we will flee the scene in sheer embarrassment, not to be heard from for days or even weeks," Katherine said, waving a hand dramatically. "Who could say?"

Although she spoke with a straight face and likely meant every word, laughter erupted from Alek at Katherine's flawless delivery. It made his brothers silence themselves at once. Even Kaëden allowed a smirk to flicker across his face, though he said nothing.

Katherine's lips curved at the edges behind the rim of her glass. She turned to Alfred. "How long do we have exactly?"

"I would say enough time to freshen up before returning to greet the council, Your Highness," the handler answered, clearly quite pleased with how she had put the princes in their place.

"Excellent!" Katherine exclaimed, getting to her feet. She took an apple from the nearest fruit platter. "Then I shall return shortly."

With a quick wink to Alfred and a final glance down the table, Katherine flashed a smile at her guests and made her way through the nearest set of dining room doors with a slight skip, heading towards the passage that led to the kitchens. As Alek and Alfred exchanged apprehensive looks, Bayne rose from his seat as discreetly as possible, with Emily quickly following. The rest remained to finish their meal, while Jennifer's gaze lingered on the departing pair, her expression dark with barely contained anger.

~

"So," Emily whispered, grabbing Bayne's arm just as he was about to disappear into one of the corridors off of the foyer. "I think you and I need to have a little talk about the other night."

She steered him into the nearest empty room and shut the door behind them. Bayne rolled his eyes and let out a long sigh, wondering how Emily would decide to torture him today.

"So, what happened?"

"Can we not get into this?" Bayne asked, despite knowing what his cousin's answer would be.

"Nope!" Emily snapped, far too matter-of-fact for Bayne's liking. "Either you tell me, or I'll ask her."

"Ask her then," he muttered, brushing past her. "It's not like she'll tell you, anyway."

"Hey! Don't you dare think that she doesn't tell me everything!"

As his hand touched the doorknob, Bayne allowed himself to retaliate, against his better judgement. The anger and hurt that had stewed in his chest of late decided to escape, even if only for a second. He rounded on his cousin, leaning down towards her, so close that she could smell the whispers of whisky lingering on his breath. As Emily's bright green eyes caught a shadow flickering across Bayne's face, a smirk curled at his lips – cold and condescending.

"If she really told you *everything*," he whispered with a sneer, "we would have had a *very* different conversation the other night. In fact, if you knew anything about it at all, you would know better than to think anyone, including you, has any right to butt in."

"But...I..." stammered Emily, not having expected this reaction.

"When the council said we'd relive and feel everything? They weren't lying about the *everything* part."

"What do you—"

"Well, let's just say that now I know one of the main reasons why she never came back to me. Why she was never honest about how she felt."

"Oh, please. You can't seriously be blaming what happened on me?"

"You. The rest of our family. Our friends. None of you ever knew anything about it, yet you stuck your noses in, anyway." Bayne's voice rose, frustration burning through every word before he exhaled sharply as if trying to force the anger out of his lungs. He shook his head. "You know what? No! I'm not doing this. Not now. For your sake, Em, don't push it."

Bayne turned and stormed off, slamming the door behind him, leaving Emily to wonder just how much of what she and her friend had discussed about him over the years he had just been privy to through Katherine's memories.

As Bayne marched down the corridor, he wished he had not reacted at all. He had always hated other people getting involved in his business. In *their* business. Knowing it would be best to take some time to calm himself, he headed to the third floor. It was certainly proving more of a struggle to balance the weight of the consequences of the task than he had initially thought it would be.

Maybe this is the real test, he thought, his footsteps echoing behind him. *Finding a way to not lose your damn sanity.*

CHAPTER 15
PRINCE ALEKSANDER
OF KELDORNE

From everything that Katherine had learnt about her and Alek's relationship, she understood why his brothers had brought up what they had at brunch. While any memory involving Alek or Kaëden was still distorted or simply missing, Katherine could tell by the stories she had read in the library that there was a tension that ran deep between the lot of them.

She willed herself to push thoughts of Bayne from her mind. She could barely contain her racing worries about everything else, let alone focus on problems that were never hers to begin with. *Finish the trial*, she thought as she descended the foyer staircase. *After that, you can do what you need to do to deal with this. Just get through it. Only two left!*

She paused at the piano tucked into the corner near the courtyard doors. Positioned in front of a window overlooking the front of the property, it stood as both a familiar comfort and a quiet temptation. As the sound of Alfred announcing the council's arrival to the others floated in from outside, Katherine took a few minutes to compose herself while they were all distracted.

The cold, smooth black of the fallboard felt like home beneath her fingertips. A deep breath escaped her lips as she forced the bulk of her thoughts behind the wall she had relied on time and time again. One built to keep her from crumbling beneath the weight of expectation. A wall so familiar, she sometimes wondered if it would hold against the pressure she placed upon it.

Thankful for the power of the trial that she sensed was acting as an added buffer between her and the force of her emotions like a layer of water holding them apart and waiting to crash, she shook off as much of the negativity as possible and put on her most convincing smile.

"Ah, Princess!" greeted Horus, turning at the sound of Katherine's footsteps on the stone behind him.

Dolos and Herlock, turning with him, followed Horus's lead and bowed as low as they could. Returning their greeting quickly, Katherine looked over at the group of mortals and other onlookers. She was impressed by their resilience, especially now that more of the past was slotting into place in her mind, revealing details about how they fit into it all. Seeing Bayne glance over to her from the far end of the clearing, Katherine's stomach lurched. It made her wish that he would leave. As she walked to the edge of the fire, taking her place, she was suddenly quite apprehensive.

From where she stood, Katherine caught Emily shooting glances between her and Bayne, as if trying to piece something together. Bayne had walked past Jennifer earlier, offering her a quick kiss in greeting before slipping towards the back of the group. Whatever Emily was speculating about, the princess had no doubt it had to do with what Bayne now knew – how it might affect his relationship with Jennifer, his friendships, and his relationship with Emily.

Alek rushed to finish off his conversation with Zachary and Marko before running to take his place. With a signal from Herlock, both Katherine and Alek took a step over the dancing white fire and met each other at the symbol's centre.

Mortal and supernatural alike, apart from the council and on-duty castle keepers, of course, freshened up their drinks in preparation for a long afternoon.

Alek looked nervously at Katherine, blushed, and looked away. Katherine let out a giggle as if she was about to have her first kiss. But it was her first kiss – her first kiss with *Alek*. The boy she had apparently been raised alongside. The man she was said to have fought beside all these years. Her best friend. He himself told her that they had never thought of each other in an intimate, romantic way. *This is going to be interesting.*

Their eyes met again and this time the pair of royals managed to compose themselves. Katherine could see Kaëden and Marko glaring at them as if they were very much displeased. She did not know what they were thinking, but if she had to guess, it likely had something to do with Alek's role as a champion, and their egotistical belief that he was somehow beneath them because of it.

The prince moved towards Katherine with some hesitancy. She moved forward, too.

From what Katherine had privately dubbed 'the viewing area,' Zachary could be heard joking around at the sight of his dear friends locking lips. Even Alfred looked quite taken aback at the sight of it. It was simply something they had never thought to imagine. Although, in comparison to the reaction of the champions, Zachary and Alfred appeared to be holding it together quite well.

"How do you want to do this?" Alek asked, grinning like a schoolboy.

"I'm almost certain that it would be the same process as with anyone else."

Alek chuckled. "Won't hold it against me if it turns out horrible?" he asked.

"Oh, shut up and just kiss me already!" Katherine said with a laugh.

She grabbed the back of Alek's neck and pulled his face towards her own, closing her eyes as their lips met for the very first time. Alek, caught a bit off guard, closed his eyes too, and simply gave in.

It was the most incredible feeling, Alek's lips on hers. Warm, soft, with the faint taste of strawberries. A rush of unfamiliarity fluttered through her, startling yet intoxicating. *No.* She could not let herself think like that. *But what if?*

From the moment their lips met, a wave of energy rolled out from where the two royals stood. Each of the onlookers could feel the presence of something brushing against them as the wave reached their bodies. Invisible though the effects of the kiss were, at the moment, every being there felt a sudden change in the air.

Marko and Alfred exchanged concerned looks as the second wave came on more clearly than the first. Each ripple of energy that met them grew more and more tangible. While not yet causing them harm, those in the courtyard certainly wondered what the strongest version of this would be.

Katherine and Alek relived the memories of their youth, and she could finally see the depths of their friendship. Whether it was how they had banded together as young children in play fights against Marko, or the way they had wrestled each other to the ground over who got to have which toy first, their earlier recollections of each other were truly something special to behold. So happy. So innocent.

From playdates to royal balls, so many of her interactions with Marko and Deacon were beginning to make sense. While there was still a distortion to most, *likely because of Kaëden*, Katherine thought, it was as though the void within her was shrinking. And it was not long before the pair was thrown into a memory that had set the course of more than one nation.

Alek joined Katherine and Marko in the war room. Marko's base of operations had certainly been well-established, and there was no longer an option of turning back. As the three discussed means of thwarting the savage dictator determined to conquer their southern lands now that they had formed an alliance, Alek felt Katherine's heart skip a beat at the thought of war. Though she seemed to loathe the idea, she was, at the same time, so full of light. In the back of his mind, Alek wondered just how right Katherine had been when she brought up how this trial could impact their relationship.

The pair re-experienced the exhilaration and complete trust that came from fighting alongside each other in battle, where their unequivocal loyalty towards each other seemed to outweigh the pain of every bruise.

Every hit.

Every cut.

Each time they had stood at the precipice of death, only to be saved by their immortality.

Soon, they were launched into a memory that even Alek had placed at the edge of his mind.

"So," whispered the prince as he and Katherine pulled off their armour, having only just returned to the safety of Keldorne's castle. "My brother?"

Alek's worry simmered in his chest, having grown over time as he summoned the courage to approach her with his thoughts. While exhausted from battle, he had pushed himself from within to mention anything at all.

"Which one?" asked Katherine absent-mindedly, the victory still fresh in her mind.

"*Markovyas*," Alek said, now crossing his arms and waiting for the princess to meet his gaze.

"What about him?"

The prince smirked, raising an eyebrow. "Do not play me for a fool."

"Alright, you have deduced it. *Congratulations!*" Katherine said, her tone dripping with sarcasm.

"Ew!" Alek blurted out, having hoped that his information was false. As his stomach turned at the thought of Katherine and Marko together, the princess felt as he fought back the desire to be sick all over their weapons.

"Do not 'ew' me!" Katherine laughed. "He is...*different*."

"Unstable is more like," muttered Alek under his breath.

Wiping the last of the blood off of her face, Katherine turned to the prince and took his arm. "If you feel the need to say something, then say it. Do not hold your tongue on my account. That is not how we work."

"I am aware. I just..." Alek trailed off, running a hand over his neck.

"Yes?" prompted Katherine.

"He has a few *complexities,* as it were."

Laughing, relief washed over Katherine as the weight disappeared from her chest.

"If that is all that is undesirable about Markovyas, then I may truly count myself as extremely fortunate."

"Kat—"

"Fine!" The princess rolled her eyes and huffed dramatically, though a smile lingered on her face. "If it goes terribly, you have my full permission to use it against me for the rest of our existence. Would that suffice?"

The pair exchanged a glance before breaking into quiet laughter, discussing the topic no further as they made their way through the dark passages of the castle. As they did, Katherine noted how Alek's concern remained ignited, merely tucking itself away in the shadows of his being, *for now.*

~

The waves of energy deepened to shades of grey as they became more visible and intense. Marko and Alfred worked alongside Deacon to create a barrier that softened the impact of the surging force on the mortals.

As Katherine and Alek's exchange continued, Greyson could be seen smiling from across the courtyard. Recalling some of his favourite stories of the two, a part of him hoped that perhaps his master could finally get the happy ending he so rightfully deserved. While many within the communities of power had thought that Marko and Katherine would end up together, perhaps, just perhaps, Fate had something else in mind.

∿

The highs and lows of their friendship and alliance were exhilarating, challenging, surprising, and unforgettable. For the most part, their memories were met with silver linings, jokes, support, and true loyalty, even when they were at their lowest.

"What do you mean when you say you are through?" Alek asked Katherine, flabbergasted at hearing the news of her and Marko's parting.

"I would very much rather not talk about it," she muttered, tears in her eyes.

The prince wrapped his arms around her and pulled her close, her tears soaking through his shirt. Guiding Katherine to her knees as he lowered himself to the floor, he held her well into the night, neither of them saying a word. Only the sound of Katherine's shallow, uneven breathing could be heard as she cried herself to sleep.

Alek had always known that Katherine's heart had broken when she and Marko parted ways, but never had he actually experienced a feeling of such profound loss in the romantic sense. He himself had experienced very few *serious* relationships throughout his existence until this point. They relived the years after until Alek nearly buckled under the sudden, crushing impact of a series of distorted visions.

He could tell by the last complete memory that they had been thrown into the time when Katherine was lost to them. She had never told Alek where she had been during this period, and he had always wondered. And now, it seemed, his questions would remain unanswered, only giving rise to fresh ones. The pair quickly passed through scenes that neither he nor Katherine could make any sense of, and the prince realised that while she may have been near him during these moments or vice versa, the distortion could only stem from one other place. *Kaëden*. Before Alek could allow his mind to explore that possibility, they were snapped into a crystal clear recollection of the night she had been mysteriously left on Keldorne's doorstep.

"And you are sure of this?" asked the prince, the desperation in his voice rolling off of his tongue without even fighting to conceal itself. His hands shook, and his mouth dried up.

"We *are*, Your Highness," came the sound of Greyson's voice from next to the fire, the handler's golden eyes serious from behind his dishevelled mane of hair. "It is definitely the princess."

Alek sighed in relief, straining his ears to welcome the sound of the familiar heartbeat from beyond the castle walls. "Well then. Speak of this to no one! Instruct them to take her to the tower. Use the secret passageways. I will not have her lost to us again!"

"Of course, Your Highness."

As Greyson's stocky frame slid out of the room, off to do his master's bidding without hesitation, Katherine's body warmed as Alek fell to his knees before the dancing flames.

"Thank you!" he said, speaking to nobody. "Just...thank you!"

He sat watching the fire, preparing himself to see Katherine again. Preparing himself for whatever had happened to her. Preparing for the worst. Unable to delay it any longer, the prince took his leave and made his way towards the castle's furthest tower.

Katherine had always valued him dearly, even more so now that she could see things from his perspective. She hoped he would walk away from the trial with a similar thought.

The cold rain soaked Alek to the bone as he walked across the outer bridge, choosing to take a long way around to avoid suspicion and to ensure that he would not be followed. His worry for Katherine's well-being almost outweighed the intense anger at whoever was responsible for this. As he pushed open the door and laid eyes on her for the first time in fourteen years, his heart eased.

Hearing footsteps approach the door, the princess tried to keep her eyes open for long enough to see who had found her. She had been in and out of consciousness for hours. Her entire body relaxed as she recognised his face.

"Kat," Alek whispered as he knelt down next to the bed.

"It *is* you," she muttered with a small smile.

It was all the confirmation she needed to allow herself to give in to the rest that beckoned her. She closed her eyes and the certainty of her safety in Alek's presence eased her thoughts.

The prince immediately took her hands in his, and with every concerned breath he took, Katherine was brought to the verge of tears as he spent the rest of the night at her side.

"Where have you been?" asked Alek sometime before dawn, having realised that she had awoken.

His tone was reassuring and supportive, making her feel as though this was exactly where she should be. *Home,* in his arms.

Without pain, but still fatigued from her rescue, Katherine sat up in the bed and searched her mind. "I could not say, I am afraid. I was taken shortly before the final battle in the War of Kings." Her brow furrowed. "Everything went dark. I...I had no power."

"And after?"

"That is all I am able to recall. Everything until today is missing."

Alek swallowed hard, his expression troubled. "Katherine, it has been fourteen years since the War of Kings."

Katherine's eyes widened in shock. "What? How is that possible? Fourteen?"

"You cannot recall anything after you were taken?" Alek asked, his voice filled with concern.

"Nothing," Katherine replied, shaking her head in disbelief. "Nothing of what happened until the moment I awoke in the forest. A sealed package addressed to Alfred lay beside me." She looked down, confusion etched across her face. "How could I have lost so many years?"

Alek's expression suddenly changed from concerned to suspicious. "What was in the package?"

"I do not know. I was found before I could call on enough energy to open it. That is when they brought me here."

"Are you still hurt?" the prince asked, grabbing Katherine's wrists and checking her arms for signs of injury.

"I am alright. *Promise.*"

As the pair recalled how they had tried with all that they had to account for where she had been, they had never been able to find any answers. And as the years went on, neither Katherine nor Alek forgot how that mystery had plagued them and how it sat in the back of their mind each time one of them had been missing for too long. Even as they relived the events leading up to the council's interference in Katherine's personal affairs, events Alek had been directly involved in, the thought of someone being capable of kidnapping a pure descendant of power lingered in the background. Even after she and Marko had reunited, the unease remained.

"Brother, please! Come!" beckoned Marko from Katherine's side as Alek entered the West Wing's main living room, having only just returned from six brutal months locked in negotiations with Keldorne's military leaders on how to quell the ongoing war.

"And this?" Alek asked, eyebrows raised as Lucien handed him and Greyson each a glass of cider.

"Oh, just wait for it, Your Highness," advised Alfred, who held his drink most reluctantly. He preferred to serve rather than be served.

"Well, please raise your glasses," said Marko, holding Katherine tightly by her waist. "Princess Katherine and I are delighted to announce that we are engaged to be married."

"What?" exclaimed Alek as the glass slipped from his fingers and shattered on the floor.

Greyson hurried to clean the mess with a wave of his hand.

Marko coughed, taken aback, as a bit of cider went down the wrong way. "I beg your pardon?"

"Forgive me, brother. I did not mean to make it seem as though I were displeased. In fact, quite the contrary. The two of you make an excellent pair. My only concern is the council and what they would have to say about this, what our *brothers* would say."

"Since when do *you* care about what anyone else thinks as long as you know it to be right in your heart?"

"It is not *I*, brother, it is the—"

"Do not begin this nonsense again. If the prophecy were true, it would have happened by now. Besides, we have the council's support in this. We will move forward with or without your blessing."

Out of the corner of Alek's eye, Katherine caught a glimpse of Alfred raising his glass to his lips as he prepared for what would surely turn into a pointless debate, just as the topic had so many times when the royals were younger. Lucien and Greyson seemed to follow Alfred's lead, joining the handler where he stood watching as the royals dived into deep conversation.

Finally able to recall the fundamental differences in the opinion that Marko and Alek had once had about the prophecy, Katherine now wondered why it was that they had allowed things to unfold as they had. Knowing that she needed more information, however, she pushed out her own thoughts as she relived times long since put out of her mind.

Even the prince had to admit that most of their final days together were filled with happiness. As they enjoyed one of their favourite experiences together once more, his heart could not have been more content.

The pie smashed into Alek's face, sending cream flying everywhere, and he felt how Katherine laughed so hard that she could barely breathe. *This* was the Katherine Alek remembered. This was the Katherine he had missed having at his side. She could be so complex, so guarded, yet so carefree and vulnerable at the same time.

"Goodness, Kat!" laughed Alek, wiping cream from his eyes as he grabbed his own pie from the counter. "I think I might just be feeling sorry for Markovyas!" Without hesitation, he hurled the pie at the princess, inciting an hours-long battle that left Eyrondale's largest kitchen in ruins.

Nearing the end of memory lane, the pair were unaware that the waves of energy caused by their kiss had suddenly ceased, that the onlookers now waited nervously for the other shoe to drop.

The door creaked open and Alek entered the room, his palms sweaty as he closed it behind him and turned to look at Katherine. His green eyes widened, and he forgot to exhale for a moment, stunned by how beautiful she looked in her flowing white gown.

Katherine smiled at him in the mirror. "Thank you for meeting me."

Alek walked towards where she stood, admiring her reflection. "Of course."

She turned to face him, her heartbeat quickening as a hint of nervousness flickered across her expression. "I need to ask something of you."

"Anything."

With a deep breath, Katherine reached forward, taking his hands in hers.

"There is nobody I would rather have at my side on any other day of the year...in any other situation. That has not changed, nor will it ever change."

Alek narrowed his eyes, suspicious.

"Would you...would you give me away?"

"I beg your pardon?" asked the prince, a wide smile growing across his face. "Are...are you certain?"

"Of course I am. I could not face the deepest hell without you by my side. How in all the realms do you think I would be able to make it down the aisle any other way?"

Alek gazed into her eyes and inched closer. Squeezing her hands gently, he mustered the courage to ask her what he had been longing to ask her for an age. His hesitation rippled through his body as he paused to catch his breath.

"And this is what you truly long for, Katherine?" he asked. "Marrying my brother, I mean. I will do whatever it takes, whatever you ask. As long as it is what makes your heart most happy."

"It is."

"Very well. What kind of friend would I be if I let you walk down the aisle alone? It would be my deepest honour."

Katherine flung her arms around the prince's neck, relieved that he was offering his genuine support. Yet, beneath it, she could now feel the cold reluctance Alek had buried deep within.

After being nearly suffocated by Katherine's tight grip, Alek was released.

"Well then, Princess," said the prince, straightening his long formal overcoat, "I have a few final preparations to oversee, including checking in on the groom next door. I shall return shortly."

Alek turned and made his way across the room, pausing with his hand on the door handle. "Oh, and Katherine?" He glanced over his shoulder, a smirk tugging at the corners of his lips. "Be sure not to stumble out there."

The prince let out a boyish laugh as he ducked out of the room just as Katherine threw a pillow in the direction of his face. The princess giggled softly, shaking her head as she silently thanked the universe for his friendship.

She took a sip of her cider. It was barely a couple of minutes before Katherine heard the door open once again.

"Have you forgotten something?" she asked, thinking that Alek had returned, making no effort to look his way.

As no reply met her ears, Katherine glanced up at the door's reflection and spun around. A sinking feeling stirred in the pit of her stomach that caused Alek's heart to ache.

"What are you doing here, Lucien?"

"I apologise for this, Your Highness," whispered the handler, making his way towards her. "However, I must see my master's will through."

"Lucien, what are you—?"

Before she could finish her sentence, the room started to spin. It quickly grew dark as Katherine dropped to her knees.

"How?" she muttered, unable to summon the strength to fight against it.

Lucien reached to take the glass from her. "All I ask is that you not hold this against me upon your return, Princess," he said solemnly.

Before she could say another word, the world around her faded.

~

Just as the crowd had begun to question where the energy had disappeared to, there was movement in the centre of the symbol.

Coughing as he tried to catch his breath, Alek took his time rising to his feet after he and the princess regained consciousness from their sudden collapse. Katherine turned onto her back and clutched her chest, gasping. Uncomfortable though their pain was, it was bearable, for the most part. Considering that they shared significantly more memories than the others, both Alek and Katherine had assumed that the outcome of their kiss would be far worse than this.

As the pair strained for air, a purple light rose at their feet. It surrounded them in a smoky haze that spun around, growing brighter with each pass. Moving along the symbol's lines until it reached Alek's marker, it flashed to reveal the symbol for spirit carved beneath, before hurtling towards the barrier flame.

Fire and light collided, merging into an intense purple that climbed towards the sky, swaying from side to side in the wind, unthreatening yet powerful. Flickering as it passed through the clouds, it lit them up before exploding into the night. The ankle-height flame that had remained at the end of each task turned calm, and the familiar call of its power could be felt by those who were bound to its magic.

~

Katherine took the outstretched hand that hovered above her. As Alek helped her to her feet, her stomach gave a light flutter as their eyes met. A wide smile spread across her face.

"*Now* it makes more sense," she exclaimed, pressing through the pain.

"So, you *do* remember me then?" said Alek cheekily as he, too, broke into a grin.

Katherine shook her head and, as if they had the exact same thought, she leapt into Alek's arms as he opened them wide and closed them around her in a spine-cracking hug. Legs around his waist, holding on as he spun her around playfully, Katherine felt more at home now than she had up until that point.

The pair came to a stop, slightly dizzy, and Katherine leapt to the ground, laughing with him as though they had never been apart.

"I don't even know what to say," came Katherine's voice through the sounds of their joyous reunion.

"What do you mean?" Alek asked, his smile as contagious as ever.

"Just – thank you! For everything. You and Alfred have kept my kingdom running and I...could never say thank you enough."

Alek's face turned a deep shade of red. He bit his lip, sighed, and muttered under his breath, "It was nothing."

"Well!" called Alfred from across the clearing as he hurried towards the pair. "I must admit that I am very pleased to see this."

"As are we, Alfred," agreed Herlock, who looked upon the royals with satisfaction.

"We feared the worst, I am afraid," added Horus.

"Nonsense! Look at you all, always assuming things will go badly!" said Alek as he and Katherine stepped away from the symbol, joining the onlookers and Alfred, who seemed quite relieved not to have to duck and weave out of the way of flying furniture this time.

"You have to admit though, brother, we *did* have cause to worry," said Marko with a slight slur.

"You alright, Kat?" Emily asked, making her way to Katherine's side, ignoring what they were all sure would turn into another brotherly spat.

Katherine simply nodded with a smile, feeling quite relieved.

"So," said Alek, folding his arms across his chest as he took a step towards the princess. "Now that you know who I am, I think it's about time we have a little chat." His eyes narrowed. "Don't you?"

Those around them quietened down in an instant.

"And what are we?" blurted out Deacon. "Chopped liver?"

"My apologies, Prince Dàikonos," exclaimed Katherine without breaking Alek's gaze. Her expression turned serious. "However, Prince Aleksander and I have urgent matters of state to discuss."

Before anyone could protest, Katherine walked past the crowd and poured two full glasses of vodka from the bar. She paused only for a moment to look back at Alek, gesturing for him to join her, before she made her way across the courtyard, heading for the grounds.

"Aaaaaaaaaand there they go," sighed Marko, rolling his eyes.

"Meaning?" asked Deacon as they watched their brother hurry to catch up to the princess.

Marko patted Deacon on the shoulder and turned to make his way inside. "You'll see, little brother. None of us will be able to get a word in now."

"Well," said Alfred over the chatter, "dinner will be served at the usual time, so please feel free to make your way into the dining room when you are ready. I shall see you all soon."

The handler turned to accompany the council as they departed, leaving the mortals to linger on Marko's words alone, while Kaëden and the others left rather abruptly.

～

"Drink, anyone?" asked Jamie.

"Um, yeah," said Layla, many of the others nodding in agreement.

"Bayne?" he asked, shooting his friend a hesitant look.

Without a word, Bayne uncrossed his arms. He pushed himself off of the wall where he had been watching the festivities alone, and marched off, shaking his head.

"What's up with him?" asked Matthew, joining the group that had formed at the outdoor dining table.

"It's like he doesn't even *want* to get out of this," muttered Jennifer sourly.

"Either that, or there's a whole lot more to this than we might realise," said Aiden, taking his seat between Emily and Matthew, whose cheeks had suddenly lost their rosiness. "Ever think of that?"

"Don't tell me you're on *her* side?"

"There are sides now?" replied Aiden, eyebrows raised.

"Well...you know what I mean," said Jennifer under her breath, avoiding eye contact. "I think I'm just going to head upstairs."

"You sure?" asked Emily, looking concerned.

"Yeah. Fine."

"Alright, then. Get some rest."

They watched Jennifer head inside, and instead of imposing their concerns on their friends, they spent the hours leading up to dinner discussing all they had discovered in their latest research efforts, debating the potential consequences of the next kiss, and swapping stories of home and those they longed for.

"So," said Alek, taking a glass from Katherine as they walked across the sprawling grounds.

"Mmm?"

"Are you ready for your kiss with Kaëden?"

"Wait!" said Katherine, snapping back to the moment. "Is that really your first question?"

"Well, it's just—"

"Just what?"

"You two have a bit of a rough past, that's all."

"Well, from what I have read, I can handle Kaëden. I'm quite sure I have pretty much felt it all by now, so what difference will a little more war make? Besides, he seems to be on his best behaviour."

"Yeah," said Alek, rubbing his hand on his chin, the large ring on his index finger reflecting the light from a group of fireflies that danced in the air nearby. "About that—"

"Here we go." Katherine rolled her eyes and downed the rest of her drink.

"I'm just saying, Kat. It's not just the possible chaos your memories of your feud with Kaëden could cause." The prince ran one of his hands through his hair. He sighed. "You have a bit of explaining to do."

"Fine." Katherine scowled. "What do you want to know?"

"You know exactly what I want to know," Alek muttered, grabbing hold of her elbow and turning her to face him.

"How could I possibly know what you mean?"

"Don't play dumb with me. Out of everything, there's one piece of the puzzle that doesn't make sense, and you know it!"

She looked at him reluctantly. "Can we tackle that one another night?"

"Fine." Alek's grip tightened as she tried to tug her arm away. "But we *are* going to tackle it, Katherine."

"I know. But not today. After the trial. Can I just be happy to see you?"

The prince released her and a familiar grin returned to his face. "When are you ever *not* happy to see me?"

"Arse!" Katherine muttered, rolling her eyes again and taking a seat on the spot.

"Hey now!" chuckled Alek, bending to sit beside her. "A princess sitting on dewy grass. Oh, what would your subjects think?"

"Luckily for me, we appear to be quite alone." Katherine laughed and took a sip of her vodka, the glass having refilled itself as it waited for the royals to get over their stubbornness.

"Cheers," said Alek, tapping his glass to hers. "It's good to have you back."

"Well, not *all* the way back," she admitted, the sting of her drink lingering in her throat. "Kaëden holds the final key. I just need to get through that and the ceremony."

"Sure you want it back?" Alek asked, setting his glass down. He lay back, folding his muscular arms behind his head to gaze up at the stars.

"Why would I not?"

"You tell me. They seem to have quite a hold on you, these *humans*."

Katherine lay down beside the prince. "When you figure out why, enlighten me too, okay?"

"Yeah, yeah. Oh...and then there is everything with you and—"

"Not touching that topic, either."

"You're no fun! Here I was, so hoping you'd want to discuss your boy drama."

They burst into laughter and continued to speak away as the night went on, dinner crossing neither's mind, and all concept of time forgotten. They spoke late into the evening about all manner of kingdom business, Katherine's mortal lives, Alek's progress with uniting the outcast species, the power struggle between the kingdoms to the south, and more, until the first rays of sunlight brightened the castle grounds.

CHAPTER 16
PRINCE KAËDEN
OF CARDINALLIS

A lek had not had much rest since he and Katherine strolled back into the castle just after sunrise. Helping each other up to the third floor was quite a task all on its own, as the pair had successfully reminisced their way through several bottles of Russia's finest. Having agreed to take an excessively long shower to wash away the evidence of their evening, they parted ways to their respective suites without waking anyone.

Alek stood beneath the gleaming showerhead as streams of hot water pounded against his bare skin, massaging his neck before cascading off his flesh in glistening beads. He leant forward, hands bracing against the marble. For a moment, Alek allowed himself to be happy, free from the worry he had been carrying for far too many centuries.

She's back! he thought, not even trying to fight off a smile. It had been too long since he was able to feel any kind of relief. Alfred, Zachary, and even Greyson could not come close to Katherine, no matter how hard they had tried to help Alek run both kingdoms in her absence. *But she's back!*

As the prince stood there, his mind wandered, even if only for a moment, to the thought of Katherine doing exactly what he was, before he cut himself off. He quickly waved the faucet to its warmest setting, trying to snap himself out of it. He was reluctant to see her as anything other than his very best friend, his partner in war, his confidant. As his skin turned red from the heat, he welcomed the sting, hoping it would burn away the thoughts he refused to entertain.

Katherine's thoughts were focused on all that she had missed out on while she was away. For seven lifetimes, everything she had ever known had been lost to her, and she wondered whether she could ever make up for lost time.

It was one thing to remember Marko and the majority of what came with the memories of him, but she and Alek had, for most of their existence, lived side by side. The experiences that came with that were many. It was proving difficult to digest.

Katherine took a little more time to herself to enjoy the comforting heat of the steam before facing the day. Aware that it was not perhaps the best idea to forgo sleep, especially with what Alek had said about her and Kaëden's history the night before, she thought it would be best to grab a quick bite to eat from one of the kitchens and then rest in preparation for the final task.

Knowing it was likely that she would be hurtled through the air or injured in some other way, based on the past few days, Katherine reasoned she would be best off wearing something comfortable for when she faced her past with the eldest prince. As she threw on a quick outfit to retrieve her meal and, perhaps, a Bloody Mary, she chuckled and set aside a pair of jeans, a white tank top and a leather jacket from her closet for the next day.

It kept hitting her how much effort Alek and Alfred had gone through to modernise her world in her absence, and to ensure that her return would be as smooth as possible.

Katherine was intelligent enough not to make any sudden decisions or take any hard-line stances while parts of her memory still eluded her. While it had been easier to sit on the sidelines before this, she now knew more than enough to take back the reins of her kingdom. *One more,* she thought as she dried her hair. *One more day – that is all!*

Her hands shook as a flurry of thoughts raced through her mind. With so much to catch up on, she worried that the whirlwind would overwhelm her. As Katherine reinforced the wall that was keeping it all from flooding in too quickly, she chose to focus on trying to just get through the day.

Kaëden is tomorrow's problem.

~

Emily almost bumped into Layla and Brian as she shut her suite's door behind her. The couple had also chosen to freshen up after lunch before heading to the courtyard for the final task.

"Hey, Em!" greeted Layla with a smile. Even without her typical heeled footwear, Layla's slender frame towered over her sister.

"Hi, guys."

"You okay?" asked Brian, his cheeks redder than usual, giving away what he and his wife had been up to.

Emily pretended not to notice and tried to hide a smile. "Yeah, just a lot on my mind."

"Seems to be a theme around here," Layla said. She pointed to the door opposite them as it creaked open. "We were just about to grab Aiden. Let's head down."

They took the staircase just off of Matthew's room, taking them past the inner courtyard. As they moved through the castle, there was a strange haze that seemed to cloud the corridors. It was as if everyone they crossed paths with was more on edge than normal. And, from what they had read about Prince Kaëden in their research efforts, Emily could understand why.

Making their way outside for what would be the final time in this trial, Emily and her friends chose to settle in at the cocktail tables nearest the dining and bar area, as far out of the way of potential harm as possible while still being within earshot of the festivities.

"So," said Jamie, his voice unable to mask his nerves as he and the others joined the group. "Today's the day!"

The mortals exchanged apprehensive glances.

"Well, at least after this, we'll know where we stand," Emily said, finally. She raised the glass of champagne that stood before her on the table and downed it in one large gulp.

The others followed suit, each lifting their glass and drinking, unwilling to discuss what might happen after today.

"Ah! Getting started without us, I see?" exclaimed Alek, glancing Emily's way as he walked up to join Alfred and Zachary, who had just arrived from the armoury.

"Big day!" admitted Emily, taking a rather large sip from her glass, which had already refilled itself.

"Now you're getting it!" said the prince, winking at her as he took a glass of whisky from a passing castle keeper. "Even us immortals are thankful for the increased alcohol tolerance that comes with living in this castle. It makes life a hell of a lot easier."

"Brother!" came Deacon's voice as the youngest prince and his handler joined the group. Rawson bowed sharply to Alek before moving to stand against the wall alongside Greyson and Daniel.

Emily's face flushed.

Alek nodded to his brother and handed him a drink, gesturing towards the nearest dining room doorway. Moments later, Marko and Lucien walked through it, followed soon after by Bayne, one of the last to arrive, who made his way past everyone in a daze.

The castle keepers in attendance, however, appeared rather excited despite the fear they had exuded in the eldest prince's presence since his arrival. The creatures considered themselves fortunate to have been chosen to serve this evening. The wars between Eyrondale and Cardinallis were the stuff of legends.

The idea of Kaëden emerging as the ultimate champion, destined to prevail, either struck fear into the hearts of those within the communities of power or was revered as the key to an unstoppable alliance. A simple kiss between the two royals would be historical enough. Even the prince's brothers seemed intrigued by the prospect, however uncomfortable it made them at the same time. There was a different kind of energy present as the Consilio Statera arrived to preside over the final task.

"Ah! Good afternoon," said Herlock, raising his hands in a warm welcome as a wide smile spread across his face.

With a flurry of greetings and a bow to the princes, the council took their usual place as they waited for Katherine and Kaëden to arrive. And as usual, they remained eerily silent, even as the wait stretched on, and soft chatter eventually broke out among the crowd.

The sun had started to set by the time Kaëden finally walked through the fluttering white drapes of the living room doors.

"Your Highness!" exclaimed Horus with relief as he and the other council members shot to their feet and immediately dipped into a low bow.

"So," said the prince, his voice quiet and precise, devoid of emotion. He rubbed his hands together and made his way towards the centre of the clearing, looking uncomfortable. "Where is she?"

"Your Highness, we—"

Kaëden's voice rose, but his gaze remained fixed on the symbol. "Well?"

Before the council could scramble for an excuse for the princess's absence, colour flooded Herlock's face as he looked over the prince's shoulder.

"*She* has arrived," Katherine said, approaching from the west.

Kaëden shifted slightly to his right, offering no acknowledgement of the princess's presence beyond muttering, "You are late."

"As are you."

"Never mind. You are here now, and we can proceed," said Herlock, visibly happier than he had been minutes before. "Please, enter the circle."

The royals nodded and stepped over the ankle-height flame. At once, the fire surged upward, rebuilding the blazing barrier that enclosed them.

~

"Are you ready?" asked Katherine, glancing up at the prince, hesitant about what was to come.

"Almost." Kaëden took off his jacket and tossed it on the floor beside them. He rolled up the white sleeves of his shirt and sighed. "Ready."

There was no ignoring the obvious care the prince took with how he presented himself. Katherine had read in Alfred's files and the library's books about his meticulous grooming habits and impeccable manners. Just as she had read of his savagery.

"Alright then," he said, his eyes, green as an untouched forest at twilight, meeting hers. "Shall we?"

As their gazes clashed, sharp as a blade's edge, tension coiled between them like a drawn bowstring. She gulped, taking a step towards him.

"There is no need to be frightened," Kaëden whispered, his voice softer and more gentle than she had heard it since his arrival at the castle. His breath was warm against her lips, his presence overwhelming, though he remained perfectly still – waiting.

Katherine's breath caught, her pulse thrumming in her ears as something stirred. Something buried, restless, clawing its way to the surface. The sensation was foreign, yet it settled into her bones as if it had always been there, hidden.

She should pull away. She should not want this.

And yet, something deep within her whispered that she already had.

As their lips met, the world around her shattered. A wave of energy blazed its way through Katherine, blinding, all-consuming, wrapping around her like fire and lightning intertwined. It was searing, electric, almost too much and yet not enough. But before she could grasp what was happening, the ground beneath her mind gave way, and she was pulled into the farthest reaches of memories, perhaps best left forgotten.

The onlookers watched in silence, their emotions a whirlwind of awe, relief, and disbelief as all eyes remained fixed on the royals' embrace.

The instant the pair's lips met, inch-high flames sprung up in the courtyard. Tiny though the fires were, the princes were not leaving anything to chance. Determined to extinguish the flames with their powers before they could spread and pose a risk, neither Kaëden's brothers nor their handlers were willing to take any risks.

Aiden and Matthew seemed intent on testing their limits, downing beer after beer as they lingered at the edge of the gathering. Jennifer, meanwhile, cast sharp glances in Bayne's direction, visibly upset that he had chosen to stand by himself, *again*, rather than engage with any of them. Everyone, from the castle staff to the mortals, even the handlers, had taken notice of the distance between the couple. No one could recall the last time Jennifer and Bayne had shared a real conversation, nor had they slept in the same bed since the night before the champion selection. The royal suites held their allure, but rumours had spread like wildfire through the castle's grapevine that Jennifer had made her choice. She preferred the solitude of being two floors away from Katherine.

As the exchange between the princess and Kaëden continued, the flames surged across the courtyard with increasing speed and intensity, igniting in multiple areas and expanding unchecked. Some of the castle keepers rushed to conjure buckets of water or bags of sand, while others used what power they possessed to subdue the fires.

Katherine and Kaëden relived the moments they had spent together as children, forced into shared gatherings with their handlers. They once again experienced the polite, measured exchanges of their youth at royal balls, when decorum kept them civil.

But as their minds drifted deeper, the memories darkened. They recalled the lessons learnt with age – the weight of their duties, the cost of missteps, and the consequences of misusing their abilities.

Kaëden's thirst for control and his proclivity for violence only grew as he built his following. His power spread like a plague, turning, infecting, and multiplying at an alarming rate. He seized territory and waged war against his siblings as they, too, carved out kingdoms of their own.

Katherine felt the fire in him, the relentless hunger for control that drove him forward. It consumed her, pulling her into the intoxicating rush of an addiction she never saw coming.

Adrenaline crashed through Katherine's entire being as she and Kaëden stood facing each other, noses so close they could have been touching. As the pair relived the final moments of their first battle, all that separated them was the thin barrier shield that Katherine had so cleverly thought to put in place at the edge of her most protected lands and properties years before.

The prince snarled in fury, the freezing rain that fell to the earth around them turning into sheets that came down with violent force. Katherine laughed as she watched him realise he had to admit defeat. Even with his large forces, she had mastered enough of the purest powers that she was able to thwart even his heavy-weighted attack on her southern communities.

Kaëden's eyes were black with rage as he backed away from the border, retreating into the shadows of the night, his soldiers following. As Katherine felt the anger radiate from within the prince, she wondered whether the present-day Kaëden still felt such hatred for her beneath all the silence he had brought with him into the trials.

"That was incredible," came Alek's voice, cutting through the rain, ringing in Katherine's ears as though he were right beside her.

"When it comes to Kaëden, I think it will only be a matter of time before we face each other in battle again," whispered the princess, the wind carrying her words back to Alek who had held back to direct the rest of the generals. "We need to be ready."

Watching as streams of blood flowed on the rocks beside her, dancing their way past her feet, Katherine's heart raced with the worry of how Kaëden would choose to retaliate. She returned her blood-soaked sword to its place on her back and cast one last look at the impenetrable force field before making her way back to her armies.

～

Between the princes, handlers, Zachary, and the castle keepers, the fires that had begun spreading faster and burning more fiercely seemed, for the most part, manageable. However, Emily and the others had learnt not to assume they had faced the worst of these tasks' effects until the very end.

The pair of royals plunged into memory after memory, and at last, Katherine understood why Alek had been so concerned. Though their shared experiences were fewer and more widely spaced than those with anyone else besides Deacon, they were far more extreme.

～

"Enough!" Katherine shouted, slamming her hands onto the table with an explosive crack that split it in half as she shot to her feet.

Kaëden stopped in his tracks, his hand wrapped around Marko's throat, both snarling fiercely at each other.

"I will not stand for this kind of behaviour while we hold council!" she said, voice quivering with anger. "We are here to discuss whether we should intervene in the escalating war between species that is devastating the eastern regions. We are not here to fight like children. And if that is your aim, take it up with me."

The eldest prince grunted and released his brother from his grip, however reluctantly. As Katherine felt his hands loosen, she feared that she would soon experience them around her own neck.

Katherine took her seat and continued as calmly as she could. "Now, the council has asked us to deliberate, and that is exactly what we will do. Do we overrule the kings and stop this war before it goes any further, or do we sit back and wait to see its outcome?"

"I say we do what we have always done," came a cold voice from the doorway.

"Prince Cartesius," exclaimed Herlock. "We had come to the conclusion that you would not be joining us today."

"Well, you know me," said Carter with a sneer, running his fingers along the table as he walked past his brothers to take a seat at the far end, shaking the raindrops from his long, black hair. "Hate to disappoint."

A chill ran down the princess's spine as if she were plunging towards the ground. Her body tensed as she watched Carter take his rightful seat at the table. Whether in that moment or all those years ago, the effect he had on her remained the same.

"Come now. Do not allow me to interrupt," said the prince as he put his boots up on the table, sprawling out as though he were there for leisure.

"As I was saying—"

"Yes, yes. You want us to fix our kids' problems for them. I say let them fight."

"Prince Cartesius—"

"Actually, Prince Dàikonos agrees," interrupted Rawson's voice, his eyes fearful at the sight of Cartesius and Kaëden together. And, from what Katherine could sense stirring within the eldest prince's insides, the handler had every right to be afraid.

"What?" said Alek, his focus drawn away from his brothers.

"P...Prince Dàikonos has asked me to vote against interference."

"Two against. What do you say, Your Highnesses?" asked Horus, glancing between Katherine and the other royals.

"Against," muttered Kaëden, his eyes fixed on Carter, lips curled in disgust.

"As expected," muttered Katherine, rolling her eyes.

"I am against it, too," said Alek.

"What?"

"Katherine, you know we should just let them figure it out amongst themselves. This is not the sort of thing we need to stick our noses into."

The princess's chalice clattered to the floor as she knocked it off the table, sending it flying across the room.

"Fine! Have it your way, then. But, so help me, anyone who spills Eyrondale blood shall have the blood of his loved ones drawn in return."

Enraged, Katherine gave the sons of Magic a final look of disapproval, her eyes lingering on Cartesius before she marched out of the room.

The royals shifted through echoes of the past, one after another, until the princess felt smoke hit her face.

A sudden wave of hopelessness washed over her as Katherine's world dimmed. Cold, heavy metal cuffs snapped around her wrists. Disoriented and drained, she could hear footsteps drawing closer, the hum of chanting growing louder with each one. Too faint to summon her power, she was lifted off the ground, then everything vanished into the deepest black before she could make sense of it.

What felt like an instant later, Katherine awoke in a damp stone room, behind a wall of bars that caged her in. There were no windows, and the only light filtering through came from a large fireplace on the far end of the area outside her cell.

With what little strength she had, Katherine moved to grab hold of the bars. As she did, a searing pain shot through her body. Thankfully, she was still able to heal quickly. Taking a closer yet cautious look, she noticed small, barely visible carvings on the iron.

"Certainly, there is no possible way for this to go wrong," Katherine muttered to herself, shaking her head. Knowing better, but determined to exhaust whatever options she had available to her, she raised her hand to create a glowing ball of blue fire. "Here we go."

She hurtled the fireball towards the cell door. Ducking for cover as it bounced off of that which kept her captive, Katherine's heart sank as the flames tore through the old cabinet that sat on the side wall of the room, reducing it to ash.

"I would suggest that you avoid using any form of power or magic in there," came a voice from the depths of the shadows. The raspy sound cut through the cold air, sharp and sudden, echoing as it hit the stone walls surrounding them.

"Who are you?" Katherine moved to peer into the emptiness, where the only light flickered violently as if enraged by the audacity of being talked over. As the fire's anger grew in the distance, its brightness did not. Katherine was unable to make out the source of her curiosity, let alone which cell contained it.

"Just another of His Highness's *special* captives. As you are. Princess Katherine, I assume?"

"You know who I am?"

"My dear, there are not many in our world who do *not* know of you. And, based on how the guards have been talking of late, I would say that anyone of lesser importance would not have struck such fear in their hearts."

A faint smile flickered across Katherine's face. "And *again*, who might you be?"

"For tonight, I have no name. Perhaps I shall have one tomorrow."

The voice faded, and Katherine took it as the end of the discussion. Exhausted, she did her best to fight against the invisible ropes tugging persistently at her eyelids. But she could not touch the bars without the iron scorching her skin. Any power she managed to summon rebounded off her cage without leaving a trace. Kaëden had thought of everything. Drained from battle and from the effects of her capture, Katherine reluctantly lowered herself to the ground and leant her back against the stone.

The prince felt how Katherine's mind remained alert, though her body slept. Her panic gripped him each time she opened her eyes when he was near, unable to tell how many hours or days had passed, and he sensed the twinge of fear that crept in as she realised she had no plan.

But nothing could have prepared him for the way her hunger ignited the moment the scent of blood reached her. Sudden. Primal. All-consuming.

Katherine's eyes widened at the sight of the werewolf being dragged through the dimly lit dungeon hall. As the fire sent orbs of light soaring towards each sconce, the dark trail of blood the creature left behind made her mouth water. Her jaw clenched as the smell grew stronger with each passing heartbeat. There was an anger inside of her that was fuelled into being at its sweet scent, longing for release.

Kaëden had, many times, wondered what it was like for Katherine to be lost in the bloodlust. And now, there was no escaping it.

"Here!" snarled the prince. He grabbed the wolf by the scruff of its neck and launched it across the floor to stop just short of the bars that kept his prisoner so safely at bay.

"What is this?" demanded Katherine, struggling to maintain her composure. She had no idea how long it had been since she had last silenced her craving – since the day she had been captured.

"Exactly what you have been longing for all this time."

"How—"

"I can see why you and my brother were so desperate to keep this little secret to yourselves. It is quite the weakness, is it not?" Kaëden breathed, moving across the room in less than a second to press himself up against the cage door, mere inches from where Katherine's eyes were starting to betray her.

Kaëden sensed the hatred Katherine had harboured towards him for so long, now drowned beneath an uncontrollable hunger.

"Weakness." The prince sneered as he watched Katherine's face contort in frustration. "Or advantage."

She narrowed her eyes sceptically, but the smell of blood distracted from her captor's words, causing a hard pounding in her head. Kaëden smiled, then, without warning, seized one of the bars. With a single, effortless yank, he tore the door from its hinges and sent it crashing into the opposite wall.

Caught somewhere between a longing for blood and a thirst for revenge, Katherine hesitated, her eyes glowing a deep gold as she searched his face for any insight into this trickery.

The prince stepped back, hands clasped behind him, a smirk playing on his lips. After a moment, he lifted one hand in a lazy gesture.

"Please," he instructed, motioning to the body sprawled on the floor, its owner battling to hold on to his last breath.

Choosing the hunger over all reason, Katherine dropped to her knees and grasped the wolf's black, hairy shoulder. It was barely able to let out a howl before Kaëden was lost in the depths of satisfying an indescribable desire as Katherine plunged her teeth into the beast's flesh, piercing the hard skin to drink from the crimson well within. The prince felt an unmatched rush as the metallic liquid slid down the princess's throat. He had never experienced anything like it.

Every encounter that followed was a battle of wills – barbed words and sharp glares, fire meeting fire, neither willing to yield.

But as the years passed, something insidious crept in. Their exchanges, once brimming with hostility, became more measured. The heat of their mutual hatred started to burn with something deeper than the urge to tear each other apart. When Kaëden ensured Katherine had werewolf blood each week, he did more than sustain her – he watched her succumb to hunger, to the darkness it unearthed in her. And each time, the prince pushed, prodded, tested the edges of her restraint, fascinated by the warrior who, aside from Carter, was the only one he had ever considered his equal.

Yet he kept her weak, never quite strong enough to be a real threat. Or so Kaëden told himself.

After just over a decade as his captive, the royals were thrown into a memory that Katherine would never have expected, given their long history. If she had not been forced to relive the events leading up to it, she would have thought the power of the kiss to be faulty.

Kaëden's chest rose and fell with steady breaths, but his hands curled into fists at his sides. He should have pulled away. He should have said something – anything – to regain control of the moment. But he only stood there, watching Katherine, transfixed.

Rising from the floor, her feet covered in the now-cold crimson that had flowed from the wolf's body, Katherine moved towards her captor. After delivering the princess her first wolf that first week, Kaëden had ordered her transfer to a more fitting cell – one buried in the depths of the dungeon, where even the guards preferred not to linger. But, with his prized flame walkers being sent to devour a city up north, there was no one he trusted to guard his most valuable prisoner but himself.

Now, for the first time since Katherine's arrival, they were truly alone.

As Kaëden sensed the princess's rapid heartbeat slow to the brink of stopping, the fire's warmth at his back was nothing compared to the searing heat threatening to burst through his veins. There was nothing he could do but surrender, letting his mind and body drown in the sheer exhilaration of it.

The prince wrapped an arm around Katherine's waist and pulled her close, their lips meeting before she could protest. She wrenched away just as quickly.

But one kiss was all it took for her descent into madness. In less time than it took either of them to blink, she seized Kaëden by the neck, her nails threatening to puncture his flesh, and dragged his mouth back to hers. The forbidden desire that ignited in her chest was a storm she had no hope of taming.

The taste of blood on their lips as they became one seemed to only fuel their fiery exchange. Ignoring all logic and history, the pair lost themselves in the thrill of the cold stone beneath them, knowing it would be unable to speak of the secrets it bore witness to.

Suddenly, it all made more sense. The missing time. The distorted memories. They were finally falling into place. Whether it had been the bloodlust, their hatred for each other, or their forced interactions during her imprisonment, somehow it had all culminated into an unbelievable passion that had brightened even Kaëden's dark soul.

~

Without warning, every flame the princes and staff had been battling in the courtyard extinguished at once, leaving behind a frigid cold in their absence.

"What's happening?" came Layla's voice as frost clawed at the castle windows.

Mere seconds after the liquor in their cups met the open air, it solidified into ice, spreading in jagged fractures across the surface.

Even the snot bubble at Aiden's nose froze where it hung, splintering. He yanked it away in alarm, but the deathly chill clung to his skin, creeping outward like an infection that stung his flesh. Alek rushed to help the mortals as Greyson and Alfred moved to contain the cold as it snaked across the floor, reaching for the walls and crawling up the furniture.

"Not sure," Jamie muttered, his gaze shifting to the gazebo in the far corner of the courtyard, where a thin veil of fog was creeping in.

Emily caught the nervous glances exchanged between Alek and Marko as they followed Jamie's gaze.

~

"They would never understand how this happened, let alone that we allow it to continue," admitted Katherine, as Kaëden paced before the fireplace.

"We cannot hide this, Katherine," he replied softly, clearly playing out various scenarios in his mind. "And we know just as little about all of this as they would."

"Going back would mean that they would bleed me out. *Starve me* until the blood flows no more through my veins. And what would you do then? Would we even be what we are now?"

"Very well. But you know that we cannot escape this."

"Well then," whispered Katherine, getting up from the chair and making her way over to the prince, "I suggest that we put it far out of mind."

Her hands wrapped around his bare waist, and the warmth of his skin increased at her touch. As Katherine placed her lips on his shoulder blade, there was little that Kaëden could do but agree.

There was no denying the feelings stirring deep within Katherine. As she struggled to reconcile her past with the present, one thing was clear – something was amiss. She understood why they would have kept it, kept *them* a secret, given their history. But now, as she relived everything they had once felt, there was no explanation for why these memories had vanished entirely from her mind for so many centuries.

Katherine had no recollection of them, even as she now lived them. It was unlike anything she had experienced with the other champions.

Kaëden growled, closing his eyes at the princess's touch, his skin tingling each time she kissed his flesh. "You do this on purpose."

"Are you protesting?" she breathed, brushing his ear with her lips.

A satisfied grin spread across Kaëden's face. "It is still under advisement."

"Well then, best I do more to convince you."

"Best we get started then, Princess. This is going to take a while." Kaëden shifted in her grasp before hoisting her into the air, their bodies aligning, as their lips met in a heated clash of desire.

After living over a decade of a life she never knew she had lived, it was the next revelations that would make everything Katherine thought she knew crumble.

The prince's heartbeat quickened as he hesitantly placed a hand on Katherine's stomach. His insides ached as if he already knew this was nothing more than an impossible dream.

"How...how can this be?" Kaëden asked, voice hushed, barely daring to speak the words aloud.

"I would not have thought that it was," admitted Katherine, waiting nervously for his reaction. "None of us would have."

Taking her hands in his, Kaëden looked deep into her golden eyes. "It matters not. As long as it *is*. That is all that should draw our focus."

Katherine's emotions surged, struggling beneath the weight of the bloodlust. Kaëden felt it too, her feelings for him growing stronger, more undeniable than either had once been willing to believe.

"Focus is exactly what we should not draw."

"I agree," he said, reaching for a thick blanket and draping it over her shoulders. The air in the cell was cold, the damp walls offering little comfort. "They would not understand."

"Where there was little to no chance that they would have understood before, there is even less now. Not when we do not yet understand it ourselves."

"This is one secret that cannot remain hidden forever." Kaëden exhaled, his grip on the blanket tightening before he met Katherine's gaze. "But I will not have you lingering in the darkness of my dungeons any longer. You will be moved upstairs while we make sense of it."

Katherine's lips parted, surprise flickering across her face. She searched for any trace of hesitation in his expression but found none.

"This does not change what you are," continued the prince, his voice quieter but no less firm. "You are still my prisoner. But for now...let us enjoy what is only ours."

～

Emily gasped as she looked out at the courtyard, watching those scrambling to contain the task's effects. The orange, yellow, and red roses that had once brightened the space ignited, their petals curling into flames that drew in and swallowed the frozen remnants of the royals' kiss in seconds.

"Wow!" exclaimed Layla from her side, following her sister's gaze.

Captivated by the beauty of the hypnotic light, the sisters seemed to forget about the potential risk the fires posed.

～

Carter threw Katherine through the air as if she were nothing to him. The wall cracked as her back hit against the stone before she fell to the floor. He advanced towards her, Kaëden experiencing every shred of dread that both he and Katherine had felt at that moment.

As Carter's fingers took hold of her throat and tightened, he raised the princess from the ground and smiled, leaning in to whisper in her ear.

"I warned you not to stand in my way, Katherine."

Struggling to break free from his chains, out of the corner of his eye, Kaëden saw a shimmer of metal as Carter reached beneath his cloak. Unable to make a move against it, the eldest prince watched in horror as the long, thin blade of Cartesius's sword plunged into Katherine's abdomen.

A sudden fury blazed through Kaëden's body, and allowed him to draw on every ounce of strength that he was able to conjure to overcome the spell-cast restraints and race to her side.

Having not expected Kaëden to rediscover his strength so quickly, Carter backed up towards the window. Smiling, having clearly seen some success in whatever plan he had dared to execute, he appeared to show hesitation only at the thought of abandoning the sword that still lingered in Katherine's gut, pinning her to the wall. But clearly knowing not to test Kaëden's thirst for vengeance, with one last sneer, Carter waved to his fuming brother and jumped playfully into the night – gone without a trace.

Kaëden grabbed the weapon's long, intricately patterned handle and pulled it carefully from Katherine's stomach. He sighed, relieved at knowing that they could not be killed by anything known to this existence. He only had to wait for Katherine's wounds to heal. But now, as the cool stone pressed against Katherine's back, his heart sank with hers the moment she recognised the blade.

As her memories returned of not only this night but those linked to it, Katherine hoped the recollections she had still to endure would not reveal the true nature of the blade that lay tainted by her life force. Not to Kaëden. Not to anyone.

Identifying it from one of the stories that she had heard as a child, the panic that she felt intensified, bringing with it a sense of fear that she had not experienced in centuries. *Impossible*, she thought, longing to be wrong. But, as she struggled to fight against the pain of the moment, her thoughts were pushed aside as the experience continued.

Katherine's wounds were not healing, not fully, and certainly not as quickly as they should have been. Kaëden's concern threatened to drown them both as he held hands over the open wound in desperation, closing his eyes and muttering an incantation that saw a burst of white light flash from his hands and disappear into Katherine's body. Minutes passed, but her wounds finally tightened.

Ignoring all reason, Katherine got to her feet and made her way towards the sword, fighting the pain. Its silver blade glistened with a gruesome sheen that was clearly a mark of its first step in the dance of war. The trinity knots on the cross guard, a symbol of what had, in more modern times, become known as a representation of everlasting love, remained unsullied, catching the ambient light of the room as if whispering secrets into the air. The heat of the recent encounter lingering on its textured, black grip, carrying the residue of a life extinguished in the fervour of combat.

The reality of what happened hit Katherine harder than any loss ever had, and her eyes filled instantly with tears that could not be held at bay.

"He is gone," she whispered, pressing her hand to her abdomen as what had once cradled the precious life within deflated with breathtaking speed.

"How?" Kaëden demanded, his voice edged with raw disbelief.

"This blade. It—"

"Katherine, I—"

She held a hand up to silence the prince.

"Kaëden, I have heard stories of this blade, and there is no arguing against it. Legend has it that it was forged by Fate as a means to maintain the balance between the Nine Strands of Power. If we are to exist, then so must a means to end us. I had always thought it to be a folktale, a story to scare us. But this blade? It *can* kill us. It is the only thing that can."

"Nothing can kill us, Katherine."

"Kaëden, touch me. Tell me if you can feel him."

The prince rested a hand over Katherine's stomach, dread coiling in his chest as the truth settled over him that she was right. Their child, heir to both of their kingdoms and the future balance of all power, the miracle that had defied the prophecy, was gone.

~

As they watched the pair in their final recollection, the mortals' eyes, as well as those of many of the castle keepers, grew wide with fear. From the centre where Katherine and Kaëden were standing, a fierce, red light spread towards the barrier flames. Kaëden's placeholder on the pentacle glowed brightly, transforming into the symbol for fire. Unlike the others, this light did not dance. Instead, it thrashed, driven by a violent need to break free.

It struck the outer circle, erupting into flames that swelled hotter and higher with each breath, scorching everything in its path. Quick to react, the princes used their power to repel the flames, keeping them from reaching those that meant so much to Katherine. The humans took cover against the far wall, fearing they would be engulfed by the flames, as the castle grew warmer around them.

"It's too strong!" Alek shouted as he tried his utmost to contain the fiery product of Kaëden and Katherine's kiss.

"We won't need to hold it for long. Just long enough!" cried Lucien, rushing forward to help. He and the other handlers worked together to create a shield to prevent the flames from spreading any further.

~

The pain of their loss was too much for Katherine to take. But there was no avoiding it. Their child dying at Carter's hand gave birth to an intense rage inside of her that would not be quelled. Kaëden felt it rise in her chest as he fought against not only the crippling torment of his own grief at that moment but Katherine's insatiable thirst for revenge. Knowing what lay ahead, that Katherine was about to know exactly how he had stolen this moment from her, the prince waited for what he knew would, once they awoke from this, turn into a reckoning.

"He will suffer for what he has done!" promised Katherine as she left Kaëden's arms and marched towards the window, intending to begin her search for the fool who had just killed her unborn child. But the prince was too quick.

"I cannot let you go after him, Katherine," said Kaëden sternly, blocking her path. "You have no idea where he is or what he is capable of at this point."

"But I—"

"No!" he snapped, seizing her by the arms and pulling her against him. His grip was firm, unyielding. "I will not lose you, too."

Katherine protested against it, but she was still too weak. "I will not stop hunting him until I see his head on a spike, Kaëden! He took this from us. We have the weapon. He *will* die for this. Only after his voice is hoarse from begging me to end whatever it is that I decide to impose as punishment."

No matter how badly Kaëden had wanted to agree with her and give in to his rage, he simply pulled her closer.

A sudden stillness seized the prince's eyes. "I cannot allow you to do this."

Katherine felt him battling against anger, his heart and mind desperately searching for a clear path forward, one where he would not lose her. Yet, at the same time, she was so furious with her younger self for admitting the truth about the blade while bearing the unfathomable weight of the loss she had just experienced that she was not focused enough to brace for what was to come – what she should have seen coming, as it was straight out of a page in her own strategy book.

"You will never know how sorry I am for this, Katherine," he whispered, brushing her hair from her face and tracing his fingers gently along her cheek. "But I know you. You will not let this be. And I cannot have you risking your life for this."

He gulped as he prepared to say goodbye to her, for what would certainly be far too long.

"What are you—"

"This will be the most selfish thing I ever do. But I would rather see you hate me and be alive than love me and be lost to me forever. I shall ensure the blade's safety and entrust it to Alfred. I will not tell him what it is, but knowing his loyalty to you, he will lock it far away from where anybody, especially my brother, could ever find it. It will be as though it never happened."

There was fear in Katherine's eyes as the prince's body went tense. "What are you doing, Kaëden?"

He kissed her forehead. "You will remember this one day when you need to. But for now, my Nightfire, this is the only way I know how to keep you."

Before the princess could react, Kaëden stepped back and extended a hand towards her. A burst of bright purple light shot forward, too fast for her to evade. In her mind's eye, Katherine watched as every memory of her and Kaëden's relationship, of their child, of Carter's attempt at their lives, began to disappear, fading into the darkness until nothing was left other than her hatred for him before he had taken her captive.

～

The flames raged into an inferno, burning out of control. Even as the princes and handlers fought to contain it, the fire only grew larger and hotter. Then, without warning, it plunged to the ground and vanished as if it had never existed, leaving only wisps of steam rising from the stone.

No barrier.

No symbols carved into the courtyard.

Only the orb that glowed from where it appeared at the royals' feet.

Their eyes snapped open as an invisible force tore them apart, hurling them through the air. Katherine slammed into the wall behind the dining table. Kaëden crashed onto the floor near the staircase leading to the grounds with a bone-jarring thud.

Katherine's mouth opened in a silent scream. The pain was so immense it stole even her voice. Her body convulsed, every nerve set ablaze as she lay frozen, trapped in agony she could not express.

Across the courtyard, Kaëden hunched over, clutching his chest. Hoarse, ragged cries tore from his throat as each fresh wave of torment struck him down. His knees buckled again and again, his limbs refusing to hold him upright as the relentless force battered him without mercy.

Then, as suddenly as it had come, it disappeared.

A dull ache remained within Katherine, leaving her weak. She gritted her teeth and reached for the nearest chair, using it to steady herself as she forced herself upright. Her mouth was dry, scraping like sandpaper with every breath.

Kaëden's chest finally loosened, and as he straightened, their eyes met.

"Are you okay?" Alek asked Katherine as he raced towards her.

She nodded her head, unable to speak. A nearby castle keeper rushed to fetch a glass of water.

She downed the icy drink, never taking her eyes off Kaëden.

She now understood why the prince had not killed her each time they had met in battle since the War of Kings had ended. She understood why her memories of him had always been so unclear. This revelation had, in an instant, changed Katherine's entire outlook towards him. It challenged everything she thought she knew. It was as though she were seeing him with new eyes. Seeing him as if for the first time. Seeing what lay beneath the savage warrior she had always loathed. It was too much.

Katherine straightened, tempering her expression as she walked past Alek, Marko, and the rest of the crowd that was desperate to see if she was okay. As she crossed the clearing towards Kaëden, he rose from the floor, preparing himself for whatever anger was about to come his way – for whatever Katherine intended to do to him for his betrayal.

Hurrying to collect the orb that had taken with it any trace of the trial, Herlock tucked it inside his cloak discreetly, leaving nothing behind.

Exchanging a satisfied look with Horus and Dolos, Herlock gave a nod to those who noticed before leading the way back through the castle, leaving the others to handle the consequences of the task without aid. Just as they always did.

≈

"Kat! Katherine!" called Alek, chasing after her. But she waved the prince off and headed towards the nearest staircase.

Alek hesitated. It was clear he wanted to follow her, just as Emily did, but they honoured her command and remained in the courtyard. She walked past Kaëden, leaving him untouched and unscathed as he struggled to fully recover from the effects of their kiss.

As Katherine descended the stairs, aware that almost every eye was on her, she fought the urge to lean against each rose-filled pot to rest and catch her breath. She paused here and there, but only when the weight of hiding the pain that threatened to burst from her chest became a little more than she could handle. She was determined to do this alone.

This was different from when she had experienced pain with Marko and Bayne in the earlier days of the trial. This was a burning within her that grasped at her very lungs with each breath she took. Katherine looked down at her trembling hands. Her vision flickered in and out of focus. One moment she was present, the next, a wave of memories crashed over her, knocking her off balance.

She moved deeper into the castle grounds, battling to keep herself upright as the pieces of her life wove their way back into place. Only when she was far enough from the ever-watchful gaze of Zachary's security cameras did she let herself collapse against the trunk of a towering oak, its roots stretching towards one of the larger ponds that led to the Forgotten Woods.

Katherine lay there for what felt like hours, memory after memory slamming into her. Everything hurt. It was as though every fibre of her being was set on fire over and over again. Recollections that spanned an uncountable amount of lifetimes flooded in without filter, and she silently endured the raw agony of stitching together nearly her entire existence in one go. As the pain grew steadily more intense, she passed out.

CHAPTER 17
THE UNKNOWN HERO

K atherine opened her eyes to near darkness. Sitting up, it took
her a minute to realise that she was no longer out in the cold.
Climbing off of the firm yet soft bed, she walked towards the
fire that flickered gently in the fireplace opposite her.

Watching the flames dance, Katherine figured that she must have
been inside for a few hours at least. *But who would bring me here?* she
thought, looking around. She recognised it as one of the guest bedrooms
on the ground floor of the castle, leading out to the northern grounds.

These rooms had always been reserved for use by general guests who
were looking for something smaller, and more intimate than the first-floor
suites. The upper floors were for her court's more prominent members,
with the first floor reserved for the general court, the second for nobility
and those in her council, and the third for royalty and those Katherine
trusted most. Even her current suite would have been easily accessible by
anyone on the grounds at the moment. *So why here?*

She whispered to the fire, urging it to grow as a chill seeped into her bones, despite not a single window being opened. Even with the extra light, Katherine found no sign of her mysterious rescuer. She crossed the room to the double doors and pushed them open with ease. *So this is how we got in.*

The tall, hedged wall, grown to keep the large patio private, hid any sign of life that might be moving about out on the grounds. No figures sat at the cast iron bistro set in the corner. No animals scurried across the area. Nothing.

Against her better judgment, Katherine accepted that this would be a mystery best left until morning. She closed the doors, locking them behind her. She moved to the exit on the opposite end of the room to confirm that it was indeed locked, just as she had suspected, before heading into the en-suite to wet a towel with warm water. Returning to the four-poster bed, she placed the cloth on her forehead and fell back asleep with ease.

∾

Katherine woke to the sound of birds chirping. Though she had been unable to escape thoughts of who had brought her in from the cold the night before, even as she dreamt, she now had more pressing matters to attend to.

Tonight would see her powers return to her, along with any recollections that may still be hiding in the depths of her mind. She would finally be herself.

The princess gave the room one last look before heading out the door, through the castle, and up to her own suite to get ready for what would certainly be a battle of a day ahead.

∾

"Has anyone seen her?" asked Alek as soon as he walked in through the dining room doors.

"No, not yet."

"Not me."

"Everyone's been asking!"

"Nope."

"Sir, one of the castle keepers said they heard movement inside her suite earlier this morning," came Alfred's voice over the crowd.

"Ah. Excellent then, Alfred," said Alek, not looking entirely convinced that everything was alright as the prince made his way to his usual seat.

An unspoken unease ghosted over their skin as they ate, many anxiously awaiting Katherine's arrival. But once it became clear that she would not be joining them for their meal, Alfred called for silence to make his announcements.

"Ahem! Each of you is aware that after every trial, a ball will be held, allowing members of the communities of power to witness the outcomes as we progress. Since Eyrondale Castle will host these festivities and, knowing our princess as we do, I have decided to theme each of these events as she most likely would have, were she in a position to do so. Therefore, before each ball, a selection of clothing will be provided for you to choose from." Alfred nodded towards the princes. "For the gentlemen, Your Highnesses excluded, of course, you are to head into the music room after this to be sized and make your selections. If you still need directions, ask a castle keeper. Ladies, please proceed to the second living room, just off the foyer, and do the same."

There was a murmur of agreement.

"Just as with the Selection by Fire, drivers will be waiting outside to transport you all to the East Wing this evening. Meet downstairs to depart at seven. Once there, I ask that you please remain aware and alert. While those in attendance will be unable to use their powers, in accordance with Eyrondale's laws, you are still mortal – and I would rather not have to explain your deaths or abductions to the princess." Alfred chuckled before leaving them to their meals.

"He's in a good mood this morning," muttered Marko, putting down the paper and taking a sip of his espresso.

"Anyone think he might just be excited that she's really coming back tonight?" Alek asked rhetorically, getting to his feet. He threw on his leather jacket and smiled from ear to ear.

Marko made no effort to look up, but a slight smile played on his lips. "I have a feeling we're in for a hell of a ride once she is!"

"You make it seem like she's going to be a completely different person or something," piped up Emily, also getting to her feet to leave.

A few of the handlers exchanged sideways glances.

"Well," started Alek, "let's just say that once she fully pieces together who she is and gets her powers back—"

"You might have a very different view of who you thought you knew," interrupted Marko, managing a full-on smile this time.

"Listen. You might have known her for a hell of a lot longer, but she's family to me. That will never change. I'll always know who she is inside," said Emily. She shrugged, refusing to believe the brothers, however confident in their words they seemed.

Kaëden raised an eyebrow from behind his steaming drink, though it was unclear which of his brothers was right. "I think we are about to see something else entirely," he muttered.

Emily shook her head, a soft laugh escaping her as she left, the rest of the diners dispersing soon after.

～

Layla met Emily outside the door to the second living room after they had freshened up in their suites. Unlike the previous event, where they had a choice of four or five outfits each, they were met with an entire room filled with racks of white ball gowns and evening dresses.

"What the...?" exclaimed Layla, her eyes widening.

"Wow!" said Emily, taking a few seconds to look around.

"Ah! Ladies," came a squeak from behind one of the racks. A tall, slender, bespectacled young man ran out to meet them.

"Um. Hi," greeted Emily as the excited tailor raced towards her, measuring tape in hand.

"You have perfect timing," he said.

With a dramatic flourish of his wrist, Emily's hands shot above her head as the tape flew forward, wrapping itself around her waist to take her measurements. It tickled.

"And you are?"

"Oh, yes! Forgive me. My name is Juan. I am Eloise's assistant. I will be taking over your gown selections and fittings for the upcoming festivities."

"Oh. Okay." The sisters shared a quick glance. "Nice to meet you. I'm Layla, this is Emily."

"Pleasure," said Juan, his hazel eyes not bothering to meet theirs as he took the pencil from his ear to note down their sizes.

He bit into the wood of the pencil for safekeeping, briefly holding it between his teeth as he gestured for them to follow him to the nearest set of freestanding mirrors and step atop the alteration podiums.

"Your other friend was in here a moment ago, but she left to go soak up what little sun we have left today. She should be back soon."

"That's okay, we'll see her later," Emily squealed excitedly as Juan hurried to find a sample selection of outfits for the pair.

Surrounded by exquisite gowns and dazzling jewels, it was difficult to deny that the castle had its charms. If this was the trade-off for all the chaos they had to endure, many of the mortals agreed there was little sense in not enjoying the luxury they had a chance to experience while they could.

The bustling young assistant soon gathered a selection of dresses that were sure to impress and hung them on a rolling rack. Despite Juan's animated gestures and frantic searching, his short black hair remained flawless, and not a droplet of sweat could be found on his olive brow.

"Alright!" he said, narrowing his eyes as he looked between the sisters. "I have chosen what *I* think would work well. I suggest we begin here."

It sounded less like a suggestion than a challenge – one he clearly dared them to ignore.

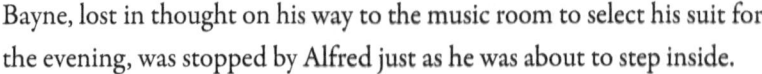

Bayne, lost in thought on his way to the music room to select his suit for the evening, was stopped by Alfred just as he was about to step inside.

"Ah! Young Master Bayne!" Alfred exclaimed, excitement in his voice.

"Y...yes, Alfred?" stammered Bayne, still battling to get used to the formal title.

"Please, come with me. You are a champion, after all. I have arranged for more top-of-the-line choices to be taken to your suite for a private viewing." The handler winked at him, a flicker of fire dancing in his grey eyes. "One of our finest is at your disposal and is waiting to assist."

Bayne was taken aback. "Um. Thank you. That's really nice of you, actually."

"Not a problem at all, Master Bayne." The handler gestured to the corridor to their left, his posture poised and attentive. "Please, allow me to accompany you."

They rounded the corner of the music room, Bayne catching a glimpse of sunlight spilling through the doors that led to its courtyard. There was still so much of the castle left to explore. But the distraction from his racing thoughts was brief. He and Alfred took the left corridor before turning right, arriving at the north-east tower. They climbed three of the floors in silence before his handler suddenly stopped and turned to face him, the firelight in the tower dimming as if straining to eavesdrop on their conversation.

"If I may offer some advice?" Alfred said.

Dragging his gaze from the tendrils of light beside them, Bayne muttered, "Um, sure?"

"As a champion, you should constantly be putting your best foot forward, especially in the eyes of those who represent the Six Kingdoms of Power. None of them knows you. You know none of their ways. Make no mistake – for you, it is about charming them just as much as Katherine."

Bayne opened his mouth to respond, but Alfred pressed on, lowering his voice.

"I am more than willing to be of assistance should you need it. I understand that you are of significant importance to the princess, and I have also seen that there are many things to be considered in these trials. It is only right that you have some of the same advantages that they do. But it is also only fair that you actually put some effort into winning this."

Bayne did not reply immediately, unprepared for such bluntness. Instead, the pair moved through the exit to the third floor and rounded the corner, heading down the first corridor. Silent, though, the champion remained as they made their way towards his suite at the far end. He paused just as Alfred reached for the door.

"This is real, isn't it?" Bayne asked softly. "*Really* real, I mean. All of it."

The handler took hold of the gargoyle handle and beckoned the champion inside as it granted them entry. "As real as I am, sir. I am relieved to see that you finally understand some of the weight of what is happening. If this first trial is anything to go by, I only hope that you keep that in mind as you progress. Because *they* will."

As Bayne passed him, Alfred rested a hand on his arm.

"And *she* definitely will," he whispered.

They held each other's gaze for a moment before Bayne gave a slight nod. Alfred loosened his grip and guided the champion further into the room, where rows of white suits, shirts, ties, shoes, and accessories awaited.

"Welcome, Master Bayne," greeted an excited, grey-haired, bat-like old woman as she ran out from behind the first rack of dress shirts.

"Hello?" said Bayne, apprehensively.

"Eloise Kernipski-Goldwing," she said, introducing herself with a bow, her canary-yellow spectacles almost falling onto the floor as her tall frame bent in half.

She straightened up and greeted Alfred, who promptly took his leave, before hurrying over to the mirrors set up beside the fireplace. She gestured for Bayne to join her, her bright green eyes scanning his overall appearance.

"Well then. Yes. *This* I can work with." Eloise beamed, clearly delighted with her new doll. "Please, step up to the platform. Sophie, we shall do the bottoms first!"

A petite, dark-haired woman with pointed ears and dark pink eyes rushed to Bayne's side, carrying a selection of white trousers for him to browse. Her curly hair bounced with each eager step, and she smelled faintly of caramel.

"Pick one, Master Bayne," instructed Eloise. "Let us begin!"

There was a knock from the other side of her suite's doors.

"Enter," instructed Katherine, walking into the sitting room and setting down her coffee.

"Ah, Princess!" greeted Eloise, entering the suite. She bowed so low that her long nose nearly touched the floor, her bright yellow spectacles still proving tricky to hold on to.

"Ms Kernipski-Goldwing, a pleasure to see you again."

"Likewise, Your Highness. Where would you like to begin? Do you have something in mind for this evening?"

"What are *they* wearing?" Katherine asked, starting to look through the custom white gowns Sophie had wheeled into the room moments before her boss arrived.

"Well, I have had the fortune to advise them all this afternoon, and I would say there are four possible contenders."

Eloise retrieved four gowns from the three racks near the fireplace, handing one to each of the two assistants, another to Sophie, and keeping the fourth for herself.

"Good!" said Katherine, her voice steady. "Whoever said that appearance is not everything never had to endure a ball full of hundreds of supernatural and magical politicians, all looking for any sign of weakness."

"Well, Your Highness, from what I remember, you have never had to worry about being perceived as weak!" Eloise smirked, eyes glinting with a hint of mischief.

"And I would like to keep it that way, Ms Kernipski-Goldwing."

"Of course, Princess. How can I be of assistance?"

"This one," said Katherine, pointing to the pearl-white satin master-piece on the far right.

Eloise instructed the assistants to pack away the rest of the dresses as she and Sophie prepared for the alterations.

Katherine stepped onto the fitting platform, staring at herself in the mirror. "Two things, Ms Kernipski-Goldwing."

"Yes, Princess?"

"First...it needs to be able to hide *those*." The princess pointed to the small table in the corner as Heleen, ever insistent despite Katherine's usual refusals, moved to help her remove the top layers of her clothing. "Just in case."

A rosy hue flushed across Sophie's copper-toned face as she tried to appear uninterested, though she was clearly listening in.

Eloise's eyes widened. "Of...of course, Your Highness. As I said. Never weak." She walked over to the table and noted down the measurements of the guns and blades neatly laid out in a row.

A hint of a grin played at the corners of Katherine's mouth. "And you, as always, *discreet*."

"And the second?"

Now, a full-blown smile spread across the princess's face as all eyes in the room turned to her, a trace of fear in each.

"Does it come in red?"

CHAPTER 18
THE WHITE AND RED BALL

The black town cars were lined up behind each other, waiting to transport their guests to the East Wing of the castle. Alfred, who had pre-assigned them to specific vehicles, was coordinating and organising to ensure that each handoff went smoothly.

"Excuse me?" came Jennifer's voice from behind Emily. "Is Bayne running late?"

"Master Bayne?" replied Alfred, raising his eyebrows as he glanced up at the pair from his tablet as they joined him on the landing. "He will be arriving at the East Wing later, escorted by me. It is a protocol for all champions, Miss."

"Oh, I...he didn't tell me," Jennifer said, looking hurt.

Emily noticed the brief flicker of recognition in Alfred's expression before he handed his device to the nearest castle keeper. Folding his hands behind his back, he settled into place.

"Miss, may I be so bold as to suggest that you talk to Master Bayne?"

"What do you mean? We—"

"He *has* shared with you the consequences of what would happen should he not fully participate in these trials, yes?" The handler narrowed his eyes.

Emily glanced from Alfred to Jennifer as Layla finally joined them, ready to meet their driver. Discreetly, she waved her sister off from interrupting.

"Yes, but—" Jennifer began, but Alfred's sharp tone cut her short.

"Miss, while I serve the master of this kingdom, I am still fair. I notice many things and share almost none. What I will tell you is that—"

"Yes?"

"Well, in truth, Fate is not a being to be trifled with. Master Bayne was chosen for a reason, and until he is released by Fate himself, he must give his whole heart to these trials. If you do not wish to lose him, you must understand this."

"But I know him. I know *her*. If he does, then I'll end up losing him anyway."

"Don't say that, Jen!" whispered Layla, giving Emily a sideways look as if asking for backup.

"But it's true, isn't it, Alfred?"

"I cannot say for sure either way, as none of us knows what Fate truly has in store. What I can say, however, is that Master Bayne would not have been chosen as a champion unless, deep down, there was a true desire for it."

"You mean for *her*?"

Alfred shrugged, visibly uncomfortable, and gestured for the trio to descend the stairs as the final car pulled up.

"Have a lovely evening, ladies."

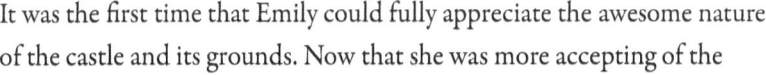

It was the first time that Emily could fully appreciate the awesome nature of the castle and its grounds. Now that she was more accepting of the world she had so suddenly been thrown into, she could better take in and process the finer elements of this fantasy.

The first time she had made her way to the East Wing, she had been deep in thought, barely believing that any of this was real. This time, however, knowing what she did now, Emily allowed herself to be more open to what this power had to offer. After everything she had seen, there was no way *not* to believe.

The towering walls were imposing enough on their own, but as Emily, Layla, and Jennifer stepped out of the town car, they paused to take in the sight of the castle, illuminated and adorned with breathtaking extravagance. They joined the queue of guests leading to the landing at the top of the stairs, relieved to have taken Juan's fashion advice earlier. Emily, taking in the opulence surrounding them – the elegantly dressed guests, the gleam of fine jewellery, and the effortless grace in their movements – quickly ensured her gown looked pristine. The others did the same.

Unlike the champion selection, which had taken place in the Grand Hall and allowed for at most a hundred and fifty guests, Alfred had informed them that all future festivities would be held in the Grand Ballroom. This venue, according to the mortals' research, was able to comfortably accommodate six hundred. For this evening, the event would be kept small, with only around four hundred attendees. This still meant, though, that Emily and the others would be surrounded by hundreds of beings or products of power, representatives of the Nine Strands, as well as numerous mortal leaders and dignitaries.

As if the security at the East Wing's outer gates were not enough, another layer of protection met them as they reached the top of the landing. Their names were double and triple-checked against the guest list, their purses were searched, and they had to pass through a sheet of blue smoke that danced through the air in the doorway, spelled to reveal any falsehoods in appearance. With each passing moment, the event's attendees seemed to shed their more mortal features, finally giving Emily and her friends a glimpse of the types of creatures and beings she had only ever read about in books and seen in films.

The red flowers that once lined their path to the Grand Hall had been replaced by archways of white, their petals shimmering with shades of blue as guests passed beneath them. Leading towards the open double doors opposite the East Wing's main entrance, the continuously blooming rose tunnel ensured that guests would only follow its direction. It appeared that the castle staff had taken every care to ensure that none would be tempted to explore the areas to which they had not been granted access – again.

The hundreds of white butterflies that had previously overseen the East Wing entranceway danced overhead as Emily, Layla, and Jennifer emerged from the enchanted floral arches and entered a scene that could have easily been plucked from the pages of a fairy tale. The sheer magnitude of the room was breathtaking, stretching out before them like a canvas of grandeur.

A band played in the corner to their right, one of the fully stocked bars greeted guests in the corner on the left, and a large dance floor invited them into the centre with open arms. As they descended into the room, which mirrored the castle's styling, they were captivated by the way the black and gold veins in the marble seemed to shift like liquid.

Layla nudged Emily in the ribs, finally capturing her attention. Reluctantly tearing her gaze away from the shimmering gold lines that reflected the ballroom's lighting, Emily followed her sister's lead, and they navigated through the crowd in search of their friends.

Opting to start at the bar and progress down the left-hand-side wall, Jennifer wasted no time in accepting a freshly poured cherry cocktail. Without hesitation, Emily followed suit, though she could not shake off the unsettling glance from what appeared to be an elderly wolf at the opposite end of the counter. Nevertheless, she swiftly grabbed two coconut cream concoctions, one for herself and one for her sister, before resuming their mission, assuming Aiden and the others had already moved on.

Along the walls, the fireplaces cast a warm, inviting glow, while the four sets of tall, oversized arched glass doors stood open, allowing a gentle breeze to trickle in and beckoning guests to explore the lush garden and tranquil ponds beyond. Cold though the night was, Emily barely felt it in the magic that emanated from their surroundings.

As they strolled past the live-edge wooden banquet tables bordering the dance floor to their right, each spacious enough to comfortably accommodate thirty, their eyes scanned the intricately decorated place cards meticulously arranged on the tables. Amidst the hustle and bustle of their arrival, the mortals realised they had overlooked their table assignments upon entering, too captivated by the beauty that had greeted them.

"Over there!" Jennifer called to the others over her shoulder as they neared the front of the Grand Ballroom, her gaze fixing on Aiden's tousled mop of hair near the landing that appeared to be the focal point of tonight's event.

Hurriedly moving past a pair of faeries engaged in rapid conversation at the base of a staircase leading to an overhead glass walkway, the mortals wove through the flurry of gossamer wings, each beat leaving a shimmering trail of dust that swirled in the air before settling like mist. They pressed on, joining their friends.

"'Bout time," Aiden said with a laugh, his mischievous smile catching Emily off guard as moonlight streamed through the circular glass window above them.

The window, stretching nearly the full height and width of the stone wall that housed it, echoed the architectural style of the oversized doors they had passed earlier. Encased in sculpted marble vines, the panels formed a mesmerising stained-glass masterpiece, depicting the timeless struggle between light and darkness within the form of a winged creature. Its design was reminiscent of the guardians that watched over the castle.

"It's quite...something. Isn't it?" said Jamie, gesturing towards the work of art.

"Always said she went from zero to a hundred."

"Aiden—"

"What? It's not like she doesn't have taste. But...could this be any more showy?"

"Think that's the point."

Aiden shrugged and took a sip of his drink. "Just saying."

"Come on," said Jamie, rolling his eyes. "We were going to check out the courtyard."

Following Jamie's lead, the group made their way past a second staircase that led up to the walkway, where a group of tall, gangly, pale-looking creatures were taking in the view through the glass.

Craving a moment of respite from the busy ballroom, the mortals moved through the crowd. With every step they took, Emily was unable to shake the curious gazes following their movements, their presence seeming to ripple through the crowd like the latest morsel of juicy gossip. The air outside promised a reprieve, a chance to escape the weight of scrutiny and ground themselves.

As the mortals passed a nearby fireplace and stepped through the nearest of the five doorways, they were met with a courtyard that surpassed even their heightened expectations. They had not been afforded a chance to enter it from the Grand Hall at the champion selection, and they were glad they had not, because it would have stolen from this very moment.

Exiting into the covered cocktail area, they were welcomed by attentive servers offering freshly poured champagne, the melodic tunes of another band serenading the space and a lively gathering of partygoers. Many had assembled on the lowered dance floor that stood, uncovered, beneath the gentle glow of thousands of fireflies.

"Wow!" exclaimed Matthew. His eyes sparkled with excitement as he spotted a trio of elegant elves, their pointed ears decorated with delicate silver jewellery, and their skin shimmering in the light. They moved with an indescribable grace, their long, flowing robes trailing behind them in a dance of moonlight.

"This can't be real," muttered Jennifer, staring out at the crowd.

"You keep saying that," said Aiden, not bothering to look at her, "and yet—"

"Come on," interrupted Jamie. "Let's do a lap before they sit us down for the banquet."

Agreeing, they navigated through the crowds of white, staying close together as they traversed past a multitude of creatures and beings. They narrowly avoided a couple of regal vampires emerging from the shadows of the grounds, their pale flesh highlighted by the glint of their crimson eyes. Despite any apprehension, the mortals placed their trust in Zachary's security system and the strategically positioned guards, choosing to satisfy their curiosity instead of cowering to the fear that many of the guests would have otherwise struck in their hearts.

One by one, the champions and their handlers arrived at the private entrance to the East Wing, the same one Katherine had used before. Aimee, the castle keeper, handed each of them a drink as they waited. When Bayne finally joined them, Alfred at his side, Aimee excused herself, leaving the champions and their handlers to their privacy.

"Good evening, Your Highnesses," said Alfred, rubbing his hands together as he straightened up from a quick bow.

Greetings met him left and right.

"This evening, you will open the dance floor with Princess Katherine, which, as most of you are aware, is tradition when a visiting royal attends court festivities. The council will advise in which order. Handlers," he said, turning to Lucien and the others. "Please make your way into the ball-room with your champions when you are ready."

Nervous, Bayne finished his drink, eager to avoid any conversation with these *people*, and gestured for Alfred to lead the way. The pair walked together down the corridor that would take them to the wing's entrance hall, and they could hear Alek and Greyson following not far behind.

With all the guests patiently awaiting the champions, Bayne was relieved that he could enjoy the tunnel of white blooms in peace before making a spectacle of himself.

Taking a fleeting moment to absorb the beauty of the butterflies that fluttered overhead, Bayne found himself overwhelmed by the thunderous applause that accompanied his announced arrival in the Grand Ballroom. Spotting his friends near the bar, he gracefully manoeuvred out of the spotlight, allowing Alek to take over as the centre of attention.

"Hey!" Bayne said, walking up to greet Jennifer. He leant in for a kiss, but she held him at bay.

"You could have said something," Jennifer said, clearly still upset that they had not arrived at the ball together.

Emily and Layla exchanged looks before backing away to join the group that Brian and Matthew were now talking to.

"Can we not do this? It's not the time," Bayne whispered with a hint of sadness in his eyes.

"She's caused more than one argument between us, Bayne. I won't stand for it again."

Biting his lip in frustration, the champion closed his eyes and paused to take a deep breath as he tried to fend off the sudden pain that had taken hold of his chest. "I understand that, believe me. I've made more compromises to stop that from happening than you know. But, Jen, she was just as surprised by all of this as I was, as *you* were. I thought we'd moved past this?"

"How could we have moved past anything if you've barely said two words to me lately?"

"And whose fault is that?" Bayne muttered before he could stop himself.

Jennifer raised her eyebrows. "So, are you defending yourself?" She huffed. "Or *her*?"

"Defending her? Defending her for what? *Not* asking for this either?"

"You know what?" Jennifer snapped, throwing her hands to her head as another round of applause rang through the room. "You're right! This isn't the place."

"Jen—"

"Bayne, I—"

Their conversation was abruptly cut short by the most deafening applause yet, signalling the arrival of Marko, the clear favourite. This was soon followed by echoes of excited, yet terrified, cheers as the eldest prince made his entrance.

There was a call for silence, which saw any chance at conversation put on hold. A few seconds was all it took to gather the crowd's focus before two of the violinists led the band in a slow instrumental arrangement to welcome Eyrondale's leader.

Every eye in the ballroom snapped towards the grand, gold-accented doorway as Katherine stepped into view. She stood alone. A striking figure in a sea of white, draped in a strapless crimson ball gown that clung to her frame like liquid fire. Jewels encrusted along its sweetheart neckline caught the light, scattering shards of brilliance across the polished floor. The cascading ruffles, fluid and untamed, seemed almost sentient as they pooled around her feet. At that moment, she was not just seen – she was dizzying, leaving more than a few jaws unhinged.

"Welcome, everyone!" Katherine smiled as the hundreds of guests and staff bent into a low bow. Her voice floated through the air, light as a whisper on the wind, yet carrying effortlessly to the room's furthest corners. "Thank you for joining us. Welcome to Eyrondale. Please, enjoy your evening."

Everyone straightened at her words, and the princess stepped back to greet Alfred and the Consilio Statera, who had made their way over to her, as chatter and mingling resumed. It was not long before Alfred encouraged the council to excuse themselves to allow Katherine a chance to catch her breath.

"How are you this evening, Princess?" he asked softly, offering her a drink from a passing tray.

Katherine smiled, accepting it happily, grateful for a moment's peace. "Better. Thank you, Alfred."

"Well enough to take a lap around the room?"

"We must all do things that we would rather not do, Alfred." She stuck her nose in the air, puffing her chest slightly in jest. "It is *duty,* after all!"

"Well then!" Alfred laughed as he reached for a drink himself. "To duty!"

They clinked their glasses and discreetly finished their liquid salvation before making their way around the room, Alfred slipping away now and then to introduce Bayne to prominent guests and ensure the young mortal did not become too overwhelmed.

Soon, the handlers were told to gather their champions at the base of the landing, and the attendees were instructed to line the edges of the dance floor.

"Silence, everyone!" Herlock's booming voice echoed over the excited crowd from where he and the other council members had taken centre stage, bathed in the moonlight that streamed through the stained glass.

"Please, join us in welcoming Prince Markovyas of Neighlore, Prince Dàikonos of Azrallus, Prince Aleksander of Keldorne, Prince Kaëden of Cardinallis, and Master Bayne McAllister," announced Horus.

The room broke into applause, and Katherine discreetly gave each of her potential suitors a once-over.

"We shall begin this evening's festivities with a dance," Horus continued. "Each champion will represent their court as they share a dance with the princess, as is customary." He turned to face Katherine and gestured towards the dance floor. "Princess, please, whenever you are ready."

The band played in the background as the princess walked over to take Marko's outstretched hand, following his lead to the ballroom's centre.

With a wave, Horus dimmed the light emanating from the flames in the room, and the band struck up a new tune.

Emily and Aiden had managed to push their way to the front of the crowd, joining Jennifer and Layla, who had left Jamie and the others at the bar. Drinks in hand, they watched eagerly as the royals turned to face each other.

Their eyes met, having not spoken since their task, and there was a clear tension that created an instant barrier between the two. Left hand at his waist, outstretching his right arm, Marko bent into a half bow, his gaze never leaving Katherine's. As was customary, she returned his gesture, determined to not allow her innermost thoughts to betray her.

Mortals and products of power alike could appreciate the pair's elegant display of tradition. They were the picturesque image of what one would expect a royal couple to be.

A traditional arrangement that originated in Neighlore's westernmost region, one that the pair had danced to many times before, led their movements. The moment the prince's hand took hold of Katherine's waist, her dress's fabric rustled, revealing itself to be made from a cascade of living roses in full bloom.

As they floated across the dance floor without a word, their eyes left each other's only when the dance demanded it. Neither willing to be the first to break the silence.

Seemingly deciding to synchronise, the blooms of Katherine's dress shifted their petals in perfect harmony with the subtle, familiar rhythm of the song. Reflecting the light with every orchestrated flutter, they cast waves of ephemeral ripples across the gown's surface.

As Marko eased Katherine into a low dip at the final bar before pulling her close to his chest, her heart quickened at the heat of his breath on her cheek. It took everything to not give in to old habits and place her lips on his, and it appeared that Marko felt the same.

The band resumed a soft tune as the crowd watched with curiosity. Many among them longed for the pair's history to triumph, having heard or witnessed the legend of their romance. Applause flooded the room as Marko reached for Katherine's hand and kissed it, bending into a bow. The look on his face told Katherine he had noticed the conflict stirring in her eyes.

The prince turned to leave the dance floor, offering a customary bow of acknowledgement to Deacon as they passed. He made a beeline for the nearest bar, the crowd parting to let him pass.

~

The youngest prince's boyish smile ignited something within her every time she saw it. Katherine remained intrigued by the air of mystery that surrounded him. Unlike the other champions, she had not spent enough time with Deacon to be able to predict his next move. As his deep brown eyes met hers, Katherine thought that perhaps it would all just be easier if she began a life with someone new. No history or baggage to cloud the air.

Deacon's smile widened as the pair bowed to each other, growing as they drew closer.

"You *do* look absolutely beautiful, Princess," he said as he took her waist, his voice so smooth that it sent a shiver down Katherine's spine.

"You are the first person to say that who is not attempting to flatter me out of fear. So, thank you," she whispered.

"And who says that I'm not?" The prince laughed as they took their first steps to the rhythm of a traditional waltz, seamlessly woven with elements of smooth jazz.

"You're not too bad at this," Katherine admitted.

"A compliment? I think I'm starting to like you so much more now. I had absolutely no interest before this." His playful and sarcastic nature made Katherine laugh as the prince lifted her in the air and spun around.

"Arrogant much?" she teased.

"Oh, honey," Deacon muttered back, lowering her onto his chest. "You have *no* idea."

"I think I might be starting to like *you* a little more now too."

"Definitely nothing wrong with that," breathed the prince as they continued to dance, a touch closer than before.

Whether it was his flirtatious nature or the sheer mystery that surrounded him, Katherine was not the only one affected by his larger-than-life presence. Even the blooms of her dress appeared to swoon at the sound of the prince's voice. But no matter how hard they batted their petals in his direction or moved them to blow soft kisses his way, he could not be distracted from the princess, who seemed to fit so effortlessly in his arms.

As the song drew to a close, Deacon spun Katherine one last time before catching her, just as a round of applause rang in their ears.

"And anyone who can't see how stunning you look this evening is a damn fool," he said softly, releasing her to bow in farewell as a devilish smile lingered on his face.

~

Alek skipped past his brother, offering Deacon a quick bend at the waist before approaching Katherine.

"So," Alek said as their eyes met, sweeping into a deep, theatrical flourish before her. "Fast or slow?"

"Surprise me." She beamed, bowing in return, her cheeks turning a light shade of pink.

"As you wish."

He swooshed his hand in the air and the band took his cue. A whimsical yet sultry arrangement filled the hall as the petals of red snapped to attention, pleating themselves into tiny fans that opened and closed to the beat playfully.

The royals had danced together at banquets, in hiding, for fun, but this was different. It was as though they were dancing together for the first time. There was an energy there that they had not been aware of, or had chosen not to feel, before.

Katherine felt every touch as though she were in a vacuum. Alek's hand on her waist, the brush of his chest, the fingertips that curled over as they held her hand – all of it. She felt comfort at the warmth of her body against his. She was overwhelmed by the peace she felt at his scent. There was something there, between them, that was drawing her in.

Noticing the change in the way she looked at him, Alek seemed to savour every breath as they moved together as one. They had always been so in sync that everything felt effortless, even after all their time apart. His mouth trembled each time they got too close, and he bit his lower lip whenever Katherine caught herself blushing and looked away. It was as though the thought of the two of them had never been one worth considering – until now.

The music faded, and the pair stopped only inches apart, allowing a giggle to escape their lips before stepping back, blood red and slightly embarrassed. Alek bowed and kissed Katherine's hand, causing the tiny flutter that had woken in her stomach to grow. The prince smiled as he turned to leave, and Katherine thought of how easy it could be if she were matched with him.

Before she could let herself dwell on it, she caught a glimpse of Alek and Kaëden dipping in formal acknowledgement as the tone among the crowd shifted from excitement to apprehension.

~

"Princess," said Kaëden, greeting her with his usual stoicism, though the faintest trace of a smile ghosted his lips.

Katherine paused, realising that she had not had time to process what she had learnt about herself and the eldest prince in the first trial. It was strange. She was struggling to come to terms with the fact that her own thoughts had deceived her about all of it.

As he bowed to her, just as his brothers had done before him, Katherine could have sworn she saw a hint of fear mixed with regret, deep in Kaëden's eyes, though his face turned hard. She bent towards him, determined to reserve any commentary or questions about her recent revelations until after her powers were restored. There were so many things onto which Katherine now needed to shift her focus. She knew that once she was completely herself again, she would be able to make more sense of it all.

Only a little longer.

Katherine placed her hand in his as the violins started up again. At his touch, the petals of her dress recoiled, closing themselves up to form hundreds of tiny thorns that longed to protect themselves as well as their princess. While the defensiveness of her gown did not seem to offend the prince, a few onlookers looked less than impressed at its blatant rudeness.

"I know this," Katherine whispered as Kaëden took her around the middle and guided them into a waltz, the soft, slow tune resonating in the depths of her memory.

"You do," came his voice, cool as ever as they danced with perfect form.

"You did this?" asked Katherine in his ear as she spun into him, identifying the song as one she had written herself – *Shadowflame.*

"I thought it may bring a smile to your face. After everything, that is the least that I owe you."

Their eyes met briefly before he looked away, barely giving Katherine a chance to search his face for answers she dared not ask. They moved with grace. Left, then right. She wondered which version of Kaëden was before her now – the one she remembered marching into countless battles against, or the one with whom she had kept a well-guarded secret for fourteen years.

The pair glided across the dance floor, ignoring the murmurings of the crowd around them. It was truly a rare occasion to see Katherine and Kaëden in the same room, let alone not at each other's throats. Many looked on with worry, glancing towards the exits in case the prince chose to lash out. Others whispered about what Katherine could be feeling as she spun into the arms of such a monster. All but those in Kaëden's court seemed to be on edge, much more so than when she had danced with the other champions. As the music slowed, the crowd quickly applauded, eager to see the exchange end before it could explode into chaos.

The prince took Katherine's hand and pressed a trembling kiss to her skin, his lips barely grazing her flesh. He looked up, his eyes lingering on hers for a moment longer than they normally would have as the band readied themselves for the final dance.

"Princess," said Kaëden with a nod as he straightened up.

Face still quite inexpressive, he returned to Daniel, who had been waiting at the edge of the dance floor, drinks in hand, and gave a half-hearted greeting to Bayne as he passed.

Katherine had no time to dwell on the thoughts of her complicated past with the eldest son of Magic, especially when it came to the idea of their child. It was a notion she found almost unbelievable.

∿

The chatter died down as everyone looked to the dance floor one last time, Horus gesturing for the final champion to come forward.

Bayne caught the slow turn of Katherine's head, her movements measured, as if careful not to reveal anything. Her expression was unreadable as he crossed the room.

As he stopped before her, there was a hesitation from each of them before they made eye contact. They had not had a moment alone since their task either, and even if they had, they probably would have avoided the topic like a plague.

Bayne's nerves seemed to grow far beyond what he could contain, but there was something about the way Katherine was looking at him that helped to drown out the world around them. The champion bowed low as the band played an instrumental rendition of a modern song that he and Katherine recognised at once. Choosing to set aside his thoughts of Jennifer for now, at least, and ignoring the weight of countless eyes on him, Bayne allowed himself to give in to the moment and smile.

Taken aback, Katherine narrowed her gaze questioningly before understanding what he was trying to do. She smiled in return as he reached to take her hand, a smile that he had not seen in person in far too long. Both trembled as their skin touched, even more so when Bayne took Katherine's waist, leading them off in a dance.

This was the first time they had ever danced together, yet it felt as though Katherine had been transported back to a life once forgotten, a life where the two of them existed in a world of their own. As the hall seemed to melt away around them, the blooms of Katherine's gown softened, and the pair moved in a way no one had expected.

Where the champion's hands met her skin, it tingled. When she felt his breath, her heart quickened. As he spun her slowly into his chest, she felt warmth. Katherine could not imagine being able to explain to anyone, not even if she tried. There was something about Bayne that made her feel things differently than she ever had. Whether it was nerves or the intensity of such pure human emotion, there was no denying the spark that existed between them.

Why? she thought as they danced effortlessly across the room, the red of her dress taking on a life of its own. She could almost hear the petals gossiping excitedly as they sprang into a continuous bloom, leaving a trail of crimson at the pair's feet. *More than a thousand lifetimes' worth of lifetimes, but he made it here. How?* Staring back at him, she had a nagging feeling that the champion was thinking the exact same thing.

All that Bayne could manage to do was smile as Katherine spun into him one last time. Taking a moment to fully appreciate the moment, she welcomed his pause before releasing his grip on her. As they bid each other farewell, something flickered across Bayne's face. If she did not know better, she might have thought it was guilt, with a side serving of regret. As polite applause rose around them, the pair left the dance floor, slipping back into the festivities to prepare for the feast, not saying another word to each other.

CHAPTER 19
THE WARNING

After her guests had overindulged in both food and drink at the feast, accompanied by the mesmerising performance of a talented fire wielder, the castle keepers cleared everything away, leaving the attendees to mingle. Katherine made her way through the crowd towards her friend, who looked stunning in a one-shouldered gown, her black hair cascading over her open back.

"Emily!" she exclaimed, delighted to see how well the mortal appeared to be handling the evening.

Emily turned around with a wide smile.

"Hi!" greeted Katherine, having only just successfully avoided a rather intoxicated group of sorcerers who appeared to be wagering the outcome of the next trial with a one-handed goblin.

"It's about time. I don't suppose you can hug at these things?"

"No. Not really," Katherine admitted. "But we *can* have a drink and catch up with a hug when this is all done."

"Well then, as long as I'm still on the catch-up list, then I'm happy!"

"Always. I—"

"Princess, pardon me?" came Zachary's voice from behind them.

"Give me a moment please, Em," Katherine said, squeezing Emily's arm to comfort her. She turned to face Zachary, who was far too red in the cheeks to be sober.

"The council has asked me to alert you that they will be beginning the ceremony shortly."

"Excellent. Please see to it that every exit is covered. Just in case. These trials are far too important to allow more slip-ups."

"Yes, Your Highness," he replied without hesitation, reaching into his white coat for the tablet hidden inside.

"That's my cue, Em. Excuse me. We need to run over a few things."

"Sure. I get it. We'll find some time soon."

Without waiting for a response, Zachary gestured for Katherine to join him, and the pair headed for the landing. He pointed out the improvements he had made to the security system since their last visit to the East Wing, summarising the upgraded surveillance and increased security personnel.

"Dead zones? Blind spots?"

Checking to be sure they would not be overheard, Zachary lowered his voice. "We have overlapping cameras. Zero and zero. I've got this. Don't worry, Kat."

"Are you certain?"

"Of course. Nothing will get by us." His gaze flickered as he looked past her. "Oh, um, Princess, it looks like you have company."

He backed away quickly as Katherine turned just in time to see Jennifer coming towards her.

"I have been meaning to talk to you," said Katherine as the fiery redhead approached with Jamie in tow.

"Oh?" said Jennifer, slightly surprised. She seemed to have expected the princess to dismiss her.

"Yes." Katherine took a sip of her champagne and gestured around the room. "All of this must be overwhelming. But allow me to reassure you that I will do everything I can to figure it out and get you back home."

"I..." Jennifer began, but trailed off, glancing at Jamie. Katherine watched the hesitation in her posture, the way the mortal seemed to steel herself before speaking again. "Honestly, right now, I just need to ask you something."

"You may ask. I shall do my best to answer."

"When you danced with Bayne earlier, how was he?"

Not having anticipated the question, Katherine paused, her body tensing. "What do you mean?"

"It's just that he's been a bit off lately and, with all of this craziness, I just need to know if it's directed at me or if he's been the same with everyone. I figured I'd come straight to the source."

"If *what* is being directed at you? Have you spoken to him about your concerns?"

"Have you ever known him to be an open book?"

"Fair point." Katherine laughed. "As far as I'm aware, he is acting as he always does. Nothing out of character, if that is what you are referring to?"

"So just avoiding me, then?"

"I couldn't say. Even if I could, it wouldn't be my place." Katherine sighed, softening her expression. "Whatever is happening between you, I apologise for my part. Never, since the dawn of the prophecy's creation, would any of us have guessed that this is where we would be when it finally triggered. Regardless, I hope for your sake that you can stand by him for as long as he wants you there. You know as well as I do that he will come around in the end."

Jennifer's face flushed, her lips parting somewhat as if searching for a response that never came.

"Is there something else?"

"I...don't know how to ask this."

"Simple. Just ask."

"Have…" Jennifer whispered, taking an anxious breath before letting the words escape her lips. "Have you ever seen him be *aggressive?*"

Wondering where this was going, Katherine moved closer to the almost trembling mortal. She lowered her voice as Jamie stood guard, ensuring they would not be interrupted. She noticed his eyes narrow as he listened in on what Jennifer could possibly want to discuss at a time like this.

"No. I have never seen him act aggressively. However, I suppose it would depend on your definition of aggressive. What are you asking?"

"Tell me, *please.*"

Straining to think of anything relevant, Katherine chose to be as honest as she could at that moment, still uncertain of Jennifer's motives. Her mind flickered to what she had heard whispered among the castle keepers of a recent exchange between Bayne and Emily.

"Well," Katherine admitted carefully, "I have heard rumours of his temper, but having never seen it myself, I found it difficult to believe."

The concern on Jennifer's face deepened at the princess's words. She folded her arms nervously across her chest. "Please, I need to know. I—"

"Why are you asking this, Jennifer?" Katherine's brow furrowed as she searched the mortal's eyes for an explanation. "Are you asking if I have *heard* anything, or are you trying to *tell* me something?"

"It's nothing, I swear."

Jennifer's words did little to provide comfort. A nagging unease twisted in Katherine's gut, and she pressed the issue further.

"What is this about, Jennifer? He is exactly who he has always been, and given the unique circumstances he has found himself in, I'm impressed at his ability to pretend to be taking things this well."

"I think it's more than that."

For a moment, the world of magic faded away, leaving Katherine simply a woman speaking to another. They had never been close and had never shared conversations like this, which only confirmed what she had already suspected. Jennifer was asking for a reason. And yet, no matter what that reason was, it was not Katherine's place to pry.

"All I have heard are whispers. Just the one about Bayne and Emily. The keepers say that his temper got the better of him, but no matter how heated their exchange was rumoured to be, it is not as if he would strike her."

"Yeah. I heard about that, too!" piped up Jamie from beside them.

"Really?" asked Jennifer, shooting him a cold look.

"Yes," Jamie said, his eyes dropping as though he had just been reprimanded. "But I mean, everyone has a temper now and then, right?"

Katherine had the impression that Jennifer had not received the answer she had been seeking.

"And you're *sure* there's been nothing else? Absolutely nothing?" Jennifer pressed one last time.

Even though Katherine knew better, she allowed the only memory she had of Bayne's temper to slip free.

"There was one other incident," Katherine said softly, not wanting to go into much detail. "Only one."

Jennifer leant in. "Yes?"

"There was an accident, years ago, at one of Jamie's parties that—"

"Oh yeah," Jamie blurted out. "I almost forgot. Everyone went on about how you were the—"

Katherine shot the mortal a warning look, and he quickly quietened down.

Jennifer frowned. "What are you talking about?"

"There was a moment when things could have spiralled out of control, but it was nothing. That night was a whirlwind of emotion, and he had every reason to react the way he did. Besides, he never actually resorted to violence. The situation was handled before things got out of hand."

"Yeah," muttered Jamie under his breath, "by you."

Sighing, Katherine turned back to Jennifer, who appeared not to have heard Jamie's statement. She relaxed her stance. "Listen. What I consider to be aggression is the needless slaughter of thousands at the mere whim of idiots in power. And trust me, Bayne is the furthest thing from that type." She paused. "Even so, this castle has a way of darkening even the purest of hearts if they are not cautious."

"Ah! The girlfriend and the ex," came Alek's voice, interrupting them. The prince had noticed the three huddled together as he was walking past.

"Alek," greeted Katherine, relieved to be rescued from what would have surely turned into a problem. "Keeping an eye on me, I see."

"Always!" He smiled, hands in his pockets. "You know, the two of you aren't supposed to be getting along."

Exchanging a slight smile with Katherine, Jennifer raised her hands and playfully took a swipe at her. Katherine avoided it and returned one of her own. Whether it was the tension being broken or just the atmosphere around them, the two, if only for a moment, enjoyed each other's company.

Alek merely shook his head. "Very unbecoming."

Katherine laughed. "I *do* actually like her."

"Sure," replied the prince, just loud enough for her to hear him, clearly unconvinced by her smile.

"Well," said the mortal, her eyes darting around nervously. "I'm going to get a different drink. See you soon, Kat...oh, I mean, Your Highness."

"Of course," Katherine replied, leaning close to her ear. "If there is something, anything, that you need, please come to me. Especially if you have any reason to feel unsafe. But while I'm still unsure of what truly haunts your mind to prompt such an inquiry, I would urge you to think twice before jumping to any conclusions when it comes to Bayne. I'm not aware of what has transpired between the two of you as of late, but he deserves the benefit of the doubt."

"Thank you, *again*," Jennifer whispered before turning to leave.

"Well, that was strange," said Jamie, moving to stand next to Katherine and Alek as they watched the mane of red hair move through the room.

"I was right in telling her all that I knew, was I not, Jamie?" Katherine asked quietly. "I could never imagine him doing anything to result in such questions, but then again, she wouldn't have asked for no reason?"

"No, you were right. She asked the question, and you answered. It's up to her how she takes it. And, as for why she asked, that's gotta be on her, too."

"Alright, then."

"Well," said Alek, reaching for a passing tray of smoking red cocktails. "Seems like a good time for a drink!"

Hesitant to ignore the worry she felt in the pit of her stomach, Katherine exchanged her empty glass with a full one from Alek and joined him and Jamie in a toast to a wonderful evening. If Jennifer's goal had been to unsettle her mind, then the mortal had been successful. However, if there was a true concern that had sparked their discussion, Katherine could not simply pass things off as insignificant or irrelevant.

"Tell Zach to keep an eye on her," Katherine whispered in Alek's ear, low enough for Jamie not to notice, never taking her eyes off her guests.

"Already done," said the prince as he raised his glass to his lips.

"Pardon the interruption, Your Highness," came a voice from over her shoulder.

"Yes, Alfred?" said Katherine, smiling as she greeted the handler.

"There are many dignitaries still awaiting an audience, and we are set to begin quite soon."

"Of course!" she exclaimed, taking the last sip of her drink. "Oh, how I have missed the politics."

Alek and Jamie snickered at Katherine's tone. Even Alfred cracked a smile as she joined him to take another lap around the room.

"It's still a bit unreal," Jamie confessed before downing his drink.

"You'll get used to it. If I were you, I would try to focus on the fun side of it," replied Alek, bumping the mortal playfully in the shoulder. "Excuse me, please. I, too, need to join in on the duty of it all."

Taking a swig of his drink, Alek spun playfully on his heels before disappearing into the crowd.

Katherine felt as if no time had passed as she made her way from greeting one dignitary to the next. While there were still parts of her that waited, quite impatiently, to be pieced together, the princess within took over, knowing it was only a matter of time before things would finally be clear.

She nodded politely, smiled graciously, laughed pleasantly, and conducted herself with all the grace she could manage. As she moved her way through the ballroom, Katherine kept a silent eye on each of the champions. Kaëden appeared to be in the midst of a serious discussion with members of his inner council. Alek had decided to head back over to drag Jamie along to meet a few of Keldorne's court representatives. Deacon looked to be trapped in a conversation with one of his military generals. Bayne seemed to be in the middle of an argument in the corner, as Jennifer pointed a finger at his face in frustration. And lastly, Marko could be overheard trying to explain the role of the mortals to some of Neighlore's more untrusting forces.

The guests danced and talked, gossiped and drank, and there was nothing else on their lips besides the trials and all that related to them. Seizing a moment between greeting a few of Azrallus's leaders, Katherine slipped off to the side to catch her breath. While she loved a good ball, she had nearly forgotten how long they could be, how draining.

"Your Highness," came Alek's all-too-knowing voice as a hand appeared from behind her, holding a tumbler of clear liquid.

She took it with a smile as Alek and Jamie joined her again. "You two appear to be getting along well," said Katherine, clinking her glass with theirs and finishing the ice-cold premium vodka in a single go.

Jamie shrugged playfully, pouting his lips. "You know, for an immortal, this guy isn't half bad."

They all let out a laugh. As always, Jamie had a way of lightening the mood.

"We figured you needed a break," admitted Alek.

"You are not wrong."

"Oh, heads up!" warned the prince quietly, gesturing over Katherine's shoulder.

She turned, quite surprised to see Jennifer and Bayne approaching. Jamie looked most uncomfortable. "Oh, bloody hell! What now?"

~

"I should be going. It's been a lovely party," said Jennifer as she did a little bow. "Thank you again!"

Katherine smiled, not wanting to appear as confused as she was quickly becoming. "Of course, it was good to see you. I hope you enjoy the rest of your evening."

Turning on her heels, Jennifer made her way for the nearest exit. With a quick goodbye to Alek and Jamie, Bayne started to follow.

"Hey!" called Katherine, reacting to the champion's unexpected coldness.

He stopped, his jaw clenched, and turned reluctantly.

"Besides the fact that you still need to participate in the ceremony, were you really planning on leaving without so much as a goodbye?" she said, her eyes narrowing into slits. "No goodnight for me?"

Bayne approached the princess and placed one hand on her hip, leaning in to kiss her cheek. His lips hovered next to her ear, and he lowered his voice. "I never fucking did what you told her I did." He released her and walked off to follow Jennifer through the doors that led out into the courtyard.

Caught off guard by the sudden turn of events, Katherine's insides froze.

Exchanging a puzzled glance with Alfred, who had appeared at his side, Alek gestured for the handler to go after the couple, while he and Jamie kept a stunned Katherine company.

~

"Master Bayne!" called Alfred as he hurried to catch up before they headed out too far.

"Seriously?" whispered Jennifer irritably as she and Bayne turned around. The cold air stung their ears as they paused beneath the dancing fireflies.

Quickly coming to a stop before the mortals, Alfred gave a slight bow. "Sir, your presence is required in the Grand Ballroom."

Jennifer rolled her eyes. "Can't we just go home already?"

"You may. Master Bayne, however, may not. As a champion, this is what is expected of him."

Jennifer clung to Bayne's arm, clutching it tighter as Alfred gave her a stern look.

"While you are here under the princess's protection, I would advise you to not interfere with these trials. I would also urge you to take care in *how* you address the princess. As well as in what you say to others."

Bayne opened his mouth to interject, but Jennifer beat him to it. "What's that supposed to mean, exactly?"

"She may have a soft spot for those she cared for while mortal, but that does not mean that she will respond as kindly to situations like this in future."

Jennifer scoffed, her expression wavering between guilt and anger.

"Master Bayne, join me," instructed Alfred coldly, narrowing his eyes at the distasteful display of human emotions. "*Please.*"

Bayne hesitated for a brief moment, his jaw tightening as if in pain, before exchanging a quick look with Jennifer. Then, with visible reluctance, he peeled his arm from her grip and strode to his handler's side.

Jennifer scowled. "Are you serious?"

"You know the rules. I have to do what I have to do," said Bayne softly.

"Well, I hope you enjoy sleeping alone," she spluttered angrily. "Again!"

"Jen, don't—"

"Master Bayne, if I may?" interrupted Alfred, raising his hand to silence both him and Jennifer, his gaze remaining locked onto the troublemaker. Without waiting for permission, he continued, "I am aware of what you did this evening, miss. Princess Katherine may not be fully dialled into all the goings on around her at present but make no mistake, there is nothing that happens in her castle that she does not, or will not, know about."

Jennifer shuffled her feet uncomfortably as Bayne's eyes darkened. Alfred could see the conflict in the young man's posture, his instinct to protect Jennifer warring with the doubt creeping into his features. Whatever words Bayne had prepared to defend her faltered as the truth of Alfred's account made him doubt.

"The princess, for the time being, seems quite willing to look past certain missteps that have occurred since her return. However, rest assured that after tonight, once her mind and power is restored, childish stunts executed in a fit of jealousy will no longer go unaddressed. The manipulation of her words and spreading of false claims is an offence to her crown and believe me, she will not be so willing to forgive and forget if this continues."

The colour drained from Jennifer's face as Bayne seemed to realise that he may have been too rash in his interaction with Katherine earlier.

"I had hoped that the discussion we had would be more successful than it appears to have been. While anyone could certainly understand your frustration, should you try to undermine my princess again, I will not be as quick to pass it over as I am now."

Alfred closed the gap between them, leaning in and feeling the fear radiating from Jennifer's skin as he brushed against her. Discreetly, his fingers slipped into her shimmering purse, retrieving the recording device he had seen her fiddling with earlier, concealed in the shadows. With a single slick motion, he stowed it safely in his pocket, careful not to let Bayne see it.

Jennifer gulped, unable to form words.

"Please," said Alfred, taking a step back and adjusting his suit, "leave if you so choose. But you are welcome and encouraged to stay should you agree to adhere to the rules of this kingdom. I warn you, however, that this is to be the final discussion on the matter."

The handler turned on his heel, leaving Jennifer speechless and flushed.

"Master Bayne?" Alfred glanced over his shoulder as he made his way back into the Grand Ballroom.

Bayne hesitated, shrugged, and then turned to follow suit. His handler's expression remained unreadable, but the tension in his movements hinted at frustration. Whatever had truly transpired that evening remained unclear, but he did not ask Alfred to explain.

Jennifer watched as Bayne disappeared back into the fantasy of the evening. Without another glance towards the celebration of *The Katherine Show*, she left, heading for one of the candlelit pathways that led down the courtyard steps, around the Grand Hall, and out to the waiting sea of cars.

CHAPTER 20
THE POWER UP

As the music softened into a gentle hum, Horus waved his hand, making the candles and flames throughout the Grand Ballroom brighten. The guests eagerly turned their attention to the council, their eyes fixed on the three beings as they ascended the stairs, their white cloaks trailing behind them. Strange though it was to see them in anything other than their familiar champagne-coloured attire, the purity of the colourless cloth seemed to be a calming force.

Bayne and Alfred slipped in from outside without drawing attention.

"Princess. Champions. *Come*!" instructed Herlock, gesturing for them to gather at the foot of the landing.

Each of the champions made their way into the walkway that had formed among the masses, accompanied by their handlers. As they took their places side by side before the council, Katherine came to a stop just a few feet away.

Dozens of servers and castle keepers wove through the ballroom, trays of chilled raspberry champagne hovering beside them as they handed out drinks to the guests.

Wine in one hand, bubbly in the other, Emily saw no reason to forfeit either, as she tried to prepare herself for what Alfred and the princes had warned them of. She wondered what kind of person this *new* Katherine would be, and she worried whether their friendship would change entirely or if they actually stood a chance in this world. In *her* world.

Even as a mortal, Emily sensed the excitement shared by everyone in attendance. Servers, royalty, council members, and guests alike. All eyes remained fixed in anticipation, waiting.

Herlock removed the orb from its home in his cloak and placed it in the middle of the landing. The council gathered around it, their voices rising in unison. A dazzling light flared from their hands, engulfing the sphere as it morphed into the unmistakable emblem of prophecy. Its ankle-high flames flickered in silent summons, calling to those sworn to its unbreakable oath. Its fires burnt more fiercely than ever before.

~

Katherine stepped into the heart of the symbol, bracing herself for whatever pain she was about to endure. Handing her the ceremonial blade, Horus signalled that it was time for the princess to press it to her palm and offer her life force up to the power of Fate.

The moment the crimson droplets touched the stone, the flames vanished, taking with them every other light in the extravagant ballroom, leaving only a faint glow that barely illuminated the symbol.

Before anyone could question what was happening, the ground beneath them quaked. Katherine struggled to maintain her footing but ensured that she remained at the centre of the chaos, just as the council had instructed earlier.

A deafening roar split the darkness as violent blasts of flame erupted from the air, water, spirit, fire, and earth markers, drowning out the panicked cries of the guests. Towering above them all, the flames twisted and surged before diving straight for Katherine's chest, the searing streams colliding with a force she had no hope of resisting.

The fire wove through her body, flowing around her, into her, and out again, as if she were both their vessel and their source. The spectacle was, for many, too bright to watch as its luminosity grew. The ground shook violently, sending some stumbling and others tumbling to the floor. Then, just as suddenly, the flames vanished, and the stone stood inert once more as the symbol reverted to its orb state.

Katherine opened her eyes and gazed out at the crowd as applause resounded throughout the room. She took a shaky but deep breath, letting the moment anchor itself in their chest.

"Your power has returned, Princess Katherine," Herlock whispered with a smile, collecting the orb. He waved his hand to reignite the ballroom's light.

Dolos narrowed his eyes, looking her up and down. "All of your power, but not immortality, it seems," he whispered, his voice so soft that Katherine and his fellow council members barely heard his words. "Perhaps Fate knows something we do not."

"Either way," Horus said, casting a sideways glance at Dolos, one that carried more of a warning than anything else. "Welcome back, Your Highness."

Without waiting for a response from Katherine, the council formally announced the conclusion of the first trial, addressing the guests with a few last words. They spoke briefly of the next stage, reminding everyone of the prophecy's ultimate outcome and the effects it would bring once all five trials were complete, before bidding the crowd a good night. With a final bow to the princess and the other royals, they turned to leave, graciously acknowledging the waves of applause that followed them as they departed.

～

A woman's voice rang out, distant yet cutting through the roars and wild jeers that filled the air. "Kat!"

"Princess Katherine?" called someone else.

Katherine looked around. She glimpsed familiar faces before her, yet they flickered and faded, slipping in and out of focus as she drifted between presence and oblivion. Wanting to get out of the East Wing and away from the beady eyes of her guests as quickly as she could, the princess headed for the courtyard, aiming straight for the candlelit pathways that led out into the grounds. Without stopping to acknowledge the party-goers vying for her attention, she even evaded Alek's attempt to halt her. As she fought through the mental and physical minefield she now found herself trapped in, her focus remained unshaken.

She felt as she had after her kiss with Kaëden, the flood of memories was almost too much to bear. This time, however, it was like parts of her very DNA being awakened, the effects coming on in waves. Not only was her power returning with every hit – each one powerful enough to cripple a lesser being – but it was also unleashing secrets and emotions she had tucked away in the far corners of her mind.

She may have recalled all she had experienced with the champions as the first trial progressed, but each fragmented memory she had struggled to piece together since the prophecy was triggered was now sharpening into view.

Katherine barely registered the sound of Alfred hurrying to catch up with her until his hand touched her back. "Is everything alright, Princess?"

She grimaced as they walked beneath the glow of the fireflies, but offered no reply. The handler nodded in understanding, his face marked with concern as he watched her descend the stairs and vanish into the shadows. Then, with a quiet sigh, Alfred returned to oversee the event's final hours. Thankfully, Katherine had always been able to rely on his ability to respect her privacy.

Katherine moved with as much composure as possible, even as the cold air wrapped around her face like a scarf, nearly suffocating her as it took hold of her throat. Seeking to put as far a distance between herself and the festivities as possible, she chose a path to the West Wing that only those who resided within the castle walls would think of taking. While not the quickest route back, it allowed her to avoid the bright lights of the spectacle. This way offered the most privacy, for the underground passages and corridors connecting the two wings remained firmly sealed. In her current state of mind, she was not inclined to attempt to unseal them.

Katherine battled past through sharp twigs and tightly spaced trees. Not many people chose to travel through the edges of the forest. Even when the castle had been bustling with bodies hundreds of years before, most preferred to use the long, connecting corridors rather than navigate the dangers of the grounds. While Alfred had done an amazing job at maintaining the property, the Forgotten Woods and its surroundings remained untouched, rugged, and natural.

∼

"How is she?" asked Alek, appearing at Alfred's side the moment he saw an opening where they would not be overheard.

"I am sure she is as well as could be expected," whispered Alfred. "She seemed to want to be alone, Your Highness."

The prince nodded, barely moving his lips as he spoke. "Understandable, given what she must be going through. Wise not to let them see her falter. Keep me informed if you hear anything more."

"Of course. Thankfully, no one seems to be questioning her disappearance."

"Yet."

Sensing the weight of too many eyes on them, Alek shot Alfred a quick glance before grabbing a glass of champagne from a passing server and rejoining the guests, pretending all was well.

Katherine was barely able to see where she was going. Her vision blurred in and out more frequently as she fought her way through the forest. What should have been a leisurely half-an-hour walk was quickly turning into an endless maze of green and brown. She stumbled and fell, a sudden pain searing through her right leg. As her face struck the ground, the scent of moist soil filled her nostrils. It was sharp and inescapable.

Katherine's eyes watered from the sting, snapping her back to the present. She pushed herself up, catching the sight of blood trickling from a fresh cut, the culprit – a gnarled tree root – jutting out from the earth behind her. Though her power was returning, her healing abilities were slower than she had anticipated. *Perhaps Dolos is onto something,* she thought.

She hiked her dress up, and the living roses faded into the material itself to allow Katherine to more easily manoeuvre through the treacherous woods. Reaching for the slip she was wearing underneath, she took off the holster that housed her weapons and used her blade to cut off a strip of cloth to wrap tightly around her thigh to slow the bleeding. She sat there for a few minutes before trying to get to her feet, determined to outthink the pain and make it back to the safety of the West Wing as soon as possible.

The leaves rustled behind her, a whisper of movement in the still night. The icy breath of air brushed against her skin as she turned, her gaze catching the slight, deliberate sway of the nearby branches. She had been beneath the canopy of these ancient giants many times before and was no stranger to the forest's inhabitants. In the past, though, they had usually chosen to leave her be, fearful of the chaos she could bring to their home – her home – if they did anything untoward. Whether it was paranoia or her vision beginning to play tricks on her again, a deep cry in her gut urged her not to dismiss it. Something, *someone,* was watching her.

Ignoring her wounded leg as best she could, Katherine resumed her journey through the trees. The panic that had set in was only worsened by her inability to remain present. It seemed to intensify the more the effects of her power and returning memories took hold.

Waves of voices crashed through her mind as the walls holding her past at bay crumbled. Yet through the noise, Katherine could still hear movement behind her as she navigated through the sea of hazy trees.

It took every ounce of focus she could muster, but she moved faster, pushing through the clutter as she tried to stay aware of her surroundings. She needed to gauge how closely she was being followed. As with the echoes of lives once lived, her power faded in and out, her enhanced hearing useless, and her speed unreliable.

Through the density of the forest, Katherine saw moonlight peeking through up ahead. She emerged from the dark into a clearing, home to a wooden cabin she knew had once been part of a small village, long abandoned.

It hit her. She had taken a wrong turn. She was about fifteen minutes away from the barrier that marked the end of the outer grounds. Though she held an inherent advantage on Eyrondale's soil, she was still twenty-five minutes from the added protection of the enchantments placed over the West Wing and its inner grounds, where she had long ago ensured that none but the invited could cross.

I don't have time for this, thought Katherine as she narrowed her eyes, peering across the clearing. Deciding to make the best of what she had, she hurried towards the crooked wooden door and thrust it open. Scrambling to close and bolt it shut, she searched the room. A flicker of ease crept in as her fingertips brushed against a lantern on the dusty table nearby.

Having nothing to light it with, Katherine's only choice was to use her power. But the worry in her gut deepened as she tried again and again to produce fire, once one of the simplest tasks for her. It took a handful of attempts, but finally, she was able to create a spark that ignited a small flame, which she sent into the holder.

Dim though the light was, Katherine saw no more than a few cupboards, a green armchair, and a rusty old washbasin. It looked like someone had occupied the shack some years before but had left in quite a hurry.

Hearing movement, Katherine reached for her gun. Her heart sank. She had been so out of it, so panicked, that she had forgotten her holsters back in the forest. Stumbling towards the nearest cupboard, she found within it a long, thin case that had been bolted and locked shut. Her gaze darted to an axe hanging on the far wall. Without hesitation, she seized it and swung at the lock. Inside was a worn shotgun and half a box of shells. No one would live here without means to survive the forest.

As the murmur of disturbed foliage grew louder, Katherine crept towards the window beside the door. It had been poorly boarded up with wooden planks, allowing whispers of the night's danger to whistle its way into the room. She stabilised herself and peeked through one of the gaps.

Katherine watched as fractured, shadow-like figures slipped into the clearing and advanced towards the decaying shelter. A soft gasp escaped her lips as she leant against the wall, realising she was surrounded. She squeezed her eyes shut, dread coiling in her chest as it dawned on her that, in her present state, she could not summon enough strength to escape.

Bang.

Her heart hammered loudly in her ears as the wood behind her trembled, shaking loose a thick cloud of dust that billowed into the air. Something was determined to get in.

Bang.

The pounding intensified.

Bang.

Any second now, the door would come crashing down.

Bang!

As it flew off its hinges, the door shot across the room, splintering apart. The cabin quaked from the force of the blow.

Katherine kept her eyes shut as the sound of deep, steady breathing reached her from the left. The musty scent of aged wood and dust was soon overwhelmed by the pungent stench of rotting flesh, growing stronger with each step the creature took inside.

She felt as though she were about to heave up her very insides. It had been many ages since she had smelled something so horrid, so putrid.

Unable to endure it any longer, she gave in. Reluctantly, her eyes opened, stinging from the powerful scent that seeped into them.

A large, black figure was moving in her direction, its frayed, tattered cloak rippling in the breeze. As its long, thin hand stretched out towards her, Katherine froze. Her focus remained locked on the gnarled appendage, its dark grey skin appearing to melt from the bone.

Noticing her stare, the faceless figure closed the gap between them and clasped its skeletal fingers around Katherine's neck. The shotgun dropped from her hands as she was lifted off of the ground. Struggling to try to free herself from the suffocating grip, Katherine was losing strength far quicker than she should have, her eyes watering from the pain as her body betrayed her.

Her breathing was strained and short, but she refused to give in as the creature's other hand pressed against her chest. Agony exploded through her as its sharp claws dug into the flesh over her heart – the very places her own nails had torn through days earlier to save Bayne – consuming her as it locked the scream in her throat.

Through her suffering, Katherine barely felt the warmth of the crimson liquid run down her body. The view before her soon faded as the floorboards creaked beneath the weight of a second visitor's footsteps. Katherine, only able to see a blurred outline before her world turned black, thought that somewhere in the distance of her mind, she heard a man say, "Take only what we need. She'll beg for the end soon enough – but not before I'm ready."

CHAPTER 21
THE AFTERMATH

E mily waited with Matthew for the others to get out of their town cars and join them on the landing at the West Wing's entrance. The pair had left before the other mortals and had beaten the rush to exit the East Wing.

"So, what do you think happens now?" asked Matthew, looking out at the winding driveway as the cars waited in line to drop off their friends.

"I'm not sure. But hopefully, now that she's back to being, well, who-ever she is, we can get some answers," said Emily quietly, unsure whether her friend was truly returning or slipping further away.

They let the conversation end there as the others gathered with them. The castle doors swung open as the final car rounded the fountain at the centre of the driveway and headed back towards the castle gates.

Alfred was waiting to greet the group with his usual welcoming smile. "This way, please," he said, leading them through the foyer into the living room.

He stopped, turned to face them, and waved open both sets of doors, allowing the hum of voices to filter in from the courtyard.

"There is an assortment of nightcaps on the table. Please feel free to enjoy the rest of the evening. I trust everyone has had a good time?"

"Yes, thank you!" Emily said, smiling as she ran her fingers over the luxurious fabric of her gown.

"Oh, definitely."

"Everything was so beautiful!"

"Excellent. The princess will be pleased to hear that," Alfred exclaimed. "Please, be sure to call should you need anything further. Goodnight everyone."

The handler waved his hand to dim the room's fires and close the curtains, offering a last smile before retiring for the evening.

"Shall we?" asked Jamie, nodding his head in time with the music drifting to their ears.

A few exchanged glances and shrugged, as if to say 'why not?'

Jamie rubbed his hands together and took hold of Matthew's and Aiden's shoulders as he stood between them, smiling. "Come on, boys, it's been a hell of a week. We could all use another round!"

Walking out to the courtyard, the mortals were surprised to see that the champions and one of the handlers were already waiting for them, drinks in hand.

As Emily approached, she could only just hear Daniel whisper to Kaëden, "No sign, sir. I will continue searching," before the handler hurried back into the castle through the dining room.

"Ah! Welcome!" greeted Deacon, a wide smile on the prince's face as he raised his drink in the air before taking a sip.

Marko turned around to face the group, his conversation with Alek at the other end of the table growing quiet. Instrumental music played on the outdoor speakers, keeping the evening's festivities and excitement alive.

"Hey, Em," said Bayne as his cousin went to hug him.

"I haven't had a chance to talk to you all night," she whispered in his ear. "Jen head to bed?"

Not the most open of people to begin with, Bayne stepped back as tactfully as he could and replied, "Yeah, uh. Been a bit of a rough one."

Emily took her cousin's response as a sign that he did not want her to pry any further. As she sighed, she noticed the way Bayne's body tensed, the rigid set of his shoulders betraying the anger still simmering beneath the surface. She wished he would just open up to her. It had been this way their entire lives, and more than once, Emily had wondered if his coldness was the very thing keeping them from being as close as she longed for.

"Everyone," called Alek as he and Marko joined the group. "If I could get your attention for a moment or two, please."

The chatter and laughter subsided a little to allow the prince to speak.

"Listen, I know that this has been surreal this far and that all of us are looking forward to getting *our* Katherine back, whatever that may mean to each of us individually. Now that she has returned, I am sure you may have endless questions you may have for her. I just need to warn you, you should still tread lightly."

The mortals exchanged sceptical looks, and Matthew piped up. "What are you saying, exactly? We get it you've warned us—"

"I think what my brother means," interjected Marko, "is that it's a whole new ball game now. So far, you've been fairly accepting of all of this, but our warnings aren't just for show."

Deacon chuckled from behind his glass as he leant against the dining table, having removed his tie and jacket. His brothers shot him a disapproving look.

"What I'm saying is that you still need to be careful." Alek exhaled slowly, running a hand through his hair as if searching for the right words. "You know Katherine in your own way, but that may not be the Katherine that walks back through those doors."

"As I've said, it doesn't matter what version of her walks back in here," came Emily's voice from one of the cocktail tables that had been set out for them.

"Oh, no?" asked Marko, eyebrows raised, amused.

"No! Either way, she's still Katherine, and we'll love her anyway. Whatever that means."

Out of the corner of her eye, Emily caught Bayne watching her, a slight smile playing on his lips. She wondered what he was thinking. He had always seemed surprised whenever she showed devotion to anyone besides herself. Her friendship with Katherine had long been proof of just how deeply she could care, even if not everyone saw it. They had not always got along behind closed doors, but she liked to believe that, deep down, Bayne respected the way she stood by her friend. Even if he would never admit it, he knew it took courage to defend someone without knowing if there was even a friendship left to save.

"It's a beautiful thought," Alek said, not quite successful in convincing Emily if he truly believed it or if he was merely humouring her. "But there are things about her you might not be able to accept."

"Say it, brother," came Kaëden's bitter voice from the bar as he searched through the bottles of liquor for something with a bit more kick.

"Say what?" pressed Emily.

Alek looked at Kaëden and scowled.

"If you refuse, I am certain someone else would be more than willing to fill them in," said the eldest prince, selecting a bottle of top-shelf whisky.

Deacon shook his head and downed his drink, his glass refilling with cognac immediately. "He means," he said, settling onto the table and pointedly ignoring the disapproving looks cast his way, "that Katherine is incredibly beautiful. She is charismatic. She is powerful."

Emily opened her mouth to speak, but Deacon took no notice.

"And with that power comes a temper," he continued, the boyish grin never fully fading from his face. "We all have them. It just means that, when it comes to Katherine, you shouldn't push the boundaries. Even I, who cherish the peace that life in the far reaches of the world provides, have witnessed the devastation she can leave behind."

Bayne uncrossed his arms as he automatically moved towards the prince. Emily and the other mortals exchanged nervous looks.

"You're going to scare them, Deacon!" said Alek harshly. Emily caught the way his gaze flicked to Bayne as if gauging his reaction.

"I just mean that I've heard the stories. And I'm sure they pale in comparison to what you've seen fighting alongside her all these years. And from what I hear, she's given Kaëden a decent run for his money on more than one occasion."

Alek huffed and shook his head, evidently choosing to hold his tongue rather than reply with a snippy retort.

"Okay, enough," snapped Marko.

"He is not wrong, brother," said Kaëden.

"Thank you!" Deacon shouted a little too loudly. "Even *he* agrees with me. Now you know it's true."

The eldest prince shot his brother a look that wiped the smile from his face. "Deacon, all I am saying is that she is one of the most powerful beings in existence. It would be best not to piss her off. Or me, for that matter."

With that, Kaëden adjusted his suit jacket, walked to an open table furthest from the crowd, and sat down with his drink, not saying another word.

"I guess that's one way to put it," muttered Deacon, downing another brandy.

Katherine's face was cold and damp. She opened her eyes, her surroundings taking a moment to come into clear view.

"What the...?" she exclaimed, finding herself not in the cabin, but under a tree, mere feet from the boundary line she had earlier been so desperately trying to reach.

Propping herself up, she looked around wildly, but there was no sign of anyone, or *anything*, else. The nearby turquoise stream trickled softly, its waters shimmering under the moonlight, rippling as it flowed.

Taking deep breaths of relief, Katherine lifted her gown, noticing that her leg had almost healed itself completely. Trying to piece together the events that had unfolded after she left the East Wing, now that her mind was more capable, Katherine wondered what exactly the figures in the clearing could have wanted with her if not to harm her. *How was it able to hurt me?* A sharp, yet manageable pain throbbed in her chest as she rubbed a hand over her heart. Even through the layers of her gown, it burnt to the touch. Only now did she realise that, despite being torn earlier, the fabric was perfectly intact.

As a sinking feeling took hold of her insides, Katherine hesitantly peeled the top of her dress away from her body. Looking down, she saw fresh scars marking the exact spots where her attacker had dug into her chest in the cabin. *There are only three types of beings who could have left these*, Katherine admitted to herself – a pure descendant, one of the twelve members of the council, or a first-born consequence of power.

She could no longer afford to remain out in the open – not on this side of the line.

She got to her feet and set off in the direction of the castle, moving towards the boundary, which glowed a deep red as she approached. As if it were a tangible shield of light, Katherine reached forward, touching it as it danced before her. She took a breath and leapt over the stream, her body tingling as she passed through the dense light, hovering in the air as the enchantment examined her worthiness to enter.

The second her feet touched the ground on the other side, the final pieces seemed to fall into place. She drew in a breath, and a frigid force slammed into her chest, stealing the air from her lungs. As the icy grip released her, Katherine's entire body felt calm.

She finally felt more complete than she had in centuries. She had finally regained both her memories and her powers. Better still, the pain faded into a faint sensation that no longer threatened to cripple her.

She was free.

Her past identity and her recently lived humanity were intertwining to shape something entirely new.

A smile spread across Katherine's face as the raw, untamed power within her stirred. While still bound by the restrictions imposed by the council on all pure descendants of power, there was a flare of purity that refused to be subdued, a force reaching for the surface. She shot a glance back at the other side of the stream before pushing off with all her might, towards the castle as fast as she could, testing the constraints enforced by the rules of the trials.

The forest passed by in a blur as she pressed the boundaries of her enhanced speed. Yet, a small part of her was unable to shake the feeling that she was still missing something important. Something that could help her make sense of it all.

Why now? Why was it so important for the prophecy to be triggered now?

Katherine's thoughts raced. She knew there was no time to waste, that she would need to find whatever it was she was missing, and *fast*.

❧

The front doors slammed shut, echoing through the foyer and out into the night's air.

"Katherine?" asked Marko loudly over the music.

"Must be," said Alek, looking around to see who was absent from their gathering.

The castle keepers never used the main entrances, and anyone not caught up in the post-festivities celebrations would already be in bed.

Bayne glanced towards the open sets of double doors, waiting for Katherine to walk through one of them. A few, including Emily, craned their necks to try to catch a glimpse of her. Moments passed, but the princess was nowhere to be seen.

They finished their nightcaps at their own pace, Alek occasionally casting concerned glances towards the castle before he, too, decided to turn in for the night.

CHAPTER 22
THE MORNING AFTER

"This seems to be becoming a theme, Alfred," commented Alek from behind his morning coffee.

"Would you like me to check on her, Your Highness?" Alfred whispered in the prince's ear.

Alek could see Emily, Aiden, and a few others steal quick glances at him and the handler as they talked.

"No, no, thank you," said Alek loudly, as if to make it seem insignificant. "But this coffee *does* need a bit more Irish!"

"Yes, sir! Of course," agreed Alfred, retrieving one of the more premium bottles of whisky from the bar behind them and topping up Alek's brew as nonchalantly as possible, spelling the cup to refill itself as needed.

"You're not fooling anyone, you know," said Deacon from down the table as he paged through the newspaper, stopping at the sports section without looking up for a second.

"Oh, yeah?" asked Alek, leaning forward to look past the line of diners between them, eyebrows slightly raised.

With a sigh, Deacon closed his paper reluctantly. "Brother, she's just been slammed with more than a thousand lifetimes' worth of memories, as well as her power. Relax! It's going to take her a minute before she goes back to fighting bad guys at your side. Okay?"

Marko let out a snicker across from Alek.

Deacon scoffed and shook his head. "And you? Aren't *you* worried?"

Marko shifted forward, crossing his arms on the table as his brother shuffled in his seat uncomfortably.

"I just mean that out of everyone here, you should be the most concerned of all, Markovyas."

"And why is that?" responded Marko, now straight-faced and staring Deacon down.

"Come on. You must have done something really bad for her to not come running right back into your arms the second she remembered you."

A loud clang only fuelled the tension as Alek dropped his fork. His brothers shot him a quick glance before turning back to shooting daggers at each other.

"You dare?" pushed Marko with a slight snarl.

"And you call Kaëden and me vicious." Deacon chuckled. "Just look at how you're reacting now. I swear, you and Alek are so touchy."

"Leave it," snapped Alek, before taking a sip of his coffee as Marko opened his mouth to retort.

"If I may?" came Alfred's voice, determined to cut off whatever was about to transpire.

"Of course, Alfred," prompted Alek, turning his attention away from his brothers.

"The council has advised that they wish to pass by here later on. If everyone could please be near the foyer this afternoon so we can gather at a moment's notice to greet them."

Nods passed around the table, accompanied by a flurry of acknowledgements, though the mortals, princes, and their handlers remained wary at the thought of an unexpected visit. The announcement silenced any bickering, snuffing out what could have been a full-blown blaze.

Jennifer could be heard letting out a loud sigh from the far end of the table as she folded her arms, clearly annoyed. Jamie and Aiden, however, seemed somewhat excited at the prospect of learning more about what was to happen in the next part of the trials.

As hurried conversation broke out over the latest news, many of the mortals cast glances between Bayne and the princes, clearly wondering when the champion would fill them in on what was happening behind closed doors. But, as expected, Bayne paid little attention to the chatter around him, intent on avoiding any form of small talk.

∼

"Pardon the interruption, everyone!" came Zachary's voice from the doorway that led to the armoury staircase.

Silence fell as all eyes turned to the slightly nervous-looking tech wizard.

"Yes, Zachary?" prompted Alfred, hands behind his back, moving forward from the wall where he had been watching the morning's events.

"There was an...um—"

"What's wrong, Zach?" asked Alek, face serious as he got to his feet, knowing that tone all too well.

With a sharp inhale, Zachary continued, lowering his voice slightly as he addressed the prince. "It seems there's been an incident out in the Forgotten Woods, Your Highness."

"Go on," Alek encouraged, his voice hardening.

"When I got in this morning, I ran a sweep across the grounds. It looks like something was out near the boundary last night."

"What kind of something?"

"Can't say for sure. But whatever it was, the traces of power it left behind suggest it's big."

Alek looked down at the table, his eyes darting from side to side as his mind raced. Finally, he pursed his lips and closed his eyes as he reached his fingertips down to touch the table as gently as possible.

"Where did you say Katherine is, Alfred?" the prince asked through gritted teeth, furrowing his brow.

Concern flooded Alfred's face. "I—"

"Surveillance shows she headed up to her suite after getting back last night," interrupted Zachary.

Alek opened his eyes, breathing deeply.

"Everything alright over there, brother?"

"Everything's fine, Deacon," said Marko harshly, his concern mounting as he studied Alek's reaction.

"And what time did she get in again?" Alek whispered, turning to look at Zachary, ignoring the others.

"Later than she should have."

Alek's nostrils flared, his fists closing shut as his face turned red.

"Damn it!" shouted the prince as he, in one swift motion, grabbed the nearest glass and threw it into a wall, shattering it into pieces.

Emily almost jumped out of her seat, as did a few of the other mortals.

"What is it, Alek?" asked Kaëden, his eyes narrowing at the sudden outburst.

"Nothing," muttered the prince as he held his hand to his forehead, doing his best to control his temper.

"But—" began Deacon.

"I said it's nothing. I'll handle it!"

Deacon looked as though he wanted to press the issue, but Kaëden silenced him with a discreet shake of his head.

"Zach, Alfred, follow me," Alek instructed, marching past them. He yanked open the door to the staircase and led the way to the armoury.

"What do you think that's all about?" asked Deacon as his eyes lingered on the closed door.

"He said he's got it," snapped Marko.

"Yeah, but what if we need to know? Plus, it's obviously about *her*."

"Listen, Alek's been keeping watch over Eyrondale since she began her first life as a mortal. He knows what he's doing. And I'm sure that *you* wouldn't like any of us interfering if something was happening in *your* kingdom. Right, brother?"

The youngest prince seemed to decide that it was better to hold his tongue, as Marko's raised eyebrows dared him to try his luck again.

"Well, I'd like to know, for one!" piped up Emily as silence fell.

The mortal could feel Kaëden's gaze shift towards her, but she was more concerned about her friend than what the princes thought at this point. While still visibly nervous around them, she had come to trust Alfred and Alek when they promised that no harm would come to her or the others while they were in Eyrondale.

"Me too!" said Layla, hurrying to show her sister support.

"Well, you see, brother?" muttered Deacon. "I'm not the only one."

"I'm sure they'll tell us if it is anything to be concerned about."

"Do you ever give a direct answer?" blurted out Emily before she could stop herself.

Marko chuckled at the human's bravery in the face of more powerful forces than she could possibly begin to comprehend.

"Wouldn't you rather have a touch of mystery in your life?" said the prince, getting up and taking his coat from Lucien.

Emily's cheeks glowed bright pink.

"I can see why she likes you." Marko paused, just about to exit through the courtyard doors. He turned back to face Emily and winked. *"Kinda."*

Layla giggled beside her sister as Aiden, Jamie, and a few others smiled at the deepening redness of Emily's face as the prince left without another word.

~

"Alright," said Alek as the trio reached the table in the centre of the armoury's main room. "Where is she?"

"Last the cameras picked her up, it was around two-forty-three this morning," said Zachary, pulling up the surveillance records from his tablet, casting as many feeds onto the screens as he could.

"You're sure she's in her suite?" asked Alek, cross-armed at the war table, staring at footage of Katherine making her way up the helical staircase in the northeast tower.

"I don't have a way to check."

"Now's not the time to pretend that you don't have every inch of this place wired, Zach."

"*Almost* every inch," corrected Zachary. "But I still can't give you what you're asking for. You know that."

"I don't care about her rules right now. It's *me*. I need to make sure she's safe."

"If she finds out about this..." Zachary's voice trailed off as he pulled up the view of Katherine's balcony from one of the outer wall cameras that overlooked the training arena. With a few adjustments, he was able to create a perfect line of sight into the princess's suite through the open balcony doors.

Alek watched as Katherine paced up and down in her bedroom.

"Yeah, I know. I'll take the heat for it. It's fine." The prince's hands tightened their grip on the edge of the table, and he hung his head, letting out a sigh of relief as he composed himself.

"At least she's safe," Zachary muttered.

"Yeah." Running his hand through his hair, Alek looked to Alfred, who seemed to be just as relieved as he was. "How did she get home last night?"

"I cannot say, Your Highness. She waved off any attempt at company. Staff mentioned seeing her head into the woods, on a path that should have led her to emerge around the far side of the Stargazer's Tower."

"Mmm. She has her memories, so she wouldn't have gone off the trails. She would have known the quickest path to take."

Alek turned to look at the large wall-size screen. "Zach, show me where exactly the incident happened."

Without hesitation, Zachary tapped away on his device, and a map of the castle grounds appeared on the screen. Next to a red glowing line that represented the protective boundary danced a little ball of blue light, surrounded by a green haze.

"These are the ones I'm worried about," explained Zachary, pointing to the collection of twinkling gold, a bit further to the left.

Alek stepped closer to the screen, his eyes narrowing. "We don't have anyone stationed out there. That village has been abandoned for ages. The forest has all but swallowed it."

"Exactly. Those lights definitely aren't werewolf, vampire, goblin, or ghoul."

"There seems to be one light here that's brighter than the rest," said the prince, pointing to a concentrated glow near the treeline.

"I would guess that's the leader."

"Send a few riders out. Find me anything I can use."

"Yes, sir!" said Zachary, moving to one of the nearest computers and typing at an astonishing speed.

"Alfred," instructed Alek as the prince made his way towards the stairway. "Make sure she's okay."

"Right away!"

~

There was a rap on the door to her suite as Katherine continued to pace back and forth in her bedroom, the fires warming her as she marched up and down the marble floor. Called back to reality, she moved into the sitting area, her focus shifting to the large wooden doors.

"Enter," she instructed, one of the doors creaking open at her command. It felt good to have that power back.

"Pardon the interruption, Your Highness," said Alfred, stopping as he entered to sink into a low bow.

"What is it, Alfred?"

"Your Highness, I simply wanted to ensure that you were alright and that nothing had befallen you."

Katherine smiled. "Thank you, old friend. But, as always, I'm—"

"Fine?" came the sharp interjection.

Her smile faltered slightly, fingers grazing the fabric of her sleeve as she hesitated. "I'm as fine as I can be. Whatever pain comes – or remains – I may be a few hundred years out of practice, but I'm sure I'm capable of handling it."

"So, you are in pain?"

"Alfred!"

"Fine?"

"As I said. *Fine.*" The princess smiled at her handler's stubbornness. "I will be down in a few hours. I promise."

Alfred said nothing, but the way his eyes lingered on hers made it clear he was not entirely convinced. Katherine held his gaze, unwavering. After a moment, he gave a slight bow and exited the room.

Pacing once again, Katherine knew that, human life aside, she needed to put her kingdom first. *No matter how much I care about these people, these trials...my kingdom – the balance must come first.*

It is all too perfect, she thought as she continued to analyse the events that had occurred over the past fortnight, trying to find a hint of what lay beneath the surface. *The timing of everything aligns too well. These trials all but guarantee that the highest leaders of each kingdom will be preoccupied for the foreseeable future. But to what end?*

Katherine retrieved the drink she had left behind in the bedroom and returned to the front fireplace, taking a seat atop the plush rug that spread out across most of the area. Cross-legged, a glass of red in hand, she searched the dancing flame for any clue that could explain what was going on.

She sat for what felt like hours, encouraging the fire with a wave of her hand each time it began to dim. Her wine glass was on its seventh refill when muffled screams filled the room, echoing from the tablet she had set to monitor the castle entrances. Abandoning her quest for answers, and the rest of her drink, Katherine hurriedly slipped on the leather jacket that hung next to the door and made her way towards the source of the disturbance.

Her boots made sharp, quick sounds against the floor as she moved through the castle, following the cries that grew ever louder as she approached the main living areas. Approaching the staircase leading to the foyer, Katherine caught what sounded like Alek yelling in the brief silences between the terrified screams.

CHAPTER 23
THE BEGINNING

"And this?" came Katherine's enchanting yet stern voice from atop the staircase.

"You're here!" exclaimed Alek, smiling as he looked up at her, ignoring the cries that echoed through the foyer.

"Of course I am. Nobody could miss that racket. Why is *he* here? You and Alfred *invited* him in?" she asked, nodding towards the man Alek held by the scruff of his neck.

"Apparently, he has information about an incident that happened here last night. I'm thinking a little gentle persuasion will do the trick."

"Now, now, brother, what's going on here?" asked Deacon as the prince traipsed into the foyer, followed out of the main living room by Marko, Emily, and Jamie.

"You're disturbing my afternoon drink, brother," joked Marko.

"What incident?" asked Katherine, suspicion creeping into her voice.

Bayne entered the room, drawn by the commotion, just as the rest of the mortals rushed in. His gaze lifted to Katherine, his expression unreadable, but a hint of sadness in his eyes lingered as if recalling the words he had spoken to her the night before.

"Something was out in the Forgotten Woods, something that shouldn't have been," answered Alek, shaking the captive wildly.

The man, his dark eyes widening at the sight of so many pure descendants of power in one place, continued to fight against Alek's grip.

"Enough!" yelled the prince, holding his free hand up in the air, quickly closing it into a tight fist.

The man's voice was cut off in an instant, muted as if snuffed out. His eyes welled with tears from the pain as Katherine descended the final few stairs and handed her tablet to Alfred.

The princess kept her focus on the figure kneeling at Alek's feet, cowering in fear at the realisation that escape was impossible. Avoiding eye contact with anyone else in the room, Katherine moved with deliberate restraint, her pace slowing as she neared Bayne. He opened his mouth, clearly about to speak, but before he could, she lifted a hand to stop him.

Nobody else seemed to want to brave trying to greet Katherine as she crossed the foyer. The other mortals shrank back, eyes darting between one another, as if afraid that even breathing too loudly might draw unwanted attention. The sharp clack of Katherine's boots fell silent as she stopped before Alek, who released his grip on the captive's neck and flung him forward at her feet.

"Rise," instructed the princess as the stranger continued to sob, Alek having unclenched his fist.

She exhaled sharply, rolling her eyes before extending a hand towards the man's head.

"I said, rise!" Katherine demanded coldly, quickly growing impatient.

The man resisted, but his body obeyed nonetheless. He got to his feet as Katherine's fingers moved effortlessly through the air, guiding him like a puppet on invisible strings. She could feel the mortals' unease radiating in steady waves. Emily, in particular, was watching with wide eyes, exchanging nervous glances with those nearest to her. But Katherine barely spared them a thought. Unlike the humans, Kaëden and the other princes were silent, their expressions inscrutable, though there was no mistaking the flicker of anticipation in their eyes.

"Now," she said, her tone terrifyingly yet unexpectedly polite as she came face-to-face with her guest. "What do you know?"

Katherine's eyes turned the shade of midnight as she waited.

"I...I..." the man spluttered, still unable, or unwilling, to speak.

A loud, theatrical sigh escaped the princess's lips as she closed the gap between them. The man's face was both dark with shadows and pale with fear, sweat dripping from his brow. Nearly touching her nose to his, Katherine grasped his tattered collar, adjusting and straightening it with unnecessary slowness.

"Don't be frightened," she whispered, a gentle smile curling her lips as if to offer reassurance. "I understand. You worry for yourself – for those you care about."

The man nodded quickly, Katherine's gaze resting on him with quiet empathy.

"I can assure you that if you share your tale, I will personally see to it that your family is taken care of."

His lips quivered as Katherine brushed the dust off of his shoulders.

"But," the princess's tone shifted sharply, "the same cannot be said if I find that you have withheld pertinent information from me about the goings on in *my* kingdom."

Looking around the room in search of some form of relief or aid, the captive's face contorted in defeat. "P...Princess," he stuttered, locks of his greasy black hair whipping back and forth. "I...I can't. He...I'll be...He'll kill me."

The smile faded from Katherine's face instantly. Anger building, she lowered her voice. "And you think that I will not eviscerate you along with every soul you have ever met if you continue to hold your tongue?"

Katherine could sense the way the mortals had frozen, their fear pressing into the space between them. She could practically hear the frantic rhythm of their hearts, each beat a quiet betrayal of their unease.

She had always been slightly quick-tempered, but this was different. Emily said nothing, but Katherine did not need words to know what she was thinking. The tightness in the human's stance, the way her throat bobbed as she swallowed, told her enough. And Katherine did not need a mirror to know what they saw – someone capable of instilling such terror into those who had never thought to fear her before.

"They...they don't have a name yet."

"Go on," Katherine prompted, folding her arms across her chest.

"There have been whispers that something, some *things*, have been born from the depths of a chasm that lies far within the boundaries of a land long ago left untouched."

Katherine's eyes narrowed as she strained to hear the next, barely audible, words. The fabric of her sleeves bunched under the pressure of her nails, the bite of her grip sharp against the leather.

"There is an evil that is coming for us all, Your Highness. And from what I understand, it is to begin, and end, with you."

A cold knot twisted deep in Katherine's insides, her pulse quickening as she glanced around the room. His words closed in around her like a dark cloud, heavy and suffocating. This was not a conversation for prying ears.

She leant in, her voice a harsh whisper laced with urgency. "Who else knows of this?"

"Only a few. The reach of their shadows has only just begun to brush against the earth's surface. Only those who have seen them believe."

"And have you seen them? These creatures?"

"A mere glimpse. But it was enough to shake me."

"And have they shaken you enough to sway your loyalties?"

"Your...Your Highness..."

"That is what I thought," Katherine breathed, aware that she had no other choice.

She took a step back and placed one hand reassuringly on the man's shoulder. He looked relieved as Katherine let out a quick sigh and searched his eyes once more for any trace of further insight. Smiling, she drew her other arm back before, in one swift motion, driving it forward into his chest, her hand wrapping around his heart as her fist broke through to the other side of him.

Pulling her bloody sleeve back through his body, she allowed both the captive and his heart to drop to the floor. Shocked gasps and strangled cries tore through the room as Katherine watched the last flicker of life drain from his already dark eyes, leaving behind nothing but empty, lifeless voids.

"What did you do that for?" Alek asked frantically, rushing towards her, ignoring the reactions of the mortals. "What did he say?"

"There was no chance of him leaving here alive. Whether he knew anything or not," Katherine replied coldly, taking the handkerchief that Alfred had hurried to give her.

As she wiped and dabbed at the blood that so desperately clung to her, Emily clutched her stomach, suddenly ill in the nearest vase at the sight of her friend's cruelty.

Jennifer moved to stand beside Emily, her hand clamped over her mouth to stifle a scream. The mortals looked as though they were barely restraining the urge to flee. Jennifer's legs trembled, and she instinctively stepped back, colliding with Marko. He barely reacted. If he was bothered by Katherine's actions, he gave no sign of it.

The faint notes of "Für Elise" barely masked the horror of the scene. Alfred tore his concerned gaze away from Bayne's wide, shock-stricken eyes, exchanging a brief look with Katherine before waving open the doors. Beyond them, the three council members stood waiting, patient yet expectant, as if the chaos inside had not unsettled them in the slightest.

~

"Good day, Your Highness," greeted Herlock as Katherine gestured for them to enter.

"Ah!" exclaimed Horus as the trio walked into the foyer, coming to a stop before the lifeless being that lay soaked in a congealing pool of red.

He and his fellow council members seemed unimpressed, yet unsurprised by the violence Katherine had succumbed to. Their expressions were calm and composed. So composed, in fact, that Katherine wondered whether they had timed their arrival a little too well. Perhaps they had foreseen how the day's events would unfold.

The council's eyes met briefly, and a knowing look passing between them before Horus continued. "We had wondered whether you felt...uh... alright."

"Yes," said Dolos, his eyes moving slowly around the room, taking in the gruesome scene. "We were concerned when you left the ball last night."

"Well, as you can see, I am fine," reassured Katherine. "Should anything become of concern, I will be sure to inform you. Or I'm sure that *Alfred* will, as is his duty."

"Of course, Your Highness," squeaked Horus, knowing better than to argue with protocols established thousands of years ago.

"I am certain that you have not taken time out of your busy existence just to check up on me." Katherine's tone dripped with sarcasm as she arched an eyebrow, almost positive that this was exactly the reason for their visit. She tossed the handkerchief onto the bloody corpse without a second thought. "So, what can we assist you with?"

Horus cleared his throat and stepped forward, taking great care not to sully his robes with the bloodshed.

"Perceptive as ever, Your Highness."

Two castle keepers emerged from the passage to the kitchens. With a wave of their hands, the body burst into flames, leaving behind a shimmering ash that they quickly scooped into a bag. It took only a few seconds for the creatures to finish up and exit the foyer, leaving the floor as spotless as ever.

"Champions, please, come forward."

As if they had been unfrozen, the champions moved around them. Kaëden peeled himself away from the main living room's doorframe where he had been leaning, watching with a rather satisfied look on his face. Deacon zigzagged through the group of mortals to stop just short of the council. Alek took a few steps forward to join his brothers as Marko stopped beside them. Bayne was the only one who remained behind Katherine, reluctant to move any closer to where the body had been. With the look of shock still evident on his face, Bayne seemed to find himself drawn in by the council's words, his steps faltering only momentarily before he settled into his place.

"Make no mistake," said Horus. "The first trial was expected to be the most simple. From here, Fate will make decisions that will shape the course of the future of all existence. The next trial is of the utmost importance as, at its end, only four will proceed."

The energy around them shifted noticeably. Until now, there had been no real competition between the champions. The stakes had been nothing more than rumours on the wind.

Alek's gaze swept the room, pausing briefly on Bayne – the *wild card*. Katherine caught the flicker of something in the prince's expression – a knowing glint in his eye. Whatever he was thinking, she could sense it. When she followed his line of sight, she saw it too – the hunger building in his brothers' eyes. Things were about to get interesting.

Herlock's eyes glowed in the light of the living flames that hovered within the chandelier above. "We will return in five days to complete the order selection and to inform you of what the next trial will require. We suggest that you all take the week to prepare for what this challenge might bring."

Alfred was the one to break the silence. "Thank you, I will inform the other handlers."

"Of course." Horus hesitated before leading his fellow council members in a bow. "Your Highnesses."

"Well, um...yes. That is all." Herlock shuffled his feet uncomfortably as he straightened, careful to avoid passing down judgement on what had transpired only moments before. "With that, we wish you a pleasant evening ahead." He nodded. "Your Highnesses, Master Bayne."

"Very well," said Katherine, fully aware she would become the topic of conversation the moment they were out of earshot. "We shall see you in five days."

They watched as the council turned as one and made their way outside, the double wooden doors of the West Wing bidding them a final goodbye as they slammed shut behind them.

~

"Well then," said Alek, turning to face everyone and clapping his hands, doing his best to seem cheery. "You heard them. We should all get some rest."

"Yes," added Alfred, making his way in the direction of the kitchens. "The night is still young, so I will have the staff send up dine-in baskets for each of you. No need to come down for dinner. You may take the evening to do as you please."

"Excellent idea, Alfred," said Alek, realising that Katherine, who was still standing expressionless, was not going to make an effort to distract her friends from the aftereffects of her display of violence.

Alfred bustled out of the room, leaving Emily and the other mortals to face their shock without reinforcement. Calling for a castle keeper to escort the mortals to their suites on the first floor to clear the scene as quickly as possible, Alek gave Emily a look that prompted her to go along with it.

As Emily turned to follow Aimee's lead, the prince felt a sense of unease in the pit of his stomach. Despite his attempts to maintain a façade of normalcy, he knew that things were far from normal. And Katherine's stoic demeanour made it clear that she had no intention of offering any comfort. He stood, waiting, as he watched the humans disappear into the depths of the castle.

There was silence among those who remained as the final footsteps retreated. Katherine stood, arms crossed, staring at her boots. She only moved once the world beyond the room was still.

"Kat—" came Alek's voice as he rounded on her.

"Finally," Katherine said, stopping the prince before he could pass down commentary on her actions. She took a step towards him, relaxing her arms. "I need to talk to you."

Alek threw his hands up in exasperation before letting them fall to his sides. "I'm definitely not stopping you."

She tilted her head, biting her lip as her fingers tightened into fists. Their eyes met.

"Wait!" the prince's tone softened. "What's wrong?"

Without another word, Alek shot Marko a look that made him straighten up, pulling his brother's attention away from the vacant stare he had been lost in.

"Come on. Best leave these two be," Marko said, his hands still in his pockets as he made his way to the living room. He gave a small gesture for the other champions to follow. "Sure you could use a drink."

Scoffing, Deacon was the first to follow, with Kaëden close behind.

"Hey. Go with 'em," said Alek, laying his hand on Bayne's shoulder and guiding him towards the next room. "I've got this."

Without so much as a glance at any of them as she passed by, the princess marched straight for the armoury staircase. Alek sighed, giving Bayne a reassuring pat on the back before following after her.

"Ah, well!" laughed Marko. He downed the drink he had just poured himself. "Lucien and the others missed a good show."

"You're telling me," muttered Deacon.

"Here, *boy*," Marko's voice drawled as he lifted a glass of scotch towards Bayne. "Drink up."

"I..." spluttered Bayne, unable to decide where his own head was at.

"Don't have the stomach for death, do ya?"

"Marko!" Deacon chuckled as he took a seat in a nearby armchair. "Don't mock the kid. I'm sure he'll get used to it quick enough living here."

The two princes laughed at the expression on Bayne's face as he dared not say anything.

Bayne hesitated before reluctantly taking the offered drink, his mind still reeling from the night's events. He took a sip, the warmth of the alcohol spreading through him and momentarily easing the tension in his muscles. As he glanced around at his companions, he wondered if they were right – if he would indeed get used to this new way of life.

~

"Excuse us, please!" Katherine instructed as she and Alek stepped into the armoury.

Zachary and his IT team stopped their work immediately. He shot the prince a concerned look before complying with his master's order. Rising from his position where he had been meticulously reviewing the previous night's camera footage at the war table – yet again – he grabbed his tablet and swiftly shut down the recording equipment for the room. As Zachary followed the last of his staff out through the back entrance, four of the monitors on the wall promptly went blank.

Alek turned his attention to Katherine, who made her way to the table and glanced over at the recordings. The prince's frown lines were more pronounced than she had seen them this past week.

"What's going on, Kat?" he asked, his eyes tracking her every move.

She ran her fingers through her hair and took a breath. "Something happened after the ball."

Alek shifted his weight, his gaze wary as Katherine started to pace. "I'm all ears."

"After my power was restored, it felt as though it, along with my remaining memories, was still falling into place. I couldn't allow the courts to see me in a diminished state and so I made my way back to the West Wing."

"Right. So—"

"I returned through the forest, Aleksander. In the midst of blurred vision, haunting hallucinations, echoes of voices, and relentless waves of pain, I grew convinced I was being followed. And it turns out, I was right."

"So, it *was* you out there last night?"

Katherine halted, fixing him with a piercing gaze.

He pointed to the blue haze on the aerial surveillance footage that Zachary had shown the prince earlier. "Outside of the boundary line?"

"In my...*state*, I miscalculated the direction back to the castle and found myself outside of the line longer than I should have been. Before I realised it, I was surrounded."

"That!" Alek hurriedly pointed to another frame that Zachary had left up on the screen. "Those golden lights. You're telling me that you saw whatever those things were?"

"Yes."

"Why didn't you say anything to anyone earlier? I—"

Katherine held up a hand to silence the prince before he could continue. "One of them, whoever or whatever they were, got inside. My power was faulty."

"And you weren't able to—"

She shook her head, cutting Alek off. Her expression sent a haunted look flickering across his face. "Just as I was about to lose consciousness, someone else entered."

The prince moved closer, reaching for each of Katherine's arms. Knowing that it took more than an encounter with a simple beast to shake her, he squeezed them gently. "Who?"

She took a sharp breath in. She had known Alek for the entirety of their existence. There was nothing he could hide from her, nor she from him. She paused before nodding, unable to bring herself to say it.

"No," Alek muttered.

"He...he said he needed something from me."

Alek's expression darkened as the realisation took hold, the same awful conclusion forming in his mind as it had in Katherine's. Silence stretched between them, each royal unwilling to give voice to what they both knew.

"There aren't many foolish enough to take on a pure descendant of power."

"No. No, there are not."

Alek hung his head briefly before enveloping Katherine in his arms. Yet even the steady warmth of his embrace did little to soften the harsh reality before them.

He exhaled slowly, his voice barely above a whisper. "Carter."

The name hung in the air, heavy with loathing. A pause. A cruel truth. "This is only the beginning."

IN THE
BEGINNING

I n the beginning, the Three Spheres of Power collided, bringing existence into being and marking the genesis of all ages. This clash of energies caused each to fracture into three distinct strands.

The Cosmic Sphere divided into Creation, Destruction, and Void. The Magic Sphere unravelled into Arcane, Elemental, and Spirit. And the Destiny Sphere shattered into Fate, Time, and Soul. However, the raw presence of these forces threatened the survival of the very existence they had created. Quickly realising the devastation their unchecked power could unleash, the Nine Strands of Power decided to part ways to establish balance. Each sphere would see one strand absorbed into all that is and would be. One would dwell beyond the tangible universe. And one would bring physical representations into being.

Destruction, Arcane, and Fate chose to seep into the world. Arcane wove itself into the fabric of reality, granting future beings the ability to wield its energy. Fate entwined with existence itself, shaping the destinies of all who would come. Meanwhile, Destruction would linger in the shadows, destined to bring an end to every beginning.

Void, Spirit, and Soul took it upon themselves to shape their power beyond the realms of sight and certainty, forming unseen planes of existence that would influence all that came to be.

Creation, Elemental, and Time were tasked with manifesting physical representations of their power to ensure the balance would endure. However, impatience grew within the Cosmic Sphere before the strands could agree on the creation of the physical worlds.

Driven by their ambition to claim supremacy in the hierarchy of power, Creation and Destruction joined forces, acting prematurely before Elemental Magic and Time could intervene. Together, they birthed the first physical embodiments of power – fully formed entities made from Creation yet tainted by Destruction – known as the Celestials. In their haste to ensure that the representations of Cosmic Power would dominate, these Celestials were brought into existence without the understanding required to wield their power with more wisdom. Before long, their missteps and misdeeds gave rise to other beings.

As the earliest effects of the Cosmic Sphere's unchecked influence took shape, the strands of Time and Elemental Magic did not immediately create their own representations. Instead of retaliating, they chose a different path. The firstborn manifestations of this upheaval emerged as gods, demigods, demons, and humans. With each ripple of creation, new forces spread across existence, further tipping the balance in the sphere's favour.

The swift actions of those with Cosmic Power had shaped physical reality according to their sphere's desires, setting the template for all subsequent life forms. But the other two strands saw this as an opportunity to introduce entities capable of doing better. They sought to restore balance by introducing their physical representations as infants – beings who would be immortal safeguards, yet vulnerable enough to grow, learn, and gain knowledge over the ages.

It was then that Time gave birth to a daughter, born of both light and darkness, while the five sons of Elemental Magic emerged to represent fire, earth, water, spirit, and air.

The rise of these beings led Fate to deliver his first prophecy – one so significant that the Nine Strands of Power gathered once more, risking all of existence. Fate foretold that these children would one day cause the lines of power to merge, bringing forth a force unlike any other, one that would forever alter the balance. In response to this prophecy, and before retreating to their respective corners of reality and beyond, the Nine Strands recognised the need to establish an authority to act as a minder for each line's influence over existence in their absence – until Fate's prophecy came to pass.

These nine guardians, each embodying a Strand of Power, became known as the "Handlers." The Consilio Statera, a council of three formidable beings, led the Handlers and held ultimate authority over each Sphere of Power.

With the Nine Strands dispersing, confident that their stewards would fulfil their purpose, a brilliant flash illuminated the sky, as if stars had fallen to Earth. It heralded the arrival of the descendants. Waves of energy surged outward from where they landed, shaping the boundaries of what would come to be known as the First Kingdoms – lands infused with the essence of the children's abilities.

These kingdoms became the original domains, each ruled by one of the six, raised under the careful guidance of their handler. As the children grew, so did their influence, and the reach of their kingdoms extended far and wide. Yet, with power came unforeseen consequences – just as had occurred with the Celestials. Every misuse of their abilities, whether born from innocence or ambition, gave rise to new beings – creatures who embodied the consequences of their actions. Each of these beings shifted the delicate balance that held reality together.

The Age of the Gods continued, marked by the reign of Celestials and first-born beings who thrived during this era, wielding their unique influence across the world. But, because of their lineage and their prophesied roles in shaping the future of existence, the six children ascended to positions of royalty. They became revered and feared in equal measure by the creatures and beings who inhabited the realms.

For a time, peace prevailed. But ambition is a seed that takes root even in the most fertile of souls. The unchecked emergence of first-born consequences of power and their descendants disrupted the fragile balance, as struggles for dominance drew even the most reserved beings into greed and anger. Fearful of the escalating threat, the council turned to the untouched energy of the strands to impose strict boundaries on the children's abilities. No longer could their powers give birth to unintended creatures or spiral beyond control.

Unable to fully limit the overwhelming influence of the Cosmic Sphere, the council solidified this newfound equilibrium by banishing the Celestials and their firstborns from the Earth. The council stripped them of their ability to take physical form, diminishing their influence on reality.

However, this measure only fuelled the flame that had ignited within the second-eldest prince. His thirst for control morphed into an obsession. Hungry for supremacy, he sought a way to manipulate the prophecy whispered by Fate himself. Though many had dismissed it as a legend, the prince remained convinced that controlling its fulfilment would grant him influence over all creation – and beyond.

It was only when whispers of a threat capable of ending even the immortals reached his younger brother that the true extent of the prince's obsession became clear. Desperate, the younger brother pleaded with the Consilio Statera for aid. Though bound to observe, the council could no longer ignore the destruction wrought by unchecked ambition. The prince's past actions had given rise to beings so powerful that even the other descendants struggled to control the chaos they unleashed. The Consilio Statera, understanding the immense danger he posed, feared that if the prince found a way to bend the prophecy to his will, he could bring about ruin – especially if he possessed the means to end a pure descendent of power.

Rather than waiting for the prince to act, the council took pre-emptive measures. As the only beings capable of enacting the first portion of the prophecy, they believed their best chance of thwarting his plans was to initiate it, and without the prince's knowledge. They sent Katherine, the daughter of Time, into the mortal world, stripping her of her powers and erasing her memories. She would be unaware of her true identity, her past, and her critical role in the universe. She would live and die – again and again – caught in a cycle of life and death, shielded from those who sought her until the rest of the prophecy unfolded as it was meant to.

But hiding Katherine was not the end.

Across seven mortal lives, the princess remained oblivious. Then, one day, everything she knew came crashing down.

She had been found.

Torn from her mortal existence, the prophecy, once dormant, stirred to life.

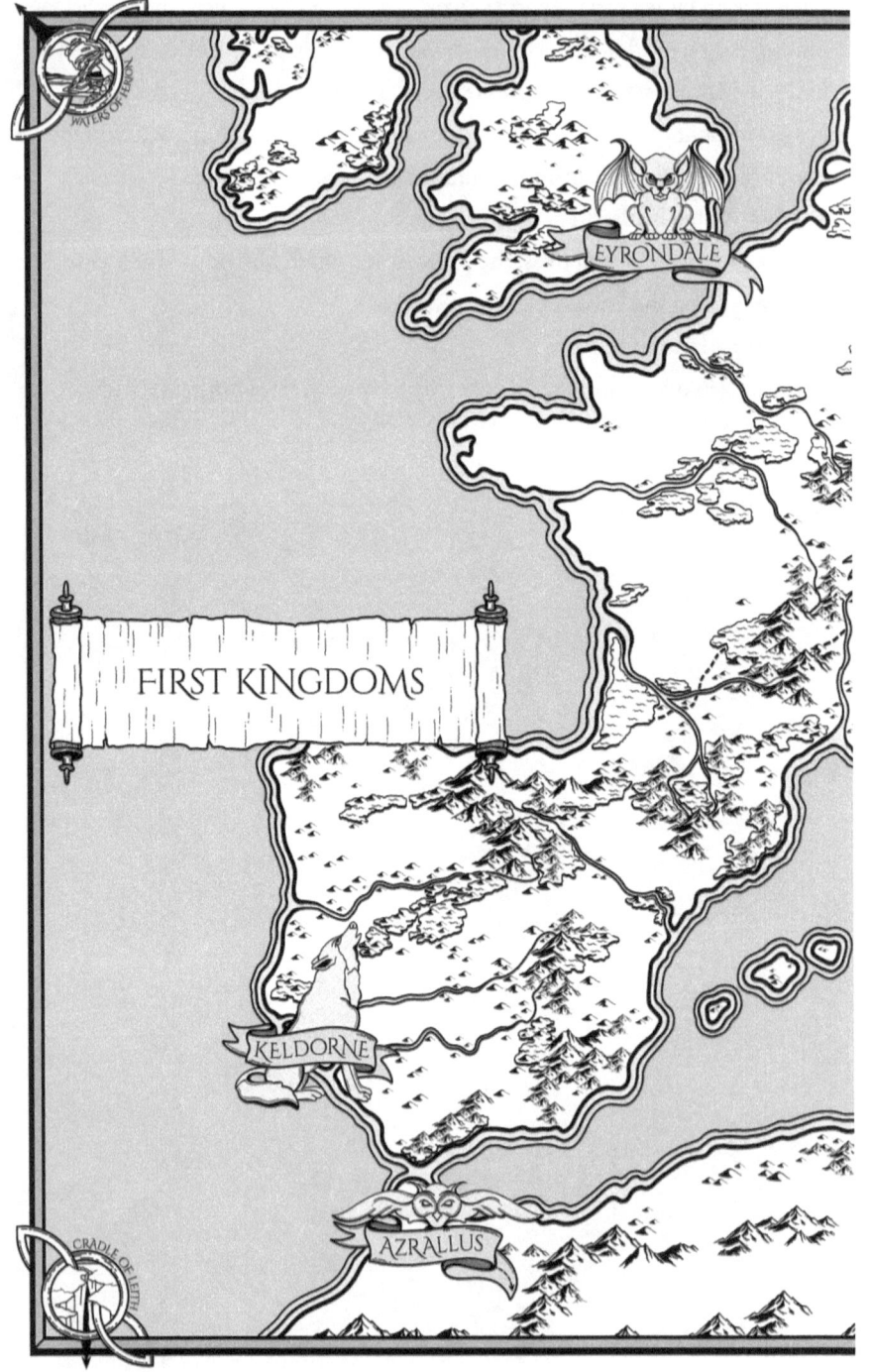

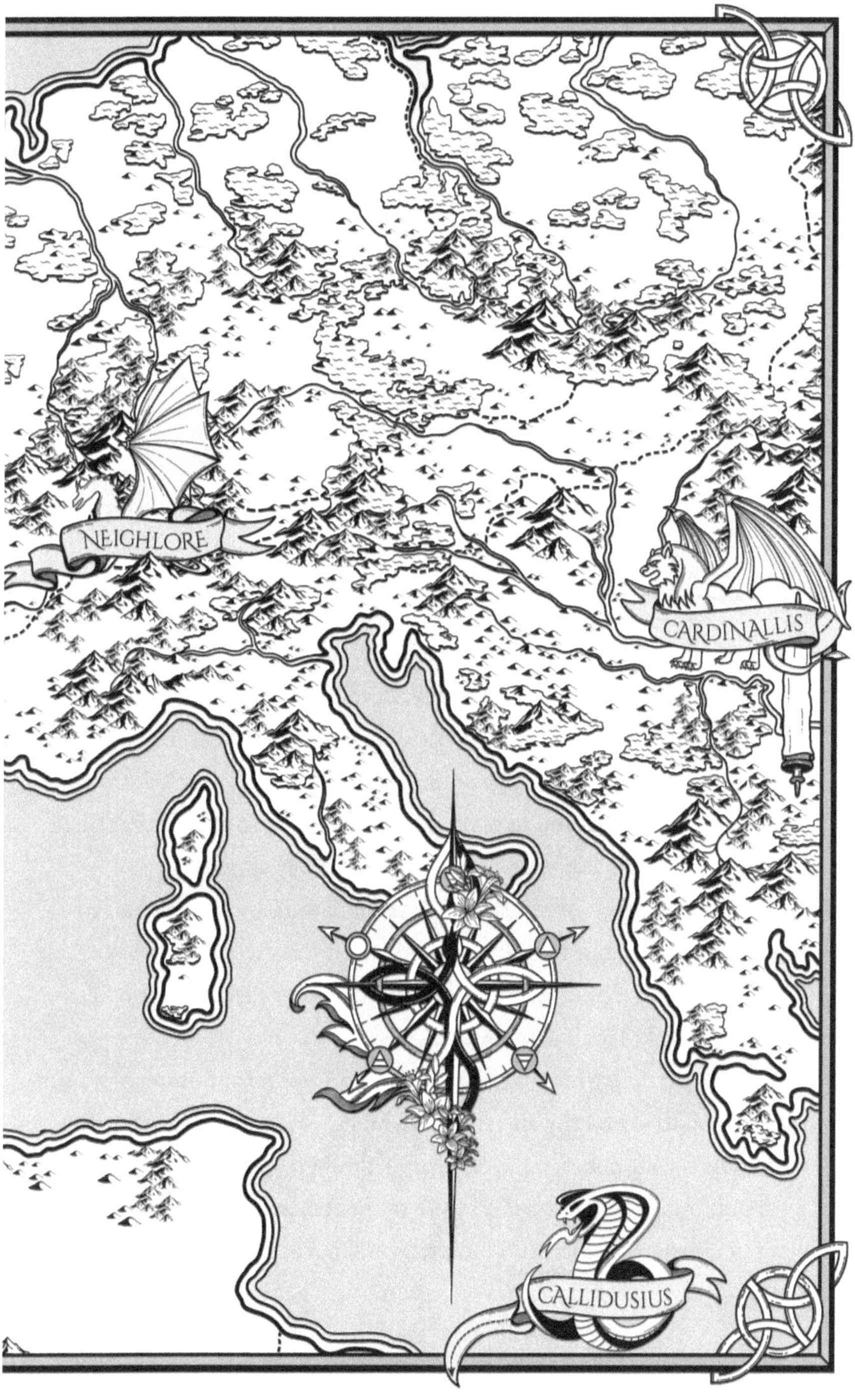

NEIGHLORE

CARDINALLIS

CALLIDUSIUS

ACKNOWLEDGEMENTS

Creating The Awakening of a Princess would not have been possible without the support of so many.

Thank you to Rebecca and Ramona, whose unique edits at varying stages of the book's development helped shape it into what it is today, and to Gareth, who brought the world of Eyrondale to life through stunning cover design and formatting, with a level of creativity, care, and attention to detail that I deeply appreciate.

To my beta readers, whose sharp eyes and honest feedback helped refine every page, your insight shaped this story in ways I will always value. And to the readers joining me on this journey, your love for stories like this is what makes it all worthwhile.

To my partner, whose unwavering support has meant more than I can express, and to my family and friends, who never tired of hearing about Eyrondale – your belief in me carried me through every challenge.

And to the characters who inspired The Ashes of Eyrondale long before I understood their story, thank you. I never meant to write about you, and yet, there you were.

Thank you.

S amantha de la Porté is the author of The Ashes of Eyrondale, a pentalogy that blends fantasy, paranormal romance, and magic realism in the modern world, where the ancient forces of Cosmic, Magic, and Destiny Power shape everyday life. In The Awakening of a Princess, the first book in the series, Katherine, the lost daughter of Time, embarks on the first of the Five Trials of Fate to reclaim her forgotten memories and regain her powers. As part of a prophecy almost as old as existence itself, Katherine must face a destiny that will determine the future balance of power.

When she's not writing or crafting digital marketing strategies, Samantha can be found painting, travelling, exploring new cuisines, or attending live music events.

Join Samantha on the journey through The Ashes of Eyrondale by visiting www.samanthadelaporte.com or by following her on Instagram: @samantha_delaporte and @ashesofeyrondale.

www.ingramcontent.com/pod-product-compliance
Lightning Source LLC
Chambersburg PA
CBHW030936120726
47906CB00002B/589